THE ONLY THING
THAT LASTS

THE ONLY THING
THAT LASTS

a novel

Tyler R. Tichelaar

Marquette, Michigan

THE ONLY THING THAT LASTS

Marquette Fiction
1202 Pine Street
Marquette, MI 49855
www.marquettefiction.com

ISBN-13: 978-0-9791790-04-4
ISBN-10: 0-9791790-4-1

Library of Congress PCN 2007932348

Printed in the United States of America

Publication managed by Superior Book Productions
www.superiorbookproductions.com

To my brother, Dan
who likes an old-fashioned book

"Land is the only thing in the world that amounts to anything….for 'tis the only thing in this world that lasts, and don't you be forgetting it! 'Tis the only thing worth working for, worth fighting for—worth dying for….And to anyone with a drop of Irish blood in them the land they live on is like their mother….'Twill come to you, this love of land. There's no getting away from it, if you're Irish."

— Margaret Mitchell, *Gone With The Wind*

PRINCIPAL CHARACTERS IN
THE ONLY THING THAT LASTS

The O'Neills

Robert O'Neill – The narrator and hero of this novel. Named for his grand-
  father. Born in South Carolina, he goes to live with his grandmother and
  aunt in Marquette, Michigan during World War I
Kathleen O'Neill – Robert O'Neill's widowed grandmother who lives in
  Marquette, Michigan
Louisa May O'Neill – Robert O'Neill's spinster aunt who lives with his
  grandmother
Cynthia O'Neill – Robert O'Neill's mother, deceased when the novel opens
John O'Neill – Robert O'Neill's father, who is away fighting in World War I.
  He and his late wife were second cousins
Robert O'Neill Sr. – The late husband of Kathleen O'Neill

The Blacks

Nellie Black – Negro servant and friend to John and Cynthia O'Neill in
  South Carolina
Martin Black – her husband

The Carters

Barney Carter – longtime friend of the O'Neill family in South Carolina

The Smiths and Hamptons

Carolina Smith – sister to the late Robert O'Neill Sr.
Judge Smith – Carolina Smith's deceased husband
Jane Hampton – Carolina's married daughter
George Hampton – Jane Hampton's husband
Mark Hampton – George and Jane Hampton's older son
Tom Hampton – George and Jane's younger son

Carolina Smith's Servants

Jones – A Negro butler
Jenny – A Negro maid

The Lawsons

Ellen Lawson – Mother of three daughters, whose husband is away fighting in
    World War I
Margaret "Mags" Lawson – Ellen's oldest daughter
Mollie Lawson – Ellen's middle daughter
Mary Lawson – Ellen's youngest daughter
Helen Neill – Ellen Lawson's niece who comes to live with the Lawsons
Helen Pierson – Ellen Lawson's unmarried sister from downstate who comes
    to visit

The Williams and Hobsons

Mrs. Williams – elderly lady who is good friends with Kathleen O'Neill
John Williams – Mrs. Williams's middle-aged bachelor son
Marie Hobson – Mrs. Williams's widowed daughter who lives on
    Mackinac Island
Eric Hobson – Marie Hobson's son who is away fighting in World War I

The Lewises

James Lewis – elderly bachelor friend of the late Robert O'Neill Sr., brother of
    Charles
Charles Lewis – elderly bachelor friend of the late Robert O'Neill Sr., brother
    of James

The Grahams

Mrs. Graham – mother of Eliza Graham
Eliza Graham – fiancée of Mark Hampton

The Mitchells

Roger Mitchell – middle-aged bachelor, brother of Mary and Florence
Mary Mitchell – spinster sister of Roger and Florence
Florence Mitchell – spinster sister of Roger and Mary

Preface

The world has nearly forgotten Robert O'Neill as one of the great twentieth century American novelists. Although he did not publish anything during the last couple decades of his life, he did write one last work while in his eighties. A few months before his passing in 1998, he described this last work to me as a "failed attempt" to write his autobiography. At age ninety-four, he realized how difficult a task it would be to encompass his entire life in one volume and to finish that work before his death, so he focused on those years he considered most formative of his character and writing. In addition, he wished to pay tribute to the town of Marquette, where he lived most of his life and which he always regarded as his true home. *The Only Thing That Lasts* captures his and Marquette's past, the world of his youth, a world at that time that was innocent despite the background events of the First World War and the Great Depression. Mr. O'Neill's memoir is both an old-fashioned story, and one that charts the growth of an impressionable young mind that would one day create some of our greatest fiction.

I am deeply honored, as president of the Robert O'Neill Historical Trust and Mr. O'Neill's literary executor, to present to the world my favorite author's final work. Mr. O'Neill graciously entrusted me to be lifelong curator of his home, which has been preserved as an historical and literary museum. The proceeds from the sale of his autobiography will be used to support that historical trust.

The Only Thing That Lasts is Robert O'Neill's final gift to his beloved Marquette and to his millions of loyal readers, both of whom he always felt gave far more back to him than his pen could ever repay.

John Vandelaare
Marquette, Michigan
August 27, 2001

PART I

1917-1918

Chapter 1

Going North

"So, you're going up North to live with those damn Yankees. How do you feel about that?"

Mr. Carter turned his head to spit out a wad of tobacco, then turned back to look me straight in the eye. We were sitting on my parents' front porch. I had known Mr. Carter all thirteen years of my life—he was an old family friend, having known my grandparents on both sides of the family—yet I had never felt overly comfortable around him. Since my father's parents had long since passed away, he had come over to our house often, to "check up on" my dad, and to give him some fatherly, if unwanted, advice. My father was always cheerful toward Mr. Carter, my mother always polite—yet many times I had caught the irritated glances my parents exchanged when they heard Mr. Carter's knock on the door. Because my parents had raised me to respect my elders, I usually did not become riled by Mr. Carter's comments—if today were different, perhaps it was because my mother had died a couple days before—or perhaps because my father was away fighting in the Great War in Europe, and we had not heard from him in weeks—or perhaps because in a couple hours I would be boarding a train with my aunt, to go live with her and my grandmother in the North, until my father returned home.

None of these events had caused me to lose my temper in the last few days—not even when Mr. Carter continually spat tobacco juice on my mother's whitewashed porch. But his comment that I would be living among "damn Yankees" now stirred me enough to retort:

"My family are Yankees!"

I sneered out the damning word "Yankees" in mockery of how all good South Carolinians spit it out. Even if my family were half-Yankees, I would not have them insulted.

Mr. Carter frowned.

"No, they're not," he said slowly, pulling out his tobacco can and putting another plug into his mouth. "Your family comes from good Southern blood—your father was born here, as were both your mama's parents, even if your mama was born up North. Your folks were probably ashamed to tell you so, but your grandpa's family were deserters of the Cause; they moved up North before the war, and then your grandmother went and married your grandfather when he was down here as part of the occupying Union Army during Reconstruction. So I guess you could say she deserted too. But your grandmother comes from one of the oldest and finest families in the South—her aunt, Abigail Richmond, could have been the first lady of the Confederacy had she wished. But instead she chose to associate with Northern carpetbaggers and scalawags. That's how your grandma met your grandpa, at some fancy party her Aunt Abigail held for those damn Yankee soldiers."

I felt incensed. How dare he spout off my family history to me, as if I did not know it! But truthfully, I knew none of this. I had never thought to ask why my mother's family lived in Michigan, or how she came to meet my father who was from South Carolina, or why we lived in the South and not the North. And now my mother was dead, and my father was overseas, so I might never be able to ask him about these things. Oddly, my parents had never spoken of the Civil War, and while I had learned plenty about it in school, somehow I had never thought to ask about our family's role in it. My schoolmates all knew about their family's roles in that war; they all could list with great pride every battle a grandfather or great-uncle fought at. I always remained silent during these discussions—perhaps because I sensed that in the South where the Confederacy lived on in so many hearts, something must be wrong with my family never to mention the war.

Could my grandmother have really married a Yankee soldier? Was I the grandson of a Yankee? Were my mother's relatives really traitors to the Cause? I could not believe any of it. I would never be able to hold my head up again at school if it were true—only I would not be going back to the local school. I would go to school in the North with Yankees! I felt my family pride dying inside me. Mr. Carter couldn't possibly be right, could he?

"Ha!" chortled Mr. Carter. "I bet I know more about your family history than you do!" He let out another stream of tobacco juice as if to affirm the statement.

I was angry, but I could not argue—he probably did know more about my family history, yet he had no right to call my family members Yankees and deserters.

Mr. Carter was about my grandmother's age—in his early sixties—too young to have fought in the war. He was of that unfortunate group of Southern boys who had hoped the war would last long enough for them to join up, so they could restore the failing Confederate Army, but by the time Mr. Carter was ten years old, Lee was defeated, the Union restored, the South occupied by Northern soldiers. But Mr. Carter could remember the South's defeat, and he had been a friend of my father's father in his boyhood—if that were the case, then he probably did know all the details of my family's history during the war, and perhaps he did speak the truth now, but he had no right to throw it in my face, to dishonor my family the day after my mother was laid in her grave.

"Excuse me," I said and went into the house.

"Robert, I'll be ready to go in ten minutes," said my aunt as I came in the door.

For a second, I considered that she might know the truth—she was my mother's sister; she lived in the North, unmarried, with my grandmother—who probably knew everything about the family. I thought of asking my aunt whether Mr. Carter's words were true—were our family deserters of the Southern Cause? But if it were true, I was not yet prepared to hear it. I went into the bathroom to be alone with my thoughts.

My mother's family Yankees? How could I think of them that way? But they did live in the North. I had seen them so rarely that I had never thought about why they lived so far away, and now I was going to live with a grandmother who had married a Union soldier, and worse, that Union soldier had been my grandfather! My father must have known this, yet he had married my mother, the daughter of a Yankee soldier. I wished I could contact my dad. I wondered whether he would have consented to my living up North if he were aware of my mother's passing. We had sent him word, but who knew when he would receive it?

Maybe I didn't have to go. Maybe I could stay with Mr. Carter until my father came home—but living with Mr. Carter wouldn't be much better than living with Yankees. Could I live in my parents' house by myself? I was thirteen now, and Nellie, my parents' Negro servant, could still come over to check on me and cook my meals.

But I knew the grownups would think such a plan impractical at my age.

I stared out the bathroom window, at the beautiful willow trees and my swing hanging from an oak. I wondered whether I would ever see our magnolia tree blossom again. I knew the North didn't have magnolias. From what Aunt Louisa May had told me, they didn't have much of anything except snow.

"Robert, we're ready!" my aunt called. "Hurry or we'll miss the train."

Who was she to decide where I lived? But I couldn't be rude to her any more than to Mr. Carter. And she had always been kind to me, and I knew my grandmother was kind as well. It was not my aunt's fault if she were born a Yankee—she could not help where she was born, and she had been born long after the war. I could blame my grandmother, but she was taking me in now. I felt rather relieved to think I wouldn't be going back to school here—I would have been ashamed if my friends found out about my Yankee connections—imagine what they would think when they heard I was going to live among Northerners? Perhaps the North was the only place I would be accepted now. But that was silly—all our neighbors knew my mother was from the North. I was making too much out of it all. The war had ended over fifty years ago—it probably didn't matter to anyone now except an old man like Mr. Carter.

"Robert!"

"Coming!" I shouted. I flushed the toilet so no one would think I had simply gone into the bathroom to avoid Mr. Carter. Why did he have to tell me all this the very day I was leaving? Why couldn't my parents have told me this before? Was our past so besmirched that they had thought it best to keep it from me?

When I stepped out the front door, Aunt Louisa May was standing on the porch.

"There you are," she said. "Hurry and say goodbye to Nellie so we're not late for our train."

Nellie stood by Mr. Carter, handing him luggage to place in his wagon so he could drive us to the train station.

I went down the front steps and walked up to her. "Goodbye, Nellie." I held out my hand, but she did not blink until Mr. Carter took the suitcase from her. Then she buried me in her arms. "Be good for your aunt, Robert," she said.

She had been like a second mother to me. I had known her all my life. Three times a week she had come to help my mother with the cooking and cleaning, and often she had postponed her work to chat or play a game with me. Now I felt as if I were losing my mother all over again.

"I wish you could come with me," I said as she released me.

She laughed and said, "What would I do up North? Besides, you know I'm a married lady now."

She had married just a year ago. I held a fierce hatred toward her husband whom I did not think good enough for her. But secretly, I felt he had partly stolen her from me.

"Then I wish I could stay, and you could look after me," I said.

I felt the childishness of this remark—I was practically a man, after all. But I had been unable to stop myself from speaking the words.

"You're getting too old to need looking after. And you'll be back before you know it—your father will be coming home soon."

She was trying to cheer me, but from all accounts, the war in Europe was far from over.

"Here's the key, Nellie. I locked the door," said Aunt Louisa May. "Let us know if you hear from Robert's father. I'll write to him again as soon as we reach Marquette."

"Don't you worry none, Miss Weesa May," she replied. "I'll keep a good eye on the place."

"So'll I," said Mr. Carter, although he had not been asked. I think he resented that my aunt had given Nellie the key over him. But it did not matter—he would stick his nose in our business anyway by driving over every few days to check on the house.

"Let me give you a hand, Miss O'Neill," he offered, helping my aunt into the wagon.

I crawled into the back with the suitcases, wishing instead we could ride to the train depot in my father's automobile. Would I ever get to ride in it again?

We had barely waved goodbye to Nellie and pulled away from the house when my aunt, as if reading my mind, said, "I'm surprised, Mr. Carter, that being such a prosperous landowner, you haven't bought yourself an automobile."

"Don't believe in 'em," Mr. Carter replied. "Dem contraptions is jus' a passin' fad."

"Well, I imagine they'll be around longer than this horse of yours," Aunt Louisa May said. Jeb Stuart was a rather run-down nag.

Mr. Carter began whistling "Dixie" to ignore her. I think it was the only tune he knew. My aunt and I exchanged amused glances. Mr. Carter was a stubborn old man, set in his ways and unlikely to change. He would not have driven that old nag any faster to the train station if Sherman's army were after him. But his whistling reminded me that I wouldn't be in the land of cotton anymore. Marquette seemed an unimaginable place, from all I had heard about it. It was like a fabled land where the snowbanks reached six feet high, where people had to snowshoe or ski to get around in winter, where even on the hottest summer days, the temperature scarcely exceeded eighty, and Lake Superior, the world's largest freshwater lake, was within walking distance from everywhere in the little town. I could not imagine living amid such cold weather, in a place so contrary to everything I had previously known.

Mr. Carter kept up his whistling all the way to the train station. We had no conversation—I think my aunt and I were both exhausted from the long days of preparing for my mother's funeral, the thought of the long trip North, and the all-consuming grief in our hearts. I had not even cried for my mother, except the day of her death; I felt numb all over, as if the world were moving on, as if I were going through the motions of living, merely going to Marquette because I was told, not really caring what became of me. I fell into a melancholy daze until Mr. Carter coughed, and then I saw we were pulling up to the train depot.

"Well, Robert, hope ya have a good time up North, and that ya come back here soon," he said, after pulling our luggage out of the wagon and handing it to my aunt and me.

"Thank you, Mr. Carter," I said. "You've been a good friend to my parents, and I thank you since they are not here to do so."

I felt very adult saying such words. Mr. Carter had always hung around our house, eating our food, amusing and occasionally annoying my parents with his shiftless ways, but I thought it best to be polite when we were parting. I felt I was being very big and gracious considering his recent degrading remarks about my family.

"Don't ya worry none. I'll keep an eye on the house while you're gone."

"Goodbye, Mr. Carter," said Aunt Louisa May. "Thank you for everything."

He tipped his hat to her, and for a moment, I saw their eyes meet and an odd smile of approval cross Mr. Carter's face. My aunt, seeing him smile, looked bewildered and quickly reached for my hand. Mr. Carter turned to spit out his tobacco.

"Well, see ya," I said to him, as Aunt Louisa May pulled me toward the train.

We quickly got on board, found our seats, and waited silently for the train to pull away. In a few minutes, my childhood world was left behind.

I felt lonely as the train headed North and familiar sites disappeared. My aunt sat quietly for a while, doubtless exhausted from all the urgent arrangements she had been forced to make. She stared out the window until long after we had crossed the border into North Carolina. Once or twice I heard her sigh. After half an hour, I pulled out a book and tried to read—I remember nothing of the book now, except that a mother was in it, which immediately made me think of my own mother. I felt less grief-stricken now than angry that my mother's death meant I must live up North. And again, I felt anger stir in me over Mr. Carter's words—what did he know? He was always exaggerating the truth—my own father had said so on more than one occasion. I could not trust Mr. Carter's words.

"I'm sorry, Robert. I've been day-dreaming," said my aunt, turning toward me. "It's just so hard for me to imagine your mother being gone. I'm sorry your life has to be so disrupted like this, but I don't know what else can be done since your father is away. We'll just have to make the best of it. I wish your grandmother hadn't twisted her ankle—I imagine she'd make a better traveling companion for you than me."

"It's all right, Aunt Louisa May," I said, wishing to soothe her. Her eyes looked red, as if she were holding back tears. "During times like these, we have to do our duty, and mine is to cause as little trouble for everyone as possible."

I was proud of how brave I sounded. I told myself that even if I were going to live with my grandmother and aunt, I would be man of the house.

She smiled. "You're a good boy, Robert. Your grandmother and I will be happy to have you with us. I still can't get over how much you look like your mother."

She meant the words kindly, although I would have preferred to resemble my father. And the mention of my mother again reminded me of Mr. Carter's words—that my mother's family had deserted the South and sided with Yankees. I decided it was time I knew the truth.

"Aunt Louisa May, how come my mother was from Marquette, yet she married my dad who was from South Carolina?" I asked the question although I was afraid of the answers. "Isn't your side of the family also originally from the South? I've never really understood that, although I know at one point my mother told me she and my father are cousins of some sort."

"Your parents are second cousins," my aunt replied. "They met when we came down South once to visit my Great-Aunt Abigail. When your parents got married, your mother decided to live down here with your father."

"But then," I said, "if they're cousins, why does half the family live in Marquette and half down South?

"To explain all that would make a long story," Aunt Louisa May said.

"It's a long train ride to Marquette," I replied.

I would rather hear a long story, and know the full truth of it at once, before we reached Marquette; hearing of my family's dishonor seemed preferable to sitting in silence and ignorance, alone with my grief and fears.

"I just want to know," I added, "if we're really Southerners or Yankees?"

My aunt laughed. "I never thought of it that way. I don't think anyone in Marquette would label himself a Yankee, but you Southerners have a different perspective I suppose."

Her saying "you Southerners" gave me hope; even if she were a Yankee, I was a Southerner. Yet I waited patiently for further explanation.

"I guess by rights you could say your mother's half of the O'Neill family are expatriate Southerners."

I did not like that term "expatriate" but it was less harsh than "deserter" or "traitor."

"How long have we lived in the South?" I asked. "Aren't we originally Irish?"

"Oh yes," said my aunt, "although I don't know anything about the family when they lived in Ireland. I only know that my father's grandfather was Seamus O'Neill, and he came to America around 1820 or so and settled in South Carolina. I don't know anything else about him except that he had two sons, Edmund and James. Edmund O'Neill was your great-grandfather on your mother's side, and James O'Neill was your great-grandfather on your father's side, but I don't really know anything about James's family, so you'll have to ask your father about that."

"But how did your side of the family end up in the North?" I asked. "When did that happen?"

"Edmund and James tried to make a living off the land their father left them, but while James was headstrong and strict about business, Edmund had no interest in farming. They owned a few slaves—not more than a dozen I would say. James insisted they would need more slaves to make the farm profitable, but Edmund refused to buy more. On his honeymoon, he and his wife Dolly had traveled to Washington D.C., where they had heard an abolitionist speaking. From that time on, he began to feel more and more that slavery was wrong."

"I don't know how anyone could ever doubt it," I replied. Yet I was surprised by my reaction—why was I so upset that my family should desert the Southern cause when I believed slavery was wrong? I would have been incensed if anyone had treated Nellie like a slave.

"Well, we live in a more enlightened age now," said my aunt. "In those days, people quoted the Bible to support slavery. James apparently didn't care whether slavery was immoral—he just knew he needed more hands to make the farm profitable. To ease his conscience and still not disagree with his brother, Edmund sold his land to James."

"What difference did that make?"

"Edmund freed the slaves he had. He said he couldn't bear to see them remain in bondage. But I doubt it made any difference because my father said the slaves couldn't find work anywhere in the county, and when Edmund offered them money so they could go North, they said they weren't going to leave their home, so they stayed at the farm, working for the minimal pay James gave them. I'm sure Edmund meant well, but his actions didn't really make any difference. Only the war made the difference."

"So then what happened?"

"James was infuriated with his brother—he purposely paid the ex-slaves low wages, and he called his brother a traitor. He said he could not operate the farm and pay wages and that he would go bankrupt, although I guess he managed to get by until the war. But I don't think the two brothers ever spoke again."

I could see James's point—why should he pay for what he had really inherited? His brother, rather than helping with the farm, had only cost the family more. Yet, I felt rather proud that my great-grandfather had stood by his principles.

"And then Edmund moved to the North?"

"Yes. He had heard about the iron ore discoveries in Upper Michigan, and somehow he got it into his head that he could make a great deal of money up there without having to own slaves, so he came to Marquette back when it was just a little village of a few hundred people. That was about the mid-1850s I guess. My father, whom you're named after, and his sister, my Aunt Carolina, were just children then. Of course, my father has been dead for years, but you'll meet Aunt Carolina when we get to Marquette."

"It must have been hard," I said, "for our family to leave everything they knew in South Carolina to move to a new town." I was thinking of my own situation.

"I'm sure it was," said Aunt Louisa May. "Edmund must have loved the South or he wouldn't have given his daughter the name of Carolina. I wish before he died, I had thought to ask him more about it, but you never think to ask those questions when you're young."

I felt proud of myself to be so young and asking questions—but I might not have asked if Mr. Carter had not riled me up.

"What happened to James during the war?" I asked.

"He must have gotten by somehow, even after his slaves were freed. I guess the farm had to be sold eventually by your father's father after James died, but I don't know much about that. That was before I ever knew that side of the family."

I thought about this for a while, wondering what it was like to own a farm full of slaves, only to lose it all.

"Your grandmother might know something about it too," Aunt Louisa May added. "She could tell you stories about life during the war since she lived through it down here."

"She wasn't born in the North?"

"Oh no, she grew up not far from where your parents live now. During the war, her parents both died, and Yankees burnt down the family plantation. She was an only child, and just a little girl during the war, so she went to live in Charleston with her Aunt Abigail. That's where she met my father."

"And your Father fought for the Union?"

"No, not quite. My father was Edmund's son. He was just a boy during the war, but afterwards, he joined the army and ended up being stationed in Charleston during the Reconstruction. My mother's Aunt Abigail was from one of the oldest families in South Carolina, and somehow, her fortune came through just fine during the war—rumor said she and her husband were trading with the Yankees. I doubt that's true. I think that after the war, they just accepted what most Southerners wouldn't—that they would have to befriend the Yankees if they wanted to survive. They had a great big house in Charleston, so they had gigantic parties for the Yankee officers; my father was invited to one of her parties where he met your grandmother. She'll tell you that the neighbors thought it bad enough she would marry a Yankee, but to marry a man whose parents had been Southerners and deserted the cause—well, that would have made her a social outcast in Charleston. But Aunt Abigail told your grandmother that she would have a better life in the North, so she married my father anyway, and once his military duty was over, they moved to Marquette."

"And then my mom and dad met when Grandma came back to the South to visit her aunt?"

"Yes, and that was a bit difficult for them as well, just as it was for my parents. My mother thought your father was a good young man, but his father, Jefferson Davis O'Neill—you can imagine why James O'Neill picked that name for his son—very much opposed the thought of his son marrying the grand-daughter of his traitor uncle. Jefferson Davis O'Neill had only been a baby during the war, but he ranted and raved that no son of his would marry a Yankee. Your parents insisted they would marry anyway. My mother tried to talk sense into your father's father, but he flew into such a conniption fit that he had a stroke and died two days later. That was a depressing start for a marriage, but once the mourning period for him ended, your parents got married anyway."

"I'm sorry my grandpa died that way," I said, "but it sounds like it was his own fault."

"He was a proud man," Aunt Louisa May replied, "and his father had poisoned him against our side of the family."

"I'm glad my father isn't ornery like his father and grandfather were."

"Well, maybe they weren't always that way," said Aunt Louisa May. "Your father knew them better and can fill in any holes in my version of the story."

It all sounded so foolish to me—that James O'Neill would refuse to speak to his brother for the rest of his life, that Jefferson Davis O'Neill would oppose his son marrying because of a feud between his father and uncle. Why couldn't people let the past rest? And why had I been so worried about it—these events had all happened years ago, so why should I care what Mr. Carter or anyone else thought?

"So," my aunt finished, "I don't know whether that answers your question about us being Yankees or Southerners. I think you could just say we're an American family."

"Mr. Carter doesn't think so," I said. "He's the one who told me your side of the family were Yankees and deserters of the Southern Cause."

My aunt pursed her lips. "Mr. Carter is a foolish old man. He—" But then she held her words, thinking better of it, and instead said, "The Civil War has been over more than fifty years. People who hold onto the past like that only hurt themselves. I think once Mr. Carter's generation is gone, no one will care whether someone's family fought for the North or the South. We're all one nation now."

I agreed with Aunt Louisa May, yet I knew plenty of Southerners who thought differently—I knew the stubborn pride of my neighbors—and I had heard the stories of hunger and homes burnt down by Yankees during the war. If the South had treated the North that way, the same anger would have existed on the other side. Would another fifty years heal the pain better than the last fifty?

"I often thought," my aunt mused, "that your mother was a brave woman to move down here, especially when she was a Yankee and descended from an apparently despised Southerner family. I give her and your father both a lot of credit for staying steadfast in their love, despite the prejudice surrounding them."

I felt pride well up in me at these words. My father had been brave to stand up against his own father and not let guilt over his father's death stop him from following his heart. And my mother had left the only world she had known in Marquette, so she could live with my father in South Carolina, in what must have been a strange place to her when she was used to Lake Superior and snow. South Carolina had no real lakes, only rivers; on the rare occasion when it did snow, it would only last for an hour and then melt, and in summer, the temperature could soar over a hundred degrees. I felt proud of my mother, and of all my family who had been willing to move from the South to the North and back again. Now, by going to Marquette, I was doing the same.

I wondered what it would be like to live in Marquette; I wished I had paid more attention to my mother's stories about her hometown, but Marquette had always seemed such an unbelievable place to me. I was about to ask my aunt to describe Marquette when she suggested we go to supper in the dining car, and once we had ordered, she began asking me about school, and telling me I would be enrolled at Bishop Baraga, the Catholic school in Marquette. We had no Catholic school back home—almost all the neighbors were Baptists— but both sides of my family had been Irish Catholic—at least there had been no religious conflict in the family. I wondered what the children in Marquette would be like—would they teach me how to ski or snowshoe? Would they make fun of me because I was from the South? Would they be smarter than me? No, they couldn't possibly because the South had such fine schools, but then, if Southerners were so smart, wouldn't they have won the war? The thought of going to school with all those Yankees made me nervous until I reminded myself they were not Yankees, just Americans.

After supper, my aunt and I retired to bed in our sleeper car. The next day, we talked little, both tired from the long journey. I wanted to ask her about Marquette, but finally decided I would just wait to see it for myself. I was too tired and anxious to read, so I mostly just stared out the window. The land of the lower Midwest was so bare and level. I had grown up in the foothills, surrounded by trees—I hoped Marquette would not be flat and lifeless like Ohio.

I kept repeating over in my mind the family story my aunt had told me; I struggled to remember all my ancestors' names—Seamus O'Neill, his two sons, who were my great-grandfathers, Edmund and James, and then Edmund's son was Robert, the grandfather I was named for, and James's son, my other Grandpa O'Neill, had been Jefferson Davis, the one who had opposed my parents' marriage. I tried to imagine what all their lives had been like, the anger some of them had felt, and the courage others had displayed. Where did I fit in amidst this family? My roots were in the North as well as the South; somehow I felt I would be more whole, more myself, once I had lived in both lands. Yesterday, I had feared being a Yankee; now I anticipated that living in Marquette would be a brave new adventure. I had promised my father I would be brave. I wanted him to be proud of me. I wanted to be good so God would make sure my father came home. And whatever obstacles faced me, I hoped my mother was watching over me from Heaven, and that the courage she had shown in moving South would now be mine as I moved North.

Chapter 2

My First Day in Marquette

A light snow was falling when Aunt Louisa May and I arrived in Marquette the day before Thanksgiving. The afternoon snow fascinated me—I had rarely seen any in South Carolina; the few times it had snowed there, it had only lasted an hour or two, and then the whole county had shut down. But here large fluffy flakes were piling up on top of a couple inches of snow already on the ground, and the people were going about their business without giving the snow a second thought. I envisioned myself sleigh riding and building snowmen, but my daydream was abruptly ended when I had to grab my suitcase, step off the train, and plant my feet onto Marquette's soil, or rather, snow.

The train depot was a short walk from where we would board a streetcar at the Marquette and Presque Isle Street Railway Station. As we walked, I gazed all around me, summing up the scenery. Everything looked rather bare and grey except for the white snow—it was a strange, cold looking world to my unaccustomed eyes; soon it would be as common to me as my own face in the mirror.

The streetcar ran despite the snow—another surprise to me. Aunt Louisa May and I rode it up Front Street hill—quite a large hill—in fact larger than any I remembered near my home in South Carolina; with relief, I saw Marquette was not flat as I had feared—in fact, I thought the hill rather steep, but my aunt remarked, "Usually I just walk up Front Street, but it would be kind of hard while carrying our luggage." At the top of the hill, the streetcar turned onto what I would later learn was Arch Street. We disembarked and walked the couple extra blocks to Grandma and Aunt Louisa May's house.

"So how do you like Marquette so far?" asked my aunt as we hobbled down the sidewalk, lugging our suitcases, trying not to drag them in the snow, although I was happily dragging my feet, enjoying how they pushed the snow about.

"I expected to see more snow," I said. I was a little disappointed—Mama had told me three feet of snow was not uncommon.

"Wait until after Christmas," my aunt replied.

"It sure is cold though," I grumbled. My right hand was freezing as it held onto the suitcase handle, while I had stuffed my left hand into my coat pocket.

"Actually, I'm rather warm with this heavy coat on," said my aunt. She had not even buttoned up her coat as I had. She would later always fuss at me to be buttoned up, but I would often see her step outside to get the mail or run an errand to a neighbor without any coat on at all. The temperature would have to be subzero before she even bothered to put on her gloves. I had a new appreciation for women's strength when they could bear such temperatures; I was less surprised by the hardy men, but I thought women were delicate—I would soon find out they snow-shoed, skied and chopped firewood just like any man in Upper Michigan.

"See that house across the street?" my aunt said as we walked along Arch Street.

"That little one?" I asked.

"Yes. That's the house the famous book *Dandelion Cottage* was based on. I'm sure you've read that, haven't you?"

"No, I've never heard of it," I replied, thinking the house didn't look like much, just a tiny little one floor square box.

"Oh!" replied my aunt. "Your mother always wrote that you were addicted to books."

"I am."

"It's strange then you never came across it, but we have the book at home. You can start reading it tonight if you like."

"All right," I said, trying to sound interested, but my fingers were really freezing. My aunt had let me pack my suitcase, and I had never thought to pack gloves—I only owned one pair and never wore them.

"I'm sure you'll love the book," she said. "It's one of the best children's books ever written, and the author lives right here in Marquette. We're very privileged to have such a famous woman in our community. The book's about four little girls who rent the house as their summer play cottage."

It didn't sound too exciting to me. After all, I was a boy, and not interested in flowers, especially not dandelions, which were really weeds. I hoped Grandma and Aunt Louisa May owned some stories by Jack London, or even the Tarzan books, but I rather doubted it.

"Mrs. Rankin has actually written several children's books, including some sequels to *Dandelion Cottage*," said my aunt. I think she would have summarized all Mrs. Rankin's books for me if we had not now arrived at her and Grandma's house.

"Hello, Robbie," said my grandma, opening the door and hugging me before I was over the threshold. "How are you? My how you've grown."

"I'm fine," I replied, not knowing what more to say—I had not seen her in two years, and now, here I would be living with her for who knew how long. Politely, I asked, "Is your ankle any better?" She would have come to South Carolina to fetch me herself if she had not twisted her ankle and the doctor forbidden her to walk on it.

"Just fine. The doctor says I'm good for a few more years yet. Come in, you look frozen. I'll make you some hot chocolate. I don't imagine you have any really warm clothes since the Carolinas are rarely cold. But first let me show you to your room so you can set down that big suitcase."

"I'll put my things away, then make the hot chocolate," Aunt Louisa May said, kissing Grandma on the cheek. Then I followed Grandma upstairs.

"I hope your mother's old room will be all right," said Grandma as we climbed the stairs. "It might have a few girls things in it—I haven't really touched it since she left, but we can change it if there's something you don't like."

"I'm sure it'll be fine," I said.

Then Grandma opened the bedroom door.

Pink flooded my eyes. Pink was everywhere—from the curtains to the wallpaper. The bedspread was white with pink flowers embroidered on it, and pink rugs covered the floor. The furniture was mahogany and old-fashioned, but still feminine. Mama probably would have cried sentimental tears to see Grandma had not changed her room. But I was not Mama.

Grandma must have seen my face drop for suddenly she was fumbling for words.

"My goodness. I—I don't know what I was thinking. I had forgotten it was so very—so very—"

"Pink," I muttered.

"I'm sorry, Robbie," Grandma apologized. "We'll make you some new curtains and a bedspread. Maybe we can even afford some new wallpaper. Do you think you can live with it for a few weeks?"

"Sure. It's not really that bad," I lied to make her feel better. "I like the rocking chair."

Quickly I crossed the room and flung myself into the chair to demonstrate my enthusiasm for it, only to tumble backwards onto the floor.

"Oh Robbie!" Grandma cried, rushing over to try and pick me up. "Are you okay? The back of that chair isn't very strong. I'll have to get some new dowels for it."

"I'm okay," I said. I was surprised she did not yell at me for being reckless and breaking it.

"Oh, I'm afraid your first day here isn't going very well," she laughed. "Let's go downstairs for some hot chocolate; then we'll try to start over. And I just took some chocolate chip cookies out of the oven. Maybe they'll make things not seem so bad."

"I'd love some cookies," I said, following her back downstairs.

"What color would you like your curtains and bedspread to be?" she asked.

"Blue, if it's okay," I replied. "Blue's my favorite color."

"It's Louisa May's favorite color too. Funny you should take after her rather than your Mom. Your mother's favorite color was pink."

"If I hadn't already known, I would have guessed it from her bedroom," I said. Our kitchen in South Carolina had been pink. Now that Mama was gone, I wished that last summer, on a day I was feeling particularly obstinate, I had not told her how much I hated the color of the kitchen. "I don't think any boys like pink," I told Grandma, but I recalled that my father had never complained about the kitchen's color.

"Well, I'm sure you take after your mother in other ways then," said Grandma, pausing for a second to look at me; then I realized she was also mourning my mother and looking for remembrances of her daughter in me. "I've noticed you emphasize your words rather like her, and you have some gestures of hers. I'm sorry you had to lose her, Robbie. I know how hard it must be for you because I lost my own mother when I was younger than you are now. When my parents died, I had to go live in Charleston with my aunt; that's not much different than your coming to stay with us. Time will heal all pain, I promise. And Louisa May and I will do our best to make you happy while you're here."

I appreciated her comforting words, but I was more interested in hearing about her childhood and having to go live in Charleston, but I didn't think it appropriate in my first hour here to ask her to fill in the blank spots from Aunt Louisa May's version of the family history.

"I'm glad to be here," I simply said. "I want to be with my family, although I don't understand why God took Mama from me."

"We aren't meant to understand that," Grandma sighed. "I tried for years to understand why your grandpa was taken from me when he was so young. But I know I'm stronger for it, and I trust I'll see him in the next life. Remember that death isn't an ending."

She said it so matter-of-factly, with such authority. I had barely had time to think about my mother's loss, to grieve her properly because of the journey here. Now I understood from Grandma's words that while I missed my mother, I did not really need to mourn for her—I would see her again—even if it were not for many more years. It would be a long time before I fully understood the truth in Grandma's words, and there would be grief to work through, but I have come to believe I will see my mother again.

"Well, let's not be morbid," said Grandma. "There's hot chocolate and freshly baked cookies to be devoured."

Soon, the three of us were assembled around the kitchen table, Grandma's cookies before us, as my aunt and I told Grandma about our trip. I was surprised by my aunt's final comments.

"I don't think I'll ever feel comfortable in the South," she said. "Not the way they segregate the railroad cars. It's not right—not when this country claims all men are created equal."

I was confused—not even knowing what segregation meant. When I realized she was complaining that the Negroes could not ride in the same cars as the whites, I was surprised—it had always been that way, all my life—I had never questioned it once, never even thought to ask why they were separated from us.

"When the Civil War ended," Grandma said, "we thought things would be better, but it seems as if the racial division in this country has only gotten worse. Segregation is hardly an improvement on slavery—I think maybe it's even divided the nation more, if that's possible."

How could she say that? Slavery had ended so long ago. Negroes had it much better now. Grandma and my aunt apparently didn't understand because they didn't live in the South. Who were they to judge us? I had never heard a white person speak against the system; I myself had often thought slavery must have been wrong. I could not imagine how anyone could have thought it was right, but that was different than segregation. Good sound reasons existed for that—hygienic and safety reasons. Why, if Grandma had been a man down South saying such things, she would have been run out of town.

"You'll find, Robbie," Grandma turned to me, "that people are less narrow-minded up here than down South."

"In theory at least," said my aunt. "There aren't many Negroes in town, and I imagine a few people feel awkward around them, but our hearts are in the right place here."

I didn't know what to say. What would my parents have thought of this? Would they have agreed? Would my mother have sided with them since she was born in the North? Did Grandma and Aunt Louisa May have any business even talking about it? I bet they didn't even know any Negroes. I began to understand why Southerners disliked Yankees so much, especially during the war when the North tried to impose its beliefs on the South.

"I guess we should just be thankful for the advances this country has seen," my aunt concluded.

"Speaking of being thankful," said Grandma, "we need to talk about Thanksgiving dinner. I'm going to make the pies this afternoon. I probably shouldn't have spent my time making these cookies this morning, but I thought Robbie would like them, and if I know Jane's boys, they'll eat up all the pies tomorrow so we won't have any leftovers."

"Who's Jane?" I asked, only interested because she had boys. It occurred to me I would want some friends in Marquette.

"Jane is my cousin," said Aunt Louisa May. "She'll be coming to dinner tomorrow with her family. She's your Great-Aunt Carolina's daughter—you remember I mentioned Aunt Carolina on the train. She'll be coming as well."

"How many children does Jane have?" I cut to the chase, not wanting another genealogy lesson.

"She has two sons, Mark and Tom. Mark is seventeen, and Tom is your age."

Perfect, I thought. Tom. I hoped Tom was a swell guy. I hoped he had some snowshoes or skis or something.

"That's all the family we have in town," said my aunt.

"But there'll be plenty of other guests," Grandma added. She began to recite the names of everyone she had invited to Thanksgiving dinner until I thought she would never get her pies made if she kept telling me about everyone. Except for Tom and Mark, I did not remember the name of a single person until I met each one the next day.

When the guest list recital was completed, Grandma asked whether I wanted to go upstairs and take a nap or unpack, but I politely offered instead to help. I did not want to be alone right then—the thought of all that family coming to dinner made me miss my parents, whom I had never celebrated a holiday without. Grandma set me to work peeling turnips and potatoes, which she said she usually did in the morning, but would not mind being a step ahead on.

We worked all afternoon until suppertime, when Grandma made a simple meal of cold cuts for us. "So we can save room for all that food tomorrow."

After supper, I think Grandma noticed I was looking tired so she sent me into the parlor to relax. There I found a little bookshelf that I perused, looking for something enticing, but I only found ladies' books—no Tarzan, no Jack London, not even Horatio J. Alger.

After I had listlessly paged through a few sappy looking romances, Aunt Louisa May came into the room and said, "Oh, I know what you can read." She ran upstairs, then returned with *Dandelion Cottage*.

"Thanks," I said, taking it from her.

"You go ahead and read it," she said. "Your grandma and I will be busy for a while yet."

With nothing else to do, I sat down and immersed myself between the covers of the girls' book. I figured no one else need ever know I had read it—provided Aunt Louisa May didn't tell Tom tomorrow. Actually, I have to admit I rather enjoyed it, and even more so when my aunt explained that the town of Lakeville in the book was really a thinly veiled version of Marquette. As I read, I wondered whether I would have as much fun living in Marquette as the novel's four heroines. So far I liked the snow—but not the cold—and despite the pink bedroom, I was glad to be with my grandma and aunt. I hoped tomorrow I would make some friends, at least with Tom.

I had read to page one hundred and just started to doze off from exhaustion when the women came into the parlor to "rest" for a few minutes before getting ready for bed.

"Well, I'm glad I have that potato salad made," said Grandma, picking up her sewing, which looked more like work than "rest" to me. "It's so much work to make, but always worthwhile when we eat it."

"You're the only person I know who makes potato salad for Thanksgiving," said my aunt.

"Oh, but James and Charles like it so," Grandma replied. "I bet they would willingly go without the turkey so long as they had their potato salad."

I had forgotten who James and Charles were from the earlier guest recital, but I asserted, "I love potato salad" just to make it clear I would not let them have it all.

"I knew you were my grandson for a reason," Grandma smiled. "You better enjoy it tomorrow, Robbie, because I'm not young anymore. This may be the last year I cook such a big meal for everyone."

"Mother, you say that every year," said Aunt Louisa May.

"Well, this year I'm serious. I'm getting too old for all this work."

"And you say that every year as well," Aunt Louisa May smiled. "Anyway, I think I have blue material in the sewing room that I can use to make Robert some new curtains. I'll just go check and see whether there's enough."

I put my nose back into my book, although I really wanted to go to bed. After a few minutes, my aunt returned with royal blue material.

"There isn't enough for a bedspread too," said my aunt, "but we can probably find some material that's the same color in the stores. Will it do, Robert?"

"Sure," I said. "I think it'll be perfect."

"My, it's already ten o'clock," said Grandma when the grandfather clock chimed. "I think we better get to bed. We have a big day ahead of us tomorrow. I'll be up at five to make sure that turkey gets in the oven on time, and you, Robbie, will have all our relatives and neighbors to meet."

"All right," I said, not protesting. My bedtime had been nine o'clock at home.

"After you've brushed your teeth and put on your pajamas, holler and we'll come up to say goodnight."

I usually just kissed my mom on the cheek and shook my father's hand, then went to bed on my own. I felt silly having two women come upstairs to tuck me in—perhaps I should lay down the ground rules now, I thought, but I was too tired to argue, and I should be polite my first night here. I remembered also that Grandma and Aunt Louisa May were grieving for my mother so I wanted to be kind. I knew they wanted to take the best care possible of me out of devotion to Mama. Eventually, we would adjust to one another.

And so I brushed my teeth, put on my pajamas, then hollered, "Good night." For a moment I hoped if I shut the bedroom door, they would stay downstairs, but I soon heard them coming up.

Playing along, I climbed into bed, stayed in a sitting position, and pulled the covers up to my waist, but I was not going to lie down to be tucked in.

Aunt Louisa May simply kissed me on the forehead and said, "Pleasant dreams." But after my aunt left, Grandma stayed behind a moment.

"I hope you'll be happy with us, Robbie," she said, sitting down on the edge of the bed.

"How could I not be?" I asked.

"I don't know. I personally think I'm pretty remarkable and a lot of fun to be around," Grandma laughed. "Still, I imagine it'll be hard for you at first. We all wish your mother were still with us, but we have to make the best of it. She would want us to be happy together."

"We will be," I said.

"I know," she replied, patting my hand. Then she leaned in and kissed me. "Good night, Robbie. I love you."

She then got up from the bed, turned off the light, and shut the door behind her.

I lay back in the bed. For a moment, I wondered whether I should have told her I loved her as well, but I did not even say that to my parents now that I was thirteen. I kind of wished I had said it to her though—maybe tomorrow night—although she had not seemed to wait, as if she expected it. I did feel grateful at that moment—grateful that I was in a warm house, despite the cold outside, and grateful to be with family. For the first time since my mother had died, I started to feel that everything would be okay.

I was even half-resigned to Grandma calling me Robbie.

Chapter 3

Thanksgiving

We were up early the next morning to prepare for the big Thanksgiving meal. After a rushed breakfast, I was in charge of setting the table while Grandma cooked the turkey and supervised Aunt Louisa May in everything from buttering the rolls and filling the creamer to making the gravy and hanging up clean hand towels in the bathroom.

Our guests began to arrive promptly at noon. Mrs. Williams and her son, John, were the first to appear. At age eighty, Mrs. Williams prided herself on knowing every tidbit of Marquette history, having been a resident almost since the town was founded. Now she was the last friend alive of my great-grandparents, Edmund and Dolly O'Neill. During her long life, Mrs. Williams had raised two children—her son, John, who lived with her, and her daughter, Marie, who was widowed and lived on Mackinac Island, off the eastern tip of Michigan's Upper Peninsula. Marie's son, Eric, was away fighting in the war. John, contrary to what his bachelor status might imply, was a handsome man in his mid-forties. Unfortunately, his life purpose had apparently been relegated to caring for his aging mother. Aunt Louisa May often remarked upon what a waste John's good looks were when no woman could have him—I sometimes wondered whether she would like to have him for herself. Grandma would comment that she could not understand why a man who could have any woman he wanted should choose his mother.

Mrs. Williams took a good ten minutes to walk from the front door to a chair and ease herself down into it. She seemed incredibly old to me; every minute I was afraid she would just crumple over from exhaustion, but instead,

Aunt Louisa May brought her a cup of tea which she sipped gingerly as our other guests arrived.

The Lewis brothers, James and Charles, arrived next. They had been my grandfather's playmates in their youth. For nearly half a century, they had worked in the nearby iron mines; then the previous spring they had retired and done nothing since but sit around, as was obvious from their protruding stomach rolls. I thought they told marvelous stories the first half dozen times I heard them, but since their repertoire only consisted of five stories between them, by spring I would have memorized each tale word for word and almost wished I could forget them.

The life of our party now arrived in the person of Great-Aunt Carolina Smith, my grandfather's sister. From the second I opened the door to her, I knew she was gracing us with her austere presence. She stepped into the house, without even responding to my "Hello." I had no idea who she was until after she had piled into my arms her fur coat and giant feathered hat. Dazzled by her red dress and a string of bright white pearls, I could only repeat, "Hello."

"Where is Kathleen?" she replied.

By the time I remembered Kathleen was my grandmother's first name, Aunt Carolina had stepped into the parlor doorway. She then stood there waiting to be noticed, or perhaps to have her entrance announced. She apparently was a very fine lady.

"Carolina, we're so glad you made it," said Grandma, coming up behind her from the dining room. I was surprised by Grandma's tone of respect, as if she were fully aware of the honor Great-Aunt Carolina was bestowing upon us. It would be weeks before I realized Grandma used such a tone to humor her sister-in-law rather than be subjected to complaints and accusations of improper neglect.

"Thank you, Kathleen; it's kind of you to invite me to your little party. Has my dear Jane arrived yet?"

"No, but I'm sure she will any minute. Why don't you sit down in the parlor until we're ready to eat? I have to go check on the turkey. It's just about ready to come out of the oven."

Mr. Williams, upon seeing Aunt Carolina enter, rose from his seat; the Lewis brothers continued to talk, while spread out across the sofa so no one else could sit there.

"Hello, Mr. Williams, Mrs. Williams," said Aunt Carolina. Then she glared at the Lewis brothers for failing to notice a lady was present.

Finally, she resigned herself to asking, "James, would you mind if I sat down?"

"You may have my chair, Mrs. Smith," said Mr. Williams. "It will probably be more comfortable for you."

"Thank you," she replied. "Mrs. Williams, you should be proud to have such a gentleman for a son."

"How are you, Carolina?" Mrs. Williams was the only person other than my grandmother whom I ever heard call my great-aunt by her first name. Mrs. Williams's advanced age left her without awe of the great lady she could remember as a little girl making mud-pies, long before she had married a judge and moved into a sandstone mansion on East Ridge Street.

"My rheumatism has been acting up frightfully since the weather turned so cold," said Great-Aunt Carolina. "Winter always makes me long for the warm days of my Southern childhood. The climate in Upper Michigan is so horrendous."

"Oh, my poor dear," smiled Mrs. Williams—I do believe had she been sitting next to Great-Aunt Carolina, she would have reached over and patted her knee. "You're far too young to be feeling such aches and pains. Wait until you're eighty."

"I'll never live that long," said Aunt Carolina. "My constitution is far too delicate."

"My ma had a good remedy for rheumatism," said Charles Lewis. "She always drank a shot of pickle juice each night before she went to bed. By morning, she wouldn't have a pain at all."

"Pickle juice!" said Aunt Carolina. "That's the most ridiculous thing I ever heard. Really Charles, all that vinegar would kill me for sure. You can't trust such wretched home remedies."

"Well, some of us can't afford to be running to the doctor every time we have a little ache," James Lewis defended his brother.

"Which doctor do you go to, Mrs. Smith?" asked Mr. Williams to divert an argument.

When the talk turned to doctors and ailments, my thoughts drifted. I thought I would fall asleep from boredom, but then the Hamptons arrived with their two sons.

"Hello, Jane, precious," said Aunt Carolina, rising to greet her daughter.

"Hello, Mother, how are you?" asked Mrs. Hampton.

"Fine if it weren't for my rheumatism. Hello, George."

"Hello, Mother," said Mr. Hampton in that tolerant tone men use for their mother-in-laws. "You look well."

"Thank you. And here are my two handsome grandsons. My, how you boys are growing! Mrs. Williams, can you believe any two boys could be so handsome?"

I then got my first good look at Mark and Tom. Neither looked all that special to me. Despite his age, Mr. Williams was more handsome than either of them. Mrs. Williams, perhaps knowing her genes were superior to Aunt Carolina's, simply smiled.

"Hello, Grandma," said Mark. "You're looking beautiful as always."

She giggled and offered him her cheek to kiss, which he did dutifully.

"Hello, Grandma," said Tom, unwilling to follow his brother's example.

"Oh Mark," Aunt Carolina gushed. "I don't know how Eliza can think she deserves such a handsome man as you. Mrs. Williams, have you heard that Mark and Eliza are engaged now. They'll be married just as soon as Mark turns eighteen this spring, although I'm trying to convince them to wait until after he goes to college."

Mark looked about to defend his decision to marry, but Grandma prevented him by returning into the parlor to greet her latest guests. "Hello, George, Jane. Robert, did you meet all our cousins?"

I muttered, "No," so Grandma officially introduced me to Mark and Tom. I shook hands with Mark, whose firm grip hurt my hand; I think he intended it to. He was tall and thin and had a look I did not trust, especially after how he had buttered up his grandmother. As for Tom, he smiled, sizing me up as being his age. When I went to shake his hand, he instead punched me in the arm and said, "Glad ta meetcha." He then started telling me all about his school, his friends, and all the winter games he would teach me to play. We were firm friends from that moment.

"There's the door again," said Grandma, excusing herself.

In a minute, she ushered the Mitchells into the parlor. All the seats were now occupied, so they stood in the room's center as Grandma introduced them to me. The family consisted of three siblings, a middle-aged bachelor brother, Roger, and his middle-aged spinster sisters, Mary and Florence. Roger and Mary Mitchell both appeared to be pleasant and easy-going, but Florence had a sharp-tongue; my guess was that as the youngest, her parents and siblings had spoiled her as a child and she had never quite been able to resist having her own way after that. She constantly found fault with everyone, never even sensing her own lack of congeniality.

Last to arrive was Eliza Graham, a beautiful, striking sixteen-year old ideal of womanhood. Grandma introduced her to me as our next-door neighbor, and also my cousin Mark's fiancée. The first moment I saw Eliza will live forever in my memory. Her glowing, cheerful smile, her gentle eyes, her siren's voice all clutched at my heartstrings. I instantly felt I would love her for all eternity.

Before Eliza could say hello to anyone, Mark came up to clutch her arm, instantly claiming possession.

"What took you so long?" he asked.

I knew then that I hated him.

"Mother's sick and can't come, so I didn't want to leave her alone," Eliza replied, although she directed her remarks to Grandma. "I only came over to say that we won't be coming. Mother said to give you her apologies, Mrs. O'Neill."

"You're always doing things for your mother," Mark whined. "I'll be glad when we're married, so I have you all to myself."

Despite Mark's obsessive clinging, Grandma pulled Eliza away to the kitchen so they could fix two plates of food for her to bring home.

Meanwhile, I glared at Mark for his selfishness, his utter lack of concern that his girlfriend's mother was ill. How could such a goddess as Eliza be interested in him? Not even his looks were favorable. In fact, I was better looking than him. Yet in Eliza's eyes, I was probably nothing but a child. I had long wondered when I would fall in love—and now, why did the first woman who ever gave me that tingling sensation have to be taken, and by a man—no, an ignorant oaf—whom I despised the moment I saw him. As Tom chattered to me, I could only dream of this woman, this goddess I had just met. When Eliza left the house, I watched her through the window, my gaze following her down the sidewalk. My trance was only broken when Grandma announced that dinner was ready.

As I sat down at the table, the sight of so much turkey, of potatoes and gravy, turnips and cranberries and stuffing, not to mention the pies I knew Grandma had out on the back porch to keep cold, made my stomach gnaw with hunger—I was surprised by such ravenous feelings when lovesick people reputedly lose their appetites. So I decided I would be lovesick after Thanksgiving—I didn't want to miss this bountiful feast. I don't think I ever saw so much food before, not even at the county barbecues back home. Holidays in South Carolina had only consisted of me, my parents, Nellie and Mr. Carter—we did not need so much food for five people, but Grandma had thirteen for dinner and had initially invited nineteen, so there was more than enough of everything except elbow room at the table.

"Now that everyone is seated," said Grandma, after we had waited forever for Mrs. Williams to get scooted in, "we'll have the blessing. Louisa May, would you say it, please?

My aunt thanked the Lord for the food, for the company, and for the new addition to their table that year—myself. She also included a special blessing in memory of my mother, and a prayer for my father's safety and the safety of all the men fighting in the war who could not share this special day with their families.

"Amen," was said in unison and then twenty-six hands reached around for the food.

"Eliza is getting to be more beautiful every day," said Mrs. Hampton to begin the dinner conversation. "She's the spitting image of her mother. Do you remember how attractive Lorna was when she was a girl?"

"Oh, yes," said my Grandma. "No girl in this town could catch a husband until Lorna was married off and the boys had to look elsewhere."

"Not me," said Mr. Hampton. "The moment I saw Jane, I didn't want anyone else."

"That's so sweet," said Mary Mitchell.

"Mr. Lewis," snapped Florence Mitchell, "the potatoes are supposed to be passed clockwise. I haven't received any yet."

Florence Mitchell's tone was unnecessary, but I couldn't blame her—sitting beside her, I was equally concerned about getting my share of mashed potatoes. But once my plate was full, I was free to block out the adults' conversation as I reveled in my food and wondered whether Eliza's mother were still beautiful—I needed to know whether Eliza would age well since I had already decided she would be my wife and mother to my children—it sounds silly now, but I cannot overemphasize how smitten I was by her gorgeous figure and flawless face.

"Robert, pass the gravy," said Mark. What a sorry rival he was to me when he could not even say, "Please." How could Eliza possibly love him? I found it hard to believe not one other young man existed in Marquette for her—but then, that only gave me a better chance with her, and I wasn't really that young—I would be fourteen in six months, and that was only two or three years younger than her. Somehow I would convince her to wait for me.

Save for Mark's presence at the table, the meal passed pleasantly. Even with Grandma jumping up every other minute to fetch someone more coffee or to get extra butter for the rolls, a general feeling of peace and contentment enveloped us. I ate heartily until I felt cheerful and began to enjoy the conversation and be amused by everyone's eccentricities.

An hour of stuffing ourselves must have elapsed before Mrs. Williams laid down her fork and admitted, "I can't eat another bite."

"You'll have to," Grandma replied, rising from the table for the thirty-seventh time. "We haven't had dessert yet. I have an apple, a lemon meringue, a chocolate, and two pumpkin pies for us to polish off."

The women all protested that if they ate anything more, they would have no figures left. But eventually each consented to having a sliver, but no ice cream. Men, being far more reasonable creatures, each had a full slice, some of us two—how can you choose only one kind from four types of pie?

Then all too soon, this grand moment of domestic feasting concluded. The men cleared their throats and sauntered into the parlor. The women set about clearing the table and helping Grandma with the dishes. Mrs. Williams insisted she would help, but Grandma told her, "No, you just sit there and rest." "But I want to do something," Mrs. Williams said. "You can supervise us all," Aunt Louisa May replied. But actually, I think Aunt Carolina had the supervision aspect of cleanup under control because she did not leave her seat; the only work she did was to lay her napkin on the table. After an uncertain moment, Mark went to join the men. Tom and I remained at the table, uncomfortably staring at one another, each wanting to leave but unsure how to ask.

"Men are such lazy creatures," said Florence Mitchell as she started to run the dishwater.

"They make me glad I never married one," smiled Mary. "Our brother is enough to look after."

"Robert was always good to me," said Grandma, "and Robbie will be a good husband someday. I'll make sure he knows how to cook, dust, and do windows before he leaves here."

Tom raised his eyebrows at me. I could feel myself blushing—what must he think of me? I had considered asking Grandma whether he and I could go up to my room, but now I realized we could not even do that. If he saw my pink bedroom, he would never be my friend.

"Robert, would you really like to do all that housework?" Tom's mother asked me. "Maybe you'll be a good example to my boys."

Tom and I had heard enough. I was about to crawl under the table, but Tom found the presence of mind to say, "Robert and I are gonna go outside and play."

"Oh, but it's so cold out there," said Florence Mitchell.

Tom just grunted in disagreement.

"Go ahead," said Mrs. Hampton, "but make sure you wear your hats. Letting cold air into your ears is what makes you sick."

"Jane, they have their good clothes on," said Aunt Carolina. "You don't want them to ruin their pants in this sloppy weather."

"We won't Grandma," Tom replied. "We'll be careful.

"Can't they stay in the house and find a nice little game to play, like jacks perhaps?" asked Aunt Carolina.

"Jacks!" yelled Tom. "Only girls play jacks!"

"Carolina," Grandma came to our rescue, "you can't expect two boys to sit quietly and listen to old women talk. I'd be worried about them if they did."

"Go have a good time," Aunt Louisa May told us.

We went before Tom's grandmother made further objections. But just as we started toward the front hall to grab our coats, Grandma shouted, "Make sure you're back in time for supper."

Supper! I couldn't imagine eating anything more today—although, I had only tried the pumpkin and lemon meringue pie, and I did want a piece of chocolate.

Then I realized my coat wasn't in the front hall but in my room.

"I have to go upstairs to get my coat," I apologized to Tom.

"That's all right. I'll come up and see your room," he said.

I did not know how to get out of it. I trudged up the stairs, embarrassed, trying to think what I might say, how I might distract him to keep him from noticing, but the moment I opened my bedroom door, he let out a whistle and said, "Holy cow! Why is your room pink?"

"It used to be my mama's room," I confessed. "But my grandma's going to fix it up so it'll be blue."

"Oh," he said. I grabbed my coat so we could evacuate the room of humiliation as quickly as possible. Tom followed me downstairs and out the front door.

"Now what do we do?" I asked, ignorant of winter's activities, but more to steer conversation away from my pink bedroom.

"I don't s'pose you got a sleigh?" he asked.

"No."

"What about some cardboard?"

"What do you want cardboard for?"

"Ta use as a sleigh. Nothin's as fast as cardboard."

"I can go ask my grandma for some," I offered.

"No, the snow's probably too wet for sleighing anyway. We'd just sink in it."

"Oh," I said, unaware of what constituted desirable snow conditions. "Then what should we do?"

"Let's walk down the street and see if Mags can come out."

"Who's Mags?" I asked. The name reminded me of the convict Magwitch in *Great Expectations*—I envisioned some sort of tough guy, perhaps a gang leader. Did Marquette have gangs?

"She's a girl in my class," said Tom. "We both go ta Bishop Baraga School. Her family was supposed ta come ta Aunt Kathleen's today, but her sister got the chicken pox so her mom didn't want her ta come over and spread it. Are you going ta Bishop Baraga?"

"I guess so," I said.

"Well, since you're Catholic, you probably will. It's not bad. Only a couple of the sisters are tough."

"I think that's where my aunt said I would go, but she said I wouldn't go until after Christmas."

"How come?"

"She thought I'd need time to adjust to moving here and getting over my mama's death."

"Ain't you over it yet?" Tom asked. "I mean, it's been a week now, hasn't it?"

I could not believe Tom's remark. I suddenly felt older and wiser than him, for I had experienced death, while he obviously did not understand its finality and the grief that rises from it. Yet I also envied his innocence.

When I did not reply, Tom apparently realized he had upset me, so he changed the subject.

"Anyway, if you go ta Bishop Baraga, maybe we'll be in the same class. You can sit nexta me if you want. I need a new best friend anyway since I hate my old one."

"Why do you hate him?"

"He's looney. Thinks I'm tryin' to steal his girlfriend. We got into a fight 'cause I told him she was too ugly for me. He was gonna hit me, but I saw it comin' and socked him a black eye. He's lucky that Sister stopped me or he woulda had two of 'em. Havin' girlfriends is stupid anyway; they just ruin your life."

"They're worth it if they're really beautiful," I said. I was surprised by my own words, but I could not get Eliza Graham out of my head. Another vision of her came before my eyes—she in a wedding gown, I standing beside an altar as she walked down the aisle.

"Beautiful girls can still be dumb," said Tom. "Trust me, women ain't nothin' but trouble."

Tom had barely finished his sentence before a snowball came flying at him, smacking him in the arm.

"Ha! I got you, Tom Hampton!" screamed a girl, running out from behind a house, as if to prove Tom right—girls were trouble.

"Hey, Mags!" Tom greeted his assailant. "I wantcha ta meet someone."

With long brown hair flying from out of a knit hat, Mags half-skipped over the snowbank to where we stood on the sidewalk.

"Mags, meet Robert O'Neill," Tom introduced us. "He's some sort of cousin ta me, and he just moved ta Marquette."

"Where you from?" she asked.

"South Carolina," I said.

She whistled in astonishment.

"His mother died so he's staying with my Aunt Kathleen. That's his grandma."

"Where's your dad?" she asked.

"Fighting in the war," I said.

"Really?" said Mags. "My old man's in the war too. So's my uncle. In fact, my cousin Helen from downstate's coming tomorrow to stay with us 'cause our other aunt doesn't want her anymore and her mother's dead."

"Do you wanna have a snowball fight?" Tom asked before I could ask where Mags's uncle and father were stationed.

"Sure, but which one of us gets Robert?" Mags asked.

"I'll take him," said Tom, "although he'll be a handicap since he's never made snowballs before, being from the South. I'll have to show him how."

I had made snowballs before. We occasionally got a light snow in the South, but since I didn't really know Mags yet, I preferred being on Tom's side.

Mags, however, had other ideas.

"I'll show him how to make snowballs," she said. "You always make crummy ones."

"Do not!" Tom barked.

"Tom Hampton, you just be quiet while I show him the right way to do it," she said, bending over to scoop up snow in her mittens and form it into a ball. "There, see, nothin' to it. You just have to be sure to pack it hard; otherwise, it'll fall apart in midair. You do know how to throw, don't you?"

"Of course," I said.

"Well, just to be sure," she demonstrated, "you swing your arm back like this and let it go!"

Like a catapult, her arm sent the snowball flying forward and smack into Tom's shoulder.

"You think you're funny, don'tcha?" said Tom. "Doesn't matter. Robert and me is gonna cream you."

"Ha!" she laughed and ran back behind her house. Before I could make a snowball, she had hers whirling toward us; she must have had a whole arsenal already made, she started to throw them so fast.

I realized I would need quick thinking for this battle, and although half a dozen hard snowballs hit my jaw before I managed to hit Mags in the shoulder with one, I refused to look anything but tough before my new friends. Tom, meanwhile, dodged his way behind trees until he was on the opposite corner of the house. When Mags popped out her head to launch another snowbomb, he belted her right in the face. Then Mags was finished with child's play. Before I knew what was happening, she had Tom on his back and was shoving snow down his shirt. He let out a roar as the cold ice touched his chest. Finally, he shoved her off him into the snowbank. Laughing, she jumped to her feet and exclaimed, "Did you see that, Robert? I got him good."

I couldn't help smiling at Tom's dismay. He stood up, looking angry, but when Mags and I only laughed harder, he slowly smiled. I suddenly realized I felt overwhelmingly happy and relieved to have made new friends so quickly. I could not remember having so much fun with any of my friends in South Carolina. I would have even let Mags put snow down my shirt because I had enjoyed the snowball fight so much.

"Margaret Lawson!"

We all turned our heads to see a middle-aged woman leaning out of the house's kitchen door. "What do you think you're doing throwing those snow-balls? Get right in this house, young lady, before you catch pneumonia."

"Mother," said Mags, ignoring the order, "this is Robert, Mrs. O'Neill's grandson."

"Oh, hello, Robert," she said, suddenly turning friendly. "Your grandma told us you were coming. I hope you had a nice trip here."

"Yes, ma'am," I replied. "Thank you."

"We would have come over for dinner today, but my girls have had chicken pox, and I didn't want them to spread it. Margaret, I told you not to go outside. I didn't want you too close to other people. You might still be contagious. You've only been over your chicken pox a couple days now."

"Oh, Mother, you know even Mary is fine now. She's just faking it for the attention."

"Come inside, Margaret," her mother repeated. "Goodbye, Robert. It was nice to meet you. I hope you like Marquette."

"Goodbye, Tom, Robert," groaned Mags. "Maybe I'll see you tomorrow."

"I don't know why you have to roughhouse with those boys," we heard Mrs. Lawson grumble as she closed the door after her daughter.

Tom mimicked her. "'I don't know why you have to roughhouse, Margaret. It isn't at all ladylike, Margaret.' Poor Mags. That ole mother of hers doesn't let her have any fun. Mrs. Lawson thinks she's some great lady and wants her daughters to grow up to marry doctors or lawyers or something. I can't figure out why she don't like me though—'specially since my grandma's so rich."

Tom and I walked back to my Grandma's house. After hearing Mrs. Lawson's comment, I understood why Mags was such a tomboy. When I told Tom I had enjoyed the snowball fight, Tom replied, "That ain't nothin'. You should have been there for the one we had in the schoolyard last winter." He then detailed to me the movements of the two armies formed during this already legendary snowball fight when his entire class at school had broken into teams.

"Look at those wet clothes," said Florence Mitchell, who just would be the one to meet us at the front door. "You better change right away before the snow thaws or you'll be all wet and catch your deaths of pneumonia. You're both old enough to know better than not to brush all that snow off your clothes before you come inside. Do you think we all want to walk in your puddles?"

"Sorry," Tom said. She only frowned and turned around. Tom stuck his tongue out behind her back, but James Lewis happened to see it as he stepped out of the kitchen. He set to giggling and Florence Mitchell turned around to demand what was so funny. But Mr. Lewis was a true pal and did not rat on Tom.

My new best friend and I went up to my room to change our clothes. I loaned Tom some of my dry pants, and we hung the wet ones above the bathtub so they wouldn't melt all over the floor. I was grateful Tom did not comment on the pink bedroom this time.

Grandma met me at the bottom of the stairs and whispered, "Just ignore Florence. She's only happy when she's made someone else miserable. I can't expect two healthy boys not to get wet when they play in the snow."

Supper was now ready. Once again, we crowded around the table. Despite everyone's protests of still being stuffed, onto the table was laid out the remains of the turkey, potatoes, cranberries, stuffing, potato salad and pumpkin, apple, lemon meringue and chocolate pies, and it all disappeared just as rapidly as at dinner. I was surprised to find my snowball fight had built up quite an appetite in me. Mark, however, had no excuse—he might have been older, but he ate at least double what I did, and his table manners were atrocious—I actually saw him wipe his hand on his pants at one point. Poor Eliza must have known she did not have a gentleman for a future husband so why did she tolerate him? Since she lived next door to me, rather than next door to Mark, I would find an opportunity to gain her affection—I was sure of it.

Dark had fallen by the time supper ended. The women set to washing the dishes one more time. Tom and I went out onto the front porch to avoid the parlor filled with the men and their cigars. Mark, after a dull afternoon pretending to be a grown man, decided to join us. We turned on the porch light and sat on the swing, but we soon grew cold, and Mark refused to let us rock the swing to keep our circulation going.

"How about we build a snowman?" Tom suggested.

"Okay," I said, "but you'll have to show me how."

"Children," Mark said, "I hope you evolve from this immature stage sooner or later. Please attempt to accomplish it sooner."

"Why don'tcha try speakin' English for once?" Tom replied.

"I do speak English. You're just too juvenile to comprehend sophisticated dialogue."

"I don't know how Eliza can stand you," said Tom, "much less wanna marry you."

"You're just jealous because the only girlfriend you have is Ragamuffin Mags."

"You better shut up!" said Tom.

"You know it's true. Mags in Rags is the only girl Tom Hampton will ever have to love."

"I'm not as dumb as you 'cause I'll never get married."

"That just further shows how immature you are," said Mark.

"Robert, let's go back inside," said Tom. "There's too much hot air out here."

I followed Tom inside, being all the more convinced his brother was my enemy. Just how could Eliza stand Mark?

The women had just finished the dishes, so everyone was gathering at the table to play cards. Tom and I squeezed in to play a few hands. When Mark came in, he sat in the corner with his grandmother, agreeing with her that card playing was immoral. Tom rolled his eyes. Everyone else kept playing.

When the clock struck ten, Mr. Hampton said, "After this round, boys, go put on your coats. I have to work in the morning."

"I hate when the party breaks up," Mary Mitchell said. "It's always so sad."

"But we all had a wonderful time while it lasted," said Grandma.

"Yes, we did," Mrs. Williams agreed.

A flood of consent came from everyone.

At the front door, Tom shook my hand and said, "I'll come over tamorrow ta see you, Robert, since there's no school."

"All right," I said, feeling a return visit would seal the pact of friendship.

Once all the guests were gone, I kissed my two female guardians goodnight and climbed upstairs to my room. For a little while, as I tried to fall asleep, I thought back over the party, and then the snowball fight. But once sleep overcame me, my dreams were blessed solely by Eliza Graham's charming smile.

Chapter 4

Helen

The following morning, Tom came over as I finished breakfast. I quickly shoveled down the last of my scrambled eggs, then put on my coat and boots, and promised I'd be back for lunch.

"I brought my sleigh," said Tom as we stepped outside.

"Good," I replied. "I'm really excited to—"

"Hey, Mags!" Tom cut me off. I saw her coming up the sidewalk with a plain-faced girl. "Who's that with you?"

We came down the porch steps to meet the girls on the sidewalk.

"This is my cousin, Helen," said Mags. "Remember I told you she was coming to stay with us until the war's over?"

"Where's she from?" Tom asked, as if Helen were unable to answer for herself.

"I'm from Flint, in the Lower Peninsula," Helen told him. "Aunt Elaine is letting me stay with her until my dad comes home from the war."

"What took you so long to get here?" asked Tom. "The war's been goin' on forever."

Helen's face crinkled up with sadness as she explained, "My mom died last year, so I was staying with my Grandma and spinster Aunt Helen, but Grandma said she thought I would be happier being around other children, so she sent me up here to be with my cousins—but I know she really just didn't want me around because I'm too much trouble for her."

"Oh," Tom said. "Mags, do you wanna go sleighridin'?"

"Can't," Mags grumbled. "My mother said since it's Helen's first day here, I have to do whatever she wants, and she wants to go to the ole library."

"Geez! Can't she go by herself?" asked Tom.

"I don't know the way," Helen said.

"What do you wanna go to the library for anyway?" Tom asked.

"To get some books." Her eyes grew in amazement that anyone could ask such a ridiculous question.

"Maybe after lunch I can go sleigh riding," said Mags.

But Tom was determined to have his way now.

"Let's walk Helen there, and then we'll go sleigh ridin'. She can find her way back, can't she?"

"I might get lost," said Helen, obviously annoyed that he talked as if she were not there; she was clearly less concerned about getting lost than responding to Tom's antagonism toward her.

"It's only three or four blocks," Tom argued.

"I haven't been to the library yet," I interceded. I sympathized with Helen since I was also unfamiliar with Marquette, and I knew what it was to lose a mother. Besides, visiting the library didn't sound bad since there were only girls' books at Grandma's house. "If you show us how to get there, I'll help Helen find the way back. I have a good memory."

"Don't you wanna sleigh ride?" Tom asked me. "You'll miss all the fun."

"That's all right," I said. "We have all winter for sleigh riding. You and Mags go. I can catch up with you after lunch."

Tom tried to object, but Mags, grateful to be relieved of her task, said, "Let them go, Tom. Robert can go with us this afternoon."

"All right, come on." Tom grabbed his sleigh's rope and pulled it down the street, the three of us trailing behind.

We walked a few blocks, afraid to say anything since Tom was now in a bad mood. Finally, we stopped at the top of Front Street's hill where a couple churches stood.

"There it is," said Tom, pointing at a majestic limestone building with great pillars in front. "Don't get lost on the way back. I'll come by your place after lunch, Robert."

"Okay. Thanks," I smiled to appease him.

"Come on, Mags," he said, leading her downhill to another side street they could sleigh down.

Helen and I started up the library's high front steps.

"Isn't it beautiful?" asked Helen, stopping after a couple seconds to admire the building. "It looks just like a Greek Temple."

"Yeah," I said, "or a Southern plantation house made of stone."

"We have bigger libraries than this downstate," said Helen, "but I haven't seen one so graceful."

"I've never even been in a library," I confessed. "I imagine there's one in Greenville, but we only go to town a couple times a year so I couldn't really check books out of it."

"Where's Greenville?" she asked.

"In South Carolina," I replied, as if all the world knew where Greenville was.

She looked at me strangely.

"I thought you had a bit of a Southern accent, but I didn't think Southerners were big readers."

"Why not?"

"I don't know. I never really thought about it—I just figured they weren't. But why are you in Marquette?"

"My mama died and my father's gone to the war, so like you, I've been sent here to live with my relatives—my grandma and aunt. I just got here two days ago myself."

Helen gasped, surprised by our similar stories. Then she said, "I guess even if Southern ladies read, I didn't think Southern boys did. Actually most boys don't read no matter where they're from."

"I read all the time!" I declared in vindication of boys everywhere.

"Okay," she said, taken aback by my enthusiasm. "Well, what books are you going to check out?"

I wanted a Tarzan novel. I had heard a new one was out where Tarzan fought the Germans in Africa. I was dying to read it, but not thinking it would interest Helen, I said, "I guess I'll have to see what they have. Right now I'm reading *Dandelion Cottage*. My aunt gave it to me to read because it was written by someone who lives in Marquette."

"What's it about?" asked Helen.

"Four girls who rent out a cottage for their summer playhouse."

"That sounds good."

"It's really a girls' book," I frowned.

"That's all right. I read books for boys and girls. It doesn't matter to me. Books broaden the mind."

By now, we had finished climbing the library steps. As we passed through the front door, we started to whisper. To the right and left of us were two rooms branching off while in front of us was the librarian's desk, and behind us on each side of the doors were stairs to the upper and lower floors.

"Robert, do you know who wrote *Dandelion Cottage*?" Helen asked.

"Her last name is Rankin," I said, "but we better ask for help. I doubt we'll ever find the book in this huge place."

"I'll find it," stated Helen. "I know my way around a library."

She led us into one side room, and then back out into the next, and up and down between aisles until she suddenly realized *Dandelion Cottage* would be with the children's books. I had thought to go to the children's section first, but she acted so self-assured I was afraid to repeat my suggestion of asking for help. Eventually, we did find the book, along with several others by Carroll Watson Rankin. Helen pulled *Dandelion Cottage* from the shelf and quietly read the first paragraph. I stood a few feet from her, pretending to read the book spines, but actually, I was silently observing her. She was only perhaps an inch or two shorter than me, and I guessed she was probably about a year younger. She had long brown hair, a green dress that went down to her knees, long socks pulled up to meet her dress, winter shoes, and a brown cloth coat. She squinted as she read, mouthing the words to herself as if trying to imagine the dialogue spoken. Her small lips moved rapidly.

"I'll check it out," she said, snapping the book shut and tucking it under her arm. "Now I want to see whether they have any Oz books."

"What are Oz books?" I asked.

"You don't know about the Oz books?" she asked. She said it so loudly I feared the librarian would throw us out of the building. "I thought every boy and girl read the Oz books. They're the most wonderfully magical stories ever written, full of witches, talking animals, and fantastic faraway countries. Anyone who hasn't read them has led an underprivileged childhood, and anyone who doesn't like them clearly has no imagination. You have to read them."

"Okay," I said, amused by her overwhelming enthusiasm.

"Come on," she said, grabbing my hand and pulling me down the aisle and into another where in the B's for, according to Helen, "L. Frank Baum, the greatest children's writer who ever lived," I saw my first Oz books. "Here's *The Wonderful Wizard of Oz*," said Helen. "It's the first in the series so you need to start with that one. Oh, sugar! They don't have *The Emerald City of Oz*. That's the next one I have to read, but I'll get *The Patchwork Girl of Oz* since it's the next in the series. I've read the first five books four times each. I've wanted to read the sixth book before the others, but I haven't found it yet, and I just can't wait to read the others any longer, especially since I see they also have the eighth book, *Tiktok of Oz*."

"How many are there?" I asked, wondering what I had gotten myself into. She would apparently expect me to read them all.

"The eleventh one, *The Lost Princess of Oz,* just came out this year. A new book comes out almost every year."

Since we were in the B's, I thought of stepping down the aisle a little to Edgar Rice Burroughs, but Helen said, "Let's go check out."

Rather than argue with her—somehow I didn't think she'd care for Tarzan—I followed her to the front desk.

"I hope you like *Dandelion Cottage,*" said the librarian. "It's already considered a children's classic." Then she saw the Oz books. "I don't know what you children see in those books with all their weird pictures and fantastic characters. They're not very useful when they're so unrealistic."

She shook her head disapprovingly as she stamped our books. I was embarrassed to be checking the books out—I suspected these Oz books were also written for girls. I hoped Tom didn't see me carrying them home.

To my surprise, as the librarian handed us back our books, Helen declared, "The Oz books will also be classics someday. You'll see. They're even better than anything Hans Christian Andersen wrote."

"Fairy tales," grumbled the librarian. "I never did like them."

I grabbed both our books and started toward the door, so Helen would follow rather than argue over the value of imagination.

She looked miffed once we were outside, but I deterred her anger by saying, "Now we'll have to figure out how to get back home."

"Since you're also new to Marquette," she said, "I suppose you don't know where my Aunt Elaine lives?"

"I think so. Tom and I actually went to visit Mags yesterday."

"Oh yeah, Mags was bragging to me this morning about how she whipped you and Tom in that snowball fight yesterday."

"She didn't whip us," I said, indignant to be thought bested by a girl.

"No, I don't imagine she could whip you," said Helen. "You look pretty strong. I think she just likes to exaggerate. I don't really know her that well, but I'm a pretty good judge of character."

"Well," I allowed, "she is good at snowball fights, and since I'm from the South, I don't really know much about them."

"We get snow in Flint, but Grandma would have disapproved if I were in a snowball fight."

"Mags's mother didn't approve yesterday."

"No, she wouldn't. Grandma raised my mom and aunts to be ladies because Grandma's a social climber and wanted all her daughters to marry rich husbands. None of them did, and Grandma's always been disappointed by it. Since my mom died, Grandma's always been downright nasty to my dad; in fact, I know the reason she sent me here rather than keep me with her was just to spite him."

"I'll never understand why people are always so worried about being rich," I said.

"Money gives you power and it can solve all your problems," Helen stated in a mocking tone. "My Aunt Elaine's just as bad as Grandma; I think she regrets not marrying a rich man, so now she expects all her daughters to marry gentlemen."

"Money does not a gentleman make," I said, repeating my father's own words. "It's being kind and having good manners." But then to cheer Helen, I suggested, "Maybe your Grandma really did think you would be happier here with your cousins."

"No, my grandma hates me!" Helen said. "She's never forgiven my mom for marrying beneath her, and she hates me as a result."

She began to sob uncontrollably. I was so astonished by her instant tears that I didn't know what else to do except pat her arm to calm her.

"Young man!" shouted an old woman, attempting to cross the street. "You leave that girl alone, or I'll tell your parents. I know what naughty thoughts you boys have at your age!"

Helen, humiliated by the old woman's words, turned and ran down the street. I was after her in a second, not thinking until later that the old woman might think I was only pestering Helen more.

"Helen, please stop!" I called. She ran nearly a block, then stopped and leaned up against a lamppost. "I didn't mean to upset you."

"It's okay," she said, wiping her eyes on her coat sleeve. "I only ran so you wouldn't get into trouble with that nosy old woman."

"Come on," I said, taking her arm and carrying our books under my other arm. "Your aunt's house is right over there."

She let me lead her for a minute before she said, "Thank you for taking me to the library, Robert. I'm sorry I embarrassed you."

"It's all right," I replied. "I'm glad to have someone to talk to about books." And I kind of was glad; I could try to get her interested in Tarzan and Jack London later.

"Helen, is that you?" shouted Mrs. Lawson from her front porch. "Where's Margaret?"

"She went sleigh riding with her friend, Tom," Helen said. "Robert took me to the library instead."

"That was kind of you, Robert. I suppose you newcomers have to stick together. Actually, Robert, your grandmother just called to invite me over for lunch. Mollie said she'd stay with Mary. Poor dear, she still feels a little under the weather. Do you want to come with me, Helen? If Robert doesn't mind waiting a minute, we can walk back with him."

"Okay," said Helen. "I'll just go put my library books inside."

Helen ran into the house while Mrs. Lawson and I awkwardly ignored each other. When Helen returned, Mrs. Lawson scolded, "Helen, it's not ladylike to run. I suppose your father didn't teach you any better, but there'll be no running in my house. You need to act like a young lady if you want to be treated like one."

"Yes, Aunt Elaine," she said, lowering her head, ashamed to be reprimanded in front of me.

As we started down the street, Mrs. Lawson asked how I liked Marquette.

"It seems nice so far," I said. "The library is really big, and I like the snow, although I'm not used to it being so cold."

"Wait until January when we get the big blizzards and subzero temperatures," Mrs. Lawson replied.

"It gets cold like this in Flint," said Helen.

"Yes, it can get this cold downstate," said Mrs. Lawson, "but it's nothing to what will come once winter is really here."

Mrs. Lawson had been born downstate, but her husband had been born in Marquette, so she related to us his tales of terrible storms during his childhood when snow had drifted to the second floor of houses, and the roads had been even harder to plow since they only used horses and no machinery. "People used to be snowed in for days," she concluded.

Days! I couldn't imagine. Why, we could all starve to death! Actually, it sounded rather exciting.

Grandma met us at the front door. By now it was apparent to me that she loved to socialize, and since the Lawsons had not come for her big Thanksgiving dinner, she had invited Mrs. Lawson for lunch.

"Hello, Elaine. This must be your niece. Hello, Helen, I'm Robert's grandmother, Mrs. O'Neill."

"Hello," Helen muttered shyly, for which I could not blame her; she apparently had reason to fear grandmothers.

Grandma had us sit down while Aunt Louisa May carried in lunch. Once the food was on the table, Grandma asked Helen about her trip. Finding a grownup actually interested in her made Helen perk up.

"It was wonderful," she said. "I loved riding on the train, over all those miles and miles of land, and wondering what kinds of lives all the people live in the houses I passed by. I was so excited to ride the ferry over the straits, especially with the ice and snow on the water—it made me a little nervous as if I were on the *Titanic*."

I was surprised by her words because Aunt Louisa May and I had also had to ride the ferry that carried the train over the Straits of Mackinac to Upper Michigan. Yet I had not thought of the *Titanic*. I had always thought myself more imaginative than others, but I was starting to wonder whether Helen were my equal.

"Weren't you nervous to travel by yourself like that?" asked Aunt Louisa May.

"No," said Helen. "I like being by myself."

"You won't be by yourself much anymore," Mrs. Lawson laughed, "not with my three girls around."

"Will you be sending Helen to Bishop Baraga?" Grandma asked Mrs. Lawson.

"Yes, that's where my girls go."

"Robert will be going there too," said Grandma. "Helen, maybe the two of you will be in the same class."

"What grade are you in?" Helen asked me.

"Eighth," I replied.

"Oh, I'm only in seventh," she said. "Mags and Tom are both in eighth grade though."

"Oh well," I said, "we can always walk to school and back together."

"Robert won't start school until after Christmas," said Grandma. "I think he needs a little time to adjust to his loss."

"Helen will start Monday," said Mrs. Lawson. "I didn't want her to fall behind."

I thought Mrs. Lawson unsympathetic, considering Helen also needed time to adjust to her new home.

Grandma said, "Robert won't fall behind. He's a very bright boy."

"Sometimes," Mrs. Lawson replied, "they place new students a class behind where they should be to make sure they won't be behind, so maybe Robert and Helen will be in the same class."

"No," said Grandma. "Robert was near the head of his class in South Carolina. I'll talk to the teachers to make sure that doesn't happen."

"I bet he'll be the smartest boy in his class," Helen said.

I blushed. She was practically staring at me, and not in the same curious way as when she had learned I was a Southerner. It was more a gaze of admiration, and it made me uncomfortable.

Mrs. Lawson, not to be outdone, said, "My Mary is so smart she'll be skipping fourth grade next year and going straight into fifth."

The door knocker eliminated further competition between the adults over us children. Aunt Louisa May went to see who was there. A moment later, Tom and Mags burst in, soaked with snow that immediately started to melt on the dining room floor.

"Margaret! Why you're drenched!" Mrs. Lawson exclaimed. "Go home and change before you catch pneumonia."

"No, we're going back out to play in a minute," Mags protested.

"I don't care. You'll change your clothes first."

"We just came in to see if Robert could go sleigh riding with us now," said Tom.

"Sure, I'll go," I said. "Helen, do you want to come?" I imagined she wouldn't go, but I thought it polite to ask her.

Helen didn't look very interested until I said, "Please, Helen; it'll be lots of fun." I was afraid if she said, "No," that Mrs. Lawson wouldn't let Mags go either.

"All right, I'll go if you do."

I almost wished I hadn't insisted when she said that. This girl made me uncomfortable, especially after the crying incident on the walk home, and now the way she kept staring at me. I was afraid if she always wanted to hang around me, Mags and Tom wouldn't invite me to play with them, and they seemed a lot more fun than Helen.

"First, you'll both have to go home and put on something warmer," Mrs. Lawson told Mags and Helen.

"Go ahead," I told the girls. "Tom and I will wait for you to come back."

"We won't be ten minutes," promised Mags, who would not have felt the need for dry clothes if she had fallen into Lake Superior.

While we waited for the girls, I finished my sandwich, and then I went upstairs to put on an extra shirt under my jacket. Tom insisted on following me up to my room. I was relieved that he didn't notice the Oz book I had checked out, especially since the main character in it was a girl, but I don't think Tom ever noticed a book in his life. He just plopped down onto my pink bedspread, despite his dirty pants. I did not care—although Grandma would— I thought the bedspread might look better with a little brown on it.

"We can watch for Helen and Mags from my window," I said while digging through the suitcase I had still not unpacked. I was destitute of winter clothes, not having needed them in the South, but Grandma had promised to take me shopping tomorrow for a hat, gloves, scarf, a winter jacket, and some long johns, whatever those were. Tom looked at my toy cowboys and Indians—the only things besides clothes and a couple books that I had brought from home. Since I had left the bedroom door open, we could hear the grownups' voices downstairs.

"Robert doesn't seem like he'll give you much trouble," said Mrs. Lawson. "I'm sure you're glad to have him. I wish having Helen were as easy."

"She seems like a well-mannered young lady," Aunt Louisa May replied.

"Well, at least she's not as wild as Margaret," said Mrs. Lawson. "I hope she'll be a good influence on my girls, but she is such a moody and depressed child. My mother and sister couldn't do anything with her. All she ever wanted to do was sulk in a corner with a book."

"Well, being around your girls will make her more sociable," said Grandma. "I'm sure it will be a mutual benefit for all of them."

"Here they come," said Tom, setting down a toy Indian as he looked out the window and saw the girls returning. "Let's go."

As we came down the stairs, we heard Mrs. Lawson say, "Maybe Helen will make Margaret less interested in playing with boys—especially Tom. I know he's your great-nephew, Kathleen, but he is rather coarse and vulgar."

"Grandma!" I shouted, hoping to cut off Mrs. Lawson's words before Tom heard them, "we're going back outside!"

"Be back in time for supper," Grandma shouted back.

As we put on our boots, then opened the door, Mrs. Lawson, oblivious that we were in hearing distance, continued, "Mark is much better behaved than his younger brother."

Tom and I went out the door, shutting it behind us. The girls were still half a block away. I did not know what to say. I did not know how much Tom had heard. Then he turned to me and said, "I know it's not right to hit girls, but

I'd like to hit that woman. What's wrong with Mags and I playing together? You can see what she's like. She's just as rough as a boy. Always has been. That's not my fault."

"I know," I said. "There's nothing wrong with your playing together."

Not knowing what more to say, I changed the subject by hollering to the girls, "What took you so long?" They really hadn't been that long. Not more than the ten minutes Mags had promised.

"Helen couldn't find her scarf," Mags moaned, "and she insisted on wearing it, even though I told her scarves are more trouble than they're worth."

"Well, let's go," said Tom, grabbing the rope of his sleigh and pulling it off the snowbank.

"I wish I had a sleigh," said Mags. "Ma won't let me have one."

"Because it's not ladylike?" I laughed.

"Exactly." She rolled her eyes. "I'd have a better one than Tom's though. I'd have one like Lon has. His is a lot faster than Tom's."

"Is not!" said Tom.

"Lon's sleigh makes yours look like a snail, Tom Hampton."

"Lon's sleigh can't even go down a hill. It gets stuck all the time."

"You're only saying that because he whooped you."

"He did not."

"Who's Lon?" I asked.

"Tom's old best friend who beat him up."

"He did not!" said Tom. "I socked him good in the eye. Cripe, even his ugly girlfriend could beat him up."

"Even so," said Mags, "Lon's sleigh is still faster than yours."

"If you like Lon so much, maybe you should go ride on his sleigh," Tom threatened.

I waited for Mags to retort. Tom was obviously hurt that she thought Lon had gotten the best of him, especially since yesterday he had bragged to me how he had socked his former best friend. Actually, knowing that made me a bit nervous since now I was supposedly Tom's best friend.

"I didn't say I liked Lon better than you, Tom," said Mags, her voice suddenly turning gentle. "Just that I liked his sleigh better."

Tom grimaced and started down the street. We all followed, Mags running to catch up with Tom. In a minute, I heard them joshing each other as if they had never argued. Then I realized Helen had drifted behind me. I slowed down to wait for her, and when she saw me loitering, she smiled and walked faster to catch up.

"Your Aunt Elaine told my grandma she thought you'd be a good influence on Mags," I said, hoping to cheer Helen.

"Figures," said Helen. "She's only interested in what I can do for her. Aunt Elaine doesn't love me any more than Aunt Helen or my Grandma do."

"She was worried Mary might give you the chicken pox when you first got here," I said.

"Mary hasn't had the chicken pox in a week," said Helen. "She just likes to make things up because she's spoiled. She'll do anything for attention."

"Well, try not to think about it," I said. "Just concentrate on how much fun we're going to have this afternoon."

"How can I not think about it? You don't know what you're talking about—how can you when your aunt and Grandma actually like having you around?"

I didn't reply. Our situations were not that different, but I knew I was dealing better with mine—maybe because I was a boy—maybe because I was a year older. I felt bad for her, but I didn't know how to make her happy.

Once we reached the sledding hill, we piled onto Tom's sleigh. Tom and Mags said all the weight had to be in the back of the sleigh. Tom and I were about the same size, but he said he had to sit in front because he had to steer. That meant I was in the back. Then I found myself with Helen in front of me, and Mags in front of her. We each had to wrap our arms around the person before us. But I had to give the sleigh a push, then hop on before I put my arms around Helen. As I jumped on, we started to soar downhill, flying like the wind, faster than a train, the cold wind nipping my nose. We went so fast and the hill was so steep that I thought we would never stop. And then we realized we couldn't stop, and Tom lost control, unable to steer away from a bump in the trail that sent us all up in the air, then down in different directions. I flipped over onto my side and Helen landed on my leg, twisting it.

Before I even felt the impact of the blow, I heard Helen laugh for the first time.

Chapter 5

Trouble

Sunday morning, Grandma woke me early, just as dawn broke.

"Hurry up and get dressed, Robert, or we'll be late for Mass," she said, opening my curtains.

A slender beam of sunlight drifted in, dancing on the wall, enhancing the room's pinkness. I wanted to ask how long before my room would be painted, but I decided to wait until I was more awake and less grumpy.

"All right," I mumbled. I hated getting up early, but I was still new here and felt I should abide by Grandma's rules. Later, when I started going to school, my body would better adjust to these early Sunday mornings.

After hastily dressing, I met Grandma and my aunt downstairs. We walked to the corner of Fourth Street, and then started down the hill to St. John the Baptist's Catholic Church, a large, dull colored brown brick church, with a bell tower in the back. We walked along its side, and only when we came around to its front door did I notice its aesthetic grandeur. Built in the Spanish Romanesque style, it was unique among Upper Peninsula churches, looking as if it belonged in Mexico or at least Texas. Stained glass windows ran along both its sides. The front doors were arched with a few steps leading up to them. Above the doors was a gorgeous rose window. But what I liked best were the statues on top of the columns and the apex of the saints, the evangelists, and of course, St. John the Baptist. The saints looked down with pensive faces upon all the church's visitors, blessing them as they passed inside.

I was not a very religious boy, only thinking to pray when I wanted or needed something, such as when my mother had died. My parents had dutifully taken me to a little stone church in our town, but they had scarcely ever said a word about religion to me. I had had no Catholic friends in South Carolina. All our neighbors were Baptists, and my parents had told me never to discuss religion with other people, probably because they feared prejudice against us as Catholics. But Upper Michigan had been settled largely by French Canadians and Irish and German immigrants, so the Catholic Church flourished here. And between going to school at Bishop Baraga and sitting in St. John the Baptist's, my heart would slowly fill with devotion to God. I loved the church's beautiful stained glass windows, the grand old hymns we sang, the ritual and the tradition, even the glorious sound of the ancient Latin tongue. St. John the Baptist had been opened in 1908, so it was quite a modern church at the time, although today it would seem very old fashioned. When it was torn down in 1986, I felt devastated, as if I had lost a family member, for I had worshipped within its walls nearly seventy years, and always, I had found peace there.

When I sat down in the pew that first day, before I even admired the stained glass windows, I looked about nervously, checking out the faces of everyone present to see whether I knew anyone. I asked Grandma whether the Lawsons went to St. John's, but she whispered back that they went to St. Peter's Cathedral, an even larger church further down the street, whose towers I had spotted as we came down Fourth Street's hill. Then I saw the Hamptons come in and sit across the aisle from us. Tom glanced my way, smiled, and waved, but after his father whispered to him, he stared straight ahead, trying to be solemn and stay out of trouble. I did not recognize anyone else in the congregation. Grandma later told me that Aunt Carolina would not attend St. John's because she claimed there was a draft inside, but Aunt Louisa May told me the truth was that Aunt Carolina liked St. Peter's better because it was showier. I don't imagine my great-aunt would have fit into St. John's parish family anyway—I doubt she fit into St. Peter's.

I sat quietly through the service, admiring the stained glass windows more than listening to the Latin service or the homily. But when I went up to communion, I remembered to ask God to forgive my sins and to bless Grandma and Aunt Louisa May for kindly taking me in. I prayed for my father's safety and asked that I would get a letter from him soon. I prayed that my mother be in paradise, and I asked that Helen find comfort from her own sadness.

After the service, Grandma suggested we light a votive candle for my mother. We bought one and placed it before a statue of the Blessed Virgin, herself a mother. She had a kind look on her face, which reminded me of Mama. I felt a fuzzy glow inside, as if my own mother were looking down on me from Heaven. I missed Mama terribly, but I knew she would not want me to grieve, only to be good for Grandma and Aunt Louisa May so my father would not worry. I asked Mama to watch over Dad, who was in far greater need than me.

When we came outside, Tom was waiting for us. His parents and brother had gone home in their automobile, but he had wanted to walk home with us.

"Tom, will your parents be home this afternoon?" Aunt Louisa May asked as we started up the hill.

"I think so," he said.

"Would they mind having company?" asked Grandma.

"I don't think so."

"Will you tell them we'll come over after dinner?"

"Okay. Will you come over too, Robert?"

"Of course," I said.

"How's school going, Tom?" asked Aunt Louisa May.

"Okay."

"We'll see whether we can't get Robert into your class, Tom," said Grandma. "Then you can show him the ropes."

"Um, sure," he said. I didn't know what showing me the ropes would entail, but Tom's face reflected uncertainty about teaching me anything related to homework. "We need a good quarterback for when we play football. Are you any good at football, Robert?"

"Sure," I said. I was really only okay at football, but I wouldn't admit it. I was nervous the boys here might be stronger or run faster, but I would do my best.

"You can't play football in the snow," said Grandma.

"Sure you can," said Tom. "There's not much else to do in the schoolyard—we can't sled or ice skate there. Well, I'll see you later, Robert."

"Okay," I said.

We had reached the top of the hill now, and he had to turn down a different street than us.

"Thanks for walking us home, Tom," Grandma called after him.

"Sure!"

He turned and started running toward home, slipped on some ice, fell down, jumped back up, turned around to wave, then went back to running.

Aunt Louisa May could not help laughing.

"He's a good boy," said Grandma. "I don't imagine he does all that well in school, but he's got a good heart. I don't know what Elaine has against him."

"I don't like Mrs. Lawson," I said before I considered that perhaps I shouldn't talk about other grownups in front of my aunt and grandma.

"Why not?"

"I heard what she said about Tom yesterday. He heard it too. She has no right to judge people like that."

"No, she doesn't. She should learn when to hold her tongue," agreed Aunt Louisa May.

"Yes," said Grandma, "but her words don't reflect poorly on Tom. They reflect on her own fears."

"What's she afraid of?" I asked.

"Not being socially accepted. She would like nothing better than to be bosom friends with your Aunt Carolina, but Carolina doesn't think Elaine's of her class, and consequently, Elaine doesn't like Carolina's grandson playing with her daughters."

"She would if she thought she could get Mark or Tom to marry one of her daughters," Aunt Louisa May said.

"Maybe Aunt Carolina will be dead by the time the girls are old enough to marry," I thought, but I knew it would be too rude to say such a thing.

"We shouldn't be too hard on Elaine," Grandma said. "She's not having an easy time of it with her husband in the war. She's got three girls to raise and now Helen as well. I know she's still angry that her husband enlisted, and I can't really blame her."

"My mama was proud of my father for going," I said.

"Yes, but your parents only had one son to provide for, not three girls. There's a big difference. And your parents are financially better off than the Lawsons. For all the airs Elaine and her mother and sisters put on, they've never owned much. We can't blame her for wanting something better for her girls."

When we reached home, we sat down for a late breakfast that would also serve as dinner. Grandma and Aunt Louisa May tried to describe to me who was who at church from what people had been wearing, but I never noticed people's clothes. After eating, we quickly did up the dishes, and then went over to visit the Hamptons.

This was my first visit to Tom's house, so I paid close attention to the direction so I could walk there on my own. We were half a block away when we saw the house; Mark and Eliza were sitting on the front porch swing.

"Hello," said Grandma as we came up the front steps. "It's rather cold to be sitting outside, isn't it?"

"Only place we can get any privacy," said Mark. His tone said we were interrupting him. "Besides, we're keeping each other warm," he added. He had his arm around Eliza's shoulder.

Eliza blushed, but she did not pull away from him. I wanted to sock him right then.

"Are your parents home?" Aunt Louisa May asked.

Mark nodded, and Grandma and Aunt Louisa May went inside, while I said, "Grandma, tell Tom I'll wait out here for him." I considered squeezing onto the swing beside Eliza, but I did not think I would fit, and I did not want to look ridiculous in the attempt, so I leaned against the porch railing, trying to think of something brilliant to say that would win Eliza's admiration. The best I came up with was, "So, how's it going?"

"Just fine, thank you," Eliza smiled.

"I hear your parents had a Negro working for them," said Mark.

"Huh?" I said. "Oh, you mean Nellie. Yes, she came in to help my mom around the house once in a while, but she was really more of a family friend."

"I wouldn't let one of that kind in my house," said Mark.

I didn't know what to say. Why had he brought up the subject?

"Nellie's a good cook," I said, as if that made a difference. I didn't know how to defend her.

"My grandma's got a couple of 'em," said Mark. "Don't know why. Jones, he's a shiftless, lazy bugger."

I was surprised to hear Aunt Carolina had Negro servants. I had not seen any Negroes in Marquette since I had arrived, but then, neither had I thought much about it—Negroes were part of my everyday world in the South.

"Nellie is a hard worker," I said. But I remembered my father saying her husband was rather lazy. Were all Negro men lazy? I didn't really know any so how could I say, but then how could Mark say either?

"I have a hard time believing that," said Mark. "My grandma's had a few of their kind over the years. She always hires Negroes, but they never work out. I don't know why she gets them except that her parents had them down South when she was a little girl. Back then, they were slaves so you could make them work. Now you can't get them to do anything."

"I've met lots of Nellie's family," I said, "and they're all nice people and hard workers."

I was surprised to hear a Yankee talk like this. I thought Northerners claimed they were friends to the Negroes and had fought the war to free them. Mark talked about Negroes the way Mr. Carter talked about Yankees. I realized I knew hardly anything more about Negroes than him, but Mark's ignorance made me despise him all the more intensely.

"Robert, how do you like Marquette so far?" Eliza asked.

I was glad to have the subject changed—and pleased to have Eliza pay attention to me.

I wanted to say something intelligent so Mark would look stupid by comparison, especially since I felt he had insulted Nellie, but all I could think to say was, "I really like it so far."

"What do you think of all this snow?"

"It's colder than I expected." I was starting to shiver from standing still on the porch. "But the snow was great for when Tom and I went sleigh riding yesterday with Mags and Helen."

"That's good," she said. "I loved sleigh riding when I was a child."

A child! Is that what she considered me? Why, in May I would be fourteen!

"Why don't you go find Tom," said Mark, as if he were Mark Antony ordering me to stay away from Cleopatra.

"My grandma will tell him I'm here," I said. "He'll be out in a minute."

"It's getting cold out here. Let's go in," Mark told Eliza.

He took her hand and practically yanked her up from the swing without even asking whether she wanted to go inside.

"Are you coming, Robert?" she asked, apparently unaware that going inside was her boyfriend's ploy to keep her from me. Before I could follow, Tom appeared on the porch, a brownie in one hand, another still half in his mouth as he spoke.

"Robert, come on in," he said. "My ma just took these out of the oven and said we could have some."

Mark and Eliza passed by Tom without a word. Then I followed him inside.

"Hello, Robert," said Mrs. Hampton when we reached the kitchen. "You boys stay in here to eat. I don't want chocolate frosting smeared all over the house."

I knew better than to make a mess, but from the chocolate smudges already on Tom's face, I could understand her worry. Tom poured us some milk, and then we sat down at the table, focused on devouring brownies.

"Anyway," Mr. Hampton's voice drifted in from the parlor, "I don't envy any young man going off to this war. I'm glad I'm too old to go and the boys are too young."

"I'll be joining up just as soon as I turn eighteen in April," Mark said. Apparently my archenemy and my future bride had joined the grownups in the parlor.

"No, you won't," said Mrs. Hampton.

"There isn't much choice," Mark replied. "I'll be drafted otherwise."

"Your Grandma knows people. She'll find a way to get you out of it."

"I don't want to 'get out of it'," Mark raised his voice. "I want to go. It's what all American men should do."

"Mark, we'll discuss it later," said his father.

"Hopefully the war will be over by spring so you won't have to go," Eliza said. "Besides, once you're eighteen, we're going to get married, and I don't want you to leave me right after the honeymoon."

I felt sick to think of such a clown on a honeymoon with such divinity.

"I don't understand why you want to marry so young," said Aunt Louisa May. "I'm thirty-seven and perfectly happy being a spinster. Neither of you are half my age. You have plenty of time. You have all your lives ahead of you."

"Let's go outside," said Tom, shoving the last half of a brownie in his mouth. "I saw Mags, her sister Mollie, and Helen walk by. If we hurry, we can catch up with them and have another snowball fight."

"Okay," I said, although I still felt a little cold from standing on the porch. I thought I could be content with a game of checkers for now, or just sitting in the parlor near Eliza. But I could not tell Tom that, so we set off in search of the girls. After walking a couple blocks, we spotted them coming toward us.

"Hey Mags!" Tom shouted.

"Hello," she called back, but she did not sound friendly.

When we were closer, Helen said, "Hello, Robert." Her face lit up when she spoke to me.

Mollie stood impatiently, not introducing herself or asking to be introduced.

"Ya wanna have a snowball fight?" Tom asked.

"Can't," said Mags. "We just went to the Mitchells to bring them some cookies from my mom, and now we have to go bring this care package to Mrs. Haslett 'cause she's sick."

"What's in it?" asked Tom, noticing for the first time what Mollie was holding.

"Banana bread," said Mollie.

"Can I have some?" he asked.

"No, don't let him, Mags," said Mollie.

"Please?" he begged.

"We just had brownies, Tom," I reminded him.

"Yeah, but Mags's mom bakes better than mine."

"No, you can't have any," Mags decided, "but if you want to wait for us, we'll be back in twenty minutes or so, and then we can have a snowball fight."

"All right," said Tom. "Robert and I'll go back to my house and build a fort and an arsenal of snowballs for when you get back."

"Goodbye, Robert," said Helen, turning to follow her cousins.

"See you later," I muttered, afraid Tom would notice the look she had given me.

Back in Tom's yard, we rolled several huge snowballs and placed them side-by-side until we had a fort nearly three feet high. Then we padded the cracks between them with snow so our fort would be impenetrable. By the time we actually started to make the snowballs for our arsenal, my fingers were getting numb with cold. I thought the girls sure were taking their time walking back. I took off my gloves and blew on my fingers to keep them from going numb. Tom told me to curl up my hands inside the gloves rather than have my fingers in each slot. I was about to suggest we go inside and wait for the girls, but then Mark stepped back onto the porch, Aphrodite on his arm. Since we were building our fortress off to the porch's end, they did not see us when they first came outside.

"I'm sorry I have to go," Eliza said as Mark walked her down the steps, "but Mother still doesn't feel well, and I promised to read to her this afternoon."

"I don't mind since I get to walk you home," Mark said. "I wish Dad would trust me with the car so I could drive you home."

"I don't mind walking," said Eliza. "It gives us more time together."

"After Grandma dies and I'm rich, I'll drive you home in a Rolls-Royce."

"We'll be married by then, so you won't have to drive me home, but I don't care whether we have a Rolls-Royce or we walk, so long as I'm with you."

"I'll get you a Rolls-Royce anyway," said Mark. "I plan to buy you lots of beautiful things."

They paused just before reaching the sidewalk so he could give her a kiss on the lips. I was stunned, never having seen anyone kiss in public like that. I started to feel infuriated when Tom nudged me in the ribs and said, "Hey, let's get loverboy."

He was molding a snowball in his hands.

"What if we hit Eliza?" I asked.

"Nah, I'm a good shot."

Before I could stop him, Tom sent a snowball flying straight at the despicably happy couple.

I heard a sudden, boisterous smash of ice against a skull. Then I saw Eliza with her hand to her temple, sobs breaking from her beautiful lips, tears streaming from her usually radiant eyes.

And I saw Mark tear across the yard toward us.

"I'll kill you, you monster!" he yelled, then effortlessly picked Tom up from the ground, lifted him into the air and flung him head first into a snowbank.

"You little brat! I'm going to kill you!" he kept shouting. Now he was sitting on Tom, pummeling his chest and slapping his face.

"Stop!" I yelled. "You'll kill him!"

I grabbed Mark's arm from behind, then tried to wrap my arm around his waist to pull him off my friend.

"Shut up!" he said, flinging me back with his arm so that his fist hit me in the eye. I fell over backwards, completely dazed, then lay there, conscious only that Eliza was standing above us, likewise telling Mark to stop.

"Boys, cut it out right now!" yelled Mr. Hampton, coming down the front steps. "I'll give you both a good beating with my belt for this."

"Why do you boys have to fight?" cried Mrs. Hampton, standing on the porch. As I struggled to sit up, I could see her wringing her hands while Grandma and my aunt peered over her shoulder.

"Oh," cried Mrs. Hampton, as her husband pulled Mark off Tom, then pulled Tom to his feet. "Oh, Tom, your nose is bleeding. Come inside. Oh, I'm so afraid you boys are going to kill one another someday. Don't I have enough to worry about without you always fighting?"

"You boys should be ashamed to upset your mother like this," said Mr. Hampton.

Mark stood panting, his entire body throbbing with anger. I looked to see whether Eliza were seriously hurt, only to see her looking at Mark, with both fear and perhaps misplaced admiration over his defending her.

"Should we call the doctor?" asked Mrs. Hampton as her husband led Tom to her. She took out her handkerchief to wipe the blood from her son's nose.

"Nah, just clean him up and he'll be fine," said Mr. Hampton. "He's been through worse before."

Mrs. Hampton led Tom inside. Mr. Hampton ordered Mark to go upstairs to his room.

"I'm going to walk Eliza home," said Mark.

"Don't you backtalk to me, young man. You'll do what I say so long as you live under my roof."

"We're about ready to go ourselves," Grandma said, coming down the front steps, with her coat on now. "We'll walk Eliza home for you, Mark."

Without replying, Mark brushed past her to go into the house.

Aunt Louisa May came down the steps and took my face in her hands. "You've got a little scrape on your cheek," she said.

"I'll be fine," I replied, not wanting to look weak in front of Eliza. If Mr. Hampton had not stopped the fight, I told myself I would have gotten up out of the snow and jumped on Mark's back, then pinned him to the ground until he cried "Uncle!" If I could take Mark—especially when I was four years younger than him—Eliza would be sure to admire how strong I was. Somehow, before Mark turned eighteen, I would make her realize I was the better man. Then she would wait for me to turn eighteen.

"What happened to you?" Mags asked. Suddenly I saw the girls standing on the sidewalk. "Robert, you look like someone socked you in the eye."

"Mark hit me," I said.

"Why? What happened?"

"Let's go home," said Grandma. She had been talking to Eliza for a minute, finding out what had happened.

"I'll explain later," I told Mags as we started down the street, the girls following us.

"Did he hit Tom too?" Mags asked.

I felt I had to explain, or she would just keep asking questions.

"Tom threw a snowball at Mark, but it hit Eliza instead, so Mark got mad and started beating on Tom. When I tried to stop him, he hit me in the eye."

"Just because of a little snowball?" said Mags.

"It was a piece of ice," Eliza told her, "and it hurt. It was a childish thing to do. Tom is always causing trouble. Robert, I hope he doesn't become a bad influence on you."

"I've been hit by lots of snowballs, and I never cried about it," Mags said.

"It was an accident," I told Eliza. I had to admit I was a little perturbed with her; I was sorry she had been hit, but it was just a snowball. She had no business telling me Tom was a bad influence considering the company she kept. Mark, with his big words and nasty comments, must have badly brainwashed her. She was going to take a lot of convincing if she were going to be my girlfriend.

"It was still childish," Eliza said, "and you're not much better than him, Robert, being his accomplice."

"Eliza, you're such a prissy girl," said Mags. "That's what your problem is."

"That's enough," said Grandma. "We won't discuss it any further."

Since there wasn't going to be a snowball fight now, I kind of wished Mags and her girl troop would get lost, but she continued to follow us, and despite Grandma's injunction not to discuss it further, she said, "I wish I'd seen it. I would have given Mark a good clobbering myself."

Eliza turned around and gave her a scornful look.

"Robert, I think your eye is turning black," said Mollie.

"Let me see," said Grandma, stopping me to look closely. "It does look a little bruised. We better put a steak on it when you get home."

"I've had three black eyes in my life," Mags said. "They don't hurt that much."

Everyone ignored her. When we reached home, Grandma said goodbye to Eliza since she only had to walk next door. "Come inside, Robert," Grandma then told me.

"I'll see you later," I told the girls.

"All right," said Mags.

"I'm sorry you were hurt, Robert," said Helen.

"Thanks," I muttered, not particularly wanting her sympathy.

Once I was seated at the kitchen table, I apologized to Grandma for fighting, and I explained how it hadn't been my fault.

"It's all right, Robert," she said. "Boys always play rough, and Mark can act just like an animal sometimes. He pretends he's all grown up, but only in size. He's as much a ruffian now as when he was little."

Then she plopped a chunk of frozen meat over my eye.

"Grandma, it's freezing!" I said.

"Good, that'll stop the swelling."

I winced but left the steak against my eye. Then I said, "Grandma, I tried to tell Tom not to throw the snowball, and then I tried to stop Mark from hurting Tom, but both times it seems my trying to help only made things worse."

"Sometimes life is like that," said Grandma.

"I know, but it's not fair; Tom wasn't smart to do it, but Mark did overreact. I hate him."

"Hate," said Grandma, "is a strong word for a young man who went to church this morning. You don't even know Mark yet. I admit he has his faults, but I shouldn't speak so harshly of him either. Work on trying to find something to like about him."

She then went into the parlor with my aunt, leaving me at the table. I thought how impossible it would be to like anything about Mark. After much thought, I finally decided I had to admire his good taste in women. Then I was off thinking about Eliza again. If I were her boyfriend and anyone threw a snowball at her, I would have thrashed that boy too, even if he were my best friend. And since Mark was her boyfriend and he was defending her honor, she had been obliged to take his side in the fight. But I didn't like how he told her what to do, yanking her around by the arm as if she were his property. I was certain it wasn't in his nature to be kind. I decided if I could create an argument between them, his true colors would show. Then I could defend her, which would mean she would side with me, and then, of course—

"All's fair in love and war," I thought.

Chapter 6

Questions

Wednesday of the following week, Grandma and Aunt Louisa May decided to go shopping while I was told I would have to stay home. Without their saying why, I knew they were going to buy me Christmas presents. Since Tom and Mags were in school, I had no one to play with during the day, so I settled down on the sofa, planning to read.

By then I had finished *Dandelion Cottage* and *The Wonderful Wizard of Oz*, so I dug through Grandma's bookshelves. The best book I could find was *Little Men*, but I quickly put it down when I realized it was a sequel to *Little Women*, and I wasn't about to read another girls' book, at least not right then. An entire shelf was filled with girls' books by Louisa May Alcott, my grandmother's favorite author. Grandma had even named my aunt after her. But those books didn't interest me. I hoped I would get some boys' books for Christmas.

Last Christmas, I had been given *The Boy's King Arthur*, which I had enjoyed enough to read three times. My father and I had read it aloud on Christmas night. If I had brought it to Marquette, I would have read it again now.

Then I remembered neither of my parents would be spending Christmas with me. Aunt Louisa May had written to my father again on Saturday to say we were in Marquette, in case he had not received her previous letter—I knew it was too soon for him to have gotten the second letter, but I still thought his long silence frightening. His last letter had come in September long before my mother had even been ill. I was so afraid he might have been killed.

Today was the first time I had really been alone with my feelings, and I suddenly felt anger overwhelm me. Of course, I knew everyone had to die, but why did my mother have to die before I had grown up, and why when my father could not be with her, and why when Grandma's twisted ankle had made her unable to travel? I knew Grandma and my aunt were also grieving, but they did not show it, and I was afraid I would upset them if I said anything. Grandma had told me my first night here to be brave. I wanted to be brave for my father's sake, but I also wanted him here, so we could comfort each other. I imagined him somewhere in Europe, crying alone in a tent after reading my aunt's letter. Maybe he would be so upset he would let the Germans shoot him rather than go on without my mother. Then what would I do? I would be an orphan.

My tears poured out. I found myself sobbing violently. I curled up into a couch corner and cried until I had to wipe my nose on my shirtsleeves. I was too overcome with crying, aching, and coughing to look for a handkerchief. My whole chest heaved up and down in pain, my throat was sore, and I felt utterly exhausted.

Then I realized someone else was in the room. I tried to sit back up, embarrassed to be found crying like a girl, but Aunt Louisa May was already beside me on the couch, her arms around me.

"Mother said to let you cry so you could get it all out," she said, "but I had to make sure you're okay."

"Thanks," I muttered in embarrassment.

"I know it hurts, Robert. I've cried too. We all loved your mother so much."

"Why did she have to die?" I demanded, wiping my eyes with the handkerchief she handed me.

"I don't know. I wish I did. But I do know she would want you to go on living and to be happy, rather than grieving her loss."

"But it isn't fair," I said. "Why did she have to die now, when Grandma couldn't come to see her one last time, and when my father wasn't home? How could God let this happen?"

"I don't know," my aunt repeated. Her arm was around me, gently trying to rock me. "Maybe because God loves her so much he didn't want her ever to be sick again or to know the pain of losing those she loved. She's lucky she got to go before the rest of us so she wouldn't have to miss us the way we miss her. We can be thankful for that. And we'll see her again someday. You need to believe that with all your heart."

I said nothing. My throat hurt too much. And I didn't know what to say.

"Let me go get you some water," said my aunt, getting up from the couch.

I blew my nose into the handkerchief. Then I drank the glass of water she brought me.

"Aunt Louisa May," I said, "do you really believe I'll see my mother again?"

"Absolutely."

"But I miss her so much now. I don't know how I can stand it."

"You will though. The first death of a loved one is the hardest for all of us, but I promise time will heal the pain, although you will always miss her."

"But how do you stand it?" I asked. Life could only get worse if I were still to lose my father, my grandma, my aunt. I could lose everyone I loved and then be all alone.

"Look at your grandma," said Aunt Louisa May. "She's managed. She lost both of her parents in the Civil War when she was younger than you. But she grew up and married and had children and a happy life despite it all. My father died, but she stayed strong, and now your mother is gone, yet I've heard her laugh many times just this past week. Bad things happen, but so do good things. We need to concentrate on the good things."

Then the telephone rang as it always does at the most inopportune moments. Aunt Louisa May went to answer it. I wiped my eyes again and tried to understand how life could hold so much good and bad at the same time. My aunt had cheered me a little; I wanted to believe what she had said—that my mother would meet me in heaven. I would try to believe it.

"That was Mrs. Lawson," said my aunt, returning into the room. "Poor Helen caught the chicken pox, so she wanted me to warn you not to go over there when the girls get home from school."

"I had the chicken pox when I was ten," I said. "I'm immune from it now."

"Oh," said my aunt. "Then maybe you could go cheer up Helen. Mrs. Lawson said she's really depressed. I could bake some cookies for you to bring with you."

Aunt Louisa May was a gem. She had the cookies baked and cooling within the hour. Right after lunch, I was on my way to the Lawsons' house. I was so excited to have someone to play with that afternoon that I didn't even mind it would be Helen rather than Mags or Tom.

"Robert, I told your aunt you couldn't come over," said Mrs. Lawson, only opening the door a crack when she saw me.

"It's okay," I said. "I've already had the chicken pox. I thought maybe I could cheer Helen up a little."

"Oh, all right," said Mrs. Lawson. "She is rather down."

I found Helen lying on her bed, dressed but buried under a quilt with a book opened before her.

"I brought cookies," I said. "I left them in the kitchen with your aunt."

"Thanks," said Helen. Her face lit up when she saw me, but after she spoke, she grimaced. "The chicken pox are in my throat so it hurts just to eat, but the girls will like them."

"All right," I said, sitting down on another bed I figured must belong to Mags. "Do you feel up to playing? I had the chicken pox a few years ago, so it's safe for me to play with you if you're lonely."

"Sure," she said. "Aunt Elaine thinks I should just sleep all day, but I'm not tired, just bored and terribly itchy."

She reached toward her arm, but I warned her, "Don't scratch. It'll leave scars. I have a dent on my arm from where I peeled one off. I had a friend in South Carolina who had three dents on his forehead from picking off the scabs."

"Then we better play a game so I keep my hands too busy to scratch," she replied.

"Do you have any games?"

"No," she frowned. "My cousins have some, but the other day when I tried to touch one, Mary had a screaming fit."

"Oh," I said. I looked around but saw nothing else in the room to entertain us.

"Maybe," said Helen, "we could play with my dolls and teddy bears. They're the only things I brought up here with me other than my clothes and a few books."

Boys don't play with dolls and teddy bears, especially not boys who are almost fourteen. But Helen was so persuasive I finally agreed, intending to swear her to secrecy before I left.

"We could pretend the dolls and animals are different characters from Oz," said Helen. "And we can make up our own plots rather than follow the ones in the books." She crawled from her bed and took off the dresser a doll in a pretty pink evening gown. "This one is the nicest, so we'll pretend she's Princess Ozma, and this teddy bear is really beat up, so he can be the Scarecrow."

"This one looks rather fierce," I said, picking up another Teddy Bear. "He can be the Cowardly Lion."

"Okay," said Helen, "and this boy doll can be the Tin Woodman."

"Which one'll be Dorothy?" I asked.

"This one," Helen said, pulling one from a shelf in the closet. "It's the only other one I have."

"Okay, but we need a villain for the plot. A wicked witch or something."

"How about the Nome King?" she said.

"Who's that?" I asked, having only read the first Oz book.

"He's a horribly wicked, fat little man who has an underground kingdom full of the riches his Nomes dig from the earth, and he hates good people and wants to conquer the Emerald City because Dorothy stole his magic belt."

"Okay, the Nome King can be the villain," I agreed. Helen was sure into the Oz books, but I was curious enough now that I wanted to read the rest of them myself.

"But what will we use to be the Nome King?" she asked.

"Something fat," I said. "How about a sock? We'll use several socks, one for the body and the rest to stuff it so it's round."

"Here," she said, pulling socks from her dresser. "I hate this pair; they're so ugly, but that'll make them work all the better for the Nome King."

"What will the story be?" I asked.

"The Nome King will kidnap Dorothy because she stole his magic belt. He managed to get into the Emerald City by disguising himself, but he still couldn't find the belt, so he's holding her hostage for it, and everyone else has to rescue her."

"Sounds good to me," I said. We soon had Dorothy locked up in the Nome King's mountain castle, which the unimaginative would have thought only the space beneath Mags's bed. The Oz people had to go through a dangerous tunnel to reach the Nome King's mountain, which meant Helen had to toss the dolls under her bed to me. We had Dorothy almost rescued and then kidnapped again by the time Mags came home from school.

"What are you doing?" asked Mags, seeing toys strewn all over the room.

"Playing Oz," said Helen. "Robert and I have made up the whole Land of Oz, but with dolls and teddy bears."

Mags bent down and started picking up the dolls. Helen said nothing, although she didn't look pleased.

"I didn't say you could play with my dolls," said Mags. We had started out with only Helen's toys, but when the Nome King needed an army, we had borrowed some of Mags's toys as well.

"But Mags, you never play with them," said Helen. "You told me you don't even like dolls."

"That doesn't mean you can play with them without asking my permission. Besides, I bet Robert doesn't want to play with girl things anyway."

"Well, I kinda had fun," I said, hoping to keep peace between them, yet afraid Mags would tell Tom what I had done.

"Let's go outside and play, Robert," said Mags. But before I could answer, Mary came into the room. I had not met her yet; I soon learned I had been lucky up until now.

"Can't we play inside to keep Helen company?" I asked.

"Mother says I need fresh air," declared Mary, although she had not been invited to play.

"It's okay," said Helen, graciously relinquishing me to Mags rather than fighting with her. "I probably should take a nap anyway. Will you come back tomorrow, Robert, when everyone else is in school?"

"Sure," I said. "We've got to make sure Dorothy gets rescued."

"Who's Dorothy?" asked Mags.

"Let's go build a snowman," I suggested, not wanting to explain everything to someone so unimaginative that she had not read *The Wonderful Wizard of Oz.*

"Great idea!" said Mags. "It's good packing snow out there today."

"You can't!" bleated out Mary.

"Why not?" Mags asked.

"You have to do your homework first."

"I don't have that much. I'll do it after supper," said Mags.

"You do so have to do it now. I'll tell Mom otherwise."

"Mom makes dumb rules," said Mags.

"Mom!" screamed Mary. "Mom! Mom!"

Mrs. Lawson came running as if the house were on fire.

"What's wrong?" she asked. "Mary, quit that screaming. You know Helen doesn't feel well."

"Mags can't go out to play until she does her homework, can she?"

"I can do it after supper," said Mags. "I don't have that much."

"No, you better do it now," said Mrs. Lawson.

"I don't have any homework so Robert can still play with me," said Mary.

I had no intention of doing that, but I waited to see whether Mags's further protestations would work on her mother.

"No, Mags, your grades have been falling lately," said Mrs. Lawson. "If you get your homework done, you can play after supper."

"It'll be dark by then."

"Then you can play inside with Helen."

"That's not fair. Helen got to play all day with Robert, and I don't get to play at all."

"It's all right, Mags," I said. "I forgot I promised Grandma I would be home early to help her with something before supper, so don't feel bad. We can play this weekend if not tomorrow after school."

"But I want to build a snowman," said Mary.

"I'm sorry but I have to go," I replied. Mary was only eight. I wasn't going to play with her even though it did mean lying about having to help Grandma.

"Now look what you did, Mary. You spoiled it for everyone," said Mags.

I said goodbye and quickly left. I passed Mollie in the kitchen, where she was devouring all the cookies Aunt Louisa May had baked for Helen. But I didn't care who ate the cookies so long as I could get away from Mary's screaming.

I still thought Helen rather odd, but I had enjoyed myself that afternoon. On the way home, I thought that tomorrow I would bring over my toy cowboys and Indians to be the Nome King's army so we wouldn't get in trouble for using Mags's dolls. Besides, cowboys and Indians weren't girlish, so if Tom found out, it wouldn't look so bad. Then I remembered how sad I had felt that morning, and I realized Helen had cheered me up as much as I had cheered her.

Chapter 7

Christmas Eve

For the next week, I was so busy entertaining Helen that I nearly forgot to buy Christmas presents. I finally came up with ideas for Grandma, Tom, Mags, and Helen. Grandma suggested we send a gift to Nellie for taking care of my parents' house. I couldn't really send a present to my father, but we sent him a Christmas card. Then I only had Aunt Louisa May's gift to think about, but I had absolutely no idea what to get her.

"I really can't think of anything either," said Grandma when I told her my problem. "But we can go shopping together and see what we come up with."

A few days before Christmas, Grandma and I went downtown and worked our way through one store after another, buying presents for everyone on my list, except Aunt Louisa May. We saw many nice trinkets and knick-knacks and books but nothing that seemed exactly right for her. As we walked past the bank on the corner of Washington and Front Streets, I was starting to feel very frustrated. Then out of the bank stepped Great-Aunt Carolina, huddled up against the cold in an enormous mink coat.

"Yoo-hoo! Kathleen!" she waved. "How are you, dear? I haven't seen you since Thanksgiving."

"Hello, Carolina. I'm fine," Grandma replied. "How are you?"

"Are you still doing your Christmas shopping?"

"No, I'm all done. I'm trying to help Robert find something for Louisa May."

"I never could stand Christmas shopping," Aunt Carolina replied. "I give Jane money to buy things for her boys, and everyone else gets money as well.

Then I only have to make one shopping trip and that's just to the bank, which is what I'm doing now. It makes life so much easier, and with my annual party, I have enough to do."

"Yes, I can understand that with all your social activities, Christmas shopping must be a burden," said Grandma, "but I wouldn't feel right just giving money."

"That's why I consider my annual Christmas party my real gift to everyone. It takes me two weeks to plan the menu and prepare everything for it."

"You do put an awful lot of effort into it," Grandma said. "It makes my Thanksgiving Dinner look small by comparison."

"Oh, you have no idea how much work it is; it's really my gift to the entire community."

Did she invite all of Marquette to the party? I couldn't imagine that. I would later learn Aunt Carolina had a very limited definition of community, which cut off people whose income was below hers; consequently, only about one percent of Marquette's population was invited.

"At least you have some help," said Grandma.

"Yes," Aunt Carolina replied, "but I only have a staff of two now—Jones and Jenny. You know since they're Negroes, it's almost more work to direct them than just to do everything myself. I certainly can't expect them to write out the invitations—that alone takes me hours."

"Jones and Jenny have always seemed reliable to me."

"Oh, Kathleen, you wouldn't understand. You haven't had Negroes working for you since before the war. I suppose if Cynthia were alive, she could explain it to you—didn't she have a Negro maid?"

"Nellie was more our friend than a maid," I said.

Aunt Carolina frowned, as if I should not speak unless spoken to. "Sometimes I think I should just hire a couple of Finlander girls—they seem to have good hygiene at least—but they're always jabbering away in that barbaric language of theirs, and I've always had Negroes since I was a girl, so it's hard to break old habits."

Grandma said nothing in reply—what could she say to such remarks?

Aunt Carolina sighed, as if completely exhausted over her servant issues. "Anyway, you should get my invitation in the mail tomorrow. You will come, of course." Her last words were more a command than a request.

"We wouldn't miss it. You always have the nicest parties in town."

I was curious whether Aunt Carolina's parties really were nice—I imagined Grandma was only being polite, and that any party Aunt Carolina had would either be laughable or deadly dull.

"Yes, the ladies in my club are always telling me how jealous they are of my parties. This year President Kaye from the Normal School is coming, and Mayor Begole, and the Clarks, the Blackmores and Richardsons of course, and—"

She rambled off the names of several other guests—all judges, doctors, professors, politicians, or business owners. She need not try to impress me with her social connections. She did not know Tarzan or the Wizard of Oz. They would have impressed me far more.

"My goodness," said Grandma. "How many invitations did you send out?"

"Oh, nearly a hundred. Last year I invited one hundred fifteen, but this year I didn't bother with those who didn't come last year."

"My, I'm glad I don't work for you," Grandma laughed. "I would hate to clean up after such a party."

"Oh, I don't do the cleaning up," my great-aunt misunderstood.

"Well, we better be going," said Grandma. "We'll see you Christmas Eve then."

"Too-da-loo," Aunt Carolina waved, then clutched her mink coat about her more tightly and walked to her automobile where her Negro chauffeur, whom I would later know as Jones, was waiting for her.

"Well, Robert, have you come up with an idea yet for Louisa May's present?"

"There's Donckers' store," I said. "Do you think I could just buy her some candy?"

"If it's chocolate," said Grandma. "No sane woman is disappointed to receive chocolate."

When we came out of the candy store, I asked Grandma, "Am I invited to Aunt Carolina's party?"

"Of course," said Grandma. Then she giggled. "But afterwards, you'll probably wish you weren't. The guests are mostly all social climbers, but Tom will be there."

"Aunt Carolina must have a huge house to invite all those people."

"Oh, yes, you haven't been there yet. She has a beautiful home on Ridge Street, where all the richest people in town live. Her late husband, your Great-Uncle James Smith, was a judge, and from a well-to-do family to start with, but he made his fortune as a real-estate lawyer. I'm sure she only married him for his money. The O'Neills were fairly well to do down South, but never prospered much up here, despite how Carolina likes to pretend otherwise. You know, Mrs. Williams was good friends with Carolina's mother, yet Carolina never once has invited her to her house."

"Why not?" I asked. "Mrs. Williams is nice."

"Because she's of no practical use to Carolina—she has no money or social connections. But I shouldn't be gossiping about others," said Grandma, "especially not my own sister-in-law."

Christmas Eve, the night of Aunt Carolina's party, came before I knew it. In the morning, Aunt Louisa May and I went to buy a Christmas tree. We then spent the afternoon decorating it while Grandma made treats for the party.

"I know Carolina will have plenty of food," Grandma fussed, "but I don't like to go anywhere empty-handed. Of course, I have a little present for her, but she'll probably just relegate it to the attic. I've never once seen anything in her house that I've given to her; I imagine my tastes just don't meet her standards."

"Oh, Mother," said my aunt, "don't get yourself so worked up before you go."

"You would think after having her for a sister-in-law all these years, she wouldn't get to me anymore. I do try, Louisa May."

"I know," my aunt sympathized.

Despite Grandma's dread of going to the party, we had a pleasant afternoon. I did feel a little down while decorating the tree; I remembered how my parents had always done it at night while I was in bed so I would be surprised on Christmas morning. But when Aunt Louisa May and Grandma started singing Christmas carols, I couldn't help joining in, and it instantly raised my spirits.

After supper, I was sent to my room to change. "Grandma, do I really have to wear my suitcoat?" I grimaced.

"Yes, you'll feel awkward without it on—Tom and Mark will both be wearing suits, and your great-aunt is very particular about such things."

A minute after I went up to my room, I heard her hollering, "Robert, Louisa May, hurry up or we'll be late."

"I thought it was fashionable to be late," said Aunt Louisa May as we went downstairs.

"When have we ever been fashionable?" Grandma replied. "Besides, we're family so we should get there early in case Carolina needs any help."

In another minute, we were out the door. I was carrying the cookies and bars, while Grandma cautioned me to be careful in case the sidewalk was icy.

When we came to Ridge Street, I felt overwhelmed by the large, ornate Victorian homes. The most distinguished house, of course, was Aunt Carolina's—a large sandstone mansion, three stories high with a tower in front. A large porch surrounded both sides of it, and a massive lawn ran behind it out to the cliff over the lake. Now I understood just how prominent the guests would be—I could well imagine Andrew Carnegie or the Rockefellers attending.

"Hello, Jones," said Grandma to the tall black man who opened the door. "Merry Christmas. I don't believe you've met my grandson, Robert."

"Hello, Mastuh Robert," he said. He seemed surprised when I gave him my hand to shake, but he returned my, "Pleased to meet you."

"I know we're early, Jones," said Grandma, "but I thought you might need some help."

"No, ma'am. We is all set. You go on inside. Oh, wait, I'll introduce you. Mrs. Carolina is particular about that."

Before I knew what was happening, in a great booming voice, he declared, "Mrs. Robert O'Neill, Miss Louisa May O'Neill, and Mastuh Robert O'Neill."

I peeked into the enormous, empty front parlor. I wondered who needed to know we were here.

Then I turned around to see Aunt Carolina gliding down the staircase. She had heard Jones's booming voice, but apparently not the names he had called out, because the second she saw us, her willowy figure stopped gliding and just walked down the stairs.

"There you are," said Carolina. "I was wondering when you would get here. Jones, go hang up their coats. Kathleen, come with me into the kitchen. I want the food all laid out for proper effect, and I'm afraid Jenny hasn't even finished the cooking yet. Could you and Louisa May help Jones arrange everything on the table. I don't want to dirty my silk gloves."

I wanted to suggest she take off her gloves, but I knew better than to be rude to a grown-up. After giving us her orders, Aunt Carolina disappeared back upstairs—probably so she could make her grand entrance for her next guest. I followed Grandma and Aunt Louisa May into the kitchen, where I was introduced to Jenny. I could not shake her hand since she was busy stirring things on the stove and pulling other items from the oven.

"Mrs. Carolina always needs the darnd'st fancy gewgobs," Jenny complained. "All this French cooking she wants, though I don't know of no French-Indians she's got comin'. She wouldn't let one of them in her door anyway."

We all chuckled under our breath.

Then Grandma volunteered to help Jenny finish up, while Aunt Louisa May and I helped Jones carry everything into the dining room where a grand banquet of hors d'oeuvres was to be spread out.

When we had everything ready, I went into the parlor and stared up at the most enormous Christmas tree I had ever seen. The parlor had an enormously high ceiling, and the tree reached to the very top. It was covered in delicate, pastel pink and blue porcelain and glass ornaments, and it must have had a thousand electric lights.

Aunt Carolina then came into the room, apparently deciding against a grand entrance down her staircase.

"I love your Christmas tree, Aunt Carolina," I said.

"Thank you," she replied. "I've had those ornaments a couple years now, so I hope no one notices. I definitely will need to get new ones next year."

"Robert, where are you?" screamed my best friend's voice before I even realized the front door had opened.

"Tom, don't be yelling," I heard Mrs. Hampton snap, but her words were unnecessary—he had already replaced yelling with running into the parlor to find me.

"Hello," I said, a bit surprised when he nearly collided with me.

"Here, Merry Christmas. I got you a present."

"Gee, Tom," I said. "I got you one too but I didn't bring it with me."

"That's all right," he said. "Go ahead and open it."

I tore off the paper and opened the box. Inside was a brand new slingshot.

"I made it myself," Tom beamed.

"Thanks," I said. "It's great."

"George," Mrs. Hampton chided her husband. "Did you know that's what he was giving Robert? What kind of a present is that?"

"There's no harm in it, Jane. I had a slingshot myself when I was a boy."

"Well," Grandma frowned, "don't you shoot any birds or animals with it, Robert."

"I won't," I replied. "Thanks, Tom. It's a swell gift."

Then I asked, "Where's Mark?" I did not mind Mark's absence—it was the woman usually clinging to his arm that I wanted to see.

"We had to walk here because Dad let him take the car to pick up Eliza. I hope he gets a flat tire."

"Oh, Tom, don't say such things," Aunt Louisa May told him. Tom's parents were talking to Aunt Carolina, so they did not hear his remark.

Jenny came in with a platter of food she set on the coffee table. "There ain't no more room on that dining table," she said, "so these'll just have to go here until everyone eats enough to make room."

"They look delicious, Jenny," said Grandma.

"I hope so. I worked on 'em hard enough, though I appreciate all your help."

"Our pleasure," Grandma replied. "If you need any more help let us know."

Jenny disappeared back into the kitchen, just as Jones's booming voice announced, "Mr. and Mrs. Roger Richardson!" followed by "Mr. and Mrs. Lysander Blackmore!"

I was impressed by Jones's deep regal voice. I was more impressed by the sophisticated and elegant airs of the guests. The Richardsons and Blackmores were apparently both very wealthy, the Richardsons actually being the parents of Mrs. Blackmore. Mr. Blackmore had a tremendously thick, black curling mustache like I had never seen before. I later learned he was a banker. I felt he was quite an imposing figure of a man. He took one quick glance around the room, realized Mr. Hampton was the only other man present, and immediately went to speak with him upon business.

With the guests arriving, the party had officially begun, so Tom figured he could go eat.

"Let's go into the dining room now before all the food is gone," he urged, nearly pushing me in that direction. "That Mr. Richardson will eat everything if we don't. Last year I saw him swallow twelve whole deviled eggs without even chewing them."

We soon filled our plates, and then stepped into the hallway in time to see Eliza come through the front door looking utterly radiant. She was arrayed in a gown of red with sparkling white trim. A set of swan white pearls enveloped her graceful neck as if it were a Christmas present waiting to be unwrapped. She would have been a vision of exquisite beauty save for the vermin who clung like a bad wart to her arm.

"Hello, Tom. Hello, Robert," her siren voice spoke through ambrosial lips.

"Hello," I said. By the time I realized I was staring at her, Mark said, "Come on, Eliza. Let's get something to eat," and yanked her into the dining room.

Tom and I carried our plates into the parlor and sat down on a sofa. When the lovebirds entered a few minutes later, all the other seats were filled by more guests, so they were forced to sit on the same sofa as Tom and me. I hoped Eliza would sit beside me, but Mark, perhaps sensing my enmity toward him, placed himself between us.

"Tom," said my goddess, "what time did your grandma plan for the dancing to begin?"

"Around eight I imagine," he said.

"There's going to be dancing?" I said in surprise.

"Sure," said Tom. "Grandma always hires a little orchestra and a piano player."

"Robert," Mark informed me, "this is the social event of the year. After all, we are one of Marquette's oldest and finest families."

Since my great-grandparents had come to Marquette in 1855, and the city was founded in 1849, a few hundred people could claim to come from "older" families than us, but I did not know enough of Marquette's history yet to point that out. Since the O'Neills were considered traitors down South, I thought it rather nice to be considered prominent in Marquette.

And then the boredom began to set in. We were the only young people present, so there wasn't much for the four of us to do except talk to one another. The adults were all too busy mingling, trying to sound witty and to impress one another with their hints of how much money they had. As more guests poured in, the room grew so crowded we were staring at people's legs and backs and could barely have walked through the room if we had wished. Mark, apparently not up to mingling with so many prominent people, despite his superior airs, could think of little to say, other than to ask Eliza every ten minutes or so whether she wanted anything more to eat or drink. Eliza kept replying, "No, I need to watch my figure."

I wanted to tell her how fine a figure she had, but I did not want to make a scene with Mark in this crowd.

Finally, Tom, who had braved the crowd to go get seconds on hors d'oeuvres, now decided he would go get thirds, so I agreed to follow him. Even Eliza's beauty did not compensate for sitting next to Mark for an hour.

Just as we returned to the sofa—Tom led me back there—it wasn't my idea to return—the orchestra players began to tune up their instruments. Mark then decided he would eat seconds.

"Oh, not now," said Eliza. "If you eat, we might miss the first dance."

"I'll just grab a few. There's lots of time," he replied.

But as soon as he disappeared, the orchestra started playing a waltz.

"Oh, why couldn't he have gone to get seconds earlier," Eliza said. "He had a whole hour. I hate to miss the first dance. It's always the best."

"I'll dance with you, Eliza!" I blurted out.

Had I thought before I spoke, I would have asked, "May I have the honor of this dance, my lady?" but I was so afraid the lout would come back before I got Eliza on the dance floor that I couldn't take the time to find the proper words.

"Oh," said Eliza. "Well, I'd be honored, Robert."

We stood up and I reached for her hand, but before I could lead her to the dance floor, Mark was back.

"Robert's going to dance with me while you finish your snacks," Eliza told him. "You don't mind, do you?"

"I don't mind if you dance with the boys. Just so long as you don't dance with any men," he said, sitting down and picking up a gooey slice of chocolate cake in his bare hands like a Neanderthal. Had I been half a foot taller, I would have asked him to step outside for calling me a boy, but I had Eliza's hand in mine; that was worth more than my honor.

Once on the dance floor, I put my arm around Eliza's waist. I could just barely peer over her shoulder, but I saw Mark slyly reach over and wipe the chocolate frosting from his fingers onto the hem of Tom's suit when Tom wasn't looking. But I could not warn Tom now, for other dancers surged around us, and although I had never danced before, I found myself twirling around with my goddess.

"Robert, you're a natural," said Eliza.

"Oh, we dance a lot down South. There's always a ball somewhere to attend," I lied.

"I'm sure the Southern ladies are all beautiful," Eliza said. "I bet they miss having a true Southern gentleman like you to attend them at the dances."

Those were the sweetest words I had ever heard. I would have returned the compliment if my tongue had not tied itself up, then slipped down my throat to block all speech. For a minute, I felt unable to breathe. I dared not even look into her stunning eyes to see what color they were from fear I would be so overwhelmed by her unsurpassable beauty that my feet would forget what to do and land on hers.

Finally, I stuttered out, "You—you look beautiful tonight, Eliza."

"What?" The orchestra had stopped and everyone was clapping so she could not hear me. I leaned into her ear and raised my voice, "You look beautiful tonight."

I still don't think she heard me. She simply smiled as if to humor me.

"Thank you for the dance," she said before walking back to the sofa. She moved across the floor so quickly I could not even take her hand, so I followed her like a puppy dog.

"Did you miss me, Mark?" she asked, sitting down beside him and pecking his cheek.

He was lucky ladies were present so I couldn't unleash my anger.

Rather than admit he had missed her, Mark said, "Hold this," and handed Tom his plate.

"Will you dance with me now?" Eliza asked.

"All evening," he said, standing up. He took her arm and led her back onto the dance floor.

"Why'd ya wanna dance with her?" Tom sneered at me.

"Why not?" I said in a tone that dared him to speak against Eliza.

"I don't know," he muttered. "Do you wanna go get more cake?"

"No, I've had enough," I said. Watching Mark whirl Eliza about the dance floor had made me lose my appetite.

"Save my seat for me then," said Tom, before returning to the dessert table.

I felt awkward sitting alone. The house had filled with dozens of people; not one paid attention to me. I did not see Grandma or Aunt Louisa May anywhere. Occasionally, I heard Aunt Carolina's cackling voice from across the room. I caught only glimpses of Mark and Eliza twirling by. She looked as if she were enjoying herself, despite his scrunched up face, filled with sour, snobbish superiority—that look was just an act now, but I hoped soon his face would be stuck in that position.

What did Eliza see in him? Even if I admitted he was tall, handsome, and strong, was she fool enough to prefer him to a real gentleman like myself? How would I tell her of my love and convince her to wait for me until I was eighteen? I would have to find a way. I could not bear to miss out on a lifetime of glorious bliss with her. I could already see us living in a house just as grand as this one, being the toast of the town, throwing the finest parties, having the most attractive children. Of course, since Mark was my cousin and my best friend's brother, we would have to invite him to our parties out of pity—it would be rather pleasurable to have him watch me spend my life with Eliza while he realized what a lump-head he had turned out to be.

I just had to be patient. Eliza was not only beautiful, but intelligent; eventually my charms would win her over—our dancing together had only been the beginning.

"Robert, why are you sitting by yourself?" Grandma asked, coming up to me.

"I'm not," I said. "Tom just went to get some more cake."

"Are you having a good time?"

"It's all right," I replied. I imagined I could be truthful with Grandma, although I would not go so far as to tell her I was bored. "Are you having a good time?"

"Actually, I'm ready to go home. Since I hurt my ankle, I don't feel up to dancing, and it's no fun sitting on the sidelines with old ladies who just want to talk about their doctor visits."

"Where's Aunt Louisa May?" I asked.

"Over there," said Grandma, pointing to the dance floor. "Tom's father asked her to dance."

We watched Aunt Louisa May and Mr. Hampton for a minute. Her cheeks glowed as she danced, and I could see her laughing—for a minute, I wondered why she had said she had no interest in marrying—she would have been a wonderful wife and mother.

"Hi, Aunt Kathleen. Do you want a piece of cake?" asked Tom, returning with three pieces on his plate.

"No, thank you," said Grandma. "I think I'll go have a chat with Lydia Blackmore. Don't you boys make yourselves sick eating too many sweets."

"Hey, Robert, you got the slingshot I made you?" Tom asked, once Grandma was gone.

"Yeah, it's in my jacket pocket," I said. "Why?"

"Let me see it," he said.

I handed it to him.

He picked up some olive pits off his plate and stuck one on the slingshot.

"What are you going to do?" I asked.

"Hit Mark with it."

"Tom Hampton, you put that thing away!" said his mother, suddenly pushing her way through the crowd. "Are you crazy? You could hurt somebody."

"Ah, Ma!" he whined. "We're just looking at it."

"You put it away. You hear me," she repeated. "And throw away those nasty olive pits. You must have eaten two dozen olives! And all that cake! You're not eating anything more this evening, you understand me. Give me a piece of that cake, and let Robert have the other one. The last thing I need is you getting sick in church on Christmas morning because you overate tonight."

"Fine," Tom growled and went off with his plate to find a wastebasket for the olive pits.

"I'll go put the slingshot in my coat pocket so he doesn't get it again," I told Mrs. Hampton.

I made my way through the crowd to the front hall where Jones had hung up my coat. Once the slingshot was safely put away, I thought about returning to the sofa, but since Tom had probably gone into the dining room, I decided to look for him in there. The dining room was empty, but the kitchen door was open, so I peeked in.

Jones and Jenny were sitting together at the kitchen table.

"What can we do for you, Mastuh Robert?" Jones asked.

"I was just looking for Tom," I said.

"He ain't been in here, though I saw him out in the dining room a second ago getting himself some more cake. He might have gone into the washroom down the hall."

I wondered whether Tom had gone into the bathroom because he was sick from overeating or so he could eat his cake in secret.

"Thanks," I said.

"Hi, Robert," said Grandma, greeting me in the doorway as I turned around. "Do you all mind if I join you in here for a minute? It's so hot out there with so many people, and I was hoping maybe you had some ice I could put on my ankle."

"I'd be happy to oblige you," said Jenny, getting up and going to the icebox.

"Mrs. O'Neill, I don't mean to be rude," said Jones, "but I don't think Mrs. Carolina would like white folks sitting in the kitchen with us."

"Well, maybe I don't like that she doesn't like white folks in her kitchen. What's wrong with her? Is her kitchen too good for white folks?" Grandma teased.

"You are a sly one, Mrs. O'Neill," Jones chuckled.

"Well, it's lonely out there," said Grandma. "Not one of those women likes to sew or quilt—they're too busy trying to help their husbands' careers, and Louisa May is busy dancing with all the men—married and bachelors both—so I had to find someone to talk to."

I heard the bathroom door open. Tom, passing by in the hall, spotted me. "Hey, you were supposed to save my seat for me," he said.

"Let's not go back into the parlor," I said. "It's too crowded."

"Can't sit in the kitchen with the help," he replied. "Let's get some more cake now that my ma ain't watchin'. You won't tell will you, Aunt Kathleen?"

"Tell what?" she smiled.

I followed Tom back into the dining room. Alas, the poor boy, who had only had five or six pieces, found that the selfish guests had devoured the rest of the cake. The situation was quite unfair. More unfair was that I found myself trapped between a middle-aged married couple who remarked, "You're the young nephew from down South that Carolina has been talking about, aren't you?"

"Yes," I said.

"You looked older from a distance," said the wife. "I thought you were our granddaughter Lucille's age, but she must be a couple years older than you."

"He's probably closer to Winston's age," said her husband.

"Is it South Carolina where you hail from?" asked the wife.

"Yes," I said.

"How very interesting," said the husband.

"Reginald," said his wife, "we do have acquaintances in South Carolina, don't we?"

"No, my dear, in North Carolina."

"Oh, yes, in Asheville. But I do think I know someone in South Carolina. Where in South Carolina are you from?"

"The biggest nearby town is Greenville. We're near the agricultural college near Pickens."

"I believe one of my college mates is from Greenville. Who are your neighbors?"

"The most famous people from our area were the Clemsons and John C. Calhoun, but I can't think of anyone living there now that you would know."

"No, I don't know anyone named Calhoun."

I could tell from her blank look that she did not realize John C. Calhoun's name, although he had been one of the greatest men the South, indeed the United States, had ever produced. Apparently, being wealthy had not made this woman very knowledgeable.

"Who else lives there?" she asked.

"Um, Mr. Bernard Carter," I said.

"Carter—I think I know that name—isn't there a Carter who made his fortune in shipping?"

"Mr. Carter has a plantation—or what's left of one. It's not much more than a farm now," I said. "It's called Marble Hill."

"Marble Hill! Is he related to the Vanderbilts then, with their fabulous Marble House? One of my cousins is good friends with a Vanderbilt cousin; she's been to both Marble House and the Breakers in Newport."

I didn't know what to say. I doubted Mr. Carter knew anyone who even knew anyone who knew anyone who knew a Vanderbilt.

"You said it's a plantation?" asked the husband. "Cotton then I presume?"

"I don't know that he plants much of anything," I said. "He mostly lives off his fortune. He's always telling me his father left him something like fifty thousand dollars. I guess it just sits in the bank and gains interest."

"Fifty thousand dollars," laughed the husband. "Rowena, dear, can you imagine anyone living off fifty thousand dollars for the rest of his life?"

Rowena let out a snort that revealed her aristocratic claims were mere pretensions.

"Why, we've a cottage in Maine we paid that much for," laughed Reginald.

"Yes, and we thought it a real steal at the time," said Rowena.

"Fifty thousand dollars. Very good joke, Robert," said Reginald.

"But seriously," said Rowena. "Do you know anyone who is in society?"

"No, and I like Mr. Carter even if he does only have fifty thousand dollars," I said. "Excuse me."

I shoved my way past a couple other guests and went back into the parlor. What did it matter how much money anyone had? Money didn't make you a good person. I remembered how angry I had been at Mr. Carter the last day I had seen him, but if Reginald and Rowena were typical Yankees, I could see why he didn't like them. Mr. Carter was a wealthy man in my corner of South Carolina, and I knew fifty thousand was more than my parents, or Grandma, or Aunt Louisa May had, and even if Aunt Carolina had more than that, she was the family member I liked least. And since when was it anyone's business how much money someone else had? No wonder Grandma didn't like Aunt Carolina's parties.

"It took you long enough," said Tom when I collapsed beside him on the sofa.

"Who were those people in the dining room?" I asked. "I got stuck talking to them, and you abandoned me rather than helping me to escape."

"The Robillards," said Tom. "She's Mr. Richardson's sister and he's some big millionaire who made his money in coal out in Pennsylvania, where the Richardsons are from originally. They live out there, but they come up here every Christmas. There's no way I was gonna talk to 'em. Last year they brought their granddaughter, Lucille, with them, and she kept chasing after me. They even suggested maybe someday we'd be married. Heck, she's a flaky thing and too old for me anyway."

Well, I couldn't blame him then for abandoning me. Even if Lucille were as beautiful and intelligent as Eliza—which would be impossible—no one would want her grandparents for in-laws.

The evening continued on in a long, exhausting, boring daze while I sat twiddling my thumbs and watching Tom eat more cake. Eliza did not come near me for the rest of the evening, and after ten o'clock, I no longer saw her in the house. Mark had probably taken her off to some quiet place, or maybe they'd had a fight, broken off their engagement, and she had gone home while he sat outside in a snowbank, crying his eyes out. But somehow I didn't imagine that had happened, and if it ever should, I hoped to witness their break-up so I could defend her honor.

By eleven, Tom had nodded asleep on the sofa, then let out a little scream, jumped up and tried to wipe off the punch he had spilled down his suit and white shirt.

"Now what am I going to do?" he asked. "My mom'll kill me."

"Hurry up and go soak it in the bathroom before it stains," I said.

"Come with me," he said. "Walk in front of me so no one sees it. I don't want my mom yelling at me in front of everyone."

After I agreed to shield him, he said we would go to the bathroom in the back of the house rather than the one off the front hall so no one would see us.

Aunt Carolina actually had two bathrooms downstairs! I could not believe it, and I was even more surprised when Tom told me there were two more bathrooms upstairs. Even Mr. Carter only had one bathroom at Marble Hill, and until I was six, my parents had only had an outhouse.

Tom led me down the front hall, past the front stairs, past the dining room and kitchen to two doors at the back of the hall. He opened one, which turned out to be the bathroom, and went inside.

"Guard the door for me," he said. "I don't know how I'll get my shirt to dry, even if I get the stain out."

Since I didn't know either, I just stood guard. At least I intended to, but then I noticed the door across the hall was cracked open. Unable to resist, I peeked into the room, nudging the door open a few more inches. Thanks to the faint light in the hall, I could see several bookcases. I wanted to turn on the light and investigate; if Aunt Carolina owned any Tarzan or Horatio J. Alger books, and if she would let me borrow them, I would like her a lot better. But then I thought I heard a step in the hallway and turned away from the door. No one was there, but I decided it was best not to take any more chances.

Finally, Tom came out of the bathroom, his suit jacket back on, buttoned up the front to hide most of his wet shirt.

"It doesn't look very bad," I said. "I don't see the stain anyway. You could just tell your mom you spilled water on it, or that the faucet sprayed you when you were washing your hands."

"Yeah, but let's wait before joining everyone just so it can dry a little more."

"Could we go in there then?" I whispered. "Is that really a library?"

"Good idea," he said. "Grandma never lets me in there so we'll have to be quiet, but no one will suspect where we are."

I didn't need to ask Tom why Aunt Carolina wouldn't let him in the library after seeing him eat cake and spill punch down his shirt.

"My grandpa's old law books are in here, and Grandma won't let anyone touch them," Tom explained, shutting the door behind us so we were enclosed in darkness. "She acts like keeping 'em will bring him back or something, even though my mom wants her to give them to my dad since he's a lawyer."

As Tom searched for the light, I felt disappointed. I could care less about old law books. But then, Tom flipped the switch and the room was flooded in electric light. A true library inside a home! To possess a library was the only reason I could think of for why anyone would want to be rich!

"My gosh!" I exclaimed.

"This is the newest part of the house," Tom said. "My grandparents bought the house from someone else when they got married, but my grand-mother added on this room and that little conservatory area."

A large rounded room, like an extensive bay window, was filled with ferns and presented a view of the backyard, Lake Superior, and Marquette's harbor. The view was beautiful in the moonlight, but not as beautiful as the books. I instantly went to the shelves. Ornately carved little bookshelves ran all along the walls with gorgeous paintings above them. Even if the library were not forbidden, I would have been fascinated by it. The room was the height of

Victorian splendor with oriental carpets, gold embossed books, and pre-Raphaelite paintings.

"My grandpa spent all his time in here—he liked working here better than his office downtown," Tom said.

I had almost been ready to change my mind about Aunt Carolina, thinking anyone who had such a library had to be a fine person, but apparently it had been her husband's room.

"Even my grandma hardly ever comes in here," said Tom. "She's left it just the way it was when Grandpa died."

Aunt Carolina had a sentimental side then. I never would have guessed it of her.

Now, as an old man, looking back, I see that hour as one of the key moments in my life. Oh, the Peter White Public Library had more books, and Eliza was more beautiful than that room, but my first entering that library has always seemed a defining moment in my life. I remember being that young boy, peeping from the hallway into that room, as if searching for something, and then the moment the lights were turned on, how amazing it all was, like a revelation, or a beacon to a new life. Looking back now, I see a young boy trying to gaze into the future, scarcely imagining how many countless hours of happiness he would spend in that sanctuary of books.

Tom must have been sleepy because he sat down without a word. I browsed all the bookshelves and admired the paintings, which I would later learn were prints by Lord Leighton, the Rossettis, and James Archer. I found no Jack London or Tarzan books, but Dickens's complete works were there. I had only read *Great Expectations*, but I longed to borrow the copy of *A Tale of Two Cities*. I would have to wait until my next visit to the public library, however, to read it. And although I did not even know the authors' names then, there were also complete sets of Bulwer-Lytton, Sir Walter Scott, Anthony Trollope, George Eliot, and William Makepeace Thackeray, all in expensive covers, bright green, red, or blue, with gold lettering and illustrations inside. I actually dared take a few volumes off the shelf to open, even to hold up to my nose so I could inhale their glorious bookish smell.

"We better go," said Tom, waking up and looking at his watch. "It's half-past eleven."

"Okay," I said, setting down a copy of *Ivanhoe*, which made me nostalgic for when I had read *The Boy's King Arthur*, sadly left back home in South Carolina.

As we shut the door, I heard laughter. We walked quietly down the hall, hoping no one would see us coming from the library. At the kitchen door, we heard the laughter again, and peeking inside, I could see Jones and Jenny waltzing about the room. Just enough of the orchestra music could be heard in the kitchen for them to dance. Their faces glowed with smiles. Jenny laughed nervously as the music ended, and then Jones leaned in and gave her a little kiss on the cheek. They were such a pleasant looking couple that I could not help enjoying the sight of them.

Then Jenny turned her head and saw us peeking in.

"Oh, you boys should know better than to spy on folks," she said. She looked afraid.

"I better go fill the punchbowl," Jones muttered.

"It's okay," I said. Were they really afraid Tom and I would tattle on them? They had been friendly earlier. But that was before they had been caught enjoying themselves.

"Please don't tell, Mrs. Carolina," said Jenny. "She doesn't know we like each other, and if she knew, she wouldn't let us live under the same roof."

"Oh," I said, now understanding. Then Aunt Carolina said, "Why is the punchbowl empty?" No one had heard her coming. "It's been empty for fifteen minutes now. What have the two of you been doing? I never knew two such lazy, shiftless Negroes."

As she said the words, I saw the look of fear and submission on Jones and Jenny's faces, and before I could stop myself, indignation rose up inside me.

"Don't yell at them," I said. "They've been working hard for you all night."

"Don't you talk back to me, young man," my great-aunt snapped.

Then I didn't know what to say. No one had ever spoken to me like that, not in that tone—not my parents, my aunt, my grandmother—no one would treat me that way.

"Jones, I'm just about at the end of my rope with you," said Aunt Carolina. "Jenny isn't very smart, so I can excuse her, but you're setting her a bad example. If you slack off one more time, I'll fire you, and don't you think I won't. You saw me fire Cook this summer."

"Yes, ma'am," he said.

I stood in disbelief. How could she talk to them like that? How could they just stand there and take it?

In anger, I stormed from the room as I heard her say, "Jones, some of my guests are ready to leave so go help them with their coats. Jenny can fill the punchbowl."

I returned to the parlor, found Grandma, and immediately told her what had happened.

"I have a good mind," Grandma replied, "to tell Carolina just what I think of her. You would think Marquette was called the Queen City of the North because she was its queen. She has no excuse to treat people like that. I'd quit if I were them."

Before I could stop her, Grandma headed for the kitchen. I followed, hoping I would get to see her tell off Aunt Carolina. But when we reached the kitchen, Jenny was busy helping Tom dry his shirt. I could hear Aunt Carolina's cackling laughter coming from the front hall where she was saying goodnight to her guests.

Grandma waited patiently for Jenny to finish helping Tom. Then she asked Tom and I to leave so she could talk to Jenny alone. We did as we were told, as far as leaving the room and closing the kitchen door behind us, but we stood outside the door to listen.

"Don't say nothin' to her, Mrs. O'Neill," Jenny pleaded. "It won't do no good. Her bark is worse than her bite."

"Tom!" I heard Mrs. Hampton call. "We're going. Where are you?"

"Bye, Robert!" he said, smacking me on the back. Then he disappeared into the front hall.

"I don't know how you can work for a woman like her," Grandma told Jenny.

"Nothing else we can do. We have to work," said Jenny. "No one else in town will hire us. Most people don't feel comfortable around us—not like down South where everyone grew up with Negroes."

"I suppose," said Grandma. I wished Grandma would hire Jenny and Jones herself, but I suspected she didn't have the money to pay them, and Grandma was not one to let others wait on her, even if her family had once been slave owners. The Civil War had taught Grandma to fend for herself, while Aunt Carolina, who had lived in Marquette during the war, had never known such suffering, so she could remain a dainty lady.

"Hi, Jones. I understand Carolina has been awful to you," said Grandma.

Through the crack in the door, I saw him enter the kitchen from the dining room.

"Oh, she's just being her usual self," he said.

"Robert said she threatened to fire you."

"Oh, she does that almost every week," he said as if it were nothing.

"Why do you keep working for her when she treats you that way?" Grandma asked.

"We've nowhere else to go," Jenny repeated. "Besides, we love each other."

"We do," said Jones. "We'll get married just as soon as we can afford a place of our own, but for now we have to work."

Grandma apparently didn't know what to say, but she must have looked worried.

"Now Mrs. O'Neill, don't you worry none," said Jones. "Mrs. Carolina's done fired me three times this past year—the first time 'cause I got mud on the carpet after workin' in the garden cause she fired the gardener last spring and even though I told her I don't know a pansy from a tulip, not that it really matters 'cause she never looks at the flower gardens anyways. Then the second time it was 'cause Cook was sick, and I burnt the bread. I don't think Cook was even sick that time, just sick of Mrs. Carolina, 'cause the next week Cook got a job workin' for the Blackmores, and Mrs. Carolina ain't talked to Mrs. Blackmore ever since—even though she feels she has to invite her because she's got her money in that bank what Mr. Blackmore is vice president at. She was awful mad to lose Cook, and claims she fired her just to save face. Jenny here was just the parlor maid, but Mrs. Carolina makes her do all the cookin' now. It's been months since Cook left so I think Mrs. Carolina's afraid to go about firin' anyone more since she's startin' to realize she's got a reputation in this town that makes no one want to work for her. I've been expectin' another firin' brewin' up in her, but seems like this time she done lost some of the wind in her sails."

"I just don't understand why you stay," said Grandma, echoing my thoughts.

"Well, someone has to stay with her. She sho ain't gonna be able to take care of herself none. It wouldn't be very Christian to abandon her when she needs us."

"Robert, are you ready to go?" asked Aunt Louisa May, coming down the hall.

"Sure," I said, hoping she hadn't noticed I was listening at the door.

"Have you seen your grandmother?"

"She's in the kitchen with Jones and Jenny."

Aunt Louisa May opened the kitchen door and stepped in. "Mother, almost everyone has left. Are you ready?"

"I guess so," said Grandma. "Well, have a good Christmas, Jones, Jenny. Let me know if you need anything."

"Thank you, Mrs. O'Neill. We'll do that," said Jones.

"Merry Christmas to all of you," Jenny added.

We said goodbye to Aunt Carolina at the front door. Jones followed us to give us our coats. Aunt Carolina thanked us for coming. She acted as if she were glad we had come—at least the daggers in her eyes were gone—but the memory of her telling me not to backtalk to her was not. If she weren't such a fine lady, I probably would have given her a good kick. No, I wouldn't have because I had better manners. But she deserved a good kick from someone.

On the way home, Grandma told Aunt Louisa May what I had witnessed in the kitchen, and then what Jenny and Jones had said.

"Aunt Carolina's always had an ornery side," said my aunt. "I wish she knew how lucky she is to have Jones and Jenny. I doubt anyone else, even her own daughter, would live with her. But it's Christmas. We won't let her orneriness ruin our holiday. Look at the stars up there, shining so brightly."

"They are exceptionally bright," said Grandma. "I could almost believe one of them was the Star of Bethlehem."

Aunt Louisa May began softly to sing "Silent Night." Halfheartedly, Grandma and I joined in, but by the time we had reached home, we were cheered up, especially when we looked at the clock and saw it was exactly midnight and Christmas Day. I went to bed that night, not sad I would spend Christmas without my parents, but anticipating my first Christmas with my grandma and my aunt.

Chapter 8

Christmas Day

The next morning, I was awake and dressed by seven. Quietly, I went downstairs to shake my presents and try to guess what they were before everyone else woke up.

But Grandma met me at the bottom of the stairs. "I was just coming to wake you," she said. "We have to be to Mass for eight o'clock and it's a bit of a walk. We thought we would give ourselves a treat by going to St. Peter's this morning since you haven't been there yet."

"Okay," I said, anxious to see the inside of the massive sandstone cathedral.

"I hope it's not too cold out," said Aunt Louisa May. "We really should buy an automobile."

"Don't be silly, Louisa May," Grandma replied. "They're much too dangerous."

"Oh, Mother, the Hamptons have one and they've never had an accident."

"Louisa May, unless you bought us an automobile as a Christmas present, we're not going to spoil the day by having this discussion again. You know my stomach gets unsettled just riding on the streetcar."

Aunt Louisa May rolled her eyes. "Mother, it's the twentieth century. Are you ever going to let go of your Victorianism?"

"I wish you would get married and have children," Grandma replied, "so someday your children will say to you, 'Oh Mother, it's 1950, not the turn of the century anymore'."

"That's one more reason not to marry," laughed my aunt, "so I don't give you that satisfaction."

I could care less what year it was. I just wanted to open my presents, but Grandma said the cathedral would be packed so we had better leave right away; after Mass we would come back for breakfast and to open our gifts.

The cathedral was a good dozen blocks away. We walked swiftly, knowing it would be crowded and hoping we would find a seat. But the walk was well worth it. A light snow had fallen overnight so everything was glistening white as the first streaks of morning sun appeared. I enjoyed the early morning calm—it truly did feel like peace on earth. But then I remembered the war, and prayed that wherever my father was, he was safe today.

"It's so peaceful this morning," said my aunt.

"We would miss this splendid silence if we had a motor car," Grandma jibed.

As we started down Fourth Street's hill, the Hamptons' automobile rattled by us. Mr. Hampton blew his horn and all four of the family waved.

"I rest my case," said Grandma, who had been startled by the automobile's noise when it first came up behind us.

A horse and wagon followed it down the hill; the horse's hooves made a clumpety-clump sound that wasn't any more peaceful than the automobile's rattling.

"Well, it was peaceful," Aunt Louisa May said.

"I hope there's peace overseas today," I replied.

Grandma put her arm around my shoulder, sensing I was worried about my father.

We continued down the hill, then reached the bottom and started up the other side of it, approaching the cathedral as it loomed up high. Not in Greenville or Charleston had I seen its equal. To me, it was as grand as any cathedral in Europe. We climbed up its tall front steps and passed through the center of its three magnificent doors. The interior was filled with stained glass windows of saints and biblical figures, statues, and giant pillars. It was the most impressive building I had ever seen, almost like walking into the court of Heaven itself. Even today, when I have been in the cathedral a hundred times, I still remain awed by its magnificence. When the interior was destroyed by fire in 1935, the Marquette Diocese felt a stunning blow, but when the cathedral was rebuilt, it rose all the more magnificent, with even higher towers and its interior even more ornate. We Americans tend to destroy our historical monuments, but St. Peter's Cathedral seems perpetually blessed to endure, perhaps because its founder, the saintly Bishop Baraga, missionary to the Chippewa and the first white settlers of Upper Michigan, rests beneath it.

For Christmas, the church was decorated with evergreen, which to me resembled the Holy Land's palm trees. When I saw the nativity set, my heart recalled the little nativity my mother had always put up, which in turn made me think of the many happy Christmases I had spent with my parents. I had feared this Christmas would be upsetting for me, but the nativity set reminded me that Christmas was not about my happiness but the gift Christ had given to us, freeing us from sin and death, and that meant my mother was in Heaven, waiting to be reunited with me, and even if my father should not come home from the war, I would also see him again.

As I listened to the centuries old Eucharistic prayers in Latin, and as I sang the traditional Christmas hymns, I felt a calm settle over my soul, a peace I had not felt since I had come to Marquette. For the first time, I knew I could accept the sorrow of the past year and have hope for the future, and I realized if I had gone all these weeks without my mother, I could continue on and even be happy; knowing I would see her again would help me manage through many difficult times to come.

When the service had ended, Grandma wanted to show me the tomb where Bishop Baraga rested. I had never heard of him before I came to Marquette, so Grandma told me how he had been born in Slovenia and could have had a prosperous life as a priest there, but his great desire had been to preach the gospel to his Indian brothers in North America. Upper Michigan has always had a harsh climate, but to imagine the saintly bishop coming to this land in the 1830s, before there were any towns, railroads, electricity, to imagine him walking hundreds of miles on snowshoes through blizzards to bring the gospel to thousands, first the native Chippewa, then the miners and lumberjacks—it was almost miraculous and spoke so strongly of his devotion to God.

"They called him the snowshoe priest," said Grandma, "but they should have called him the snowshoe saint. I never had the chance to meet him myself, but as a boy, your grandfather was an altar server at some of the Masses he said—your grandpa told me that even when Bishop Baraga was seventy years old, he was as strong and devoted to the cause of Christianity as a man one-third his age."

"Whenever I think I have it rough," Aunt Louisa May said, "I always think of Bishop Baraga and the difficulties he faced. My little troubles seem insignif-
. icant by comparison."

I have always kept my aunt's words in my heart, often remembering the bishop's perseverance when faced with my own troubles.

"Well, I'm starving," said Grandma. "Let's go home and have breakfast. I know Robert must be anxious to open his presents."

Once home, I set the table while Grandma made us eggs and sausages and Aunt Louisa May put the pumpkin pie in the oven for Christmas dinner. For breakfast, Grandma had made a huge Christmas coffee cake, complete with candied cherries and tons of frosting, and for the first time, she let me drink coffee, not even blinking when I put in three teaspoonfuls of sugar—in fact, she did the same. As we ate, I grew anxious to open my presents. I had not asked for anything, yet I was hoping I would get some interesting books or at the very least a new bedspread and curtains since my room was still pink.

"Just let me wash up the dishes," said Grandma when we finished eating. "Then we can open the presents."

"Can't you wash the dishes later?" I groaned. I had been patient all morning, but even I had my breaking point when Christmas presents were waiting.

"No, I can't stand the thought of letting all that egg yolk harden on the plates. It'll just take me ten minutes or so."

She was twenty minutes—an eternity for a boy on Christmas morning. I asked Aunt Louisa May whether I could at least look in my Christmas stocking, but she said Grandma wouldn't want to miss any of the excitement. I asked whether I should go into the kitchen to help Grandma, but she said no. Then I wondered why my aunt didn't stay in the kitchen to help Grandma, but instead she had come into the parlor and put a Christmas record on the phonograph.

When I heard the back door slam shut, I became really impatient.

"What is she doing now to hold us up?" I couldn't help asking.

"Probably just putting out the garbage," said my aunt.

Finally, Grandma came into the parlor with a giant box in her arms.

"Robert, come get this from me," she said. "You're stronger than me, and it's yours anyway."

I jumped up and grabbed hold of the giant package.

"Can I open it now?" I asked, as excited as if I were a little boy.

"I think you better," said Grandma.

I started to pull off the ribbon, but not without first noticing the curious glances my aunt and Grandma exchanged.

I barely had the ribbon untied when the box lid popped off by itself. I was momentarily stunned until I saw a furry brown head appear.

"Merry Christmas, Robert!" said Grandma.

"Oh, Grandma," I replied, overwhelmed with pleasure. I cuddled the little cocker spaniel puppy in my arms as it reached up its head to lick my face.

"How did you manage to hide him from me?" I asked.

"That was easy," said Grandma. "Eliza agreed to keep him next door for us, but I had to promise she could come over to play with him once in a while."

I was so excited by the puppy that it did not register in my mind until later that now I had a ploy to see my goddess.

"He's just the most adorable puppy ever," said Aunt Louisa May when he started to wiggle. I set him down so he could run to her.

"What will you name him, Robert?" Grandma asked.

"I don't know," I said, suddenly puzzled.

They made a few suggestions, but none of them seemed fitting.

"Well, let's open the other gifts and you can decide later," Grandma said.

"I think we better open the gifts before the puppy does," Aunt Louisa May agreed. He was nipping at the paper on one of my packages and soon had torn a piece from it.

"He must have good taste," I said, taking the present from him and pulling the paper from a box of chocolates. I opened the box and passed the candy around, while my little friend contented himself with batting about a ball of wrapping paper.

Then we all started opening packages simultaneously. There were new clothes, books, and perfume for the women, fruitcake from neighbors, Christmas ornaments and jewelry, a sled for me, and records for Grandma, and inevitably pairs of socks. And yes, I got a blue bedspread and blue curtains and the latest Tarzan book and an Oz book as well, which Grandma somehow knew I had wanted although I had never mentioned it. I suspect she asked Helen for suggestions.

"Thank you, everyone," said Grandma after the last package had been opened.

We sat contentedly for a moment, looking at our presents and feeling fortunate.

"Well, let's get this mess cleaned up," said Grandma, "so I can get the dishes done."

I looked up from a page of my new Oz book.

"I thought you did the dishes already," I said.

"No, I was over getting your puppy from Eliza," Grandma replied.

"I didn't know I had a fibbing grandmother," I smiled.

"Well, I'm full of surprises," Grandma laughed. "Why don't you go upstairs and try on your new clothes?"

"I think he better take the puppy out first," said Aunt Louisa May.

"Good idea. He's not housebroken yet," Grandma replied.

I was glad to get out of trying on my new clothes. I put his collar and leash on the puppy, then put on my boots and coat.

"Remember to wipe his feet before you bring him back in," Grandma said.

The puppy willingly followed me out the door and down the front steps. Eliza must have already acquainted him with winter since the first thing he did was bury his snout in the freshly fallen snow, then roll around in it until his coat was full of little hard snowballs. Not yet realizing what work it would be to clean him off, I laughed, told him he was silly, then knelt down in the snow and rolled about myself, making snow angels and feeling quite content. After a minute, the puppy came and sat beside me, and I lay there, gazing up at the white clouded sky, wishing life could always be this simple.

Finally, when I started to feel cold, I stood up, brushed the snow off both of us, and returned inside.

As I opened the door, I heard Aunt Louisa May exclaim, "Oh no!"

She sounded so upset that I kicked off my boots and ran to the kitchen.

"What's wrong?" I asked.

"I was just going to put the ham in the oven when I found the pumpkin pie in there. I forgot all about it. It's completely burnt."

I looked at the pie as she set it on the counter—I didn't know which was blacker, the crust or the pumpkin itself.

"Now we'll have nothing for dessert," cried my aunt.

"It's all right, Louisa May," said Grandma. "We have coffee cake left over and plenty of candy. We can do without pie. We'll make one for New Year's instead."

And then a light bulb went on in my head.

"The puppy's the same color as the pie should have been, so I'll name him Pumpkin. That way we'll still sort of have pumpkin pie for Christmas."

Aunt Louisa May could not help laughing at this suggestion, so Pumpkin became the puppy's name, and my aunt was cheered up after that.

I had helped to solve the dessert crisis, but now I had to face my own. I was sent upstairs to try on all my clothes, which I did reluctantly and dawdled at since I carried Tarzan up with me, intending to read the first chapter and hoping my extended absence would go unnoticed. Not that I would mind helping to make dinner, but when the jungle calls, a true boy will answer.

But Tom arrived before I could answer the jungle's call. I had just started to unbutton my shirt to try on my new clothes when he burst through my bedroom door and said, "Merry Christmas! Wanna go for a walk? I'm bored."

How could anyone be bored on Christmas Day? Yet I said, "Sure, I got my own sled for Christmas so we could take that."

"No, I want to walk down to the lake. It's starting to freeze over. I like to watch the ice cracking and floating on it."

"We won't go out on it, will we?" I asked nervously.

"No, not yet. It's not that frozen, but we can eventually. My dad will take us ice fishing then. It's just neat when you can hear it cracking and dripping."

"Can we take Pumpkin?" I asked.

"What?"

"My puppy. He's named Pumpkin."

"Oh, yeah, sure," he said.

"Go ahead," said Grandma, when I asked permission. "It'll be a couple hours before we eat, and Louisa May and I can handle making supper. You boys get some fresh air."

"We're going to go see the ice—" I started, but Tom interrupted, "Did you have a good Christmas, Aunt Kathleen?" and he chatted with my aunt and Grandma while I put on my coat and put Pumpkin on his leash.

"Never tell the grownups you're going near the lake," Tom warned me once we were outside. "They always think you're dumb enough to fall in."

"Oh," I said.

Pumpkin walked about a block, then sat down and started to hold up his paws.

"He must be cold," I said, so I ended up carrying him down the hill that sloped toward the lake and the harbor. We came down the hill on Ridge Street and walked out to the shore, not far from the lighthouse. Snow covered the beach, although it was rather brown from the sand mixed in with it, and at its edge, huge chunks of ice had been pushed up that looked like little mountains. I felt as if I were in Antarctica, or perhaps even walking on the moon since everything was white and crater-like gaps spread between the ice chunks.

"I don't believe in that stuff," said Tom when I suggested the landscape resembled the moon.

"Don't believe in what?" I asked.

"In traveling to the moon and Martians and all that. It's stupid."

"It doesn't matter if it's real," I replied. "It's fun to dream about. The man who wrote Tarzan has also written some books that take place on Mars."

"Books are boring," he muttered. "I'd rather be outside sleigh riding or ice fishing—that's what's real."

I could not blame Tom for feeling that way when Marquette had such breathtaking views, but I wished my best friend liked books at least a little. I felt I had been rather quick to name Tom my best friend when we didn't have much in common. But I still liked him.

Finally, although unwilling to show we were not as tough as we would have liked, we admitted we were cold, so we turned toward home.

"We can try out your sled tomorrow," said Tom as we stopped in front of my house.

"Sure," I agreed. "I almost forgot to give you your Christmas present."

I ran inside and brought it out to him. It was a new wallet with a dollar in it; he said he had never owned a wallet, so he was very excited to get it. Then we wished each other Merry Christmas and he headed for home.

I cleaned the snow off Pumpkin's paws while watching Tom walk down the road. It was only four o'clock but already starting to get dark. Realizing Christmas Day was quickly ending, I started to feel sad. When I opened the door, the lights of the Christmas tree and the smells coming from the kitchen should have cheered me, but instead, I only felt tired. I suddenly wished the day were over so we could go back to our normal routines. It had been a happy Christmas in many ways, but it still wasn't the same without my parents.

"Robert," called Grandma from the kitchen. "We'll be ready to eat in a second if you want to go wash your hands."

"All right," I called back, before going into the bathroom to clean up.

As I sat down at the table, I told myself I probably felt down just because I was hungry, and once I ate supper, I could go read my Tarzan book, which would cheer me.

"Robert, we forgot to check the mail yesterday," Aunt Louisa May said as she set the potatoes on the table, and Grandma came behind her with the ham. "I didn't think about it until a couple minutes ago, but a letter from your father was in the box."

"Really?"

"Yes. I wanted to read it, but it was addressed to you."

"Where is it?" I asked.

"On the buffet," said Grandma.

"I'll read it after supper," I decided. I didn't want to make Grandma and my aunt wait while the food got cold. It was enough to know my father had written—to know he was alive.

"We'll do the dishes while you read the letter out loud to us," said Grandma when we had finished eating.

I then ripped it open. For a second, I felt disappointed by how short it was, but the words were comforting nevertheless.

My son Robert,

I just got at the same time all the letters your aunt has written to me. Please tell her I thank her and your grandmother for all they've done, and I know my boy could not be in better hands during this difficult time.

I am deeply saddened by the loss of your mother. I cannot even find words to express such sorrow. My commanding officer told me I could go home on leave, and I ache to see you, but everyone says we are so close now to the end of this war, and I know we need every able bodied man to succeed. Your mother would want me to do my duty, and as long as I know you are safe, I will strive to do so. Please write to Nellie and Mr. Carter and tell them I appreciate their looking after our house while we are away. Also please give my deepest sympathies to your grandma and aunt on the loss of your mother. It is inconceivable to me how I will go on without her—right now I have this war to keep my thoughts occupied, but to think of returning home not to be greeted by her—I cannot imagine such a future.

Robert, my fine son, I am proud of you more than I can ever tell you. I want you to know that I am safe in England where there is no fighting, although I imagine I will be shipped to the continent soon. Should I not come back, I want you to be brave and to know how much you were loved by both your mother and me, and I want you to go on with your life and make us proud of you, which I know you will do anyway.

The mail is to be shipped out within the hour so I will say no more now except that I pray for you each day and hope you will do the same for me.

With great affection, Dad

"That's a fine letter," said Grandma.

"Yes, it is," Aunt Louisa May agreed.

"He's safe," I said. And then I started to tear up, and Pumpkin, worried, jumped about at my feet, whining, until I picked him up and buried my tears in his fur.

"We're all relieved to know he's safe," said my aunt.

I could not have received a better Christmas present than my father's letter. And he had said the war was almost over now. I prayed it would end soon so he could come home to me.

That evening Aunt Louisa May read aloud to us from Dickens's *A Christmas Carol*. When I went to bed, I realized Christmas could have miracles—even a simple letter from my father was one, and I felt hope for the New Year.

Chapter 9

Surprises

After the holidays, I had plenty of time to play with Tom and Mags. Even Helen, who was tired of being cooped up in the house during her illness, joined us in our constant snowball fights. And then it was time for school to start again. Since Bishop Baraga was a Catholic school, we had nuns for teachers. The sisters meant well by us, but often they thought being strict was in our best interest, and while I never got the ruler from any of them, I'm afraid Tom did more than once. After a couple days of my sitting beside my best friend, Sister separated us because she said she could see I was a well-mannered boy, and she did not want me picking up Tom's bad habits. I felt incensed, although I could not quite say why—perhaps because I feared Tom would think I thought myself better than him. But thankfully by the next day, Sister seemed to have forgotten her threat. I was careful not to pick up Tom's bad habits, although I wasn't always sure what counted as one, and I did my best to be an example to him and keep him out of trouble. Whatever his faults, Tom kept his promise to be my best friend for life, and I never wanted to trade his friendship for anything. We had almost nothing in common, but I think we liked each other all the better for it; he respected, even if he could not understand, my love for books, and I admired his courage, even if I thought him a bit foolhardy when he sleighed down hills that were nearly cliffs or told people just what he thought of them.

I only remember one day when I got annoyed with him, and Helen was the reason for it. She was in the grade behind us, so I only saw her during recess, but often Tom and I would walk to school with her, Mags, Mollie, and

Mary. One day I asked Helen whether I could carry her books, thinking only that she had more than she could handle that day. Tom let out a loud, "Ha, Ha!" which I doubt even he knew the meaning of, but I instantly interpreted it as my being mocked. Before he could say more I stepped up to his nose and looked him in the eye. He muttered, "Sorry, Robert." Never again was a word said about it, but somehow after that, I found myself carrying Helen's books quite often—she would just hand them to me as if it were expected I would carry them, even when I had five or six of my own which I then had to tote in a bag.

I do not want the reader to assume that at this time I had developed any romantic feelings for Helen. I was simply trying to be polite; I figured she was new at school like me, and she seemed to be having a hard time making friends. Sometimes during these walks, Mollie and Mary would decide to walk by themselves, and then Tom and Mags would run ahead, throwing snowballs at one another, leaving Helen and me more or less alone to talk.

Helen and I would then speculate about where our fathers were stationed overseas, and sometimes she would confess to me how worried she was about her father; since my father had told me to be brave, I never expressed my own fears to her. My father's letter on Christmas had cheered me, and I received a couple more letters from him in the next few weeks that kept my spirits up. Helen had only received one letter from her father since she had come to Marquette, but I encouraged her to believe all would be well.

Winter was now at its worst. Michigan's Upper Peninsula can easily go for days at a time without the temperature rising above zero. On such days, even with scarves, mittens, wool coats, boots, hats, and long underwear, we were afraid of frostbite in the long trek to the school across from the cathedral. Tom would walk to my house in the morning and step inside to warm up while I put on my winter clothes; then we would walk to the girls' house, although we preferred the cold to going inside and talking to Mrs. Lawson. We then would stop at St. John's, walk in the side door and go out the front—even if it took us a little out of our way, it warmed us up for a moment, although the custodian occasionally got upset with us for tramping snow across the church floor.

Now, looking back, I don't know how I managed all those long winter walks—there were no school buses then, and we could not all have fit in the Hamptons' automobile. As for the snow, it piled up, up, up until we could barely see out of our houses' front windows, and nearly everyday when I got home, I would have to shovel off the steps and front walk. Grandma declared it was the best winter ever because she had me to shovel for her, and I really didn't mind since I felt like the man of the house when I shoveled.

Then one day we received news that Helen and Mags's grandmother had passed away. Mrs. Lawson and all four girls went downstate for the funeral. The day they were expected to return, Tom and I had walked to school alone, as we had all week, but that afternoon, he had to stay after school for shooting a spitball at his ex-best friend, Lon, who really seemed like an okay fellow to me, although I never would tell Tom I thought so. I walked home by myself that day, feeling quite bored that I would have no one to play with that afternoon.

As I approached our house, I saw Eliza out shoveling her front walk. Instantly, I thought of going over to shovel for her, thinking I would be gallant to do so. I had barely said a word to Eliza since the Christmas party, despite her telling Grandma she would come over often to see Pumpkin. I thought my perfect chance had come—I would go inside to fetch Pumpkin and pretend I was taking him for a walk, then approach Eliza, and while she pet Pumpkin, I would gallantly shovel her front walk.

But my plan was not meant to be. As soon as I opened the front door, Pumpkin started jumping on me. And then from the silence of the house, I realized no one was home. Thinking this odd, I went into the dining room where I found a note from Grandma.

> Robert,
> The Lawsons returned home this morning, and Mrs. Lawson's sister, Helen Pearson, has returned with them to visit. Louisa May and I have gone over to give them our sympathies. Come over to see the girls if you wish, but first please take Pumpkin outside so he doesn't make a mess in the house. If you don't want to come over, we should be home by five o'clock to make supper.
> Love, Grandma

I can't say I looked forward to going over to the Lawsons' house, considering they were grieving, but I was curious to see Helen's Aunt Helen, whom I knew she did not like. I imagined Helen would need comforting, and I felt obligated as a friend to pay my respects.

"All right, Pumpkin," I said, as he continued to harass me, "I'll take you out, but then I have to leave again."

By the time I got Pumpkin's leash on him and we were down the front steps, Eliza had gone back inside. I would have rather spent two minutes talking to her than two hours with Helen, but I knew that sometimes being a friend means not doing what you want. After taking Pumpkin to the nearest tree, I returned inside, raided the cookie jar, and then walked over to the Lawsons' house. As I knocked, I remembered how my own mother had recently died, and then I started to feel awkward, but Mags ended that when she opened the door.

"Hey, Robert! Come on in," she said. "I've missed ya. I never thought I'd miss going to school, but Ma hasn't let us do anything 'cept sit around and look glum these past two days. Grandma always did have a way of ruining people's fun."

"I'm sorry to hear about your loss," I said, afraid her mother would hear her remarks.

"It's all right. I only saw Grandma a few times, and I don't think she liked me much anyway."

Apparently Helen had not exaggerated about her grandmother.

"Hello, Robert," said Helen, coming to the door.

"Hello," I said shyly.

"Everyone's in the dining room having coffee and cookies," said Mags, elbowing me in that direction.

"There you are," said Grandma as I tripped over the rug from Mags pushing me into the room. "Robert, this is Miss Pearson. She's Helen and Mags's Aunt Helen."

"Hello," I said. "It's very nice to meet you."

"It's nice to meet you as well," she nodded. She did not look as horrid as I had expected, just plain and quiet.

"Robert, you may sit down if you like," Mrs. Lawson offered.

I squeezed into a chair beside Aunt Louisa May, who asked me how school had been just as another visitor knocked on the door.

"I'll get it!" shouted Mags. "Hope that's Tom!"

"Thank you, Margaret," her mother stopped her, "but I prefer to answer it myself."

Mrs. Lawson returned a second later, followed by John Williams.

"You must be quite the curiosity, Helen," Mrs. Lawson told her sister. "So many people are calling on us today. This is Mr. Williams."

"How are you?" he asked Miss Pearson, removing his hat and scarf to reveal his handsome face.

"Fine, thank you. How are you?"

"Just fine," he replied. He looked very fine. The cold January air apparently agreed with him for it gave his cheeks a ruddy glow. He is the only man I've ever met who truly exemplified the statement that a man gets more handsome with age. And Miss Pearson apparently thought him quite fine for as she spoke, she turned to look at him and let out a little gasp almost of awe, and then the plain, bored and tired expression on her face turned into a smile and a twinkle in the eye.

"Won't you sit down with us?" she asked.

"Thank you," he said, quickly stepping to the chair beside her.

"How is your mother, John?" Mrs. Lawson asked. "I haven't seen her since before Christmas."

"She's fine," said John. "I left her baking cookies. My mother," he explained to Miss Pearson, "is eighty, and although it frightens me, she insists on using the stove and oven; there is no stopping her. I hope I have half her energy at that age. I'm sure tomorrow I'll be sent over with a plate of treats for all of you. Today, I'm afraid I only have a card and our deepest sympathies on your loss."

"Thank you," said Miss Pearson, taking the card from him.

"Mrs. Williams was one of the first settlers in Marquette," Grandma told Miss Pearson. "She was a great friend to my husband's parents."

"Do you live with your mother?" Miss Pearson asked John.

"Yes, there are just the two of us," he replied.

"That's how it was with my mother and me," she said, "but now that my mother is gone, I'm all alone in the world."

"I'm sorry," he said. "I can't imagine how awful it must be to lose your last parent. I know it will be a difficult day for me when it comes."

"You need to find a wife, John," said Mrs. Lawson. "That'll make it easier for you."

"Robert, do ya wanna go outside to play?" Mags asked, bored with the adult conversation.

"May I, Grandma?" I asked.

"Go ahead. Just be home in time for supper."

Mags headed for the door while I asked, "Are you coming too, Helen?"

Helen simply got up from her chair and followed us outside.

"What are we going to play?" I asked, once we all had our boots on and were outside.

"Snow's no good for sledding today," said Mags. "How about a snowball fight?"

Helen and I looked at each other. We'd had just about our fill of snowball fights by now, and it was only January with at least two more months of winter to go.

"Let's go ice skating," said Helen. "I still haven't worn the skates I got at Christmas."

"Can't," said Mags. "Mine don't fit me anymore."

"Well, it's cold out anyway," said Helen. "We could go inside and play Oz again."

"I don't want to play that stupid game," said Mags.

"You would if you read the books," said Helen.

"I just finished *The Lost Princess of Oz*," I said, "but I forgot to bring it over for you to read, Helen."

"Oh, I've been waiting for it too," she said.

"Why don't we walk over to my house to get it, and then you can see Pumpkin too."

"All right," she agreed.

"If you two are going to talk about books, I'm going to go find Tom," said Mags.

"We'll just get the book for Helen," I said. "You can come and see Pumpkin too."

"No, I'm going to go find Tom," she said. "After you get the book, if you want to, you can join me at his house for a snowball fight. I don't really care what you do."

She walked off in a huff. Apparently, two days inside was all her snowball fighting spirit could handle.

Trying to compromise, despite Mags already being gone, I said to Helen, "We could go over to Tom's, and you could pick up the book on the way home."

"All right," she said.

At that moment, Mollie and Mags came out the door, fully dressed for a winter experience.

"What're you two doing?" asked Mollie.

"We're going over to Tom's house to have a snowball fight," I said. "Mags already left."

"Can we come too?" asked Mollie.

I could see Helen was about to say, "No, because Mary's too little," but Mary, anticipating the answer, already began to argue.

"It's not fair that you and Mags get to have all the fun just because you're older! If you don't let us come, I'll tell my mother that you pushed me into the snowbank!"

"I never did," Helen replied.

But it was too late to argue. Mary threw herself backward into the snowbank, and then rolled over onto her stomach, trying to attach as much snow to herself as possible.

"Helen, you better let us come," Mollie warned, "or Mary will make sure no one is allowed to go."

Helen pinched up her lips, then inhaled deeply through her nose.

"All right, but Mary, you have to promise to be nice."

"I'm always nice," said Mary, jumping up and brushing the snow from her.

"You know what your mother will say about you playing with rough boys," Helen added. "She'll be worried you'll pick up their bad habits."

"Rough boys?" I laughed. "Mags is rougher than Tom and me put together."

"Robert," Mary asked, "what bad habits do you have?"

"Robert doesn't have any bad habits," Helen replied. "He's a perfect gentleman. But you know how your mother feels about boys."

"He must have some bad habits or else Mom wouldn't warn us against him."

"Mary, just be quiet for once," said Mollie as we walked down the sidewalk. "Anyone can tell Tom has more bad habits than Robert."

"Then I'll have to ask Tom about his bad habits," said Mary.

"No, Mary, that would be rude," said Helen, "and you promised to be nice. Try to act like a young lady."

"I don't have to," said Mary. "I'm already Mom's favorite."

"You are not," Mollie said. "Mom loves us all equally."

"Then how come the dress I got for Christmas is prettier and more expensive than the dresses the rest of you got?"

"It isn't," said Mollie.

"Is so. Don't you ever look at your clothes? They're all cheap. Cheap! Cheap! Cheap! Cheap! Cheap!" she peeped like an obnoxious little chick.

"If you keep acting like that," I said, unable to bear the irritation any longer, "Tom won't let you play in his yard."

"Tom'll do whatever I say," Mary replied. "He's got a weak spot for beautiful women, and I'm the beautifullest he knows."

My tongue almost slipped that Eliza Graham was the most beautiful girl on the planet, but Mollie's tongue slipped first.

"That's a lie. Tom's in love with Mags! And she's not beautiful."

"Mags doesn't love him," Mary retorted. "And besides, who could love Mags? She's just a tomboy."

"At least she's not a sissy like you," said Mollie.

Afraid that name-calling would make things worse, I joked to Mary, "You don't want Tom to love you. He'll teach you all his bad habits."

"That's true," said Mary. "Then I guess I'll have to love you. You're better looking anyway."

"You can't love, Robert," said Mollie. "Helen's in love with him!"

And then there was silence.

I was so embarrassed I'm sure I blushed, although if accused of it, I would have said the cold air turned my cheeks red.

I was afraid to look at Helen. I felt embarrassed for her, but more so, I hoped what Mollie had said was not true. I liked Helen too much to hurt her by telling her I was in love with someone else.

"There's Tom's house," said Mollie, perhaps to end the awkwardness she had just created. Tom and Mags were kneeling in the yard, building up their snowball arsenal. Both looked up when they saw us approaching.

"What are the two of you doing here?" Mags asked her sisters. "You weren't invited."

"Helen said we could play," said Mary, "and if you don't let us, I'll go home and tell Mom."

"All right," Mags frowned, "but we're gonna have a snowball fight, and if either of you get hurt, don't come cryin' ta me. Especially you, Mary; you're such a tattletale."

"I am not!" she screamed. "Why is everyone always calling me names?"

"I wonder," groaned Tom. "Just be quiet so we can pick teams. I get Mags and Robert on mine."

"That's not fair!" said Mary. "We need a boy on our team."

"All right, then Robert can be your captain, and he and I'll pick teams, but since it's my house, I pick first, and I pick Mags."

"I'll take Helen," I said.

"Tom, pick Mary," Mags said. "She's so mean we could whip them easy with her."

"That's fine because we want Mollie," I said so she wouldn't be hurt to be picked last. I was soon to regret my decision.

"You three take the snowbank on that side of the driveway," Tom said, "and we'll take this one."

Helen, Mollie, and I climbed up the snowbank and positioned ourselves behind a little ridge at the end. I realized we didn't have any snowballs. The ready-made arsenal was in Tom and Mags's possession, so I quickly started to make snowballs, but my concentration was broken when Mollie said, "I'm not very good at snowball fights, so you two better help me rather than be kissing back here."

"Mollie!" cried Helen, having reached her limit of embarrassment for the day.

"You ready?" Tom yelled from across the driveway.

"Ready!" I called, ignoring Mollie's remark.

"Fire!" hollered the enemy. Instantly we were bombarded with icy shells, the best of them able to blind an eye or give a Lawson girl a concussion.

From the start, our cause was hopeless; Helen, despite experiencing twelve Michigan winters, still couldn't pack a decent snowball, and Mollie was lucky if she could propel hers halfway across the driveway. Mary wasn't much more help to Tom and Mags. Rather than pack a snowball, she'd pick up a handful of snowdust and toss it in the air. But even with Mary's incompetence, Tom and Mags were still creaming us. Finally, in frustration, Mollie summoned up all her strength and managed to get a snowball, not only clear across the driveway, but smack into Mary's unsuspecting face. I still wonder whether she did it on purpose.

"Owwwww!" Mary screamed while rubbing at the tears pouring from one eye while her other hand caressed her bruised jaw. "You did that on purpose! I hate you!"

She darted out from behind her snow fort and charged toward Mollie, but as she stepped into the driveway, her foot landed on ice, and she went gliding forward on one leg, wobbling all the way, until she fell and smashed into the opposite side of the snowbank.

"Owwwwww!" she repeated.

"Mary!" cried Helen, crawling down the snowbank to her cousin's side. "Are you okay?"

"No! I think I broke my back and both my legs and arms! Get me a doctor before I die!"

"I warned you that you'd get hurt, but you wouldn't listen," said Mags, walking up to her sister and standing over her.

"I'm sorry, Mary. I didn't mean to hit you," Mollie said, less contrite than fearful her mother would punish her.

"You did it on purpose!" said Mary, pushing herself into a sitting position against the snowbank. "You broke my back. I know you did. I hate you!"

"Mary, your back isn't broken," said Helen. "If it were, you wouldn't be able to sit up."

"Shut up! You're not a doctor!" she screamed. "Mollie tried to kill me!"

Mary then grabbed Mollie's leg and yanked her to the ground. She slammed her fists into her sister's foot, all the while declaring, "I hate you! You tried to kill me!"

"That's enough from all of you!"

It was an adult voice, and it caused much needed silence.

"Tom Hampton," said his mother, coming down the front steps, "how many times have I warned you that your snowball fights are dangerous?"

"But Ma, Mary's just overreacting!"

"I am not!" Mary screamed, and she turned on new tears for effect.

"That's enough of your cackling as well!" Mrs. Hampton snapped at her. Mary was stunned. For a moment, I wished Mrs. Hampton were always around, until she added, "Tom, you're grounded. Go in the house. I don't want to see you throw another snowball this winter."

As I watched Tom trudge toward the house, Mark appeared on the front steps.

"Now what kind of trouble have the immature children caused?" he asked.

"We don't need your comments, Mark," his mother replied. "Help me lift Mary. We'll bring her inside to make sure she's all right."

"Don't you touch me," Mary warned Mark, as he came up to her. "No boys are allowed to touch me. If you do, I'll tell my mother."

"Mary, Mark's only going to help you," Helen said.

"No one's touching me!" she said, getting to her feet.

"Look, you're fine," Mags said. "I bet you don't even have a bruise."

"Ha!" said Mary. "I wouldn't show you if I did."

"I think you better all go home now," Mrs. Hampton said. "It's almost suppertime anyway. And I'm especially surprised at you, Robert. You're the oldest, so you should know better. I thought you might be a good example to Tom and the girls."

I was stunned to be blamed. Had I been an adult, I would have defended myself, but I did not want to get into further trouble by being disrespectful. "Let's go, Helen," I said.

"You may have to carry me home!" Mary shouted, but I ignored her, as did Helen and her sisters. Finally, she quit whining and moped her way down the sidewalk after us.

We had just reached my house when Mags said, "Now that Tom is grounded I won't have anyone to play with, and if his mother tells mine, I'll get punished even worse than him."

"Don't worry, Mags," said Mary. "I'll make sure Mom knows it's Mollie who tried to kill me, not you."

"I didn't try to kill you!" said Mollie, starting to sob from fear of being punished.

Glad to be home and almost free of the girls, I told Helen, "I'll just run in to get that book for you."

"All right," she said.

Helen followed me up the porch steps while her cousins, too tired and crabby to wait, said they would keep walking home.

"I s'pose," Mary said as they walked away, "Robert and Helen just want to get rid of us so they can kiss."

"Shut up, Mary!" said Mags, giving her sister a shove forward.

Again, I pretended not to hear these remarks. I went inside, ran up to my room, grabbed the newest Oz book, went outside, handed it to Helen, and quickly said, "I'll see you at school tomorrow." Then I shut the door before she could reply. I did not want a private conversation with her.

It had been a trying afternoon.

Chapter 10

Winter Fades Into Spring

Winter seemed never ending. We were all developing cabin fever. January, February, March were all cold months, all filled with snowy days, always snow to shovel, always shivering long walks to school, always frozen fingers, always spending nights in the house, wrapped up in quilts, trying to read to stall the overpowering evening boredom. Snowmen, snowball fights, sleigh riding, and ice skating had been exciting at first, but now everyone wanted spring to come. Grandma was starting to fear the roof would cave in because so much snow was piled on it. Anxiously we all prayed for warmer weather.

And the war continued in Europe. Lives were ravaged abroad and at home. Until it ended, I could never be free from fear that I would become an orphan. I knew Grandma and Aunt Louisa May would continue to look after me, but even an almost fourteen-year old boy wants a father around. Everyone in town knew someone fighting in Europe; every American prayed for the safety of family and friends and for their swift return home, and occasionally, if we knew a happy day and forgot about the war, we later only felt guilt over our own happiness when our loved ones were in danger.

Prayers would not suffice; besides our daily work, we supported the war effort. We knitted hats and socks in school for the soldiers, and we planned victory gardens to plant in the spring. Grandma and Aunt Louisa May bought three hundred dollars worth of war bonds, a great contribution to their country, but not, they told me, as great as my courage in understanding my father had to fight for freedom rather than be home. I felt less concerned about my bravery than his safety; every night I prayed my mother would watch over him.

Amid all this work, Aunt Louisa May and I painted my room blue. Then I could finally ask Tom to come over and play in my room during the coldest days, once he was done being grounded. We played with my cowboys and Indians, or played checkers or cards, but we often found ourselves bored, especially on stormy days when it was too cold and windy to play outside. We longed for spring, and I already anticipated all the fun summer activities Tom promised we would do, from hiking and swimming, to riding bicycles and exploring the nearby forests.

In the evenings, I would read aloud while my ladies did their sewing. Grandma insisted we reread all of Louisa May Alcott's books, but we also found time for some Mark Twain, a couple Oz books, which the ladies didn't complain about too much, and the latest novel by Willa Cather.

One day in late March, I was walking home, thinking how, like Pip in *Great Expectations*, I should like to be a gentleman, to live in a grand manner, even surpassing Aunt Carolina—wouldn't Mark then be envious of me. I distinctly remember that day, as I turned the corner onto my block, because it was the first sighting of a patch of grass peeping up through the snow in the front yard. Bursting with spring fever, I ran up the porch steps to announce winter's power had been broken.

"I told you the thaw would start this week," Grandma said. "It always comes the week of my birthday."

"Your birthday?" I said.

"Yes," Grandma replied.

"It's on Friday," said Aunt Louisa May, "and we'll have a party to celebrate."

"Oh, no," said Grandma, "I don't want to make a big deal out of it. I've had so many birthdays, they don't excite me anymore."

"Grandma," I replied, "after all you've done for me this winter, you're going to have a birthday party. Aunt Louisa May and I will plan it."

"Oh, I don't want you to bother," she repeated, but I could see she was pleased.

The rest of that week, Aunt Louisa May and I kept ourselves busy buying Grandma's presents, wrapping and hiding them, buying decorations, and baking the cake. The war meant we had a limited supply of many things, but we did quite well because Aunt Louisa May confessed she had been saving money since Christmas to make sure the day would be nice. When we drew up the guest list, Aunt Louisa May said we would invite Aunt Carolina, but I said, "She'll just ruin the party."

"We can't not invite her, Robert," insisted Aunt Louisa May.

But the day of the party, Aunt Carolina had Jones come over to say, "Mrs. Carolina has a bad cold and begs her apologies that she can't come."

I was relieved.

On a warm, cheerful Friday evening, the spring sunlight filling the room as suppertime arrived, we set the table, frosted the birthday cake, and opened the door to all Grandma's guests. The Mitchells arrived first; they were habitually late, but upon entering, Florence said, "For once in my life I insisted we be on time." Then she added, "I'm sorry I didn't have anything decent for a party, Kathleen. This old rag is the best dress I own these days."

"Don't start that again," said her brother, Roger. "I told you to buy a new dress if you want one."

"And where am I supposed to get the money?" she asked.

"I don't need that new suit you're always after me to buy. Take the money for it and buy a dress if it'll make you happy."

"Roger, I've altered your best suit three times now; if I do it one more time, you'll look like a ragamuffin. It's bad enough to know we're poor, but we don't need all of Marquette to know it."

"We're not any worse off than most people," said Mary Mitchell, embarrassed by her siblings' bickering.

"I should have accepted that marriage proposal when I had the chance," said Florence. "I never wanted to be a burden on my brother."

Roger ignored her and went into the parlor to be alone.

"It doesn't hurt us to do without a few things," Mary said as we stood around the dining room table. "We'll get our reward in Heaven."

"Not Florence Mitchell," I thought to myself. "She should only be rewarded for not getting married and raising up children like herself." I wondered whether she really had once received a marriage proposal, or did she just pretend so she did not appear completely pathetic?

The Lewis brothers came next. They hemmed and hawed for ten minutes about the weather, then went into the parlor to sit with Roger Mitchell. Next arrived the Grahams and Hamptons together; Eliza was on Mark's arm, of course. I glared at him until he saw me and glared back. Was he on to my secret? Well, so what, I thought. He should be quaking in his shoes because he must know I'm the better man.

We were all surprised when Mr. Williams arrived, not only with his mother on his right arm, but on his left, Helen's Aunt Helen, who seemed to be making an extremely long visit to Marquette. A few minutes later, when the

Lawsons arrived, I drew Helen aside to ask why her aunt had come with Mr. Williams.

Mags, overhearing my question, said, "That ain't nothin'. Last Saturday they went to the Opera House together, his mother with 'em, and on Sunday, he came by to take her for a drive in his auto."

We all sat down to eat. Grandma said she was embarrassed by so much attention, but I could tell she was pleased. Aunt Louisa May had cooked up a masterpiece of a meal, and I was proud to have helped with the cake. Grandma was able to blow out all her candles at once, "even if I am an old lady at sixty-three now."

Mags was the first to finish eating; she did not want to sit while Grandma opened her presents so she suggested to Tom they go outside to play before it got dark.

"No," he replied. "I've got a stomach ache from eating too much. I'm going to lay down on the sofa."

"Lie down," Mrs. Lawson corrected.

"That's what I said," he replied.

He went into the parlor and Mags and Mollie followed him. "You better take off your shoes if you're going to lay on the sofa," I heard Mags say.

"Lie on the sofa," Mrs. Lawson repeated.

Grandma began to open her gifts, but before she had the paper off the first one, we heard a screech from the parlor.

"Tom Hampton, if you ever do that again, I'll clobber you!"

"What's wrong?" shouted Mrs. Lawson and Mr. Hampton together.

Mollie came running into the dining room to tattle.

"Mags offered to take Tom's shoes off for him, but when she did, he put his feet on her lap and asked her to rub them!"

"Doesn't your son have any manners?" Mrs. Lawson asked Mrs. Hampton.

"It seems to me," said Mrs. Hampton, "your daughter is rather fast if she's taking off boys' shoes."

For a second, Mrs. Lawson's nostrils flared. Then she hollered, "Margaret, come here this instant. Sit down at the table and act like a young lady."

"Tom, you come in here too," called his father. "You don't need to be rude and ignore us all."

"But I have a stomach ache," he moaned.

"It's all right, George," Grandma told Mr. Hampton. "I don't mind if he lies on the sofa."

"Tom!" Mr. Hampton repeated.

"Comin'," muttered Tom, who soon slid into the chair next to me.

"I know how awful a stomach ache can be," laughed Charles Lewis. "I remember a really bad one I had when I wasn't no older than Tom."

"Here we go again," I thought, although I had actually not heard this story.

"It was when I went swimming one time. Our family and the O'Neills, we went on a picnic. Robert"—he meant my grandfather—"didn't want to go in the water because Lake Superior was freezing that day, but I was obstinate and went in anyway. My mother yelled at me because no one else was in the water, and we had just finished eating, but I ignored her and walked out into the lake until unknowingly I came to a drop off and sank. I remember watching the water close over my head."

"You always were rather foolish," said his brother, "especially considering you never were much of a swimmer."

"No, that's not true," said Charles. "I could have swam just fine, only I was so surprised by the drop off that as I sunk, my mouth opened and filled with water, and all that picnic food I had just eaten made me like a lead weight. I struggled to pull myself back to the surface but just kept sinking. Then out of nowhere, Robert appeared underwater. He'd dived in, and he pulled me up to the shore. I don't know where he found the strength."

I was quite impressed to hear of my grandfather's heroic deed, and I hoped to hear more of his courage, but Charles Lewis stuck to the topic of his stomach.

"When Robert got me back to shore, I collapsed on the beach and lay there, my gut full of water, just moaning and moaning for the rest of the afternoon. My ma said I should go get my stomach pumped, but Pa said that's what I got for not listening."

"That's nothing," said James Lewis, who always had to best his brother in storytelling, "it couldn't have hurt as much as the time I broke my leg."

He paused for effect, waiting to be asked how he broke his leg. No one really cared, but out of politeness, Aunt Louisa May asked.

"It was when I was playing one time with your father and his sister. I climbed up this apple tree, see. There was this beautiful ripe red apple on the end of a bough, and Carolina, well, she was determined she wanted it, but she wouldn't climb up there in her hoop skirt—afraid someone would see her unmentionables I guess."

James Lewis let out a lurid chuckle at this thought. I couldn't help but smiling. I would have paid a quarter to see Aunt Carolina in that compromising position.

"Anyway, I told her I'd go get that apple for her, and even though Robert told me it was too high up, I climbed up that tree like nothing. But the branch was mighty thin so I had to try and slide myself out to reach that apple. Before I knew it, I had flipped upside down, and though I tried to wrap my legs around the branches, down I fell and broke my leg."

"Well, James," said Mr. Hampton, "I never thought you would have fallen for my mother-in-law."

Everyone laughed and then Grandma said, "It's a good thing Carolina isn't here or she'd be embarrassed."

"She always was a fuss-budget," said Charles Lewis, oblivious to her family's presence.

I saw Mrs. Hampton frown. Then I looked to see whether Mark felt offended, but instead, I saw he was holding Eliza's hand, openly, on top of the table. In disgust I turned my head, only to catch Miss Pearson blushing as John Williams looked into her eyes.

"I saw the first crocuses in my yard today," said Mary Mitchell. "It looks like spring is finally here."

That was when I recalled that in the spring, a young man's fancy turns to thoughts of love.

Chapter 11

Goodbyes

Love only grows stronger as spring progresses; that year, it was strong enough that John Williams proposed to Miss Pearson. Surprising as it seemed, a woman whom everyone believed to be destined for spinsterhood accepted the confirmed old bachelor's proposal, and I believe, in waiting so many years until their true sweethearts were found, they were a far happier couple than many who marry young. Despite what Helen thought of her aunt, everyone said Miss Pearson was a charming woman, and people were pleased when it was announced she and Mr. Williams would make their home in Marquette. Their wedding became the highlight of the spring for our little circle.

As for old Mrs. Williams, her own happiness may have surpassed that of the bride and groom now that her son had found his special someone. She wished to do everything to make "her children" happy; they promised she could live with them the rest of her days, but she insisted that since John now had "a good wife to look after him," she would go live with her widowed daughter on Mackinac Island, who was very lonely since her only son had gone to fight overseas. Mr. Williams and his bride tried to argue with Mrs. Williams, but eventually they gave up and settled down to nest happily.

Marie Hobson, Mrs. Williams' daughter, came to attend the wedding, and then the next morning, Grandma, Aunt Louisa May, and I went with her and Mrs. Williams to the train station to say our farewells.

"Goodbye, Kathleen," said Mrs. Williams, giving Grandma a great hug. "I'll never forget what a wonderful friend you've been to me all these years."

"Nor I you," said Grandma. "You were my first friend when I came to Marquette."

"Those were happy days then."

"So are these days," said Grandma, alluding to Mr. Williams's marriage.

"Not with the war on," Mrs. Williams replied, "but now that General Pershing has invaded France, it should be over soon and my grandson, Eric, and all our other dear boys will be coming home, God willing."

When the old woman started to tear up, Grandma said, "Don't cry, dear. Think about all the new friends you'll make on Mackinac Island. And I promise we'll come visit you this summer."

Mrs. Williams and Mrs. Hobson then boarded the train for St. Ignace, where they would disembark to take the ferry over to Mackinac Island.

When we got home, Grandma complained she was tired.

"We've been so busy lately with my birthday, and then the wedding, and Mrs. Williams leaving that I'm plumb worn out. I think I'll just sit and knit the rest of the day, and hope no one comes over."

We were all in favor of a quiet day at home, so Aunt Louisa May and I closed ourselves up in our bedrooms to read, while Grandma sat in the living room, knitting and listening to the Victrola.

Lying on my bed, I opened *Wuthering Heights*. I was soon immersed in the novel and had reached the scene where Cathy dies in Heathcliff's arms. With every sentence, I anticipated that Edgar Linton would burst into the room and find his wife with her lover. But Edgar was beaten by Tom, who ran into our house, slamming the door open with a loud bang. I jumped up and ran downstairs, followed by my aunt, to see what was wrong.

"Aunt Kathleen, come quickly please!" said Tom. "Grandma's had a stroke, and the doctor doesn't think she has long ta live."

"My goodness!" cried Grandma, tossing her knitting aside and running to the closet for her coat. I reached the closet first and handed her and my aunt their coats, then grabbed my own.

In a minute, we were rushing down the street on foot while Grandma asked Tom for the details.

"It was Mark's eighteenth birthday yesterday," he said, "so this morning he went and enlisted in the army. When he told Grandma, she went inta hysterics, then said she was dizzy and fell ta the floor. My mom managed to wake her up, but the doctor said her heart was givin' out, and she probably won't make it through the night."

"What can I do?" Grandma asked.

"I don't know," said Tom, "but my mom said ta fetch you. Grandma says she wants ta see you."

By the time we had practically run the several blocks to Aunt Carolina's Ridge Street mansion, we were all out of breath, but Grandma did not pause a moment, only walked through the front door without knocking, ignored Mr. Hampton standing in the front hall, and hurried upstairs to Great-Aunt Carolina's room. Mrs. Hampton must have already been upstairs with the doctor. Aunt Louisa May and I sat in the parlor with Tom, Mark, and Mr. Hampton.

My aunt asked Mr. Hampton for the latest news. He said the doctor was giving Aunt Carolina medicine for her pain, but she only had at best a few hours to live. Tom and I sat glumly, staring into space, not knowing what to say. I searched for words of comfort for him, knowing how I had felt when my own mother had died, but words would not come. Instead, I felt all over again the pain of my own mother's loss.

After Mr. Hampton explained everything to my aunt, several uncomfortable minutes of silence followed. Then Mark got up and walked to the window.

"She didn't need to overreact like that," he said. "She's always telling me what to do."

"No one's blaming you, Mark," said his father. "If her heart is that weak, anything could have set this off."

"It's my patriotic duty to enlist. She ought to understand that. After all, Great-Uncle Robert was in the service. She should be proud I want to serve my country. I'm no coward. I don't know why she's so flighty."

"Shut up, Mark," Tom snapped. "Don't talk about Grandma like that. You were always her favorite and you never appreciated it. Now you've killed her, and you don't even care."

"That's enough, Tom," Mr. Hampton warned, although he put his arm around Tom to console him. "Blaming each other won't help anything."

"I'm going out on the porch to get some fresh air," said Mark, sauntering out of the room.

No one spoke again until we heard footsteps on the stairs. Mrs. Hampton came into the parlor.

"How is she?" asked Aunt Louisa May.

"She's not in too much pain. She can barely speak, but she keeps trying. She wanted to talk to Aunt Kathleen alone."

Mr. Hampton frowned sympathetically.

"Where's Mark?" Mrs. Hampton asked.

"He went outside to get some fresh air. He's pretty upset," said Mr. Hampton.

"Well, he and his grandmother have always been close," said Mrs. Hampton. I knew better than to repeat what Mark had said about his grandmother.

"When will Mark be joining the army?" Aunt Louisa May asked.

"He's leaving for training camp in a couple weeks," said Mr. Hampton.

"I don't know why he wants to be a soldier and go get killed," said Tom, shaking off his father's arm. "He's been talking about it for the last year, but I thought that was just his big mouth trying to impress Eliza."

Despite their conflicts, I heard sincere concern for his brother in Tom's voice.

"Is Mark still planning to marry Eliza before he leaves?" asked Aunt Louisa May.

"Yes," said Mr. Hampton. "They'll be married next week. Eliza is disappointed because she always wanted a big wedding, but Mark told her she would have to sacrifice that during wartime."

I did not hear whatever else was said. My beloved was about to be married to another, and not just any other, but to a toad, a conceited windbag, a belligerent, arrogant fool! And next week! It made my skin crawl to think of it. If I were five years older, I would have gone out on the porch that very second and pounded in Mark's nose so Eliza would be disgusted by the mere sight of him. Or I would also join the army, whip the Germans, receive many medals, save the world for democracy, and then return home a hero to impress Eliza while Mark did kitchen duty for the army. I could create for myself the most wonderful fantasies in those days, all inspired by boyish infatuation and the beauty of my goddess. But I was miserable whenever I realized my daydreams could not be reality.

In half an hour, Grandma came downstairs. As she stepped into the room, Mrs. Hampton stood up and headed for the stairs, but Grandma caught her in her arms and held her for a minute until Mrs. Hampton started to sob. We knew then that Aunt Carolina's pain was over, leaving only grief for all those who had loved her despite her flaws.

Grandma and Aunt Louisa May went into the kitchen to help Jones and Jenny make sandwiches. The doctor came downstairs and assured the Hamptons that Aunt Carolina had gone peacefully; he stayed to have supper while the coroner came and then the funeral home director took away Aunt Carolina's remains. Mark telephoned Eliza, who came to eat with us. Within the hour, Mrs. Graham had told half of Marquette, so a stream of guests arrived, bringing food trays and sympathy cards for the family. I was struck by the outpouring of grief, even though I had a hard time believing even half of these people had truly liked my great-aunt.

The sun was setting by the time Grandma, Aunt Louisa May, and I walked home.

"Mother," said Aunt Louisa May. "Did Aunt Carolina say anything when you saw her?"

"Yes," said Grandma. "I didn't quite know what to say to her, other than just to listen and pat her hand. She kept saying how hard her life had been, how ever since she had been uprooted as a little girl from her home in the South, she had felt like an exile in Marquette, no matter how many guests she had or what clubs she belonged to. Then she told me it was always a comfort for her to know me as someone else raised in the South; she said I had always been her one true friend and that I had been a good wife to her brother and kind to her parents, and she was sorry for any hard words she had ever said to me. I just told her to hush and forget it all, but I was surprised by her apologies. Then I think she just lost track of what was going on—she started babbling practically, and I couldn't make out the words, but she said something about her parents' plantation house and all the slaves they had owned, although I know from what Robert told me that their parents only had maybe a dozen at best—she always exaggerated the family's status down South—and she talked about a new pink dress her mama had given her for her birthday, and how happy she was to be back home there—I think she thought she was in the old South at that point. She could scarcely have remembered much of the South since she left there when she was only four or so, but I think she romanticized it as she grew older. I never understood her attitude, yet it was the same attitude everyone had when I lived down there—anger really, anger I understood since I saw the Yankees burn my parents' house and our crops and steal everything we had. Yet I let go of the past long ago. Carolina always clung to it for some reason. She just couldn't change with the times."

"At least she's at peace now," said Aunt Louisa May. "I'm sure she had her good points and that God will be merciful to her."

I'm afraid I did not think about Aunt Carolina much more that night. My sympathies were less with my great-aunt's family than with Eliza Graham, about to enter into a marriage that could only bring her misery.

Aunt Carolina's funeral was held the next week, and two days after, Mark and Eliza were married. Mr. Hampton said Mark could have put off his term of service to take a honeymoon, but Mark insisted on leaving right away. I could not believe Mark had so little regard for his bride, but Mark liked best to do whatever he chose, and he usually chose to be inconsiderate toward others.

That whole week until the wedding, I was heartsick and could barely sleep. I tossed and turned in bed, hatching elaborate schemes to stop the wedding, making up great professions of love to declare at the ceremony when the priest asked, "Does anyone present know any just cause why these two may not be lawfully joined?"

"Yes!" I would declare. "There are two just causes! The first is because Mark Hampton is a fool!"

"And the other?" Eliza would ask, already accepting the first as obvious.

"Because I love you madly, Eliza!" And then I would run to the altar, push Mark to the ground, clasp her in my arms, and press my lips to hers. Once I released her from my embrace, she would profess equal love for me, and the priest would unite us forever in holy matrimony.

But secretly, I knew this fantastic melodrama could not be. If I did such a thing, Eliza would probably only cry that I had ruined her wedding, and I would become the laughingstock of Marquette. I was grateful when the wedding was only a private ceremony inside the Hampton home for the bride and groom's immediate families. I spent that hour alone in my room, determined I would never love again because I could not bear the heartbreak. I told myself I was above loving any woman foolish enough to love Mark Hampton, and when Mark left the following week for training camp, I felt so indifferent to the entire event that it barely even crossed my mind to hope he would be gassed in the trenches.

Chapter 12

The Play House

If Great-Aunt Carolina's death had been unexpected, the events that followed were even more so. Because of Eliza and Mark's wedding and his departure, Aunt Carolina's lawyer had forestalled settling the estate. Now Aunt Carolina's Last Will and Testament was read. The old woman had left one sole heir—the only family member absent from the reading—her eighteen-year old grandson, Mark Hampton, to whom I attributed her death. He had inherited her fabulous Ridge Street mansion as well as enough money that he would never need to work a day in his life. In her typically selfish and thoughtless manner, Aunt Carolina had snubbed both her own daughter and her youngest grandson out of preference for her favorite.

This impossible bequest became Marquette's primary gossip that spring. Mark's innocent young wife's name was also on the tongue of many an old biddy.

"Eliza hasn't any right to that house," was the general consensus.

"It ought to go to her mother-in-law, Jane Hampton. Mark and Eliza are nothing less than thieves to his mother," I heard Mrs. Lawson say to her sister.

"That little gold digger. I wish I could marry a rich man just for his money," was reportedly Florence Mitchell's remark.

To which Mary Mitchell had said, "Poor Eliza, imagine how guilty she must feel, knowing her mother-in-law must resent that she will be mistress of that house."

Grandma and Aunt Louisa May both simply said, "Eliza is such a sweet girl that we should be happy for her."

I felt the truth lay somewhere between all these statements. To her favor, Eliza did think the house should have gone to her mother-in-law, yet she felt obligated to side with her husband, and when he wrote to her, upon hearing he was now a wealthy young man—Eliza showed Grandma Mark's letter—he said, "Eliza, you are to move into Grandma's house. We don't want to live with any of our parents now that we are married, and I imagine we'll be very happy there."

After the initial shock, even Mrs. Hampton realized she didn't want the responsibility of keeping up that gigantic house. "Eliza," she told her daughter-in-law, "in a few more years, Tom will also marry and move out, and then it will be just George and me. That house would be far too large for us. You and Mark live there and just be sure to fill it with my grandchildren."

Despite the gossip, once Eliza took up residence in the house, she found herself the toast of the town. Everyone who considered him or herself a blooming flower of Marquette society, even those who could scarcely hope to bud, appeared at the door of "the little gold digger." Eliza's old friends hesitated to visit her now, feeling uncomfortable rubbing elbows with the socially elite. As I would later learn, Eliza soon found herself lonely and miserable.

After several weeks of this discomfort, Eliza received an invitation from the late Judge Smith's relatives, asking her to visit them in Lansing for the summer so they could get to know her. She had only met these relatives once before, and Mark had not been close to his late grandfather's family, but Eliza's mother insisted she go, thinking a change would do her good. Eliza would find these relatives as stuck up as the social climbers in Marquette, but once downstate, she did not know how to end her visit early. For Eliza, it was doubtless the worst summer of her life, but for me, it became one of the most memorable.

A few nights before her departure, Eliza came over to Grandma's house.

"I'll be glad to get away for a little while," she said. "That house feels just like a prison."

"I'm sure it's a difficult adjustment for you," said Aunt Louisa May.

"Yes," said Grandma, "but you'll be a fine mistress of it one day."

"I hope so," said Eliza. "I want to be a good wife to Mark."

"You will dear," Grandma assured her.

I thought she should worry less about being a good wife and more about whether Mark would be a good husband.

"I need someone to check on the house while I'm gone," said Eliza. "I thought of asking Tom, but Mark never thought he was very responsible, so I wondered whether you would mind doing it, Robert. You'd only have to go over twice a week to water the plants and open the windows to let the house air out, and I'd pay you for your trouble."

"What about Jones and Jenny?" asked Grandma. "Won't they look after it?"

"No," said Eliza. "They told me they had stayed on with Mrs. Carolina because they knew she needed them, but that I was quite capable of taking care of myself."

"But then what will they do?" Aunt Louisa May asked.

"They said they would go to Chicago—Jones has a sister there, so you see, I have no one else to ask. Do you mind, Robert?"

I was surprised by the request. I couldn't imagine being responsible for that giant house, and since it was Mark's house, I almost wished it would be swallowed into the earth. But it was also Eliza's home now, and while I could no longer hope to attain her love, out of pity for her ill-chosen marriage, I kindly agreed. I also figured I could buy some books or a new swimsuit with the money.

Once I began the job, however, I felt it was trouble. I had to go over to the house a couple times a week, and it was several blocks to walk, so it cut into my free time. I started to walk there directly from school, but even then, by the time I had opened all the windows, watered all the plants, then shut all the windows again, and collected the mail, it was suppertime, and then with homework to do, I had no playtime. The first few visits were especially dull because I was afraid to touch anything.

Then one day, I went into the library to water the Boston ferns in the large bay window. The sunlight was streaming into the room in such a friendly manner that I could not help just sitting in one of the elegant Victorian chairs and gazing at all the sparkling gilded book spines. The rest of the house was stiff and formal, but those books seemed like old friends, with all my favorite authors present from Dickens to Mark Twain, and many I had yet to discover such as Thackeray and William Dean Howells. I could only feel at home in that room.

Carefully, that day, I pulled *A Tale of Two Cities* from the shelf and slowly turned over the pages, surprised to find they had never even been cut! When I looked at Thackeray and the other authors, I noticed the same was true of their books. All these volumes had been invested in for show, yet not one ever read. While one shelf held a number of law books which had been well worn by the hands of Judge Smith, apparently the judge and Aunt Carolina had been uninterested in literature. I thought they must have been philistines to live so, but I could not help admiring how perfectly they had decorated this room. The other rooms were strict showcases, but this room reflected a more individual taste, complete with slightly sensuous pre-Raphaelite paintings, knick knacks cluttered about the shelves, and the conservatory room around the bay window that made this room half an Eden and half forbidden knowledge—yet I felt intuitively that someday I would dare to read all those splendid volumes.

The library made me wonder what other interesting clues the house might hold to Aunt Carolina's true personality, so as I walked about the house, shutting the windows, I paid more attention to the various rooms. Her bedroom had no plants in it, so I had not yet entered it, and I felt a bit odd doing so because she had died there, but earlier that day I had gone in to open its window. Still sensitive about my own mother's death, I avoided looking at the bed that had been Aunt Carolina's last resting place and went straight to the window to shut it. The same sun shining into the library was sparkling on Lake Superior that May afternoon, so I paused to look out to Marquette's harbor and marvel at the view.

Then, as I turned around to leave, I noticed a painting across from the bed. Paintings were spread all over the house, but this picture grabbed my attention because of the giant Spanish moss trees in it that reminded me of the Southern spring I was currently missing. For a moment, I could almost smell the magnolias, and then I stepped up closer to the picture of a large white farmhouse with a veranda and little pillars in the front. Peering closer, I saw painted in the bottom right corner "Our Old Home—Dolly O'Neill." Dolly O'Neill had been my great-grandmother—my grandpa and Aunt Carolina's mother. Had Dolly O'Neill actually painted this picture? I had never seen the old O'Neill farm—or plantation, as Aunt Carolina had liked to call it. Aunt Carolina had left South Carolina when she was just a little girl, yet she had placed this picture here so that every morning when she woke, it would be the first thing she saw. She could have first looked out the window at the lake, or placed any other painting across from her bed, but her old Southern home was what she chose to see first each morning when she woke.

At that moment, I don't think I understood my great-aunt any better for seeing the inner recesses of her home. All of Marquette was still new and intriguing to me, even exotic considering the first winter I had just spent there. I did not feel sadness or nostalgia for my childhood home, so I did think it odd Aunt Carolina held onto her Southern childhood so firmly. Even if I didn't understand my great-aunt then, and I'm not sure I ever did understand her, it occurred to me that no matter how blatant her faults, her money-grubbing, her snobbery, and bigotry, she had wanted to make a beautiful home for her husband, and she had left it to a grandson for whom she apparently felt great affection, even if he failed to return it. And she must have been discontented in her social world if she had to romanticize her childhood to such an extent. I thought she must have had some good points, a soft side she was afraid to show to the world, if only because she clearly could show love for some people and her childhood home. I found I had suddenly softened toward her a bit. Perhaps I am giving Aunt Carolina too much attention here, but I will leave what I have written about her, and move on with my story.

After that day, I went to the house often, usually just to sit in that beautiful library and read the gold embellished books. I took my penknife and carefully cut some of the book pages, telling myself, after all, that they were meant to be read. Then one day, Helen complained that she hardly got to see me anymore, and since she had no other friends, she had nothing else to do but sit in the house and try to read, which was nearly impossible with her noisy cousins. I don't know what possessed me, but I let her into my secret that I had found a beautiful place to read, and if she promised not to tell anyone, she could come with me every day after school, and we would sit and read to our hearts' content.

But after a few visits to Aunt Carolina's house, Helen and I no longer got much reading done. We felt awkward sitting together quietly rather than talking to each other, so one day, Helen suggested we should find a book of plays and read them out loud. But no matter how we searched that library, we could find no drama books. In trying to impress people, Aunt Carolina had somehow neglected to buy even one volume of Shakespeare.

"Let's just read out loud then," said Helen, "but we'll each read different characters' parts in the book so it's like we're acting."

I agreed. We decided to start with J.M. Barrie's *Sentimental Tommy*. I read Tommy's parts and Helen read Grizel's, and we took turns with the minor characters. And then, as I read about Tommy wanting to be a writer, the strange notion was born in my mind, and Helen suggested it, just as I was thinking it, that we should write our own plays of the books. "After all," she said, "Barrie's *The Little Minister* and *Peter Pan and Wendy* were made into plays."

Of course, Helen decided she wanted to act out the Oz books, and before I knew it, Aunt Carolina's library had become the Emerald City, while the rest of the house allowed us to have all manner of adventures in Munchkinland or the Quadling country. Perhaps we were acting a bit childish, for I was to turn fourteen that month and Helen would be thirteen in June, but I have always looked favorably upon children being actively imaginative; it reflects children's attempts to give meaning to their experiences, and I know play-acting has been the earliest form of writing for many an author.

"You make a great Nome King," Helen said one day as we locked up the house and headed home for supper.

"Not as good as your Ozma," I replied.

"We really mixed up the plot though," she said.

"I don't think L. Frank Baum would mind," I said. "I think our version is almost as good as his."

"We should write it down," said Helen. "Maybe we could send it to him to use for a future Oz book, or even another Oz play. I know they made *Tiktok of Oz* into a play."

We never were to write down that particular storyline, but in the evenings after supper, and occasionally to the neglect of my homework, I started to write little plays for Helen and me to perform in Aunt Carolina's house-turned-theatre. Our acting was far from professional, yet as an adult who has seen hundreds of stage productions, I still think the most amusing acting I ever saw was the day Helen solely performed *The Hunchback of Notre Dame* as a birthday present to me. By herself she played all the roles: the wicked priest, Esmeralda, even Quasimodo. The front hall staircase became the bell tower, and Helen Hayes could not have been more dramatic running up those stairs, then nearly stumbling down to affect the hunchback's demeanor. To this day, I often think if Helen had lived in New York, she might have become a professional actress, or even been discovered and gone on to be a star of the silver screen.

"Helen, it was marvelous!" I said, clapping and laughing simultaneously.

"I'm glad you liked it," she smiled, "and I even wrote out the script for you to keep as part of your birthday present."

She handed me a neatly handwritten script, complete with illustrations of the main characters, and with a cardboard cover to make it resemble a real book.

"Thank you," I said, stunned by the gift. I am sure I received many other presents on my fourteenth birthday, but I have forgotten all the others now. I also know at that age, I would have been too self-conscious to show anything I wrote to another, so I was all the more moved by the gift. I still have it now, nearly eighty years later.

Chapter 13

The Blue and the Green

The first day of summer vacation had come! Summer in Marquette! Winter may be Upper Michigan's more memorable season, but summer is breathtakingly beautiful. I did not know what I would do all that summer, but I knew it would probably be my only summer in Marquette since the war was likely to end soon and my dad would then bring me home, and so I was determined it would be the best summer of my life to date.

At breakfast, just as Grandma was asking me what I planned to do that day, Tom came over.

"Do you want to go swimming?" he asked as he came into the kitchen.

"Isn't it rather cold today?" asked Aunt Louisa May.

"Nah," said Tom, "it's seventy and it's supposed to hit eighty today. We can go for the whole day, Robert. My ma made me up a basket with sandwiches and juice and ice so it won't spoil, and if we put it in the lake, it'll stay cool—the lake'll be cold, but we'll stay active so we won't be. We'll go out to Presque Isle on the streetcar; do you have money for it, Robert?"

All through this speech I felt myself starting to tremble with excitement—swimming in Lake Superior—South Carolina has no real lakes, only wide rivers, which just aren't the same—and Superior is such a big, gorgeous deep blue lake; even later when I found myself shivering in it, my enthusiasm did not diminish.

"I can give you money for the streetcar," said Grandma, "but Robert, do you have a pair of swim trunks?"

"Yeah," I said. Not having had any idea what to pack when I left the South, I had just dumped a drawer full of clothes into a suitcase that surprisingly had included my swim trunks.

I gobbled down the rest of my breakfast, then ran upstairs to put on my swim trunks beneath my pants.

"Have a good time," said Aunt Louisa May as Tom and I went out the door.

"Make sure you stick together in the water, and you don't swim out too far, and be careful of the waves and currents," Grandma added.

"Yes, Grandma," I said, shutting the door.

"Must be a family thing," Tom said as we went outside. "My ma always warns me about all the same things."

"I think it's women in general," I said. "They're always worried."

"Well, I s'pose that's cause they're women," said Tom. "They're not tough like us. That's why they marry us, so we can protect 'em."

Tom seemed to have it all figured out. Rather than pursue the conversation, I asked whether Presque Isle were far.

"Don't you know where Presque Isle is?" he said. "How can you not know that?"

"I'm not from here, remember?" I said.

"It's not far," he replied. "Only about ten minutes on the streetcar—it's just north of town."

Soon I would learn that Marquette's very best place is Presque Isle Park. And once we had reached it on the streetcar, I asked myself the same question Tom had asked. "How could I not have known about Presque Isle?"

At first, the trip there on the streetcar did not seem promising. The lakeshore in those days was full of commerce, businesses, factories and just a large mess in general. Not that the lake itself appeared polluted, although perhaps it was, but the land along the lake was rather a mess, while now it has been cleaned up. The streetcar passed all this industrial hodgepodge, however, and left it behind, and then we crossed over the Dead River Bridge, and suddenly, we were at Presque Isle Park. It was actually the first time I had been outside of Marquette since I had arrived at Thanksgiving. It was my first time in the outdoors of Upper Michigan, and although most of the Upper Peninsula is a great rugged forest, this little island was a small wilderness in itself, with several remarkable features, including its famous black rocks, its high cliffs overlooking the lake, and its grave of Chief Kawbawgam, the last Chief of the Chippewa Indians.

But that first day, and everyday since then, my favorite part of Presque Isle was its cove. It was a fair hike from Presque Isle's entrance to the cove on what was hardly more than a trail along the lakeshore, amid pine and birch trees. We circled around the curve of the island and had to walk down a steep hill to the shore, and there it was, a cove, a small opening between two cliffs, not more than fifty feet wide if that, filled with rocks where the tide had pushed them up onto the shore to create a rock hound's paradise, and curving off to the left, the cliff rose up just high enough to be a perfect diving spot. The cliffs beside the cove were red sandstone with pine, birch, and oak trees growing atop them, and the rocks in the cove were a mishmash of every colored pebble imaginable. My first thought was that it resembled a pirate's cove, and it would be a perfect hiding place for stolen booty. Although I knew Tom was unimaginative, when I mentioned that it seemed like a place out of an adventure novel, he said, "That's nothing; there's a cave just over there. I'll show you."

He walked me back up from the beach to where we could climb up the side of the cliff, and then through the woods and over several large rocks jutting up out of the earth, all the while passing through bushes that scratched at our clothes. Soon we came to a pile of rocks, and a small opening in them led into a true cave—a grizzly bear probably would have felt cramped inside it, but it was a cave nevertheless.

"Sometimes I think I'd like to stick Mary in here, roll a stone over the entrance, and never tell anyone," Tom smiled, "only, she's got such a big mouth her voice would be heard all the way into town, even with the rocks trying to act as a sound barrier."

It wasn't a nice thought, but I fully understood the feeling.

"Geez, it's hot," said Tom, wiping his forehead with his shirtsleeve. "Let's go swimming."

He smacked me on the arm as a sign to follow and then raced back to the cove, letting the tree branches whip me in the face, but I was tough and fast—I would have reached the cove ahead of him if the cliff had provided room for me to pass him as we ran.

But just as we jumped down from the hill into the rock bed, we were surprised to see our secret swimming hole had been discovered, and by none other than Helen and Mags.

"Hey!" shouted Mags. "We went over to your houses to see if you wanted to go swimming. Who'd a thought you'd be here?"

"Hey!" Tom called, looking pleased, but rather than talk more, he took off his shoes and pants, then ripped off his shirt and ran into the lake, screaming because the water was so cold.

"Gosh, he's brave," said Helen. "That water's freezing."

"Come on, Robert!" he yelled.

"All right," I said, and I likewise took off my shoes, socks, pants and shirt. But with a bit more trepidation over the water's coldness, I only waded in.

I have never known a lake so cold as Superior. Even those raised in Marquette find its water often unbearable save for summer's hottest days. To me, it was like bathing in ice, and once I was in past my knees, a giant wave hurled toward me, completely soaking me, sending a complete shock to my system so I could not help but swear—the only time at that point I had ever sworn in my life. Then I felt myself blush in embarrassment, but Tom and Mags only laughed, and Tom hollered out, "Cold, isn't it?" and then I felt very pleased, as if I had been initiated, or rather baptized into the ways of the North. Now I was a true Northerner—I will not say Yankee, for I felt Tom, Mags, and Helen were my true friends—not at all Yankees, as Mr. Carter would have branded them.

Truthfully, I was a bit embarrassed that the girls had found us. They had already removed their clothes and were in their bathing suits, and I had felt shy about seeing them so dressed. In those days, bathing suits were not very revealing, especially for women—but to a fourteen-year old boy, a girl in a bathing suit was enticing nevertheless. Once I was in the water, I heard Tom yelling, "Come on, girls," and then I turned around to watch them wade in.

I really noticed Mags first. She was such a tomboy that her clothes were usually disheveled, but the bathing suit she wore stuck tightly to her, especially to her chest. By comparison, Helen did not look like she had really started to develop. For the first time, I truly realized Mags was not a boy, not even really a girl, but very much on the verge of being a woman, and I had to turn my head away to keep from staring.

She waded out and passed me to go where Tom was far enough out to be treading water. As soon as she got close to him, he gulped a mouthful of water, then sprayed her with it. She screamed, but laughed and splashed him. I watched their horseplay for a few minutes, and then Tom dove under the water, and Mags, looking about in confusion, suddenly found him behind her, his arms around her, giving her a good dunking. But being Mags, of course, she came up laughing and let him do it again.

"Hi, Robert," said Helen.

I turned around to find her beside me.

"Hello," I said.

"Are you glad school is out?" she asked.

"Yes," I said. "Are you?"

"Yes. I like school, but now I'll have more time to read."

"We do read in school," I said.

"Only what the grownups think we should, most of which is really useless like all that stuff about worms and rocks and math. I'm not going to use any of that stuff in my real life. Novels are more important because they help you understand the meaning of life. What do I care about how an earthworm grows a new tail? I'm not going to be a scientist."

"What are you going to be?" I asked.

"A writer."

"Oh," I said. I wondered how I could not have known that, recalling the play she had written and given me for my birthday.

"What do you want to be?" she asked.

"Um, I—"

"Hey, Robert!" yelled Tom. "Let's go dive off the cliff. Mags doesn't believe we will, so let's prove it to her."

"I think you boys would be crazy to do it," said Mags.

"You only say that 'cause you're scared," Tom replied as he swam toward me, splashing water all about him in his hurry to prove his courage.

"I'm not scared. I'm just not stupid," said Mags. "I'm braver than you, any day, Tom Hampton, and smarter too, aren't I, Helen?"

"I'm not getting involved in your arguments," Helen replied.

"Let's go," I said, as Tom passed me and I ran up the beach right behind him. I had felt a little uncomfortable talking to Helen. I did not know what I wanted to be—I had a good idea, but I felt awkward confessing it to her at that moment. I was glad for the opportunity to follow Tom to the cliff.

"Go ahead," I told Tom, once we had run around to the cliff's edge and stood above the lake.

"Hey, Mags, are you going to watch or not?" he hollered. I looked toward her, but she was just talking to Helen. "Mags!" he shouted.

"Mags!" I shouted in unison, and then found myself add, "Hey, Helen! Aren't you going to watch?"

Tom obviously wanted to show off for Mags. I was embarrassed by it, so I felt I had to include Helen.

Once the girls turned to look, Tom stepped back to give himself a head start; then he ran forward, was suspended in air for a couple seconds, and splashed feet first into the lake.

"Ha ha!" he shouted when he surfaced, and he turned to look at the girls and wave, who somewhat lamely waved back.

"Your turn, Robert!" Tom shouted.

I stepped back and took less of a running jump, but I successfully went over the cliff and into the water, landing just a few feet from him.

I came up from the water laughing.

"Let's go again," I said.

We swam to shore and told the girls, "We're going again!" Tom added, "Come on, Mags!"

"That's all right," she said. I sensed she wasn't afraid, just didn't want to join us. As I followed Tom again, I looked back to see Helen and Mags had waded out to where it was shoulder deep. They watched as we continued to jump many times, but they did not join us. The way they smiled made me feel awkward, as if they were busy with girl talk, yet every time I looked, they were watching us.

Tom and I ran and jumped off that cliff so many times we nearly forgot about lunch. We had put the container for lunch in the very edge of the cove, between some rocks where the water gently lapped up to the container, so the cheese in our sandwiches would not melt. Tom apparently had a large appetite since his mother had made two sandwiches for each of us, but one was enough for me, and when I said the girls could split my extra sandwich, Tom agreed to relinquish his as well.

"You're a bit of a gentleman after all, Tom Hampton," said Mags.

"I'd say you were a bit of a lady, if I wasn't afraid of you clobbering me," he smirked.

I expected Mags to clobber him then, but she only looked down at her sandwich.

"So what will we do all the rest of the summer?" asked Helen.

"I don't know," said Tom. "Go swimming I guess. Go blueberry picking when the berries are ripe. I'll teach Robert to fish."

"I'll be going to Mackinac Island for a few days," I said. "Grandma promised to go visit Mrs. Williams there."

"That's nice," said Helen. "I was there once, a few years ago. It's one of my favorite places."

"Why'd you go there?" asked Mags.

"My dad took me one summer, just for a vacation, and we always intended to go back. My dad and I used to go places together all the time. He was always trying to give me little treats. I really miss him."

I thought she was going to cry as she said the last words.

"Have you heard from him lately?" asked Mags.

"Not for a month now."

"That doesn't mean anything. I didn't hear from my dad for over two months just before Christmas," I said. "Sometimes the mail just doesn't get through quickly because of the war."

She smiled, then tried to recover from her sadness by saying, "Anyway, you'll like Mackinac Island, Robert. It's really beautiful."

"Is it as beautiful as this place?" I asked. "I can't imagine it is."

"I would say it's about the same," said Helen, "only since it's an island, there's even more blue around. You can see the lake almost anywhere on the island, but I like Marquette too."

After lunch, Tom said his mother always warned him not to go into the water after he ate, and I remembered James Lewis's claim that he had nearly drowned while swimming right after a big meal. We decided we would walk around Presque Isle while our food digested.

"It won't even take an hour to hike around," said Tom, "and then we'll come back hot from walking, so we can cool off by swimming until it's time to go home."

We all agreed and set off on our walk back up the hill to the road. We soon left the main road and made our way along the wooded trails. Sometimes we walked along a hillside trail above a giant valley in the middle of the forest, at other times on rocky cliffs towering above the lake. We came to the grave of Chief Kawbawgam and his wife Charlotte, and we rested there on the grass for a moment while marveling at the spectacular striped stone that marked the final resting place of the last Chief of the Chippewa.

"Someone ought to write a book about them," said Helen. "Can you imagine he lived to be over a hundred, and lived in three different centuries? Imagine all the changes Chief Kawbawgam saw in his lifetime."

"Imagine all the changes we'll see in ours," said Mags. "Why there weren't hardly no automobiles when we were born."

"I think Presque Isle would make the perfect setting for a romantic novel," said Helen. "Don't you, Robert?"

"Sure," I said, but added—so Tom would not think me soft—"or a great adventure story—the cove would be a great place for pirates to hide out."

"Let's go," said Tom. "I'm hot and want to go back in the lake."

We got back to the cove and spent the rest of the afternoon swimming, except when Tom and I were diving off the cliffs. For a minute, I thought we would convince Mags to join us, but she would not be persuaded. Then Helen dug out her watch and said it was nearly five o'clock.

"We better get home for supper," she said.

"One more jump!" Tom yelled and ran to the cliff to jump again.

While we waited for him, we put on our clothes, and then once I had my pants on over my swimming trunks, I reached into my pocket just to make sure I had my coins for the streetcar, but they were gone. I immediately told everyone, and we searched all over the beach and the rocks for the money, but it was nowhere to be found.

"It must have fallen out, maybe when I was sitting on the streetcar," I said.

"Maybe," said Tom.

"I guess I'll have to walk home."

"I'd walk with you," said Tom, "but we eat at five-thirty, and I already got in trouble for being late for supper yesterday."

"We eat at five-thirty too," said Mags.

Helen looked sympathetic, as if she would walk home with me, but of course, she had to be home at the same time as Mags.

"It's all right," I said. "We don't eat until six or sometimes a little later, so I have time to walk home."

"If you tell the man on the streetcar, maybe he'll just trust you to pay him later," said Tom.

"No," I said. "I wouldn't feel right doing that."

So we walked to where the streetcar would stop, and although I could have waited with my friends, I thought I better get a head start, so I left them there to wait while I headed back on foot. The streetcar passed me going to Presque Isle before I had walked a hundred yards, and as I reached the bridge over the Dead River, the streetcar passed me going back into town.

"Bye, Robert!" shouted Mags.

"See you, Robert!" Tom hollered.

Helen simply waved.

I waved back, but then paid it no more attention. I avoided looking at the industrial sites to my right, and instead gazed up at the tall Lombardy poplars lining Lakeshore Boulevard all the way from Presque Isle back into town, noticing the refreshing contrast between their green leaves and the lake's sparkling blue waves.

Since my earliest memories, blue has always been my favorite color, although I'm not quite sure why—the northwest corner of South Carolina barely has any blue, not even in the sky, which tended to be a hot, humid, hazy gray that hung over our heads, always promising rain and almost always breaking its promise. While I always loved blue, I cannot say I had a reason for it until I came to Marquette and saw the great Lake Superior. Perhaps my inner spirit had already foretold my future beside that great lake, even when I was a small child in the South. As for green, green has always been second only to blue for me, and no other color has approached either of them for third place. I do have a reason for loving green, a sense it may be an affection passed down to me from my Irish ancestors, but blue, it is just an inexplicably magical color to me, and I prefer that my preference for it remain a mystery.

The blue and the green—that moment, as I walked home from Presque Isle, along the beach, and saw the noble lean white birches, the enormous maples, and the shimmering poplar trees, saw how their vibrant green leaves so perfectly contrasted yet enhanced the changing deep and light blues of the lake behind them, and how they were also in contrast with the sky's own lighter blue and the green drifting patches of the lake—all like an emerald mixed with a diamond, or perhaps like the lustrous Connemara marble my Irish forebears had once mined—all that priceless blending of color suddenly bolted through my eyes and dazzled my very soul until I felt so exhilarated I nearly thought my soul would leave my body, my heart leaping up with joy over such grandeur.

I am tempted to belittle the experience, to make light of it by saying perhaps it was only the cold water from my swim or the heat making me almost hallucinate, but it was neither of these. It was a deep felt appreciation for Nature's wonders, for their constant reminders that if only we will look, we can be assured all is well with the world. How can it be otherwise? How can anyone doubt, when standing on the shore of Lake Superior, a magnificent lake before him, a plenitude of plant life behind him, trees, bushes, a diversity of vegetation, and the billions and billions of grains of sand on the beach, the roaring of waves capped with white, the wisps of cloud adding texture to the sky, and sunlight sparkling over it until all is so magnificent one can scarcely stand such good—how can anyone see all this and doubt that the Creation is not the greatest piece of art ever made, and that a master plan exists for all?

And I knew, just knew then that the master plan is so perfect, so well-crafted in its every detail, that I was meant to walk along the beach by myself that day, not to have Mags or Tom or Helen accompany me, for their conversation would have distracted me from all this glory. It could not be just a coincidence that I had lost the money for the streetcar. That loss was an investment for which I had been more than amply rewarded.

And so, whenever life has felt close to falling apart, I think back on that day and think of the blue and the green, the two colors that made my soul leap up in me, that made me feel I had a deeper, inner life I was only beginning to understand. For me, it was while walking along Lake Superior's shore, rather than while sitting in a yoga position or kneeling in a dark cathedral, that I became overwhelmed with the sense of my own being and the universe's magnificence. I wish this story, my own life story, despite whatever sorrows are contained in it, to be a celebration of life. Blue and Green are the colors of life, the colors of lakes and grass, vegetation, and the water that gives the vegetation life. On that day, that summer day, I awoke from a long sleep and felt that now my life, my very vibrant life, had just begun, and although I did not know yet what that life would entail, I felt I had a purpose, a reason why I was part of all this wonder. Helen had asked me what I wanted to be when I grew up. I still did not know, but I was excited for the future.

That day encompassed my first visit to Presque Isle. It was one of what Wordsworth called "spots of time," those gentle moments of joy, when we sense that all is right with the world, those moments that our minds go back to over and over again for comfort. Because of that solitary walk home, I had time to process my visit, to appreciate it fully, and each visit to Presque Isle that followed was also one to be treated with reverence. Later that summer, there were picnics on the Black Rocks and amid the park's many trees. Nothing do I treasure more than those festive times with friends and family as we rested in the beauty of Nature, whether having our photo taken by an arching rock beside the lake, or sitting around a picnic cloth, our stomachs full, our souls content to be with one another. Those are the moments I go back to now in my old age, the moments I replay again and again, thankful that within them existed life, a life more vibrant and joyful in that moment than existed in many later long years rolled together. And even today, in my mind I can go back and be a boy of fourteen again, walking over the Black Rocks, swimming in the cove at Presque Isle, picnicking under the birch trees with those friends and family, now gone, whom I loved so well.

Chapter 14

A Hot-Blooded Day

My eyes opened the next morning to the sight of my pleasant blue room filled with all the familiar objects I'd grown increasingly fonder of each day I spent among them. Yet I did not feel completely pleasant; already I could feel it would be a hot sticky day. Marquette natives will tell you that any day over seventy is too hot, and the humidity only makes summer's heat even more miserable. After having lived through my first bone-chilling winter in Marquette, I found myself surprised to feel miserable during an eighty-five degree day I would have thought comfortable in the South. I may have been born a Southerner, but my blood had grown colder during the long Northern winter.

I went downstairs to breakfast rather late, having enjoyed sleeping in until nine o'clock.

"I didn't think you would ever get up," said my aunt, drinking coffee regardless of the heat. "I don't know how anyone can sleep in this weather. I only had the sheet on me last night, and I still woke up sweating."

"Robert, you should probably go check on Mark and Eliza's house," Grandma said as she set pancakes in front of me. "You didn't go yesterday or all weekend."

"I know. I will," I said. I was annoyed to hear Great-Aunt Carolina's house referred to as Mark and Eliza's.

"You should probably go this morning before it gets any hotter so you don't get dehydrated walking there and back."

"Okay," I said.

"I was hoping you would go after breakfast and stop by the grocery store for me on the way home."

"All right," I said, but I did not like that I would have to return home right away. None of the grownups knew Helen and I played there; not even Tom knew since I was afraid he might slip and tell his mother, who would feel we were desecrating her mother's house.

When breakfast was over, Grandma and Aunt Louisa May did up the dishes, while I went into the front hall to call Helen. But the operator told me the line was busy. Then Grandma came into the hall to give me the grocery list; the only way I could stall so I could try to call again was to say I had to brush my teeth; so I headed back upstairs, waited a couple minutes, then headed back downstairs, only to hear the phone ring and Grandma answer it. I listened until I could tell she was talking to Florence Mitchell—that would mean an hour of gossiping, no matter how Grandma tried to get Florence off the phone. It was hopeless now that I would be able to call Helen before I left. And I certainly didn't want to walk all the way to the Lawsons' house in this sweltering heat. Aunt Carolina's house would probably be too hot and stuffy anyway; playing could wait for another day.

Grocery list in hand, I set out for "Mark and Eliza's house." I felt extremely irritable—I told myself it was the heat, but I knew it was really because I had wanted to see my best friend—I didn't even realize it until that moment—it was not Tom but Helen I missed. I had just seen her yesterday, but we had not spent much time talking alone. I had felt awkward and tried to avoid her questions while we were swimming, but that was partly because Tom and Mags were around, and I did not want Tom to mock me for having things in common with Helen. Yet I found myself secretly wanting to be alone with her. It didn't make sense to me. I dismissed the thought by telling myself the heat today was just messing with my brain.

Once inside Aunt Carolina's house, I felt lonely. None of Helen's laughter would be heard to cheer me. The rooms were as hot as Nebuchadnezzar's fiery furnace. Climbing up to the third floor to open the windows was like climbing an Aztec pyramid in the sultry jungle. I saved myself the exertion of walking downstairs by sliding down the banister, which created a momentary breeze and gave the banister a dusting in the process. But when I reached the bottom and no one saw me tumble off, I only felt lonelier. I did not even spend time in the library beyond what was needed to water the plants. Then I headed for the grocery store, wishing I had brought my swimming trunks so I could cool off in the lake before returning home.

"I'm back!" I shouted when I stepped inside. I nearly dropped the groceries as I struggled to open and close the door, and I felt annoyed when no one came to help me carry them in. Since I had carried two sacks, sweat had dripped down my forehead all the way home; I could not have stopped to wipe it from my face, without setting down a sack, and I was afraid the heat would make the milk spoil if I delayed even a minute.

"We're in here, Robert," Grandma called from the parlor. "Put away the groceries and then come join us."

"All right," I muttered, fearing Florence Mitchell had only telephoned so she could come over to gossip in person; I was in no mood to listen to her tongue in this heat. But as I passed the parlor door, I saw Mrs. Lawson and Helen inside.

"Hello," I muttered and headed for the kitchen. Why had I not sounded happy when I saw Helen? Why did I feel so shy suddenly?

"Robert, do you need help?" Helen asked.

I pretended not to answer. I did not want her to see how sweaty I was. But I left open the kitchen door to overhear the conversation.

"Robert, if you want to go find Margaret," Mrs. Lawson called, "she's gone over to play at Tom's house."

"She's out playing in this heat?" asked Aunt Louisa May.

"Children don't feel the heat the way we older folks do," said Grandma.

"I told her," said Mrs. Lawson, "that she would get sunstroke in this weather, but what can I do? She's so headstrong, just like her father, and I can't seem to keep her from playing with that Tom Hampton. I guess I should just be grateful that two of my daughters are growing up to be young ladies."

I suppressed telling her that Mags was the most normal and certainly the most delightful of her daughters.

"Let me help," said Helen, whom I suddenly found behind me as I wiped sweat from my face and my neck with a towel.

"Um, thanks," I said, embarrassed. I lay down the towel, although I could still feel myself sweating.

"I'll take stuff out of the bags," said Helen, "and you put it away since I don't know where it goes."

"Okay," I said, "but you don't have to help. Not that I don't appreciate it, but I mean, you're a guest after all."

"I don't mind," she said.

"I, um," I said speaking low enough that the grownups could not hear, "I just came back from Aunt Carolina's house. I tried to call you but the line was busy and then Grandma was on the phone."

"Oh," she said. "I came over because I thought you might want to go over there, but it's all right; we can go tomorrow."

When we had the groceries put away, I asked whether she wanted to go find Mags, but she said, "No, it's too hot. Let's just go sit on the porch swing and talk."

"I'll get us some lemonade to take with us," I said. I was relieved not to go find Tom and Mags. It was too hot even to walk to Tom's house, and I felt too irritable to listen to Mags and him arguing, although most days I found it amusing. For now, I found it far more pleasant to sit in the shade with Helen, to drink lemonade, and to rock the swing to create a much-needed breeze.

We sat and talked about our favorite books and the plays we had made from them. And then we talked about what other plays we would like to make up.

"I think we should make a play of J.M. Barrie's *Sentimental Tommy* and *Tommy and Grizel*," Helen said.

"I don't think there's enough action in them for a play," I replied.

"Don't you like the books?"

"Yeah, except I thought it silly how Tommy died at the end."

"I suppose," said Helen, "but I loved Grizel. I feel I can relate to her. All through the first book it seemed like she was lonely and had no one to love her until she found Tommy, and then as soon as she got him to love her, he had to die. I understand that. I know what it's like not to have anyone love you and to feel like no one ever will."

I could not understand Helen when she said such things. She made me uncomfortable. Her grandmother was dead now, so even if the old woman had neglected her, I thought she should let go of the pain.

"Helen," I said. "You're loved. I'm sure your father loves you."

"He's the only one," she said. "And I may never see him again."

"You will," I said. "The war will be over soon."

"Everyone keeps saying that, but it's been months and months and it isn't over yet."

"Still," I said, "your Aunt Elaine wouldn't have taken you in if she didn't love you, and I'm sure Mags and her sisters love you, even if they don't say so."

"How am I supposed to know I'm loved if no one says so?" she asked. "Aunt Elaine never even kisses me good night. I thought once Aunt Helen married Uncle John, I could live with them since they're probably too old to have children, but they have that whole big house to themselves and they haven't even suggested it."

"Maybe they think you're happier being with your cousins rather than living as an only child."

"I doubt it," she said. "In fact, I bet if my father were killed, Aunt Elaine and Aunt Helen would decide between them to send me to the orphanage."

"Oh, Helen, it's not really that bad. Everyone likes you—Mags and Tom do, and—"

"They just tolerate me," she said. "I don't have any real friends."

"I'm your friend," I said. "I enjoy spending time with you more than anyone else, even more than Tom, even though he says I'm his best friend."

"I thought Mags was his best friend," said Helen.

"She should be, but he told me he can't be best friends with a girl."

"But you can?" asked Helen. "You mean you really like me better than Tom?"

"Yes," I smiled, "but don't tell Tom. It'll just be our secret."

I was trying to cheer her up, but rather than smile, her tone became serious.

"Then at least I know how you feel. Now I know at least one person in the world cares about me."

"Two," I said. "You can't doubt your father cares. Part of why you're so upset is because you miss him. I know because I also miss my dad."

"Do you hear from him often?" she asked.

"About once a month," I said, "but he can't say much in his letters. He can't even say where he is in case the enemy gets his letters. About all he ever says is that he misses me."

"That's enough," said Helen. "That's what my dad writes to me, but I haven't gotten a letter now in forever, although I write him once a week. I would write him everyday, but Aunt Elaine says we can't afford to spend that much on stamps."

I was about to laugh at this horrific reason when we suddenly heard Mags screaming. We both looked behind us to see her storming down the street in our direction. Tom was running behind her, trying to catch up.

"I hate you, Tom Hampton!" she shouted.

Then, seeing Helen and I on the porch, Mags marched up the steps and grabbed Helen's arm to pull her up from the swing. "Helen, why are you talking to Robert? How can you stand any boy? They're all so stupid I hate them all. They spoil everything! Let's go home."

She was so upset I could feel hot air blowing from her nostrils. Her pupils flamed and she glared at me.

"Mags, calm down," I said. "You'll make yourself sick in this heat."

"No one's talking to you, Robert O'Neill!" she snapped.

"What's wrong, Mags?" asked Helen, yanked to her feet and leaning against the porch railing.

"That Tom Hampton!" she said, pointing at him as he walked up the steps. "I hate him! That's what's the matter!"

"Mags," Tom pleaded, his face pale with fear.

"What happened?" Helen asked.

"He tried to kiss me!" Mags spat.

"No, I didn't," said Tom, but his quaking voice betrayed his guilt.

"Helen, you better get away from Robert before he tries it on you," said Mags. "I wouldn't doubt it if he and Tom are conspiring together. I don't trust either one of them farther than I can spit!"

For a girl, Mags could spit quite far, so I could have taken this remark as a compliment, but not when her face was pulsing with rage.

"Come on, Helen," Mags said, pulling Helen toward the steps. For a moment, I thought Helen and she would both topple down the steps because Mags pulled so hard.

"Mags, I—" Tom protested, but she ignored him and yanked Helen down to the sidewalk.

"I'll see you later, Robert," said Helen, being led away.

"Robert, I—" Tom said. I could see he was afraid I had lost all respect for him. But I could not blame him.

"Mags is quite beautiful when she's angry," I said, now that she was out of hearing. He smiled, now understanding that I didn't care he had kissed a girl.

He plopped down on the porch swing beside me and wiped sweat from his forehead. Neither of us said a word, but just sat rocking the swing together.

After a minute, Mrs. Lawson came outside.

"I thought I heard Margaret out here," she said.

"She and Helen just left," I replied.

"Oh, I'll see you boys later then." She lifted her skirt in a dainty manner to descend the porch steps and then strolled toward home.

Tom and I continued to rock the swing. After a couple minutes, he began to whistle. He wasn't much for keeping a tune, but I could make out the refrain, which he repeated over and over.

> And for Bonnie Annie Laurie
> I'd lay me doon and dee.

Chapter 15

A Visit

Summer vacation was passing happily but quickly. Tom and Mags patched up their disagreement the next day of course, so they and Helen and I made many trips into the woods for picnics and to climb trees, and we continued to go swimming, despite Lake Superior's freezing waters. Helen and I played in our oversized playhouse, or should I say we performed in our theatre, and Helen did write her play version of *Sentimental Tommy* to entertain us.

And then came the Fourth of July. At the parade, we cheered those U.S. troops who had been wounded and already returned home from the war; even a couple Civil War soldiers marched down the street. The sight of the soldiers made me recall my father, and my heart beat proudly to think that at that moment he was fighting to make the world safe for democracy. Even if my father should not return home, I felt I would always be proud of the sacrifice he and all my family had made for the nation.

When we returned home after the parade, we were surprised to find a strange, shiny new automobile parked in front of our house. None of our neighbors owned an automobile, so we had no idea whose it could be. We grew more curious when we saw its apparent owner sitting on our porch swing. And we grew almost alarmed when upon seeing us, he jumped up and ran down the steps.

And then confusion was replaced by happy wonder.

"Mr. Carter!" I shouted, and I ran up to him, gladly clasping his hand in mine with more enthusiasm and affection for him than I had ever felt before. I could scarcely believe he was in Marquette, and I could barely stutter out the question of how he had he gotten there.

"Why, I came in my automobile," he laughed.

I looked over at that shiny new vehicle and felt dumbfounded. "You said you would never own an automobile! You said they're just new contraptions that won't last!"

"Well, I guess I was wrong. They're a darn good way ta see this fine country of ours."

"But—but I mean, why did you come?"

"You never told us you were coming," Grandma said; her tone expressed concern that she hadn't had time to clean the house for guests. "Louisa May, come inside and help me fix up the spare room."

"Now, don't start fussin' already," said Mr. Carter. "I got myself a room down at the Hotel Marquette."

"And you came all this way to visit us?" I asked in astonishment.

"Yeah, sho," he said. "It's been pretty lonely down South without any O'Neills around."

"Come inside," Grandma said. "I'll get us all some lemonade, and then we can have a good long visit."

We found our way into the dining room and sat around the table. Once the lemonade was poured, I found I still could not conceal my astonishment over Mr. Carter owning an automobile.

"What kind of vehicle did you buy, Mr. Carter?" I asked.

"What else?" he said. "A Model-T, the finest and best on the roads. I traveled twelve hundred miles in it in only seven days and only three flat tires on the way. It's a total marvel I tell ya."

Aunt Louisa May and I nodded our heads in agreement, but Grandma said, "I don't know. Those contraptions make me nervous. I still don't feel safe on the streetcar."

"Safest thing in the world," said Mr. Carter, "because ya're the one behin' the wheel, so ya don't have to rely on one of those fool train conductors."

"Still, I wouldn't trust myself to drive one," Grandma said.

"Well, Katy, how's 'bout I take ya out for a spin in it and prove ya wrong?" said Mr. Carter.

Aunt Louisa May and I exchanged surprised looks. No one called Grandma "Katy." Grandma looked embarrassed herself. I was waiting for her to tell him her name was Mrs. O'Neill, but she only blushed and said, "Maybe some other time, Barney."

Grandma and Mr. Carter were on a first name basis! I thought they only knew each other from a couple visits Grandma had made down South. But I was less curious about their former acquaintance than anxious to ride in that automobile.

"You can take me out for a spin, Mr. Carter," I said. I envisioned us driving over to the Hamptons' house so I could show the automobile off to Tom—it was far more grand than the one his parents owned.

"Good, we'll go for a ride later, Robert," he said. "I've always thought there just ain't nothin' like a horseless carriage."

I could hardly keep from laughing at this remark when I knew well he had denied it before. He must have been extremely lonely to buy an automobile just to come visit us. I was rather touched, really, having known him all my life but never paying him much heed, except to think him rather whimsical. I had been angry with him when we parted, but now I was glad just to see an old friend from home, and that he cared enough to come all this way made me soften toward him. Just recently, I had started to think Aunt Carolina might have been more than the superficial person she presented to the world; it was too late now for me to find out who she had really been, but it wasn't too late to find out more about Mr. Carter's true character. His traveling so many miles to visit me made me think he had a more sensitive heart than his usual comical, laziness suggested.

"You know what? I left something outside," he said, then got up from the table and went out the door before anyone could ask what it was. I looked out the window in time to see him return to the house, his arms overflowing with packages he could scarcely carry, primarily because he had brought a fine baseball bat for me, which I appreciated nearly as much as his thoughtfulness. For Grandma and Aunt Louisa May, he had brought nightgowns, neither of which looked as if it would fit its destined owner. He had also brought us what must have been nearly a bushel of pecans from the South, which made Grandma and Aunt Louisa May squeal with delight before they launched into talking about everything they could bake with them.

"Well, this has all been a pleasant surprise!" said Grandma.

In reply, Mr. Carter's stomach let out a loud growl.

"Oh, Mr. Carter, I never even thought to ask whether you were hungry. It must be almost suppertime. I'll make something right away."

"I can make something, Mother," Aunt Louisa May said. "I know you're tired from walking to the parade and back."

"No, I have to move around or my legs will stiffen up. That's one of the problems with getting old."

"Ya ain't ole yet, Katy," Mr. Carter smiled.

"Oh, Barney, you've always been such a kidder," Grandma laughed, then got up from her chair and went into the kitchen. Without seeking leave, Mr. Carter got up and followed Grandma, saying, "If I'm gonna eat, I guess I bettuh help the cook."

"Katy!" whispered Aunt Louisa May to me.

"Barney!" I said, sharing her surprise.

"I never heard them use first names before," said my aunt, "and I certainly never heard anyone refer to my mother as anything but Kathleen."

"Well," I said, "it's a day of surprises. I never thought Mr. Carter would buy an automobile; after that, I don't know what to expect."

We hushed as Mr. Carter reappeared, carrying the silverware to set the table. I had never before see him do anything he would have considered women's work, and he obviously didn't know how to set a table since he dumped all the utensils on the left side of the plate. Perhaps he was so hungry he thought setting the table would help us to eat sooner, or perhaps he just wanted to be a good guest, to make up for his unannounced visit.

"That's fine, Mr. Carter," said Grandma, coming in with the glasses. "You sit down and visit with Robert and Louisa May. I'm just going to make some cold cut sandwiches and serve the potato salad I made up this morning; it should only take me a few minutes."

"I'll help you, Mother," said my aunt. "Then Robert and Mr. Carter can have a chance to catch up."

Mr. Carter sat down at the table across from me. I had been thrilled to see an old friend when he first appeared, but now that we had talked about the car, I didn't know what more to say to him. He had often visited my parents, or rather my father, who had an affection for him, based on his peculiarities, but I had generally avoided him. Now I realized we were really quite strangers.

"How is my parents' house, Mr. Carter?" I asked.

"Okay, I guess."

What else was there for us to talk about?

"Um, how's Nellie?"

"Don't know. Haven't seen her."

"Oh," I said.

How could he not have seen her if he was going to check on our house and she was too? In seven months, they must have bumped into each other at least once.

But I didn't want to interrogate him. We sat staring at the walls. I was about to resort to discussing the weather when Aunt Louisa May came in with the lemonade pitcher to refill our glasses, and then she stole the weather topic from me. Finally, Grandma brought in the sandwiches.

When Grandma set Mr. Carter's plate before him, he said, "Looks damn good, Katy."

Grandma must have seen the glance Aunt Louisa May and I exchanged because she frowned and said, "Mr. Carter," in a disapproving tone while her face blushed red as the Confederate flag. We all knew she wasn't blushing over Mr. Carter's swearing.

His face fell, and his jaw locked up. He realized he had stepped beyond the bounds of propriety, although a few minutes earlier, Grandma had not seemed to mind and even called him by his first name. An embarrassed silence followed as we all spread napkins on our laps, sipped our lemonade, and nibbled on our sandwiches.

To restore comfort, Grandma asked, "How is Marble Hill, Mr. Carter? I always remember it as such a charming house."

I nearly snorted out my lemonade. Grandma sounded so serious about it. When was the last time she had seen it? I doubt it had been painted once in my lifetime. That house was a disaster, nearly a firetrap, badly needing repairs, loose boards on the front porch, no plumbing at all, the entire downstairs reeking of mustiness.

"All right I guess," Mr. Carter replied, "other than the roof leaking, but I ain't got the money to fix that."

I thought to ask how he could have afforded an automobile then? Was he so lonely he would sacrifice the upkeep of his house just to visit us?

"How's your cotton crop?" Grandma asked.

"Ain't none. I got enough money to live on, so no sense in doin' all that work raisin' cotton. Ain't got no one ta leave the place ta anyway. Sold all the farmland off years ago. Now it's just me, the few acres the house is on, and my Negro, Jude, who keeps a garden for our meals."

"Mr. Carter," Grandma said, "do you mean to say you've let the place go like that when it was once the finest cotton plantation for miles around? Your father was always so proud of Marble Hill."

"It's too much work for just two old men," he replied.

"You could at least paint it," I said. "I don't know when you did that last."

"I'm too old to be standing on a ladder now, and Jude's 'fraid of heights."

I knew Jude would gladly have painted the house if Mr. Carter spared the money.

"I just painted this house last fall," said Grandma, "and I'm the same age you are."

"You ain't got my rheumatism," said Mr. Carter.

"To be fair, Mother," said my aunt, "it was while painting the house that you hurt your ankle."

"Mr. Carter, why don't you just hire someone to paint Marble Hill?" I asked. I was surprised by the frustration in my voice—he had come all this way to see me, yet I was already feeling irritated with him.

"I ain't got the money," he repeated. "Ever since those damn Yankees came through the South, no one's got the money to keep things up the way they was. Those creatures stole nearly everything the South had."

"Oh, I don't want to hear any grumbling about the war," said Grandma. "That's all I ever hear about when I'm down South. Your father made sure Marble Hill remained the finest plantation in South Carolina for years after the war."

"Well, he had me to leave it to. I ain't got no wife or kids to pass it on to, and that ain't none of my fault."

Grandma pursed up her lips but did not reply. Apparently, the Civil War was not a favorite subject of hers. I had never asked her about it since I had arrived in Marquette, but now I remembered what Aunt Louisa May had told me on the train, how Grandma's family had lost everything, and then how she had bravely married a Northerner, a Yankee soldier, someone even worse than a Yankee, a Southerner whose family was viewed as traitors in the South. How odd it seemed that across the ocean, a World War was raging, yet here in my grandmother's dining room, the Civil War, which ended more than fifty years ago, was the more present event to her and Mr. Carter, for their childhood had been shattered by it, as I still feared mine would be shattered by the current war.

Aunt Louisa May changed the subject by asking Mr. Carter which states he had driven through to reach Marquette. While he detailed his travels for us, I felt a heaviness about his visit, perhaps because he had brought some familiarity from home with him, but its momentary pleasure had now turned to longing for my father. And after the initial enthusiasm in Grandma's voice, I now felt she was annoyed by his visit, although I wasn't quite sure why.

It was a relief when after supper, Mr. and Mrs. Hampton and Tom came over to visit. We all sat out on the porch, discussing the parade and the sites Mr. Carter could see in Upper Michigan. But other than Mr. Hampton offering to take Mr. Carter fishing some day, which Mr. Carter did not look interested in, the Hamptons made no offers to amuse him.

When it started to get dark, Tom and I walked down to see the fireworks, then returned home to find Grandma and Mr. Carter sitting alone on the front porch. Just enough light shone from inside the house for them to see one another. They were scarcely speaking; Grandma said they were simply "enjoying the breeze."

"Tom," Grandma said, "your parents said for you to go straight home when you got back."

"All right. Let's go swimming tomorrow, Robert," he said.

"Can I, Grandma?" I asked, afraid she would expect me to stay at home to entertain our guest, but the thought did not seem to cross her mind.

After Grandma gave her consent, Tom said good night, and then I sat down on the porch.

"Where's Aunt Louisa May?" I asked.

"She was tired, so she went to bed early," said Grandma.

I wondered whether she had grown tired of Mr. Carter's conversation.

"That's all right," said Mr. Carter. "It's given your Grandma and me time ta get reacquainted, but I better go get some shuteye for now. I'll see y'all in the mornin'."

I said goodnight while hoping Tom would come over tomorrow before Mr. Carter.

"Did Mr. Carter say how long he's going to stay?" I asked Grandma once we were inside the house.

"No, I don't imagine he knows himself," said Grandma. "He never was one to make up his mind about anything."

I sensed Grandma was relieved Mr. Carter was staying at a hotel rather than in the guest room. I was glad to see him, but if he stayed long, I feared he might just ruin the rest of summer.

Chapter 16

Secrets

In the morning, I set off right after breakfast to go swimming with Tom. Aunt Louisa May was supposed to meet with her women's group that morning—I don't know how she thought it would be accomplished, but she said her group was going to get women the right to vote—so Grandma was left at home to entertain Mr. Carter. He showed up just as I was going out the door. Aunt Louisa May suggested that in the afternoon Mr. Carter could take us all for a ride in his automobile, although Grandma said she would not enter the vehicle. I promised to be home for lunch, and then set off with Tom for the lake.

We went to the beach alongside Lakeshore Boulevard rather than go all the way to Presque Isle. We had barely taken our shoes and socks off when the entire Lawson clan, including Helen, appeared. Soon the girls joined us in the water. Mary and Mollie, being younger and smaller than the rest of us, were insisting that Tom and I let them jump into the water from our shoulders, which we agreed to halfheartedly; luckily, I got Mollie and not Mary, since if Mary got hurt, I did not want to be blamed. After a little while, however, Mollie swallowed a bunch of water and wanted to stop. She went to talk to Mags, who was now trying to convince Tom to let her jump from his shoulders, although I was sure she was too heavy for him. Mary was protesting that she wanted to jump more, and soon the three girls were in an argument while Tom stood, bemused by them all. And then I noticed Helen sitting on the beach, reading a book and looking lonely.

"Tom, I better go home now," I said. "I have to check on your grandma's house before lunch."

"All right, see ya, Robert!" he said, not thinking twice about it, although I did.

I had wanted him to ride in the automobile with me, but now I found I just wanted to talk to Helen. She never seemed fully able to join in the fun. I could not understand that, but to make her feel wanted, I asked whether she would like to walk home with me.

"Okay," she said. We quickly put on our clothes over our wet bathing suits.

Once we were out of the others' hearing, I told her if she would wait while I went inside my Grandma's house to get the key, she could go with me over to Aunt Carolina's house. She protested she was a little wet and didn't want to get sand in the carpets, but it was a warm day, so I convinced her she would dry off before we reached the house so no harm would be done.

When we got to the block before my house, we cut through the backyard to the backdoor. Helen said she would wait on the steps. I told her I would be back outside in a few minutes.

When I entered, I found the house silent. Wondering whether anyone were home, I peeked into the parlor and dining room and found them both empty. Then I had the humorous thought that maybe Mr. Carter had talked Grandma into going for a spin in his automobile, but Pumpkin was not inside either, so more likely they had taken Pumpkin for a walk. Once in my room, I changed my clothes, then looked outside and saw Mr. Carter's vehicle was still parked before the house. I thought Grandma and Mr. Carter must be out on the porch, and as I came back downstairs, I heard their voices coming through the window. I walked to the window, thinking I would just tell them I was going over to Aunt Carolina's house and would be back in time for lunch, but before I could say anything, I heard:

"Mrs. O'Neill? Dag nab it! I'm gonna call ya Katy!"

Mr. Carter had said it. I heard it plain as day, and when I heard it, I froze. I waited to hear Grandma reply, but when she didn't, I saw him step across the porch, sort of stamping his feet, and I pulled back from the window, where I could hear but not be seen.

"Katy, why do we have ta be so formal every time we see each other? Why can't it be like the ole days?"

I heard Grandma moan. My heart nearly stopped. What was he talking about? Grandma's voice was almost timid as she said, "Mr. Carter, I think our youthful follies are best forgotten now."

"How can ya say that, Katy?" he asked in a voice more mournful, even more desperate than hers. "Those were the most wunnerful days a my life; we was in love so much. I still love ya."

"If you plan to break my heart again," Grandma whimpered, "it won't work."

I could not believe what I was hearing! I had to cover my mouth to keep from shouting my astonishment. I quietly sat down in the chair beside the window to hear better.

"Don't ya believe me, Katy? I do love ya. How can I ever help but love ya?"

"If you loved me," Grandma said so softly I had to strain my ears, "you wouldn't have given up."

"What more could I do? Ya know my parents and your aunt woulda just kept tryin' to prevent it."

"We could have found a way," Grandma repeated. "We could have eloped."

Eloped! I couldn't believe it. Grandma and Mr. Carter?

"Eloped?" Mr. Carter half-laughed. "You're talkin' crazy now. Ya know ya never would have done that. Ya know what my father was like, and your Aunt Abigail didn't approve of me. We never coulda shown our faces in public again, and ya was always afraid of what people thought."

"I wouldn't have cared if I could be with you," Grandma said. "I thought you wouldn't have cared either. I learned from the sorrow of those days that it's not worth my personal happiness to please others. That's why I found it easy to marry Robert, even if people thought him a Yankee, and everyone was against the marriage, including my Aunt Abigail. I knew I had to marry him anyway."

Mr. Carter was silent a moment. "Well, I'm glad then that you found the courage to follow your heart, even if it weren't with me. I wish I'd been brave enough then, but I wasn't, and it doesn't seem like much of anything in life has mattered to me since then."

Grandma's voice grew tender. "I know. I felt that way for a long time after I lost you. I thought you would come to rescue me. When you didn't, I cried for weeks. I'm still amazed I found courage to give my heart again."

"I never saw another woman I wanted ta give my heart ta. Ya were luckier than me. I never stopped carin' for ya."

"I never stopped caring for you," Grandma replied. "I told myself just because I loved Robert, it didn't mean I couldn't love you still. I never meant to be cold to you when I saw you at John and Cynthia's house—I was just afraid of being hurt again—I thought you didn't care anymore."

"All those times you came down to visit, I was achin' everytime ta talk with ya, especially after your husband died. I was just afraid ya would think me a fool ta have held onta it for all these years."

As they talked, I wished I could see their faces. I heard the swing screech as Mr. Carter must have sat back down beside her. I could picture Grandma taking his hand in her own to comfort him while looking at him tenderly. I could not picture Mr. Carter's expression, not when I had never thought him anything but sluggish and indifferent. I had never known he could be so sincere.

"I guess," said Mr. Carter, "that none of it really matters now, but somehow I feel bettuh havin' talked about it."

"I feel the same," said Grandma. "I don't have anyone left who remembers the old days of our childhood. You were my first friend. I'm glad you've come to visit and that we can be friends again."

"I s'pose," he said, sounding afraid to say the words, "I s'pose it's too late for more 'tween us now than just bein' friends."

It seemed forever before Grandma answered.

"I don't believe in too late," she said.

"I ain't much ta look at," said Mr. Carter, already afraid of her decision. "I'm old, and gray, and got my rheumatism an' all."

"I'm old and gray and plump," Grandma replied. "And much as I love my family, I still get lonely and wish I had someone to talk to who remembers the old days."

"I'm lonely too," said Mr. Carter. "Lonely a lot of the time. Only company I got is Jude, and he'd go live with his sister in Greenville if he weren't so worried 'bout me."

"Barney?"

Grandma's voice trembled.

I felt agony, a never-ending moment.

"Barney, why don't you move here—move to Marquette?"

"Oh, I—no—I," he stammered.

"Why not?" said Grandma. "You have no family left, and when Robert's father comes back from the war, I'm going to talk to him. I love Robert too much to be so far from him, and they have no family left in South Carolina. I'm hoping they'll move here permanently, and you being their closest friend, and practically family, you might as well move here too."

"Maybe," said Mr. Carter.

I was too thunderstruck to hear what Mr. Carter said next. Grandma and Mr. Carter's secret past was enough of a surprise, but that my father might agree to live in Marquette! Would he agree? I realized I wanted him to.

"I'll go inside and get us some more lemonade," said Grandma. "You just think about moving here until I come back."

These words made me bolt to the backdoor. I did not want her to know I had been eavesdropping.

"What took you so long?" asked Helen, as I came outside, quietly closing the door behind me so Grandma would not know I had been in the house.

"I misplaced the house key," I said. "I had to look all over for it. Sorry."

I started walking through the neighbor's backyard to the street. Helen followed, not realizing I wanted to get away before Grandma might see me.

We walked across the block and onto the sidewalk, then headed down the street toward Aunt Carolina's house.

"You're awful quiet," said Helen after we had walked a block.

How could I be otherwise when my thoughts were bursting with what I had just heard? I was only fourteen! How could I keep such a huge secret! Grandma and Mr. Carter had been in love! I just couldn't keep it! Yet I felt that other secret, that I might live in Marquette permanently—that one I was afraid to speak in case it didn't come true.

"Helen," I said. "I didn't really misplace the key. I took so long because I overheard Grandma and Mr. Carter talking, and I just couldn't believe what they were saying."

I didn't need to ask her to keep it a secret. I trusted she would not tell a soul. But I expected her to act surprised once I had told her everything. Instead, she smiled, and her eyes took on a soft glazed look as she said, "How romantic."

"Yeah, but, it's weird," I said. "It's just weird to think Grandma loved someone before my grandpa, and especially, that it was Mr. Carter. He's just so different from her."

"Opposites attract," Helen stated.

"Maybe," I said, "but it's still odd."

"Well, I think it's wonderful," said Helen. "They should have told each other how they felt years ago rather than holding it in. Don't you think if you love someone, you should tell that person rather than worrying about what will happen?"

I did not know how to answer that question. I loved Eliza, but I had never told her. I had imagined proclaiming my undying love, but now I could not tell her since she was married. But what did Helen know? She had never been in love, only read about it in books, and I was old enough to know most of the stories in books were romanticized rather than realistic.

"Don't you think you should tell someone if you love them, Robert?" she repeated.

"I suppose," I said, just to answer her. Inside, I cursed my fate that made me younger than Eliza, and then I was surprised to find that I really did not care about Eliza anymore, but was reacting out of habit. I felt very puzzled at that moment.

We were soon at Aunt Carolina's house. Once inside, Helen and I parted, splitting up my duties to water the plants and open the windows so we would have more time to play. When I finished upstairs, I found her in the library, reading a volume of J.M. Barrie's plays that I had left behind the other day.

"Are you ready to finish acting out *Quality Street*?" I asked.

"No, I don't really care for it," she replied.

"Well, I have to bring it back to the library tomorrow," I said.

"That's all right," she said. "Let's make up our own play and just act it out as we go along."

"All right," I said.

We had recently read Dickens's *David Copperfield* and been struck both by the comical characters and the happy sunshine glow that alternated between the novel's more tragic moments. We knew acting out the scenes of the master novelist were beyond us, but we loved the story so much, we had not wanted it to end, so we started to act out a sequel. In our version, David and Agnes, Mr. Dick and Aunt Betsy go to Australia to visit the Micawbers, only to end up shipwrecked in Borrioboola-Gha, the site of Mrs. Jellyby's missions in *Bleak House*. It was a rather far-fetched and poor sequel, and we soon grew tired of it. I think my heart was just not in the game that day, and later I would understand equally why Helen's heart was also distracted. I began to wonder whether I should tell Aunt Louisa May about Grandma and Mr. Carter, wanting to confide in a grown up who, unlike Helen, would not have silly romantic notions about love. I was glad when it was time to go home for lunch.

As we walked home, Helen asked, "Do you want to play tomorrow?"

"I don't know," I said. "It depends on whether I have to help entertain Mr. Carter."

"Well, why don't you call me then?" she said. "I wouldn't mind helping to entertain him, and I'd like to watch love blossom between him and your grandma."

Love blossom? I really doubted that would happen.

"No," I said. "Mr. Carter can be pretty dull. I don't want to bore you."

"Really, I wouldn't mind."

"Well, we'll see. I'll call you tomorrow," I said, feeling irritated when she persisted asking after I had already told her "No." Sometimes it seemed as if Helen wanted to spend all her time with me.

I went inside and sat down with my family and Mr. Carter for lunch. As we ate, I saw no indication that Grandma and Mr. Carter's earlier conversation was going to be mentioned. Finally, just to see whether anything had changed, I asked, "Grandma, have you changed your mind? Will you go for a ride in the automobile with us?"

I thought if they were in love, they would want to spend every moment together.

"Are you crazy?" she said. "I'm a nervous wreck just thinking of you and Louisa May riding in it."

"Aren't you worried about Mr. Carter too?" I asked.

"Well, he knows how to drive the contraption," she said. "But you all better wait a half hour after eating so you don't get motion sickness."

After lunch, I went upstairs to brush my teeth. I had carried home with me the volume of J.M. Barrie's plays and left it on the table in the hall. Now I picked it up to bring to my room, but halfway upstairs, I accidentally dropped it, and from it flew a piece of paper.

Curious, I picked up the paper, but when I saw it was a note from Helen, I quickly stuffed it in the book and went to my room. I locked my door and sat down on my bed. Then I read in private what I had only glanced at and already dreaded.

Dear Robert,

You said today that you thought if a person were in love with someone, then that person should say so. Robert, I've been trying to tell you for months, but I was afraid you didn't feel the same way, but today I felt you were hinting that you like me. I can't keep it in anymore, Robert. I love you. I love you more than anyone and I know you love me more than anyone else ever loved me. But I'm still not sure you love me as a boy loves a girlfriend. You're my best friend, but I want to be more than friends. Please tell me that you love me. I want to be your girl.

Love, Helen

At first, I could only wonder how the note got in my book. Then I remembered her reading it in the library at Aunt Carolina's house while I was upstairs—at least, I had thought she was reading it. And what if I had returned the book to the library tomorrow without finding the note inside it—everyone in Marquette would have known!

And then I thought about what really mattered. Helen loved me. At least, she thought she loved me. I didn't know what I thought. What would I say next time I saw her? I certainly wasn't going to tell her that I loved her. I had admitted to myself and to her that she was my best friend, even more so than Tom. But I should have said she was my best friend who was a girl, while Tom was my best friend who was a boy; I hadn't meant more than that, had I? Helen thought I had. Just what did she mean by saying she thought I was trying to say I liked her that way? I had never suggested such a thing. We had been talking about Mr. Carter and Grandma. Why did she have to read things into the conversation that hadn't been there? I couldn't believe this. What was I going to do? I didn't want to hurt her feelings, but I wasn't going to tell her—

"Robert, hurry down. Your aunt and Mr. Carter are waiting for you!" Grandma shouted upstairs.

"I'm coming!" I yelled. But I sat on the bed another moment. What would I do? What would I say the next time I saw Helen? Should I ask Grandma what to do? But I couldn't. She had to sort things out with Mr. Carter. She didn't need my problems as well. And Aunt Louisa May had never been in love, so it was pointless to ask her for help. I wished my father were here.

"Robert, come on!" called my aunt.

"I'm coming!" I hollered back.

"So's Jefferson Davis Day!" yelled Mr. Carter.

I stuffed the note back into the book, and then stuffed the book under my pillow. I would have to figure it out later.

I was relieved when I got into Mr. Carter's automobile. We rode all over Marquette, three times over, and the automobile was so noisy it allowed me to think silently, trying to come up with an answer. But after two hours of riding about, I still did not know what to do.

All evening I felt despondent, barely joining in the conversation as Mr. Carter talked about all the places in Upper Michigan he wanted to see before he went back to South Carolina. I was relieved when he did not mention moving to Marquette, and more relieved when he left finally, and it was time for bed. I did not want to think further on Grandma and Mr. Carter's potential romance. I had my own love problems.

Chapter 17

Love?

In the morning, I still didn't know what to do. Was I overreacting to the entire situation? After all, Helen and I were hardly more than children. And to me, Love meant being together for the rest of our lives. I had thought I wanted that with Eliza, but since she had married Mark, I had given up on her. Helen was my dear friend, but I also knew our friendship was partially based on my feeling sorry for her because she was always so sad. I enjoyed her company more than anyone else's, but I did not think I could live with her sadness the rest of my life.

I didn't feel right asking Grandma and Aunt Louisa May for advice. I would have asked my father, but since he was absent, I went to my next male role model. No, not Mr. Carter—he had obviously botched up his romance. So I went to Tom. I'm not sure what I thought Tom's qualifications as counselor were, other than that he clearly liked Mags and was trying to get her attention. He had denied kissing Mags, but I was fairly certain he had. If nothing else, we could commiserate with one another over our relationship problems. Even if he laughed at me, as my best friend, he was bound to keep my secret.

It was pouring rain that morning. I wanted to visit Tom right after breakfast, but Grandma wouldn't let me go out in the downpour. We nearly got into an argument over my going because I was afraid Helen would come over before I got the chance to talk to Tom.

"Why is it so necessary you visit Tom?" Grandma asked. "You see him all the time. It won't hurt you not to see him for one day."

I didn't reply, just got up and shoved my chair under the table.

"Don't be surly, Robert," Aunt Louisa May said.

"Robert, you'll get pneumonia like your mother did if you go out in this rain," Grandma said. Then I understood why she wouldn't let me go, but it didn't make me feel any better. I felt ridiculous—I was old enough to have romance problems, yet I still had to obey my grandmother.

"Besides, Robert," added my aunt, "Mr. Carter is coming over. He came all this way to visit you, yet you've hardly spent any time with him."

I was so irritable I wanted to retort that Mr. Carter had come all this way to see Grandma, but I held my tongue.

Mr. Carter soon after telephoned to say he wouldn't come over in the rain.

All day, whenever the telephone rang, I was afraid it would be Helen, calling to demand my reply to her note. I would have just called Tom to tell him my troubles, but I knew the women would overhear my conversation.

Finally, around three o'clock, the rain began to let up. Only then did Grandma consent to let me go out, provided I take an umbrella and avoid the puddles. I felt ridiculous to have her fuss at me over such little things when my life was in a state of crisis, yet I tolerated it so I could get out the door.

Before I had walked a block, the rain started up again, the wind blowing it sideways. Despite the umbrella, I was soaked and dripping like a waterfall when I reached the Hamptons' house. I didn't care. I would finally have someone to talk to.

Mrs. Hampton was good-natured enough not to worry about the water I dripped on her rug, but I was annoyed when she said, "Robert, you better get out of that jacket before you catch pneumonia."

Then she hollered, "Tom, Robert is here!"

I turned to go up to Tom's room, but she stopped me by asking, "Robert, have you heard from your father lately?"

"Just last week," I said.

"We got a letter from Mark today. He'll be done with his training in another week and then shipping out overseas, although he doesn't know where yet."

"Oh," I said, uninterested.

"I thought this horrible war would be over before he had to fight."

"It'll be over soon," I said. That was the standard answer we all had; we could not bear to think otherwise.

"My poor boy was never away from home for even one night before, and now he'll be across the ocean with people shooting at him. I—I—"

She started to cry and sat down on a chair by the door. When she could not find her handkerchief, I handed her mine.

"Thanks, Robert. I'm sorry. I don't mean to be hysterical, but you don't know what it's like to be a mother."

"It's okay," I muttered. I was relieved to hear Tom coming down the stairs.

"Hey, Robert," he said, then saw his mother sniffling and said, "Ah, Ma, don't start that again. Mark'll be just fine. You'll see."

"You boys go on upstairs and never mind me," she said, getting up and going into the kitchen.

I followed Tom up to his room, glad to escape from Mrs. Hampton's presence. Mark was someone only a mother could love—but I did feel sorry for his mother.

"So what do ya wanna do?" Tom asked. "How about playin' a game a checkers?"

"Sure," I said, sitting down on the floor while he found the game. As we set up the checkerboard, I trembled, but I forced the words from my throat.

"Tom, I need to ask you a question."

"Sure, what?" he asked.

"Tom, are—" I couldn't ask it straight out. I would dance around my real question first. "Are you really in love with Mags?"

"Yeah," he said, as if resigned to it. "I mean, I can't imagine bein' with any other girl. I'm pretty sure she loves me too, though she's 'fraid ta admit it."

"But how can you be sure you love her?"

He had finished arranging the checkers. He raised his head from the board, looked at me strangely, then said, "Smoke before fire. You go first."

I pushed forward a checker.

"Why are you asking?" he asked. I waited for him to move a checker then looked at the board, pretending to think of my strategy, but really I was avoiding eye contact with him.

"I don't know," I said.

"Are you in love too?" he asked. "I know Eliza's beautiful, but she's taken ya know. I've seen how you've looked at her."

"No, not her," I said, embarrassed that I had been so obvious.

"Then who's the girl?" he asked.

"I'm not sure I'm in love with anyone, but I think someone's in love with me."

"Who?"

"Helen," I mumbled, hoping he wouldn't laugh.

"Helen? That shy thing?" He frowned.

I felt furious.

"What's the matter with her?" I asked.

"Nothing, nothing," he said. "You don't have ta get angry. If you love her, that's okay. Here, don't be sore. Wanna piece of chewin' gum?"

I took the stick of gum to show I had no hard feelings. He now knew I would not hear a word against Helen.

Trying to be nonchalant, I said, "Why are you surprised Helen likes me?"

"I'm not. I'm surprised though that you like her."

"I don't know whether I do. But why should it matter?"

"I don't know. I guess just 'cause lots of the girls like you, so I don't think you should settle for her."

"Lots of girls like me?" I was astonished.

"Oh sure, half our class at Bishop Baraga—Sally O'Rourke, Frances De-Frain, Elizabeth Mulloy, all those girls."

"How do you know?" I asked. I doubted it was true. I started to doubt Tom would be any help in figuring out my dilemma.

"Mags told me. She saw Sally writing 'Sally O'Neill' all over her tablet one day, although I think she'd a written 'Sally Hampton' if she weren't afraid a Mags. The girls don't chase after me 'cause they know I'm Mags's man, even if she won't admit it."

What could I say to this egotistic statement? I let Tom be deluded about his own popularity. As for me, I didn't care how many girls were in love with me. It was Helen I was worried about; she was my friend, and I didn't want to hurt her, whatever I decided about loving her.

"But I just want to know," I said, "how a fellow is supposed to know whether he's really in love?"

"If you are, you just know it," said Tom.

"But that's the problem! I don't know it!"

"Then you ain't," said Tom, jumping his king over my checkers to take my king.

"Are you sure?"

"Trust me. Mark tol' me all about it. For an older brother, he was good for that anyway—I mean, somehow he was smart enough to get Eliza to love him. He tol' me how ta get a girl ta like you before you even ask her out."

Normally, any advice from Mark I would have dismissed, but Mark had gotten Eliza to marry him; maybe he wasn't as stupid as I had always thought.

We played checkers until five o'clock. We didn't say much more about love. Tom was not the type to analyze anything deeply. To him, everything was black and white. When I left, I made him promise not to tell anyone what we had talked about.

"I ain't no snitch," he said. "But do ya think you'll end up marryin' her?"

"I don't know," I said. "I'm too young to think about that yet."

"Soon as Mags and me turn eighteen, I'm marryin' her," he replied. "Just like Mark married Eliza."

"How do you know Mags'll marry you?"

"She will. She wouldn't act the way she does if she didn't love me, and by then, she'll have gotten used ta the idea."

"Well, good luck then," I said as I stepped out his bedroom door.

"When you and I are old enough to be marrying," Tom said, "we'll be each other's best man."

"Deal," I said. Then I went downstairs to put on my coat and go back out into the rain.

I arrived home in time for supper. Mr. Carter was there, chatting away with my aunt and grandmother, and obviously less shy than the day before. But my interest in Grandma and his relationship had waned since I became obsessed with my own love life. I still didn't know what to tell Helen. Tom said either I was or I wasn't in love with Helen, but I didn't think it was that simple. When the telephone rang during supper, I feared it would be Helen—I was surprised she hadn't called already since she must be equally nervous about her note. Usually I jumped up to get the phone, but I was afraid to now.

After three rings, Grandma went to answer it. I was so absorbed in my own thoughts that when I heard her talking, I could tell it wasn't for me so I didn't pay further attention until I noticed Aunt Louisa May and Mr. Carter had stopped eating to listen.

When I heard Grandma say, "Poor Helen," my ears perked up. But I didn't understand what the conversation was about until she returned to the table.

"That poor little girl," said Grandma, shaking her head as she slid back into her chair.

"Her father?" asked Aunt Louisa May who had heard more than me.

"Yes," said Grandma. "They heard this morning. I'll do up the dishes quickly and then we should go over to see them. Oh dear, what will we bring with us?"

"The chocolate pie meant for dessert," said Aunt Louisa May. "We don't need it."

Mr. Carter grimaced, as if his heart had been set on that chocolate pie, but he could have a piece at the Lawsons' house. I felt as if I were only watching all of them, not participating in this unfolding drama. Helen's father was dead—killed in the war. I felt numb. How selfish I had been all day with my silly fears when other people all over the world were hurting from the war, and especially my dear friend. She had always been so worried about her father, far more than I was worried about mine, and now I worried that my father—no, I would not think about that now. I would just have to be a friend to Helen, to try to comfort her. My father was going to come home just fine. I wouldn't think otherwise.

As we cleared the table and quickly washed up the dishes, Grandma and Aunt Louisa May pondered what would become of Helen now.

"Elaine already has three daughters to take care of," said Grandma, "and I did think she was overextending herself by taking Helen in. Now she'll really have her hands full if she keeps the girl."

"Maybe John and Helen will take her," said my aunt. "They don't have any children."

"I don't think they want any," Grandma replied. "Besides, Helen would be better off with other children."

I did not live with other children, so I didn't see why that mattered, but I said nothing.

"Elaine sure doesn't need the burden of caring for another child," Grandma added.

I could not believe what I was hearing! Helen a burden? No wonder she was so sad. How could grownups, even my own grandmother, think that way about a child? I knew she did not think me a burden. Had Mrs. Lawson told Grandma that Helen was a burden on her?

"It would be easier if she weren't such an odd girl," said Aunt Louisa May. "She's always so quiet and serious."

"Is she the sickly, pale lookin' one Robert walked home with the other day?" asked Mr. Carter.

I was furious. Helen was a beautiful girl. Maybe a little thin and not yet fully developed, but she wasn't sickly. I went upstairs to my room and didn't come down until Grandma hollered that they were ready to leave.

Since it was still raining, we all piled into Mr. Carter's automobile. Grandma didn't even make a fuss about it since the Lawsons were only a few blocks away and Mr. Carter promised to be careful.

"I'm so glad you brought Robert over," said Mrs. Lawson at the door. "Maybe he can talk to Helen."

"How is she?" asked Grandma.

"In a state. She won't eat anything. The girls are afraid to go near her since she just sits in her room and cries; they don't understand. I tried to talk to her, but she won't say a word to me, and when John and Helen were here this afternoon, she refused to come out and see them."

"Poor girl," said Aunt Louisa May, shaking her head. "We brought you over a chocolate pie. Maybe she'll feel like having a piece later."

"Thank you," said Mrs. Lawson. "I've been so distraught I didn't even make supper so I'm sure the girls are all hungry."

Before I could protest, Mrs. Lawson set the pie on the kitchen table, cut it into eight pieces, hollered for her daughters and divided the pie between all of us, not leaving a piece for Helen. I could not believe Mrs. Lawson was so thoughtless.

"I'll bring my piece to Helen," I said, taking the plate she handed me.

"Thank you, Robert. I was hoping you would go talk to her," said Mrs. Lawson.

She handed me a fork, and then I headed for Helen and Mags's room. The bedroom door was shut. I knocked and waited for an answer. I knocked again and waited. Finally, I said, "Helen, it's Robert." When I still got no answer, I turned the knob and stepped into the room. It was gray inside, the evening having come early because of the rain. I closed the door behind me.

Helen was lying on the bed, her face buried in a pillow. When she heard the door shut, she reclaimed some dignity and sat up against the wall in a crumpled position.

"My grandma made a pie," I said. "I thought you might like a piece."

My words sounded stupid; I groped for more appropriate ones.

"I'm—I'm sorry about your dad. I—I don't—I can't imagine how—"

"Thank you," she said, looking frozen as she pulled a blanket around her. "I don't want any pie."

"Can I get you anything else?" I asked.

"A handkerchief," she said.

I dug in my pocket for mine, but not finding it, I remembered Mrs. Hampton had not given it back to me. What a waste that it had been used for tears shed over Mark when Helen's tears were more important to me.

"I'm sorry. I don't have one," I said.

"Robert, why is my life always like this?" she asked. She wiped her eyes on the edge of her sheet, only then to burst into more tears.

I stood helplessly as her body heaved with grief.

"Why, Robert? My father was the only one who loved me. The only one. The only one," she sobbed until she started to choke.

And then, before I knew what I was doing, before I could stop my feet from moving, before the words could form in my mind, I found myself sitting beside her on the bed, found myself holding her, found myself saying, "Helen, don't cry. Your father wasn't the only one who loved you. Please don't cry. It's okay. It's okay, Helen. I love you. You have me. I love you."

Chapter 18

Across the Peninsula

I don't remember how I managed to leave Helen's room that night. I felt in a fog during the following days as we went to her father's visitation and funeral. But I do remember that two days after I made my declaration of love, we received a long distance phone call from Mrs. Hobson, Mrs. Williams's daughter, on Mackinac Island.

"Marie's son has been wounded and is in a hospital in Washington D.C.," Grandma said. "She needs to go to him. He's okay, but she wants to stay with him until she can bring him home. Mrs. Williams can't possibly make the long journey to Washington D.C. so I told Marie we would go to the island and stay with her mother until she returns."

I was more than willing to go. I felt scared to hear of another of our small circle having been wounded in the war, but I was also relieved to get out of Marquette. The funeral for Helen's father was that afternoon, so Grandma said when we got home from the funeral, we would pack, then leave for Mackinac Island the next morning. I had not been alone with Helen since the night I told her I loved her, but I knew once the funeral was over, she would come over and expect me to behave as her boyfriend. Leaving town would give me time to figure out how to deal with the mess I had gotten myself into.

"Of course we'll go stay with Mrs. Williams," said Aunt Louisa May, "but Mother, Mr. Carter came all this way, and now he'll have to cut his visit short."

Before Grandma could reply, Mr. Carter, who had come over for breakfast, said, "Ain't no reason for that. I'll just go along with ya. In fact, I can drive us all there in my automobile."

Aunt Louisa May and I looked at Grandma, waiting for her reaction.

"We-ell," she said, "I guess I do have to keep up with the times. We can all go in the automobile."

The next day, at the funeral luncheon, I sat with Helen. I waited on her, I filled her plate, and I let her hold my hand under the table. I was relieved when she never said a word about our relationship to anyone. When we were surrounded by people, I told her I was going to Mackinac Island. I was afraid she would be upset by this news, but she didn't comment. I think she was still in shock over her father's death, but I also noticed her aunts constantly hovered over her. I told myself she would be fine—that her family would take care of her, despite her feelings toward them. I told myself if I went to Mackinac Island, it would teach her how to deal with her problems on her own.

After the funeral, Grandma, Aunt Louisa May, and I went home and packed for our excursion. It was a hundred and sixty-five miles to St. Ignace, from where we would have to take a ferry to Mackinac Island. Even if we didn't have a single flat tire on the trip, which was highly unlikely, we could not expect to reach St. Ignace in less than ten hours. We hoped to get there at a decent hour so we could have supper and sleep overnight, then take the ferry the next morning to Mackinac Island. We arranged for Mr. Carter to pick us up at seven the next morning.

Mr. Carter was never known for punctuality. I warned Grandma of this, but she made me get up at six anyway, and fussed at me all the while to get ready. I was ready by ten minutes to seven, then spent forty-five minutes sitting on the sofa reading while Mr. Carter did not appear. Meanwhile, Grandma kept fussing about how we would never reach St. Ignace before midnight. At seven-thirty, she finally broke down and called the Hotel Marquette, only to hear Mr. Carter honking his car horn out front.

"Good Lord, he'll wake all the neighbors!" she said.

I got up and started to carry out the luggage, Grandma behind me, as Mr. Carter came up the front steps.

"Mr. Carter, I thought you were going to be here at seven sharp," Grandma scolded.

"Tain't more than a couple minutes past," he replied.

"It's seven-thirty-four," she said, looking at her watch. "Thirty-four does not a couple minutes make."

"Well, it's gonna be a long day so I thought I needed a little extra shuteye."

"Mother, we can make up the time on the road," said Aunt Louisa May.

"And drive like maniacs all the way!" Grandma replied. "I don't think so."

"Grandma, I warned you he wouldn't be on time," I said, trying to calm her down.

"Mr. Carter, this is just like the time you—"

But then a funny look came over Grandma's face, and she bit her lip.

"Like what time, Grandma?" I asked.

"Nothing," she snapped.

I smiled. She still hadn't said anything about her relationship with Mr. Carter, but I knew it was going to come out eventually.

"Robert, get those suitcases in the car. Louisa May, do you have the lunches?"

"Yes, Mother," said my aunt. "I'll just lock the door."

"I'm nervous about Tom coming to water the plants," said Grandma, "especially if he's going to water those at Mark and Eliza's house too."

"It'll be fine, Grandma," I said. But I was a little nervous too because we had brought Pumpkin over the night before so Tom could take care of him while we were gone—I hoped his parents would make sure Tom didn't forget to feed Pumpkin or take him for walks.

"The worst that can happen is the house'll burn down," smiled Mr. Carter, "and if it's gonna do that, it's better that you're not in it anyway."

"It might just be a blessing if it did," smiled my aunt. "We sure have enough junk in it."

"Don't talk like that," said Grandma. "You're inviting bad things to happen."

From the way Grandma was looking at the automobile, I could see she was less concerned about the house burning down than about riding in Mr. Carter's modern contraption.

"Mother, you sit in the front with Mr. Carter," said Aunt Louisa May. "You need the room so your legs don't stiffen up."

"Oh, no," she said. "Let Robert sit up front so he can watch the scenery."

"No, I'm fine," I said. And my aunt and I crawled into the back seat while giving Grandma stony glares that declared we would not move. When Aunt Louisa May winked at me, I realized she had guessed Grandma's secret and planned to have her sit next to her secret beau all the way to Mackinac Island.

"Well, if you're both sure you don't mind sitting in the back," Grandma muttered.

And then to everyone's surprise, Mr. Carter opened the car door for her. It was the only gentlemanly move I had ever seen him make. Grandma seemed embarrassed, but she quickly thanked him and got into the front seat. Then she got out her scarf and wrapped it over her head to keep the wind from messing up her hair or blowing away her hat.

"That's a beautiful hat, Katy, but not so beautiful as your hair," said Mr. Carter.

I had to restrain laughter at this point, considering Grandma had long ago gone gray.

"Let's go," she replied.

Mr. Carter turned and gave her a big grin that seemed to say, "I'm so glad you'll sit beside me all the way." Then he turned on the motor.

"Are ya ready, Katy?"

"I've been ready for the last hour, Mr. Carter. Let's go or we'll never get there."

"We'll be in St. Ignace before suppertime," he replied.

Grandma looked doubtful, but when we started to roll down the street at five miles an hour, she clutched the door handle for dear life; I was unsure whether she were steadying herself or preparing to jump out if the terrible speed increased.

But Grandma had nothing to fear. In those days, the Model-T was the finest vehicle on the road, superior even to my father's Pierce Arrow, which could reputedly tackle the worst mud holes. Mr. Carter's automobile rode so smoothly that once we had driven through Marquette and then Harvey, I pulled out a book to read, and Aunt Louisa May daringly pulled out her knitting needles, not at all concerned that if we hit a bump, she might poke out her eye. As for Grandma, I don't think she even saw Lake Superior to our left because her eyes were focused so intently on the road, save for when she closed them in a state of panic as we came down the curving hill into Munising.

"My, I didn't realize automobiles went so fast," she said. "That clunker the Hamptons own wouldn't have made it this far in twice the time. We're going as fast as a train. The trees are becoming a downright blur. I don't even remember passing through Au Train."

"That's because you had your eyes closed," laughed Mr. Carter.

"Well, yes, after you nearly hit that jack rabbit," said Grandma.

"That was just a piece of paper blowing over the road," he replied. "No danger at all."

"It's fun to ride in an automobile, isn't it, Grandma?" I said.

"Well, it's not as bad as I expected. It does ride smoothly. I could almost take a nap."

But at that moment—I suspect it was intentional—Mr. Carter hit a bump that made Grandma jump in her seat and grasp the door handle.

Truthfully, Mr. Carter could be rather reckless. He reminded me of Mr. Toad from *The Wind in the Willows* the way he swerved around corners at thirty miles an hour until I thought we might topple sideways. Sometimes, he was nearly off the edge of the road, then would yank the steering wheel so hard to pull away from the gravel that I feared we'd roll over. Other times he was driving down the middle of the road, especially when another vehicle, or worse, a horse and buggy were coming in his direction. He would wait until the last minute to move over, and then shake his fist, insisting automobiles had the right of way over "ole farm nags."

I am still amazed that we managed to drive nearly five hours without an accident. We were all so anxious to get to Mackinac Island that none of us wanted to stop, but finally, Grandma said, "Barney, can we take a little break? I'm getting a little dizzy from riding for so long."

"You're just hungry," said Aunt Louisa May. "It's lunchtime."

"Maybe I am hungry," said Grandma. "I feel as if I have butterflies in my stomach."

"That's just motion sickness," said Mr. Carter. "I had that clear from the Carolinas ta Kentucky until I got used ta drivin'. Had to pull over a couple a times and throw up actually."

"Really, Barney," said Grandma.

Mr. Carter said he would stop when we reached Seney, but Grandma protested that the lumberjack town was not safe because it was filled with rogues and scoundrels.

"Let's eat at that restaurant there," said Mr. Carter as we came into Seney.

"No, Louisa May packed sandwiches," Grandma replied.

"Well, just for a cold drink," said Mr. Carter.

"Not there," Grandma said, looking at the building as it got closer. "That's a tavern. It'll be filled with drunken loggers."

"Mother," said my aunt, "how could they be drunk? You know prohibition is on."

"In Marquette County, but not here necessarily. You don't know what goes on in Seney. I know. I've heard the horror stories, fights in the streets and all, and rough men always know where to find a drink."

"Seems like the whole country's moving toward prohibition," said Mr. Carter. "It's a shame, not letting a man enjoy himself. Nothing's better than a cold beer."

"Lemonade is enjoyable enough for anyone," said Grandma.

Mr. Carter started to turn into the establishment's parking lot.

"Mr. Carter, I will not stop here!" Grandma repeated.

He flashed her a look of annoyance and pulled back onto the road. The rest of us looked back longingly, the dust from the road making us thirsty. Aunt Louisa May had a thermos of water, but by now it was no longer cold.

We kept driving, through forests, and then past acres of cleared land.

"See, there's lumberjacks all over here," said Grandma.

"Well, we have to eat," said my aunt.

"We'll just eat here," said Mr. Carter, pulling into a cleared forty. Aunt Louisa May got out and spread a blanket on the ground for us to sit on. As we ate, she noticed a blueberry patch.

"We should stop and pick some berries," she said. "Maybe Mrs. Williams would enjoy them. We could make her a pie."

"I got a pail in the car," said Mr. Carter.

"We can't afford to lose any more time," said Grandma. "Besides, the berries will spill all over if we hit a bump."

"The pail's got a lid, Katy," Mr. Carter frowned. I could tell he was still irritated not to have gotten himself a beer in Seney.

"We could pick this patch in half an hour," said Aunt Louisa May, "and it's the height of blueberry season. By the time we get back to Marquette, the season will be over, and you know how I love picking berries."

"We need to get to St. Ignace before dark," said Grandma.

"It's only one o'clock," said Mr. Carter. "Won't be dark till ten."

"What if we get a flat tire or hit a deer?" said Grandma. "We can't risk losing time."

"You women worry too much," he seethed.

"I'm not worrying," Aunt Louisa May said.

"Mr. Carter, please remember yourself," said Grandma. She started putting everything back in the picnic basket to indicate that the blueberry picking discussion had ended.

After a moment, Aunt Louisa May started to help her.

"I'm gonna check the oil," said Mr. Carter. He stood up and spit, then walked back to the car.

Once we were back on the road, my stomach started to hurt, probably from all Mr. Carter's swerving, despite the Seney stretch being a long straight line. I was also thirsty, but we were out of water now. I thought it a shame Mr. Carter hadn't had his beer—it couldn't have made his driving any worse.

"Mother, is your stomach any better?" asked my aunt.

"No," said Grandma. "If I'm going to feel this way every time I ride in an automobile, I never want to set foot in another one after today."

"Are ya gonna walk back ta Marquette then?" Mr. Carter asked.

Grandma didn't reply. I could see they were both irritated with each other.

"I'm going to read," said Grandma, "so I don't get sick from watching the road."

"That'll only make ya more sick," said Mr. Carter.

Grandma sighed and opened her book anyway, but after a few minutes, I saw her close it and go to sleep. I was feeling sleepy myself, so I likewise closed my book and then my eyes.

I couldn't actually rest. Every few minutes, I was jolted awake as we hit a large rock or plowed through a mud hole. And my aunt's clicking needles did not help matters. But somehow I managed not to open my eyes again until we were driving along a giant lake.

"Is that Lake Superior?" asked Mr. Carter.

"No, Lake Michigan," said my aunt.

"I thought ya'll lived 'long Lake Superior," said Mr. Carter.

"We're on the other side of the peninsula now," said my aunt.

"Oh, I thought it was all the same lake."

"Mr. Carter, didn't you pay any attention to geography in school?" Grandma asked.

"How was I supposed ta learn geography when the damn Yankees burnt down the schoolhouse, and I had ta work in the fields ta feed my family?" he demanded.

Grandma did not reply, for which I was thankful. I was starting to fear Mr. Carter would tell her to walk the rest of the way.

Thankfully, the sighting of Lake Michigan meant we were almost there, and after another two hours, without one flat tire the entire trip, we rolled into St. Ignace just in time for supper.

We found a hotel, and Mr. Carter and I got a room together so the ladies could have their privacy. I didn't want to share a room with him, imagining he would snore, but I was too tired to argue. We found a restaurant to eat at, then went downtown and bought some of the area's famous fudge, which Grandma declared we did not need, but which Aunt Louisa May insisted on. Inside the fudge shop was a picture of Mackinac Island's Grand Hotel, which Mr. Carter said he would stay at, having read about it in a newspaper.

"It looks expensive," said my aunt.

"Looks like a big plantation house," he said. "It'll keep me from feelin' homesick."

"Barney, you're not homesick already?" asked Grandma. Her voice sounded gentle. Now that she was no longer in a terrifying automobile, she was more her old self.

"Not a bit," he said. "Just feel I'm grand enough ta stay at the Grand."

"I trust you won't be disappointed, sir," said the fudge shop clerk. "It's a marvel to see. The finest hotel north of Detroit and Chicago."

"I doubt it's as fine as Marquette's Hotel Superior," said Aunt Louisa May. As a Marquette native, she would not be disloyal to her hometown.

We went back to our hotel. Mr. Carter and I said goodnight to the ladies in their room. As we left, Mr. Carter pushed the door wide.

"Mr. Carter!" screamed my aunt. "You just let in a gigantic moth!"

It was a monster too—it's body must have been three inches long—I never saw anything like it.

"Sorry," he said, the door still wide open.

"Quick, shut the door before another one comes in!" my aunt shouted. "I hate moths. I bet there are bats out there too."

"They won't hurt you, Aunt Louisa May," I said.

"I won't be able to sleep with that creature in here," she replied.

"Louisa May," said Grandma. "We've had plenty of moths at home."

"Not as big and ugly as this one!" she shrieked as it flew toward the lamp beside her, then up to the ceiling to bask in the light.

"Honestly, Louisa May," said Grandma, "you act as if it were a vampire bat or something."

"Don't worry none," said the gallant Sir Barney Carter. "I'll get 'im for ya."

"Oh, Barney, be careful," said Grandma as he stepped onto a chair to swat the moth with his hat.

"Just anudder inch an' I'll have 'im," Mr. Carter said, swinging his straw hat at the wall, missing the moth, reaching too far, and tumbling off the chair.

"Barney, are you all right?" Grandma asked, running to pick him up off the floor, while Aunt Louisa May huddled in a corner.

"You should have used a newspaper," I said. "You wouldn't want that moth smooshed all over your hat."

Mr. Carter ignored me. Grandma had her arms around him, and I noticed he did not get up as quickly as he could have, despite his rheumatism.

"I hope you didn't break anything," she fussed, rubbing his shoulder.

"I'll get the moth," I said, just wanting to go to bed. I grabbed a newspaper, raised my arm, jumped and swatted it in one blow.

Aunt Louisa May shrieked over the murder, although she had sanctioned it. I scooped up the dead moth and dumped it in the wastebasket.

"Oh, don't leave it in here," said my aunt. "What if it resuscitates?"

"It ain't gonna do that," said Mr. Carter.

"Fine," I barked, taking the wastebasket outside to dump the moth in the grass, all the while thinking my aunt would deserve it if I let another moth in.

"Can we go to bed now?" I asked, returning to the room.

"Can you walk all right, Barney?" Grandma asked. "You didn't hurt your leg, did you?"

Mr. Carter slowly pulled himself to his feet, leaned against the dresser, and then limped to the door.

"I'll help him," I said, letting him put his arm around my shoulders.

"Well, goodnight," said Grandma. "We'll see you both in the morning."

"Thank you, Robert," called my aunt as I helped the wounded hero from the room.

Once the door was shut, Mr. Carter stood up straight and said he was fine. He had apparently faked being hurt to gain Grandma's attention.

When we were in our room, he said, "Ya sure are lucky in that grandma of yours."

"I know," I mumbled. "Which bed do you want?"

"Don't matter none."

I plopped down on the nearest one.

"Yes suh," Mr. Carter repeated, "that Grandma of yours is one special lady. She cares a lot about people. Anyone can see that."

I got out my pajamas and went in the bathroom to change.

"She sho was worried 'bout me takin' that fall," he shouted through the door as I brushed my teeth.

When I came back out and crawled into bed, he said, "Wish more women were carin' like her. Maybe I woulda married then."

"Goodnight, Mr. Carter," I said, turning out my light. I heard him go into the bathroom. Next thing I knew, he was trying to hum to himself, "I'll Take You Home Again, Kathleen."

I felt exasperated with all three of them that night. But as I fell asleep, I thought of Helen, and what had happened between us. Then I decided I should count myself lucky to be going to Mackinac Island because bad driving, monstrous moths, and nervous grandmothers were nothing compared to the distress of love.

Chapter 19

Mackinac Island

The morning air was filled with anticipation when we embarked on the ferry for Mackinac Island. With the war on, the island's visitors were few in number, but for us, the lack of crowds was an advantage while we spent one of the finest summers there. As the ferry skimmed over the sparkling, deep blue waters of the Mackinac Straits, where Lake Michigan meets Lake Huron, I strained my eyes to make out the handful of buildings on the wooded island. Aunt Louisa May stood beside me along the rail, and the seagulls soared beside us, happy to race the ferries that ran back and forth from the island to the mainland. Grandma and Mr. Carter sat together on a bench, oblivious to the beauty around them in their contentment to be together. Grandma trusted the boat captain more than she trusted Mr. Carter behind the wheel, so peace was able to exist between them on this journey.

The boat slowly approached the island, coming around the west bluff and moving toward the island's little village harbor. Several large, elegant homes rose up on the high bluff, homes to rival Aunt Carolina's house on Ridge Street. Then came the Grand Hotel, the most impressive and massive hotel I have ever seen, a classic monument to the Midwest, an emperor surrounded by a court of small mansions. Its extensive columned sun porch stretched wide, as if to welcome its visitors with an embrace; its patriotic American flags waved in the breeze, symbolizing the peace and prosperity of our nation; its wealthy patrons strolled about its grounds, oblivious to the war. The bustling little village next came into view. The crowds were small that season, yet the sidewalks still had many visitors walking from gift shop to fudge shop, then up the hill to the remains of historic Fort Mackinac. Sailboats filled the harbor, their giant masts only surpassed in height by the steeples of whitewashed churches on the hill.

The minute we stepped off the dock, Mrs. Hobson had her arms around Grandma's neck, then shifted to Aunt Louisa May's neck. She said hello to me, and then Grandma introduced her to Mr. Carter.

"I was afraid I would miss you, not knowing which boat you would arrive on," she said, "but Mother said, 'If I know Kathleen, she'll be on the first boat in the morning'."

Grandma refrained from saying we had almost missed the first ferry because Mr. Carter had taken forever grooming his mustache.

"Well, we could hardly sleep in the hotel, it was so infested with insects," said Aunt Louisa May.

I rolled my eyes, remembering the moth incident.

"I guarantee we don't have that problem at our house," Mrs. Hobson replied. "Let me help you with your luggage. We'll have to walk home, but it's only a few blocks."

"Could ya point me toward the Grand Hotel?" asked Mr. Carter.

"Oh, I'm sure we don't mind if you stay with us as well," said Mrs. Hobson. "The Grand Hotel is very expensive, but a few of the other hotels are not quite as bad. Mother is looking forward to having a houseful to cook for, though Kathleen, I hope you won't let her overdo it."

"Of course not," said Grandma.

"I don't wanna be in the way," said Mr. Carter. "I'm a family friend, but no blood relative, so I can't impose. 'Sides, I've got loads of cash and have a hankerin' ta stay at that hotel."

"We live in that direction anyway, Mr. Carter," Mrs. Hobson smiled. "Come with us, and once I get the others settled, I'll walk you there myself."

"Much obliged," Mr. Carter said. Then he insisted on carrying Grandma's luggage, even though he had his own to carry. Mrs. Hobson and my aunt divided the other suitcases between them while I carried my own as we passed restaurants and gift shops.

"Everything looks so old fashioned," I said. Most of the buildings were wooden, many of the stores having fake fronts like those out west. The architectural change was curious when I had become used to Marquette's many sandstone buildings, which spoke of solidarity, while these buildings spoke more of elegance. In the distance, as in Marquette, but here on all sides, were a lake and a beach stretching all around the town's edge. I could hear the waves rolling in time with the horses trotting by. "I feel as if I'm in the last century almost," I added.

"Yes, we want to preserve our past here," said Marie. "We've been a popular summer resort for many years, but now we're apparently becoming known as a historical place as well. They banned automobiles from the island a few years back when one scared a horse, and it doesn't look as if the ban will ever be lifted."

"Sounds like the perfect place for you, Mother," Aunt Louisa May smiled.

Grandma did not reply.

"I hope I haven't inconvenienced you too much," Marie said as we turned off the main street into a residential area. "I've been so worried about Eric. I was afraid he would get gangrene and need to have his leg amputated, but the doctors say there's nothing to fear. The poor boy will probably limp the rest of his life, but that's better than what many a mother has suffered during this war."

"Or what daughters have suffered," I thought, remembering Helen's loss of her father.

"I'll be leaving tomorrow," said Marie. "Hopefully we'll be back in a couple weeks. I'll send you a telegram when I get to Washington."

"We're happy to help out," said Grandma. "Marquette's been rather lonely without your mother to keep us company."

"There's the house," Mrs. Hobson said.

"It's charming," said my aunt as we turned to look at it. "And what a beautiful location, with such a great view of the lake."

The house was up on a little hill a few blocks above the main street. It was a Victorian cottage, rather large, but not massive, ornate in its decorative exterior work, painted pink and light green, gentle soothing colors that already made me feel restful. It looked out at the lake like a young maiden waiting for her sailor to return.

"My late husband built it here for the view," Mrs. Hobson said. "He was a sailor you know. Lost at sea eventually, but I think he would have rather gone that way than live to be old and feeble. I thought of moving back to Marquette after he died, but I feel close to him here where I can see the lake. The view is magnificent, although the scenery is gorgeous all over the island."

We had turned up the little driveway now, and as we approached the steps, the door opened and Mrs. Williams came out, one hand clutching the doorknob to hold her up, her cane in the other hand, but her smile said she wished she could run to Grandma with open arms.

"Kathleen!" she called. A second later, they were hugging, and then there were hugs for my aunt, and even for Mr. Carter and me.

"Mr. Carter, Kathleen has told me so much about you," she said.

Aunt Louisa May and I exchanged glances. Had Grandma confided her lost love to Mrs. Williams? I saw a nervous look on Grandma's face, but Mrs. Williams only smiled at her, as if to say her secret was safe.

"Mother," said Mrs. Hobson, "if you would show Robert and the ladies to their rooms, I'll walk Mr. Carter over to the Grand Hotel."

"The Grand Hotel!" said Mrs. Williams. "Are you going to stay there? Why, it's so elite! I wouldn't even dare set foot inside of it. We have plenty of room here for you."

"Naw," he said. "I'll be just fine there."

"Oh, well, be sure to come back for lunch," said Mrs. Williams. "I made egg salad sandwiches since I know how much Louisa May likes them."

Mr. Carter promised to return in a couple hours, and then set off with Marie. Later, when I visited the Grand Hotel, I would envy Mr. Carter getting to stay there, but I was glad not to have to share a room with him; I was afraid he would further try to make me his confidant in his romance with Grandma.

Mrs. Williams showed us our rooms. She slept in the first floor bedroom, but as hostess, she insisted on climbing upstairs with us. Grandma would have Mrs. Hobson's room, while Aunt Louisa May would have the guest room. As for me, I would sleep in Eric's room, up in the attic. Mrs. Williams said a second flight of stairs was beyond her, so I went up to the attic by myself.

It strikes me now that when I first arrived at Grandma's house, I should have taken more interest in my mother's childhood bedroom rather than being so anxious to change it. I wonder what I missed learning about her by letting Grandma pack up my mother's belongings and put them away. I wonder now because when I first saw Eric's room, I felt I liked him instantly. He had a window seat so he could sit and look out at the lake. But this view being insufficient for him, the room had been painted deep blue with a wallpaper border of great masted ships, as if the lake flowed right into his room. Although the eaves curved up so the walls did not reach full height, nestled into the walls were bookshelves with knickknacks, family pictures, high school sports trophies, and a few boyhood toys. I instantly felt at home, and after quickly emptying my suitcase into the empty drawer of the dresser, I sat and stared out at the lake for several minutes. But I was less keen on nautical than literary items, so my eyes soon went to the bookshelves. Looking behind model automobiles and a ship in a bottle, I discovered Tarzan and the Boy Fortune

Hunter series, *Tom Sawyer* and *The Sea Wolf*. I could tell that Eric and I had a lot in common, even if he were nine years my senior. I could hear the women chatting downstairs, so I took time to explore the room, reading the books' spines and looking at the family pictures. I recognized photographs of Mrs. Williams, Mrs. Hobson, Eric's Uncle John, and a sailor I assumed was Eric's deceased father. I knew the young man in the football uniform must be Eric, posing as if he were ready to take on the world, happy and fearless, unaware of the war he would soon fight in. I hoped we would be great friends when he returned.

After an hour, Aunt Louisa May came upstairs to see my room. Then I went to see her room before we went down to the kitchen where Grandma and Mrs. Williams were preparing lunch. As Grandma set the table, Mrs. Hobson returned with Mr. Carter, who said the Grand Hotel was truly grand, and he was very pleased with it.

Once we sat down to eat, Grandma asked for more details about Eric's health.

"He seems in good spirits," said his mother. "I got a letter from him yesterday; he assured me he's fine. The doctors think he'll always have some slight paralysis in his leg, but as long as he doesn't have to have it amputated, I'm grateful. Lots of boys have lost limbs or their eyesight or been gassed, and those are the ones who have lived, so I'm just grateful he's coming home whole."

"It's terrible to think he'll have difficulty walking," said Grandma. "He was always such an active boy."

"I remember babysitting him when you used to come to Marquette to visit," Aunt Louisa May said. "I could barely keep an eye on him, he was always running all over the place, but he always minded me. He was never any real trouble."

"No, he was always a little gentleman," said Grandma.

"He's not little anymore," said Mrs. Williams, "and quite a looker. Marie worries his limping will keep him from finding a wife, but any woman will be lucky to have him."

"He is brave like his father," said Marie. "I'm thankful his spirits are still high, and that he's alive, of course."

"Yes," said Grandma. "I take it you heard that your sister-in-law Helen's brother-in-law was just killed. And now his poor little girl, Helen, is an orphan."

"Yes, John wrote and told us about it," said Mrs. Hobson.

"Poor thing," said Mrs. Williams.

"I lost my own father when I was about that age," said Mrs. Hobson. "It's terrible she lost her father. I'm so grateful my son is coming home to me, wounded or not."

Mrs. Williams patted her daughter on the arm, swallowing her own sadness over her grandson's wound.

"If women were allowed to vote," said Aunt Louisa May, "we never would have entered this war in the first place."

"Women vote!" laughed Mr. Carter. "That'll never happen."

Grandma glared at him.

"Well, it's not likely," he mumbled.

"President Wilson kept us out of the war as long as he could," said Mrs. Hobson, "and I don't begrudge having sent my son. Eric told me when he left that we can't consider ourselves Christians if we're not going to standup and protect the innocent. He wanted to do his duty, not just to his country, but to his fellow man."

"It sounds like you have reason to be proud of him," said Grandma.

"I am proud of him," Mrs. Hobson replied. "But I hope he never moves away from me again. I don't think I can bear such another long parting."

"I can't imagine Eric or anyone would want to leave this beautiful island," said Grandma. "All my life I've wanted to visit here because of the wonderful stories I've heard about it. I'm thankful I've finally made it."

"Then you have a treat in store for you," said Mrs. Hobson. "Mackinac Island is the jewel of the Great Lakes, and you'll have time to explore every nook and cranny of it."

The next morning, Mrs. Hobson left for Washington D.C. Grandma said she would spend the day with Mrs. Williams so they could catch up—I wondered whether catching up meant that Grandma would tell Mrs. Williams of her current romantic predicament because she insisted Aunt Louisa May, Mr. Carter, and I go sightseeing without her. Mr. Carter didn't seem interested in doing anything without Grandma, but we badgered him until he agreed to meet my aunt and me at the Grand Hotel that morning.

Aunt Louisa May and I arrived at the hotel right after breakfast. I had never seen such an enormous building. Only up close could I truly conceive how large it was, with its enormous sun porch stretching hundreds of feet, so long a dozen plantation houses could have fit inside it. Horses and carriages rode up to it, where they were greeted by impeccably dressed doormen. Then the steps from the porch went down several stories to extensive luscious gardens below.

We found Mr. Carter seated on the sun porch, patiently awaiting us. I was surprised but glad he was ready since I had doubted we would ever find him inside the hotel.

"Came down ta breakfast early," he said, "and got the bellboy ta tell me the hotel's history."

He then proceeded to rattle it off to us.

"The Grand Hotel was built in 1887 by two railroads and a navigation company that wanted tourists ta visit the island so they'd use transportin' facilities up here from Chicago and Detroit. The hotel never made much money though, and it's had five different owners since then. As recently as 1910, there was plans ta tear it down, but the islanders have always rallied to save it. Just this year it was sold again, and the new owner, a Mr. Ballard, has got all kinds a big plans and is spendin' a bundle ta improve the place."

"My goodness, Mr. Carter," said Aunt Louisa May, "you certainly have gotten a lot of information from people."

"Ya jus' need ta know how ta make friends," said Mr. Carter. "I've always had the kinda personality that attracts people and gets them ta open up ta me."

He made this statement so proudly you would have thought the bellboy was a German intelligence officer who had revealed military secrets to him so the allies could win the war. But I was impressed by Mr. Carter's interest in the hotel, considering how lazy and dull he usually was. He had been altogether more animated and quick-witted since he had arrived in Marquette. All day he chatted away happily to my aunt and me about everything he actually knew nothing about including horse breeding, botany, fur trading (the island's original enterprise), and the French-Indian War, whose conflicts had been felt in the region a century and a half earlier. Aunt Louisa May and I enjoyed ourselves perhaps all the more because of these humorous if ignorant speeches.

We navigated the Grand Hotel's mighty sun porch for half an hour, exclaiming over the view from various vantage points. Then we entered into the hotel lobby filled with countless arrangements of tables and chairs for the guests. Graceful chandeliers hung from the high ceilings. Everything had an air of decorum, of quiet efficiency, dignity, and relaxation as waiters and bellboys served the guests.

My adult life has led me to many monuments of historical importance, from Windsor Castle to the White House, from the Palace at Versailles to the

Vatican, but no place evokes such tranquility for me as the Grand Hotel. Its history may be less significant than those monumental places, but its visitors leave, reinvigorated, and with an appreciation for the elegant possibilities in life.

Eventually, we descended from the sun porch into the great gardens below where everything was fragrant, romantic, and breathtaking. Along the lawn's edge rose up the mighty forest, shading the flowers, creating a borderland from which the hotel rose like a fairy castle in an enchanted wood. The cool lake breezes, the shadowed forest, the sunlight on the white pillars, seemed to hold time still; each visit I have since made to the Grand Hotel has only made it appear more timeless.

If I had seen no more of Mackinac Island, I would have gone home happy that day, but we had only just begun to explore the island's wonders. We exited the hotel gardens and returned to the street where carriages and bicycles rolled along. We entered the Little Stone Church, where Mr. Carter, already tired from walking, sat down while we admired the stained glass windows. The church's simplicity was as spiritually impressive as the Grand Hotel was imposing. I was especially interested in the stained glass window depicting Father Marquette among the Indians. While the City of Marquette is named for that brave Jesuit priest, and he traveled throughout the Great Lakes, Mackinac Island and St. Ignace are where he had his greatest influence. I felt proud that despite all the harm white men had done to the Indians, one of the first white men had come as a bearer of goodwill. When we came out of the church, I saw the fort up on the hill and could suddenly imagine myself there more than two centuries before, a French voyageur, paddling the remarkable Jesuit missionary across the Great Lakes. What an adventure for any young man!

We went to Marquette Park to eat lunch and sat in front of the Father Marquette statue, a duplicate of the one in our own city. We rested only long enough to eat, anxious to see far more of the island, yet taking time to look at all the beauty around us. Periodically, one of us would remark, "I wish my geraniums would grow as well as those in the hotel's gardens," or "I've got a hankerin' ta buy us all some fudge this afternoon," or "I wish I could have seen the island when it was full of fur traders and Indians, and soldiers at the fort."

Fort Mackinac, looming up above the park, was our next destination. In more recent years, it has been wonderfully restored and turned into a magnificent historical site, but even during the First World War, when much of it was little more than ruins, it was interesting to imagine the lives of those soldiers, whether French, British, or American, hundreds of miles from their homes, trapped on an island through long winter months, struggling to survive, afraid of war, longing just for a letter from a loved one, yet there to do their duty and get the small compensation their individual governments would pay them. It made me appreciate my father all the more to think he was one of thousands of American soldiers who had fought for his country; through him I felt connected to my nation's past.

From the fort, we started back to Mrs. Hobson's house. Rather than return by the main road to town, Aunt Louisa May suggested we take a trail through the woods that looked like a possible shortcut. The trail wound around bumpy little hills and through a forest providing glimpses of the lake in the distance. Then we came to a clearing with a marvelous view of the lake, but more marvelous to me was a large stone plaque we found in the clearing; at first we though it was a grave, but then we saw the three stone benches surrounding it.

"Good, I need a rest," muttered Mr. Carter, plopping down on the nearest bench, and pulling off his shoe to shake out a pebble.

Aunt Louisa May sat down on another bench and asked me to read the plaque to her. The stone was raised and tilted. Carved on it was the picture of a girl looking out at a landscape with her hands raised.

"It's a memorial to Constance Fenimore Woolson, whom it says expressed her love of this island and its beauty in the words of her heroine, Anne, and then there's a quote as well."

"What'd she do, write some kinda book or somethin'?" asked Mr. Carter.

"I guess she must have," I said.

"Oh, yes," said Aunt Louisa May. "I've read *Anne*. It was partly set on Mackinac Island."

As I went to sit on the third bench, I said, "There's writing on this bench too. It lists all the novels she wrote."

"Oh," said Aunt Louisa May, looking closely. "Mine also has a list of her works, and so does Mr. Carter's."

"Maybe we shouldn't be sittin' here," said Mr. Carter.

"They wouldn't have put benches here if we weren't meant to sit on them," said my aunt. "Robert, read us what the quote on the stone says."

I got back up and read the passage from *Anne* inscribed on the plaque.

She used to whisper to them to tell them how much she loved them "her old friends." She loved the island and the island trees; she loved the wild larches the tall spires of the spruces bossed with lighter green. The gray pines and the rings of the juniper. Hear the rustling and the laughing of the forest and the wash of the waters on the pebbly beach.

"Sounds like poetry," said Mr. Carter, a rather observant comment for him.

"Yes," said Aunt Louisa May. "I think we could say this spot is the very heart of the island. It's more than just a monument to an author; it's a tribute to the island whose spirit inspires art."

"Well, let's mosey back," said Mr. Carter. "I could use a little nap 'fore supper."

He stood up and started down the path, oblivious to whether we followed. I didn't want to leave. I had never visited a literary site before, and I was struck by Aunt Louisa May's statement that this place was the heart of the island. I remembered Helen saying she always wanted to travel to the East Coast to visit literary sites; she had even been to Mackinac Island, but she had never mentioned being here. Of course, Marquette's Dandelion Cottage was also a literary site. Realizing I had seen two literary places gave me goose bumps as I cast a parting glance upon the little clearing, shaped by the benches, memorial stone, and Constance Fenimore Woolson's beloved trees. I wondered whether someday I might be remembered so fondly.

We soon came out of the forest and walked back into the village. When we reached the house, we were pleased to find Grandma and Mrs. Williams on the front porch with chocolate chip cookies and a pitcher of cold lemonade.

"I expected you would be thirsty when you got back," said Grandma upon seeing us. As we partook of the refreshments, she asked about our day and we described for her the Grand Hotel and Fort Mackinac, but while I had enjoyed the memorial to Constance Fenimore Woolson the most, I let Aunt Louisa May mention it.

"I'll have to go see that myself," said Grandma. "I remember reading that book years ago; I never read another that so vividly described a northern winter. And I bet Constance Fenimore Woolson is one of the first female writers in this country to have a monument. When I was younger, I always wanted to be a female novelist myself, just like Louisa May Alcott."

"Ain't worth it," said Mr. Carter. "There's no money in writin'."

"I wouldn't mind being a writer," I stated, partly because it was true, partly to spite Mr. Carter.

"Don't be silly," he said. "Ya'd starve ta death in an attic."

"Robert can grow up to be anything he wants," said Grandma, "and writing is a noble profession."

"Hmm," mumbled Mr. Carter, unwilling to argue with Grandma.

"Well, I think I need a little nap before supper," said Mrs. Williams. "I hope you will all excuse me."

"Do you need any help?" asked my aunt.

"No, dear. You young people stay here and enjoy the beautiful afternoon."

Mr. Carter enjoyed himself by falling asleep in his chair. Aunt Louisa May and Grandma took out their never-ending knitting, while I went up to my room to find a book to read. I wanted to read *Anne*, but settled for rereading one of Eric's Tarzan books.

I didn't concentrate much on what I read. Yes, I had dabbled in writing a few plays for amusement, but after seeing Anne's Tablet, as I later learned the literary site was named, I suddenly felt the desire to be a professional writer. At that time, I envisioned fame and fortune as the rewards for writing fabulous books. I had no idea how many lonely hours of hard work it would require. Yet even now, I would do it all over again, for when I could divorce myself from the lonely outside world, I found nothing more satisfying than to create my fictional worlds and fill them with characters, and to hope that in doing so, I was modeling the real world and providing stories to inspire others. That evening, however, I sat pondering what I could possibly write about to win fame and fortune. I became so obsessed with wanting to write that I did not sleep half the night, even though I knew the next day, Aunt Louisa May, Mr. Carter, and I had agreed to walk all the way around the island, a walk of several miles.

The next day was equally gorgeous, the sun dazzling, the lake sparkling; the forest was rich and green, almost in defiance of the putrid trenches and booming cannons overseas. That day, the American Revolution and the War of 1812, fought around the Straits of Mackinac, was more real than the gas masks and air warfare in Europe. In this peaceful setting, it was difficult to believe any man would choose to kill another. Even with Mr. Carter's rattling tongue, I found the walk peaceful. In fact, I was surprised at how willingly Mr.

Carter plodded along the forested trails. I had never known him to be so amiable down South during his visits to my parents.

We were halfway around the island when lunchtime came. Aunt Louisa May was about to suggest we stop to eat when Mr. Carter exclaimed, "Look at that!"

"It's Arch Rock," said Aunt Louisa May. "Remember, Mrs. Williams told us about it. Isn't it magnificent?"

It was a giant rock with an enormous hole in it that framed the lake.

"I wonder what did that," I mused. "There's that little arched rock at Presque Isle, but it's right along the lake. The lake's far off from here."

"Glaciers did it," said Mr. Carter. As if he were a Harvard Ph.D. in geology, he lectured us on how the elements weathered rocks. Aunt Louisa May politely listened. I munched on my sandwich.

Then it happened. That strange occurrence that would happen to me many more times until it became a daily event. On this particular occasion, I saw Arch Rock. Then I saw an Indian walk through its arched opening. Then I saw a young lady on top of it. She was hiding from the Indian, who was pursuing her. He spotted her and began to scale the rock so he could capture her. She was trapped. She was too frightened to scramble down the rock. She screamed in terror as he reached the rock's summit. Then a shout! A British soldier tore through the forest! He told her to jump. She never would have had the courage if her hero did not promise to catch her. She had barely reached his safe arms and been set on her feet before the Indian pulled out his knife and jumped through the air, intent on stabbing the soldier, but the soldier jumped aside and caught the Indian's wrist in his arms. A struggle ensued while the girl stood helpless and terrified. The hero wrestled the Indian onto his back, and then grasped his wrist tighter until the brave was forced to drop his knife. The soldier struck several mighty blows to the Indian's skull until the Indian fell dead to the ground. The soldier grabbed the knife, and then took the girl's hand. Together they raced through the forest toward the fort, fearing the Indian's fellow braves would soon pursue them.

"Are you ready to go, Robert?"

"What?"

"Are you ready to go? Mr. Carter and I are done eating."

"What are ya doin'? Day-dreamin'?" asked Mr. Carter.

"No," I blushed. "I just didn't hear you. Yes, I'm ready to go."

I helped pack up the picnic basket. Then we started back down the trail. Mr. Carter and Aunt Louisa May began discussing the bird warbles they heard, but I was wondering whether the girl and the soldier had escaped the Indians, and why she was at the fort, and why the Indians wanted to kill her, and whether the soldier loved her, or he simply felt it his duty to protect her.

It was a silly, unoriginal, melodramatic plot, especially considering I knew nothing about the Indians or soldiers who had been on Mackinac Island. But it was the start of my first novel, and that evening I locked myself in my room and drew up an outline of the tale. It was a poorly constructed romance I would never publish, but nevertheless a historical literary event, for that was the day I decided I would become a world famous novelist.

Chapter 20

A Start

The next morning, Mr. Carter and Aunt Louisa May decided they would take a break from sightseeing. Mrs. Williams did not feel well, primarily from the heat, but Aunt Louisa May went to the drugstore to get her some medicine and run some other errands. Since we weren't going on an excursion, I decided it was the perfect opportunity to begin my illustrious writing career. At some point that morning, I heard the doorbell and knew Mr. Carter must have arrived, but I did not go downstairs. Instead, starting immediately after breakfast, I wrote steadily. I was impressed by my own diligence, yet disappointed that all my efforts only produced one chapter of ten pages, and not a very good chapter at that. I wrote until quarter after twelve, and then looked at the clock in surprise that no one had called me down to lunch. I set down my pencil, shook out my cramped hand, wiped the pencil smudges from my fingers, and went downstairs.

I found no one in the kitchen or dining room. I saw the sliding parlor doors were closed. Not knowing whether Mrs. Hobson or Mrs. Williams usually closed them, I thought nothing of sliding them open.

"Oh, my gosh, Robert, you startled me!" cried Grandma, laying her hand on her heart.

Mr. Carter jumped to his feet, less from surprise than to hide how closely he had been sitting beside Grandma on the sofa. But he was not so fast that I failed to see him pull his arm from behind her waist.

For a moment, I was speechless. So Grandma and Mr. Carter actually were carrying on a secret love affair!

"I'm sorry," I said. "I was just wondering when we were going to have lunch."

"Oh, my goodness," said Grandma, grabbing her knitting from off the coffee table. "I've been so busy knitting I lost track of the time. Is it noon already?"

"It's quarter after," I said, knowing full well she had not been knitting.

"Well, maybe we should wait for Louisa May," said Grandma.

"I wouldn't mind a sandwich myself," said Mr. Carter, getting up and heading for the kitchen.

I stared at Grandma. She cast her eyes down.

"I'll make you a sandwich, Barney," she said and rushed from the room.

The front door opened and Aunt Louisa May entered with a sack of groceries.

"Robert, will you take these into the kitchen? Tell Mother I'll be there to help her with lunch in a minute."

I hesitated a moment, wondering whether I should tell my aunt what I had seen, but then I heard the pounding of Mrs. Williams's cane on the stairs. I would keep my secret until a more opportune time.

"Robert, what did you do all morning?" Grandma asked at lunch.

"Read *Treasure Island*," I lied. I didn't even like Robert Louis Stevenson, but it was the first title that popped into my head. I shouldn't have lied to my grandmother, but I wanted to hide my writing until I had finished my novel, which I now realized was going to take a lot longer than I had expected. Nor did I feel guilty about lying—after all Grandma and Mr. Carter were keeping their own secret from me.

I never did mention to my aunt what I had seen, but in the days that followed, I spent many hours in the attic room, penning my novel. Often I would glance out the window to see my aunt sitting alone in the gazebo. Knowing Mrs. Williams was napping at those times, I imagine my aunt knew what I knew, so she was letting Grandma and Mr. Carter have the parlor to themselves. Perhaps Grandma and my aunt had even discussed it and decided I was too young to understand. They had no idea how much I already knew about love both from my declaration to Helen and from penning a fictitious romance upstairs while a real one unfolded below.

During those days, I often thought of Helen, debating whether I should write to her, even just to tell her I was writing a novel, but I was afraid that would only encourage her to think I was interested in her. If I did not write to her, cruel as it seemed, perhaps she would realize I had only made my profession of love under duress while she was suffering from grief. And why didn't she write to me? Mr. Williams was now her uncle so she could easily get the address.

Our third week on the island, Mrs. Hobson telegrammed that she and Eric would be arriving the day after next. Grandma told Mrs. Williams we would leave the day after Marie and Eric returned, but Mrs. Williams insisted we remain a few days after that to visit, and she assured me Eric would not mind sharing his room.

But I minded. How could I write a novel while sharing a room with a complete stranger? I had initially hoped Eric and I would be friends, but now I only wanted to write. I knew my novel was a complete mess, the writing atrocious, the plot going nowhere in some scenes and moving too quickly in others. I needed every minute possible to concentrate on improving it. I would rather be back in Marquette, in my own room, where I would have privacy to write. But then, of course, Helen or Tom would come to interrupt me. And once school started, when would I have time to write?

I went with Grandma and Mr. Carter to greet Eric and Mrs. Hobson at the dock. I recognized Eric the moment he stepped off the boat. He was a head taller than anyone else, terribly handsome with thick black hair that curled around his forehead. His mother smiled more than I had ever seen anyone smile as she held onto his arm and joyfully introduced us.

"Last time I saw you, Eric," said Grandma, "you were smaller than Robert is. I don't suppose you even remember me."

"I sure do," said Eric, in so deep a voice that Grandma looked flustered in a way I knew Mr. Carter had never flustered her. "I remember the wonderful cookies you gave me at your house when I was a boy."

Eric had a cane in his hand, and he leaned heavily on it as we walked up the dock, but it did not seem to slow him down, his long legs easily making up for the slowness in his step. He might be wounded, but he struck me as a great hero the way he smiled with disregard for his pain, just like the soldier in my novel, whom I now imagined looking like this real life war hero. But Eric also reminded me that my own father could be hurt or not return home at all. I would not care if my father came home blind or mangled so long as he returned. I began to understand what a blow Helen must have felt in losing her father. I did not know whether I could bear such a loss, especially when not even a year had passed since I lost my mother.

I almost broke into tears when Mrs. Williams saw us coming up the walk and actually ran down the front steps into her grandson's arms. Both forgot they needed canes as he scooped her up, clear off the ground.

"Eric, she'll lose her breath," Mrs. Hobson scolded, but she was smiling and crying together.

"I can do that just by looking at him," said Mrs. Williams. "He just keeps getting more handsome."

Eric laughed and helped her back up the steps.

"Let's go have breakfast," said Mrs. Hobson, and although we had already eaten, we all willingly gathered around the table for an early lunch of eggs, sausage, and toast.

"I'm glad to hear you'll all stay a few more days," said Eric. "It's good to see all of you. Robert, I hope you don't mind sharing a room with me."

"Not if you don't mind," I said. "It's your room."

He was a returned war hero! How could I mind? Think of the stories he could tell me—all material for my books, as well as letting me know what my father was going through in the war. But for now, Eric wanted us to catch him up on everything that had been happening on Mackinac Island, a place where nothing much happened compared to the war, and therefore, all the better to hear about.

I sat listening to everyone, finding I did not mind not writing. I was glad at least someone I knew had returned home safely from the war.

But when bedtime came, I lay on the spare cot in Eric's room while he put on his nightclothes in the bathroom. I tried to read, but I couldn't concentrate on my book. I was nervous to be alone with Eric, unsure what to say, afraid I might see his naked wounded leg.

When he came to bed, he had his nightshirt on so his legs were only visible from his knees down. I was relieved not to see a scar, although I heard him groan as he got into bed.

"Does your leg hurt much?" I asked. I instantly felt it a stupid question, but I did not know what else to say.

"Sometimes," he replied, "but mostly only if I move it quickly. It's more just weak than painful. And complaining won't change anything."

After he turned out the light, I felt brave enough to ask, "What is the war like?"

"Awful," he said. "You don't want to hear about it. Just hope you never have to fight in one."

He had a fatherly tone to his voice. He sounded protective toward me; his tone both hurt and comforted me when I had not heard my father's voice in so long. But I had a father, and Eric was not that many years older than me, so I decided to think of him more like a big brother. He asked me what I liked to do, and I confessed I liked to read and swim and have snowball fights. He listened to me as if I were an adult, not a boy. I felt I could trust him.

"What will you do now that you're out of the army?" I asked.

"I think I want to be a history teacher," he said. "I've always been interested in history, but after fighting in this war, it strikes me that humans have not learned from their past mistakes. I want to make sure this war isn't forgotten or glorified, and I want to educate people about it so it doesn't happen again."

"That's a good idea," I said. "I hope there's never another war."

"I think people will always have conflict because they're always afraid of each other. Most war is based on prejudice and the fear that someone else has something that deprives you of it. I want to teach people how to be tolerant and to understand one another to eliminate that fear. Then I think we can stop wars from happening."

I knew I was not as articulate as Eric, but I managed to confess, "That's a lot like what I want to do. I want to write books to make the world a better place. But," I said, afraid he would laugh at me as Mr. Carter had, "I know most people don't succeed as writers, so maybe I'll be a teacher instead."

"You seem very bright, Robert; if you work hard at it, there's no reason why you can't be a writer. Do you write now?"

"Yes," I confessed. "I'm writing my first book."

"That's impressive at your age," he said.

I was pleased, but too embarrassed to elaborate, so I asked, "Will you teach school here on Mackinac Island?"

"Maybe, but first I'll have to get a teaching degree. I thought maybe I would go to the Normal School in Marquette to do that—maybe stay with my Uncle John and Aunt Helen. Do you know them?"

"Sure," I said. "Your Aunt Helen is my girlfriend Helen's aunt." I had not thought to say that, had not even dared use the word "girlfriend" to refer to Helen in my own thoughts, but now I said it naturally because it needed to be said, and I felt safe saying it to Eric. And Eric did not sound surprised that I had a girlfriend. Instead, he asked what Helen was like. I told him everything about her. I told him about my fears and confused feelings, and finally, I asked his advice, certain I would get a better response than I had from Tom.

"You have a good heart, Robert," Eric replied, "and I know you don't want to hurt Helen, but you'll hurt her more by keeping the truth from her. You don't have to decide how you feel now. Just be honest with her that you don't yet know how you feel; maybe then, the two of you can talk it out. Keeping things from someone never makes those things better."

"I never thought of it that way," I said.

"Helen sounds like a smart girl," he replied. "She'll understand. Anyway, it's late, so we better get some sleep."

"All right. Good night," I said.

In another minute, I heard his breathing change, so I knew he was asleep. I was relieved to find he did not snore. For a little longer, I stayed awake, my soul feeling tempest-tossed, but I knew he was right—I had to tell Helen the truth. I was surprised it had taken me so long to realize it, yet thankful I had a friend to help me figure it out. I fell asleep hoping Eric would come to Marquette for school—it would be good to have another friend in Marquette if I stayed there after the war. I hoped—but I had hoped enough for one day, so I rolled over and went to sleep.

The next day, Eric and his mother went for a walk together. The doctors had ordered him to get plenty of exercise so his leg would not stiffen up or suffer paralysis. Mrs. Williams admitted she had been so excited to have Eric home that she had barely slept that night, so she went to take a midmorning nap. Aunt Louisa May went into the kitchen to bake Eric a "Welcome Home" cake. I would have gone upstairs to write, but since Mr. Carter had not yet appeared that morning, I decided to follow Grandma into the parlor where she instantly began knitting.

"Grandma, why don't you quit making those scarves for the soldiers?" I asked. "The war is going to be over before winter comes."

"I hope to God you're right," she said, her knitting needles not pausing for a second, "but ever since that archduke was assassinated four years ago, everyone keeps saying the war will soon be over, and it hasn't been soon yet. Until a peace treaty is signed, these fingers will stay busy."

"Well, Eric did tell me that getting things from home was always a highlight for the soldiers."

"See, and for all we know, one of my scarves might end up being used by your father, or your cousin Mark."

For a moment I thought of Mark, then pushed the evil thought from my head.

"Grandma, Eric wants to go to the Normal School in Marquette to become a teacher."

"Good. Teaching is a noble profession," said Grandma.

"He'll need a place to stay. He said he would ask his Uncle John and Aunt Helen, but I was wondering whether maybe he could stay with us—we do have that extra guest room."

She knitted a full half-minute before she said anything. I wondered whether she had heard me, or was she annoyed that I should expect her to be imposed upon?

"I imagine," she finally said, "that it's difficult for a young boy like you to live with only women."

I didn't know what to reply.

"Robert, I pray everyday your father will come home, but I'll admit I've been selfish and haven't prayed as much as I should have because when he comes home, I don't want you to go away."

"I've really enjoyed being with you, Grandma," I said, unsure what more to say.

"If Eric wants to stay with us," said Grandma, "I'm sure we'll find the room. But I was hoping maybe the guest room could be for your father. I was hoping maybe the two of you would come live with us permanently."

"Oh," I said, understanding and suddenly wanting the same.

"But I'll talk to Eric when he gets back and we'll arrange it. I can't presume to know what your father will want until he tells me."

I smiled. "Thank you, Grandma. Eric's a really swell guy. You won't regret it."

"I will if he's teaching you words like 'swell'."

"Sorry," I said. I almost added that I had picked the word up from Tom, but I would not incriminate anyone.

"Of course, we'll have to ask Louisa May whether she minds having Eric stay with us."

"I'll go help her bake the cake," I said, "to soften her up a bit before I ask."

Grandma smiled, then jumped up nervously when the doorbell rang. I let in Mr. Carter, who quickly made his way to the parlor while I joined my aunt in the kitchen.

"We could use a man around the house," said my aunt after I told her I would like Eric to stay with us. "There's always something that needs fixing."

I wanted to tell her I was the man around the house, but I was not going to argue if I were getting what I wanted. I understood Eric wouldn't play with me like Tom did, but I could use someone to ask for advice, and I was getting too old for playing anyway. I had serious things going on in my life now—a girlfriend, a novel to write, and trying to figure out how to convince my father we should stay in Marquette after the war.

"Go tell your grandmother I said it was all right," said Aunt Louisa May, "and considering the frosting you got all over last time you helped me, I can manage baking the cake on my own."

"Thanks, Aunt Louisa May," I said. "I'll tell Grandma, but then I'll come back to help you anyway; someone has to lick the frosting off the spoon."

But it was more than a minute before I returned to the kitchen. I had not shut the sliding parlor doors after me, and Mr. Carter had apparently been too nervous to think of it. He had good reason to be nervous since I found him down on one knee.

"Say ya will," he pleaded as I realized Grandma's right hand was clasped in both of his.

Grandma looked up as I started to speak her name. She blushed in embarrassment while Mr. Carter, unaware of my presence, went on with his lovemaking.

"Katy, I've loved ya for fifty years. Every single night of all those years I've wanted ta be with ya. I can't bear ta go back South and maybe never see ya again. Let's not waste any more time. Just say ya will."

"I don't know what to say," said Grandma, her face puffing up.

"Say yes, Grandma!" I told her.

And then tears burst from Grandma's eyes, and Mr. Carter, despite his rheumatism, got up and put his arms around her and pressed his lips to hers, and I shouted, "Aunt Louisa May, come quick!" and Grandma did not even push him away when her knitting fell on the floor, and my aunt came in to ask, "What's all the fuss?" and I said, "Look!" and pointed, and she looked, but she was too late to see the kissing, only Grandma's tears, but that was enough for her to understand. Aunt Louisa May rushed to Grandma, and Grandma jumped up and went into her arms, and Mr. Carter sat smiling, and at that moment, Eric and Mrs. Hobson came in, and many explanations followed so that Mrs. Williams woke up, saying it was too noisy for her to sleep, and Aunt Louisa May apologized to Eric that his homecoming cake would have to be an engagement party cake instead, and he only laughed, and Mrs. Williams asked what had happened, and we all let Mr. Carter explain it, and he took twice as long as he should have with his stammering Southern drawl, and all the while, Grandma looked at him with puppy love in her eyes.

Plenty was celebrated that day. Eric was home from the war and going to become a teacher. Grandma and Mr. Carter were to be married. And secretly, I celebrated that I was going to become an author. Now if only my father would come home, everything would be perfect.

Chapter 21

Changes

Summer vacation only had a few days left by the time we returned to Marquette. Our first day back, Mr. Carter took Grandma out and bought her an engagement ring with a tremendous diamond. Grandma insisted she didn't need a ring at all, but Mr. Carter said, "Aftuh all these years, if I'm gonna get married, I'm gonna do it right," and since he wanted to go down South to Marble Hill before the wedding, he added, "And while I'm away, I don't want any men thinkin' you're a free woman."

Grandma told him he was talking foolish, but I could see she was flattered by his devotion. Mr. Carter's Model-T had barely disappeared down the street to head South before she was running to all the neighbors' houses to show off her engagement ring. Aunt Louisa May declared she had never seen her mother act so happy and carefree. And when Grandma got the Mitchell sisters to go shopping with her, she came home with quite a youthful looking wedding gown.

"I know it's my second wedding," she said, "but it's Barney's first so I want everything perfect for his sake."

That first day we were back, I visited Tom so I could fetch Pumpkin and get the key to Aunt Carolina's house. I could have gone to see Helen that day, but I didn't. Aunt Louisa May went to tell John Williams that his nephew would be moving to Marquette in a few weeks, so I imagined his wife would tell Mrs. Lawson we were back home, and then Helen would come looking for me before I knew what I would say to her.

When I got home from Tom's house, I went to sit on the front porch, still feeling tired from the long trip back to Marquette. I tried to read a book, but I found myself instead imagining what I would say to Helen. I had not written to her once from Mackinac Island—nor had I written to Tom, but that wasn't the same thing. Nor had Helen written to me. Part of me wanted to see her—to tell her all about Mackinac Island, especially Anne's Tablet and that I had started to write my first novel, although I did not think it yet good enough to show her. But mostly, I tried to think how I would explain my feelings to her. Eric had told me it would be wrong not to tell her the truth, and I knew he was right, but I did not know what words to use, and I was afraid she would cry or be angry, no matter what I said.

And then I saw Helen walking up the sidewalk. If she had not seen me at the same moment, I think I would have bolted inside and pretended not to be home, but instead, I awkwardly walked down the front steps to meet her.

"Hello," I said, surprised by my clear voice although I trembled inside.

"Hello, Robert," she said.

"Do you want to come sit on the swing?" Not waiting for an answer, I went back up the steps, assuming she would follow. I could feel my legs weaken at the thought of what I would say.

"Thanks," she said. She followed me onto the porch and then sat beside me, which only made the situation more awkward.

After a moment, as I struggled to find my courage, Helen said, "Robert, I missed you."

I didn't know what to say to that. I could feel my will power failing.

"I missed you too," I said.

Then I steeled my nerves, prepared for the wrath of a woman scorned. I knew she would lash out at me, telling me I was selfish not to have written to her, telling me I was like everyone else who had failed to love her. But she said nothing. I could feel myself sweating although it was a cool day. 'Helen, say something!' my pounding heart begged. Tell me you hate me! Tell me you love me! Tell me anything, anything. Just say something! I can't bear this silence! Such agonizing, murdering, extremely silent silence.

"Robert, I'm sorry," she said. "I didn't mean to make you say you loved me. I know I manipulated you. I'm sorry. I was so lonely that day my father died. I know you only want to be friends. You never gave me reason to think otherwise. Please forgive me."

"Helen, are you sure? I thought you'd be mad at me." I was surprised by how easy she was making this for me.

"No," she said. "I've just been stupid. And when you didn't write me from Mackinac Island, I knew you were trying to avoid me."

"I did miss you," I said. "I wished all the time you were there, so I could share with you all the wonderful things I was seeing. I just didn't know how to explain the way I felt—I think I just want us to be friends."

"That's sweet that you missed me," she replied. "You're a good friend, and I don't want to lose our friendship. Do you forgive me?"

"Of course, if you can forgive me for not being honest with you."

"Yes," she said. "I was just so stupid. I thought no one cared about me so I tried to attach myself to you. But since my father died, Aunt Elaine has been wonderful, and Uncle John and Aunt Helen have let me visit them overnight and taken me for drives and bought me ice cream. These last few weeks have actually been some of the happiest of my life, except that you weren't here to see how well I was doing."

I was touched that she had wanted to share her happiness with me, and I was simply glad that she was happy.

"I think we're too young yet to know about love," I said. "Maybe someday when we're older, we can try again, but for now we should just be friends."

I was not totally sure I would want to try again when we were older, but I would leave that to the future.

"Can we go over to your Aunt Carolina's house?" asked Helen.

"Sure," I said.

On the way to the house, I told Helen all about Mackinac Island. She was impressed to hear I had been inside the Grand Hotel, and pleased to learn of Grandma and Mr. Carter's engagement, but of course, her greatest interest was the memorial tablet to Constance Fenimore Woolson.

"Oh, I wish I had been there," said Helen. "To think I've been to Mackinac Island and I didn't even know it was there. On the way home, we'll have to stop at the library to see whether they have any of Woolson's books. Oh, by the way, Robert, while you were gone I started to write a novel. I've already got one hundred and ten pages done."

"Really?" I laughed. "I started writing one too. But I've only written about eighty pages. Mine is about Mackinac Island in the colonial period when the British held the fort there."

"Mine was going to be based on my dad's life, since I really miss him, but once I started, it didn't turn out to be much about him. It's about a soldier who comes home from the war to find the world he knew changed, but changed for the better. I figure if I can't have my father come home for real, I can pretend he did in my writing."

I thought about my new friendship with Eric; I was going to suggest she talk to him about what it was like to return home from the war, but first I had to ask the more important question.

"Does anyone know you're writing a book?"

"Mags knows I scribble, but she doesn't know what I'm writing. I don't think anyone would understand."

"I know what you mean. Grandma and my aunt would understand, but I'm still too shy to tell them. One day I commented that I wanted to be an author, and Mr. Carter told me I would end up starving in an attic."

"I would write even if it meant starving," said Helen. "I can always work at something else and write on the side until I can support myself just by writing."

I was going to say that she could always get married and then write while her husband supported her, but I thought marriage would be a good subject to avoid.

We had now arrived at Aunt Carolina's house. As I turned the key in the door, I said, "It's a good thing we're busy writing novels since once the war is over, Mark and Eliza will be living here again, and then we won't be able to perform our plays."

"It seems such a waste that they'll live here," said Helen. "I don't dislike Eliza, but I can't imagine Mark really appreciates this house."

"I doubt it too," I said, "but let's just enjoy the house while we can."

It turned out to be our last happy day there. Grandma received a telegram that afternoon that Eliza was returning on the train tomorrow. But it was a fine last day. Helen and I ran about, sacrilegiously sliding down the banisters, acting out scenes of gothic gore and intrigue in Aunt Carolina's inner sanctum library. We laughed continually and enjoyed ourselves so much it was almost as if the awkward words of love had never been spoken between us—even if they remained buried in our hearts.

Eliza came to visit us with her mother the day after she returned to Marquette. I was relieved that spending a summer with Mark's snobbish relatives had not changed her sweet nature. She congratulated Grandma on her pending nuptials, joking that now Marquette would have two young brides.

Eric arrived in town a few days later, although he did stay with his Uncle John and Aunt Helen. I still saw him frequently, and with Grandma and Mr.

Carter getting married, I agreed that they did not need a fifth person in the house. However, Mr. Carter refused to be indecorous and live with Grandma before they were wed, so he put himself up again at the Hotel Marquette, then spent his time walking about town, getting to know everyone and having supper with us each evening. He quickly befriended the Lewis brothers, who were thrilled to have a new ear to listen to their stories, and unlike Aunt Carolina, Mr. Carter didn't blink an eye when they told him to drink pickle juice for his rheumatism.

Despite his eccentricity, or perhaps because of it, Mr. Carter soon endeared himself to all our little circle. The only exception was at Aunt Louisa May's birthday party that fall when Florence Mitchell told Mr. Carter he was the epitome of everything that was wrong with men.

"Maybe so," he replied, "but I've found a woman ta love me, and I don't see any men wearin' their hearts on their sleeves for you."

Florence opened her mouth, trying to find words to reply, but she was so surprised to have someone talk back to her that she could only formulate little growling sounds in her throat, which made Mr. Carter add, "I know a good horse doctor that can help ya with that whinny of yours."

At this remark, Roger Mitchell laughed so hard he spit coffee out of his nose. While Roger wiped his face with his handkerchief, Florence told him, "You should be ashamed to let that beast of a man talk to your sister like that."

But before Roger could speak, Mary Mitchell put her hand on her sister's arm and said, "Florence, I think you've had it coming for a long time now. Sit down and forget about it." Florence opened her mouth to reply, but when the whinny sound burst out again, she grew pale and sat down, humbled at last. A week later, her tongue was sharp again, but never quite so sharp.

I pass over most of the autumn—dreading to think back on all those days of conjugating Latin verbs at school—until that tremendous day, November 11, 1918, when the peace treaty was signed. Marquette's citizens poured out into the streets, shouting with jubilation and relief. After years of sacrificing, crying, worrying, writing letters, knitting scarves for the soldiers, planting victory gardens, and more than anything, praying for peace and the safety of our men, the war was finally over. Fathers, brothers, sons were coming home! Yes, I knew that meant Mark would soon be holding Eliza in his arms again, but I tried to block that thought out by imagining the joy of my father's return, of us all being together as a family.

"Maybe your father will be home by Christmas," said Grandma one afternoon when Helen and I were in the kitchen eating her freshly baked cookies. "Barney and I will hold off the wedding until then so he can give me away."

"Grandma," I asked, "do you think Dad will make me leave in the middle of the school year so we can move back to South Carolina?"

Helen stopped munching on her cookies. We both nervously awaited Grandma's answer.

"I don't know, Robert. I didn't say anything earlier because I didn't want to get your hopes up, but I wrote to your father a month ago, telling him Barney and I were getting married, and I suggested the two of you should live in Marquette permanently, but he's never replied."

"We'll just have to wait and hope for the best," said Aunt Louisa May.

"He probably won't want to live here," I said, trying not to raise my hopes. "He's from the South, so he won't like the cold winters."

"I'll do all I can to convince him otherwise," Grandma promised. "I have yet to meet a man who isn't afraid of his mother-in-law."

Thanksgiving came, marking one year since I had arrived in Marquette. This year I did feel thankful. I would never quit missing my mother, but I had gained so many new friends. That Thanksgiving was different from the last. Aunt Carolina was not there to make a show, but Mr. Carter replaced her with his odd humor. The Lewis brothers came and told their dull stories. Florence Mitchell managed not to snap at anyone, but she still fussed about most things. The Williams came, along with old Mrs. Williams and Mrs. Hobson, who had risked traveling in inclement weather to spend the holiday with their family. The Hamptons arrived at the same time as the Lawsons, and I could almost swear I saw Tom and Mags holding hands when they passed through the door. And like the previous year, Eliza and her mother were absent, but this year, Eliza did not come to make excuses.

Dinner was fabulous, as was every dinner I think my grandmother ever made. We ate until we were stuffed, then lingered at the table to talk. Even at that time, I think I was aware of the wealth of comfort in those large family gatherings, storing the memories up to use in my future books. A family meal exudes a warmth, a sense of safety and belonging not to be found anywhere else, and despite all the fussing that went into the meal, and all the cleaning up afterwards, that moment when everyone is stuffed and content and beaming at everyone else, even though it may last only a minute, is worth it all.

And it did last only a minute that day. We were just about to start clearing the table when the doorbell rang. I ran to answer it, hoping it was my father—come home already, come to surprise us.

But it was Eliza on the front porch, her face pale. She had been crying. Then I saw her mother beside her, pushing Eliza inside; then Mrs. Graham brushed past me to go into the dining room. I looked at Eliza, afraid to ask what was wrong.

"Kathleen," I heard Mrs. Graham say, "I'm sorry to ruin your gathering." Some of the women had started clearing the table already, so she said, "Please, would everyone sit down." They did as they were told, all stunned by her somber face as I stepped into the doorway to listen. Mrs. Hampton had already gone into the kitchen and when Mrs. Graham saw this, she said, "Robert, please ask Jane to come here."

But Mrs. Hampton had heard and come into the dining room. She could not get past the Lewis brothers to her chair.

"Jane, sit down please," said Mrs. Graham.

Initially, I had feared Mrs. Graham knew something terrible about my father—that he would not be coming home—I could not think of anything else that could cause her somber tone—but when Grandma got up to give Mrs. Hampton her chair, I realized what had happened.

"I'm so sorry to ruin everyone's holiday. We didn't come earlier for dinner because we just got a telegram from the government. They didn't tell us much, but—"

"My boy!" cried Mrs. Hampton. It was more than a cry. Aunt Louisa May grabbed her before she fainted sideways from her chair.

Grandma ran to get her water.

"What is it?" asked Mary Mitchell. "Is he?"

"Yes," said Mrs. Graham. "Mark died in an army hospital of pneumonia he caught in the trenches in France."

Later, I would think it ironic that Mark did not die a true hero's death, not being killed in action, but dying of pneumonia, the same disease that had killed my mother. Today, I see the childishness of my enmity toward Mark. I also feel that his willingness to fight for his country made him a hero. I understand that now—after all, he was my cousin and I respect his memory—but at that moment, I felt confused, sad for his grieving parents and brother, and sad for Eliza, although in her case, I could not help thinking it was for the best.

I remember watching Mr. Hampton talking to his wife, making her drink the glass of water, patting her hand, telling her she had to live, that he and Tom needed her. I remember putting my own arm around Tom's shoulder to comfort him. Terrible as my own grief had been over my mother's death, at least grief takes over your whole being—it is devastating, but not as awkward as standing by helplessly, unable to relieve the hurt of others. Finally, Mr. Hampton told his wife they should go home. He was a brave man, hiding his own pain to console her.

I hugged Tom goodbye, as did Helen, feeling again her own father's death and wanting to console him. Mags hugged Tom and even kissed his cheek, yet he was in no mood to use her affection to his advantage. The party broke up soon after that. The Mitchell sisters stayed to help with the dishes and then departed last of all. Mr. Carter remained to talk with Grandma, but I went up to my room to kneel and pray that my father would come home.

The following morning, Grandma and I went over to the Grahams' house with a sympathy card and Thanksgiving leftovers.

Grandma went into the kitchen to help Mrs. Graham spread out food for all the guests who would be coming over.

"Robert," said Grandma, "why don't you go into the living room and give Eliza the card from us."

I was afraid to confront the newly widowed woman. What would I say to her? But I did not want to be rude and ignore her grief.

"Hello, Robert," she said upon seeing me. "How are you?"

I was surprised by her welcoming voice, despite the handkerchief she clutched in her hands, a sign she had been crying.

"I'm really sorry to hear about Mark," I said.

"Thank you."

"Here, we brought you a card," I handed it to her, and then retreated to sit down on the opposite side of the room. "Grandma's helping your mom lay out some food for when company comes over. The Hamptons called us to say they would be here soon."

"Thank you," she said.

"Do you know what Jane Hampton said to me?" asked Mrs. Graham. Her voice drifted in from the kitchen; she sounded angry.

"No, what?" asked Grandma.

"She said that even though Mark and Eliza were only married for a few months, since Eliza was Mark's wife, they want her to keep Carolina's house anyway. As if they have any right to give it to her. Of course it's Eliza's. She'll live there the rest of her life I imagine. And in a year or two, if she wants to remarry and live there with her second husband, it's none of their business is what I say."

Eliza's face fell. I was embarrassed for her. I imagined Mrs. Hampton had only been trying to assure the Grahams they would not have any problems, but Mrs. Graham, in her stress over Mark's death, was overreacting.

I felt sorry for Eliza, to think she would now live in that enormous house alone. I had idealized it as a wonderful, happy playhouse, but now with a grieving widow inside it, a cloud settled over its wonder.

"I imagine you're looking forward to your father coming home?" said Eliza, probably to drown out her mother's words.

"Yes," I said, "although I don't know when that will be yet."

"I hope it's soon," said Eliza. "The war has brought enough unhappiness without it having to be prolonged any longer."

I heard the front door open. The Lawsons came with banana bread, and the Hamptons came right behind them. A flood of callers soon filled the house. I stayed away from Eliza the rest of the day. I talked to Tom some, but we didn't mention Mark. I decided that since Tom had lost his brother, I would be a brother to him now.

I can't pretend that I felt any real sorrow over Mark's death. Later I realized I had never gotten the chance to know him, and I wondered whether had he lived, when we were older, perhaps at age thirty or forty, we might have been friends. But any thoughts I had, any sense that I should feel guilt or sorrow, were soon forgotten when a letter arrived a couple days later.

"Robert, it's from your father," said Grandma, bursting into my bedroom so that I did not even have time to hide the manuscript of my novel; she was so excited she did not notice I was writing, and I had already planned to say I was doing homework if I were ever caught.

"Hurry, tell me what it says," she insisted as my fingers fumbled with the envelope. Quickly, I ripped it open, unfolded the letter and read aloud.

Dear Robert,

As you must know, the war is now over. Thanks be to God for it! I hope to be home very soon, by Christmas if possible. Much work is still to be done, but I got special permission for early leave. I am looking forward to seeing all of you and should arrive in Marquette in the next couple weeks. Give my love to your Grandma, Mr. Carter, and your aunt. I've missed you so much, Robert, and I can't wait to make up for all the time we've been apart.

Love, Dad

"That's sure a short letter," said Grandma. "He didn't even mention my suggestion that you move to Marquette."

"Maybe he just wanted to wait until he gets here to talk about it," I said. I was exhilarated that he was coming home, but I was also bewildered to think my life would soon change again.

"Well, let's just be glad he's safe," said Grandma.

And then I unexpectedly found myself crying. Grandma instantly buried me in her arms. We seemed to hold each other for a long time, and I know her eyes were not dry when she released me.

"It's been a long hard wait," she said, "but it's almost over now."

We went downstairs to tell Aunt Louisa May and Mr. Carter the news.

"Thank God he's safe," said Aunt Louisa May.

"And we'll get married as soon as he's here," said Mr. Carter, giving Grandma a peck on the cheek, which still made her blush.

December passed away quickly. The usual holiday bustle, confusion, and cheer occupied us. But even when the week of Christmas arrived, we heard no further word from my father. No letter, no telegram, no telephone call. Every morning I woke up, hoping I would find him downstairs. I lay awake for hours each night wishing the doorbell would ring. I began to fear something had happened to him, some terrible accident while he was traveling to Marquette, and with the Christmas season near, I did not think I could bear another tragedy.

When Christmas Eve arrived, I think even Pumpkin was depressed— either that or Mr. Carter had fed him too much of Grandma's fruitcake. I couldn't even look at the fruitcake. I was heartsick. I wished we could put off Christmas for another week or two until my dad came home.

"It'll seem like Christmas when he does come," said my aunt, "even if it's not until February."

"He'll come home, Robert," Helen told me when she stopped by to bring over another fruitcake her mother had made for us. "I know he will. You've always been luckier than me." Rather than console me, those words only made me feel selfish.

We went to Midnight Mass. As we sat in the pew waiting for the service to begin, I anxiously looked at every face, hoping to see my father there searching for us. As we walked home, I glanced at every vehicle that passed by, in case it was him on his way home. When we reached the house, I went right upstairs and crawled into bed, only able to sleep because my disappointment weighed so heavily on me.

"Robert, aren't you going to get up?" asked Grandma, shaking me in the early morning hours. "It's almost eight o'clock. Don't you want to see what Santa Claus brought you?"

"I don't care," I growled.

"Robert, you're not going to have that attitude in my house," Grandma stated. "You're going to come downstairs and have a Merry Christmas whether you want to or not. Now hurry up and get dressed. Breakfast will be ready in five minutes."

I had no choice but to obey although I felt I could have slept until the New Year. I quickly got dressed, leaving my bed to be made later.

As I started down the stairs, I heard some whispering below, and then a man's voice, and I knew it wasn't Mr. Carter's. Could it be—then I remembered that Grandma had invited Eric to have breakfast with us.

"Merry Christmas, Robert!" shouted Eric as I went into the parlor. But it wasn't Eric. Instead, a strange bearded man stood in front of the Christmas tree.

"Dad!" I shouted.

I had never seen him with a beard. He would shave it off that afternoon so I would never see him with one again. But I remember how his beard rubbed against my cheek as I held him tightly. I thought I was dreaming. I had dreamt this dream before, and the dream was only worse now that I was dreaming he would arrive on Christmas morning. I waited to wake up crying as I had done before. His absence had hurt that much all the while he was gone, although I had never admitted it to anyone.

Only, this wasn't a dream. My father had finally come home!

Once Dad released me, Grandma, Aunt Louisa May, and Mr. Carter were all laughing and slapping my father on the back and then pulling us into the dining room to eat, and Dad was sitting there beside me, and constantly reaching over to muss my hair.

"He only just came two minutes before I went upstairs to wake you," Grandma said.

I just kept looking at him, not believing it, and yet happier than I had ever felt before.

Everyone started talking at once. Our eggs and coffee were cold before we had said half the things we wanted to say. Eric came by, late for breakfast, and was astonished by our guest. I introduced my father to Eric, and they shook hands with great cheer and started talking about where they had been stationed, while Aunt Louisa May cooked up a whole new batch of eggs for all of us.

I don't know how we ate anything. We all just kept talking at once. I told my father all about Marquette, and my friends, and Grandma told about the trip to Mackinac Island, and Mr. Carter told how he had proposed to Grandma, and Eric talked about his plans to teach, and I told Dad about my plans to write—everyone looked astonished at this revelation—but even Mr. Carter only smiled and said, "The boy's got a good head on his shoulders."

That morning, I thought my father's homecoming was the best Christmas present I could receive.

But that afternoon, before all the company came over for supper, Dad and I went upstairs and sat quietly in my room for an hour. He sat down on the bed with me and asked me about Mama's last days, and then we cried and held each other. And I told him it was all right now, because he was home, and he promised he would never leave me again no matter what might happen.

And then when all the tears were wiped away, and we saw from the clock that the guests would be coming for dinner in a few minutes, he said to me, "Robert, now that Mr. Carter is moving here, and your mother is gone, we really don't have any close family or friends left in South Carolina."

I did not say anything, anticipating, but fearful I would not hear what I wanted.

"What would you think," asked my father, "if we moved to Marquette?"

He had already gotten up from the bed. In fact, he was at the door, the doorknob in his hand, about to exit. But I jumped up and ran to him again, and throwing my arms around him, I said, "Dad, I never want to leave here. I want to live here forever. I think Marquette is the best place in the world!"

PART II

1926-1934

Chapter 22

Catching Up

"It's too bad it has to rain on their wedding day," said Dad, straightening his tie. "I remember the day I married your mother was a gorgeous day, full of sunshine, but even if it had rained, I wouldn't have noticed; your mother was so beautiful I don't think I saw anything else that day."

"Mama was always beautiful," I agreed. "Are you ready to go, Dad?"

"Ready," he said. "You can drive. Let's see whether we can beat your grandparents to the church."

We went out onto the porch, and I shut the front door behind us. Dad had bought the house for us the summer after he returned from the war; we had wanted to give Grandma and Grandpa Carter, as I now called him, their own space, although Aunt Louisa May stayed behind to keep house for them, when Grandma would let her help. Once Dad and I had our own place, Eric came to live with us while he finished school, so it was three bachelors, hanging out and having a good time together. Eric stayed until he graduated and found a job teaching history in the Marquette schools. During those years, he was like an older brother to me, and a second son to Dad. But Eric had eventually wanted his own place.

"It's a good thing I bought this new suit," said Dad as we got into the car. "I'll need it for your graduation anyway. I still can't believe you're all grown up and almost done with college. Do you think you're going to like teaching English?"

"I think so," I said, pulling the car out onto the street, "but I'll keep writing as well. Eventually, I hope to support myself just by my writing."

"I'm sure you'll be a writer yet," said Dad. "That book you just finished astonishes me at how good it is. A publisher's bound to pick it up."

My great ambition was no longer any secret. I had already sent my first two novels to publishers, only to collect rejection letters; however, I felt the book I had just finished reflected a new maturity in my style. I was confident this book would make it, but it took time to publish and sell a book, so teaching would pay the bills until then, and I was going to have bills to pay once Helen and I set up housekeeping together.

Yes, Helen and I were going to be married. She had a year left before she would finish her own degree, and we would marry once she was done. In the meantime, I helped my dad with odd carpentry jobs—he had contracted to build houses when he moved to Marquette—and Helen worked part-time at the Peter White Public Library. We wanted to save all we could so when we did marry, we could move into our own house, although Dad kept insisting we could stay with him.

Tom and Mags laughed at us, waiting to finish college and worrying about money. Neither of them had gone to college, and they had a meager income, but they managed. Mags had worked in a department store since she graduated from high school, while Tom helped my dad and me with carpentry work. Mr. Hampton wanted his son to become a lawyer like himself, but Tom wanted no part of that. Eliza had suggested giving up Aunt Carolina's house for Mags and Tom to live in since their children would carry on the family line, but Mags refused any form of charity, saying, "No, we'll stand on our own two feet or go to the poor farm." Dad got Tom a deal on some cheap lumber for building a house, so Tom bought a small lot in North Marquette in one of the new residential areas near the Normal School. All spring and summer, Mags and Tom had pounded nails and raised walls. And now that they had a home of their own, they were ready to become Mr. and Mrs. Tom Hampton.

Dad and I arrived at St. John the Baptist's Church just in time to be hit by the thunderstorm's climax. Soaked to our skin, we found the pew where my grandparents sat with Aunt Louisa May, who clutched her handkerchief, fully anticipating tears of joy. Dad found a seat beside my aunt, while I went in search of Tom.

"How's my best man?" Tom asked when I found him in a back room of the church.

"Fine," I said. "How are you? Nervous?"

"Naw!" he said, trying to comb his hair with a trembling hand.

"Let me help you," I said. I took the comb and managed to keep his cowlick from sticking up after much effort.

"Have you seen Mags yet?" Tom asked.

"No, but Helen told me she looks ravishing in her wedding dress."

"She always looks ravishing to me," said Tom. "Can't believe someone that beautiful wants anything to do with funny lookin' ole me."

"After all the years you chased her, she knows no other man will be so devoted."

"I hope she's in a good mood. She hates fussing about her clothes—I don't want that dress to make her cranky."

"She'll probably make an exception today."

"She warned me I better not smear her lipstick when I kiss her in front of everyone."

Laughing, I said, "Remember that first time you kissed her? How she shouted that men were awful and then yanked Helen down the street from fear I would do the same to her."

"Yeah," said Tom, but he did not laugh. He was nervously watching the clock.

"It's time, Tom," said Eric, popping his head in the door.

"All right," Tom said, dazed and stumbling over the carpet as he left the room, followed by Eric and me. He found his place in front of the altar. Eric and I, as his groomsmen, went to the back of the church, then started down the aisle, Helen on my arm, Mary Lawson on Eric's.

The wedding march began. Down the aisle came Mr. Lawson linked arm-in-arm with his daughter Mags, the vision of a perfect lady in her mother's eyes—although had we been able to see beneath her veil, she was probably grimacing from the tightness or itchiness of her dress. We were all very proud of her for behaving so well that day, and Tom was right—she did look ravishing. Tom was never exactly handsome, but he was the perfect husband for her—appreciative of what he was getting, his eyes adoring her throughout the ceremony and the reception that followed.

That night, Tom and Mags were the happiest couple in the reception hall, but other couples were nearly as happy. Helen and I shared many dances together, and Eric had Mary Lawson on his arm all night. Even the brightest man can become weak for a pretty face, and while I thought Mary as spoiled as ever, despite the thirteen years difference between them, her face had won Eric's heart. Helen confessed to me that Mary had said she thought Eric "sexy" because of his limp, and she clearly worshipped him, speaking in a meek voice when he was near, no matter how demanding she was at other times. Neither Mrs. Lawson nor Mrs. Hobson found any reason to frown on the relationship. Eric had his own house in Marquette, and one day he would own the house on Mackinac Island as well, which Mrs. Lawson was already referring to as "my daughter's future summer cottage" when she bragged to friends of her daughter's engagement. No one was surprised when a month later, directly after Mary's graduation from high school, Eric and Mary also wed to the envy of Marquette's young ladies, and to the advantage of its young men, who had difficulty enough finding courage to ask out a beautiful girl without having to be bitten by her sharp tongue when she rejected them. I can say that Mary made a wise choice in her husband, and over the years her temper softened and she became a good wife to Eric.

Only Mollie Lawson now remained single of the three Lawson girls, and she declared she would not marry for a long time to come. She was still plain looking, yet she ignored the couple boys who expressed interest in her. Her mother warned her she would be an old maid, but she said she would rather be a spinster than some man's slave. She endeared herself to my aunt by that remark, although my aunt told her women were no longer slaves now that they had the vote. "They still are in marriage," Mollie replied. At Tom and Mags's wedding, she preferred to sit in the corner with Eliza Hampton, widow, rather than dance with the eligible bachelors. I never did understand her, yet if I were not writing my own life story, perhaps I would have written hers for it ended up being perhaps even more interesting.

As for the rest of our friends, several things had changed. When Mrs. Williams had died, Mrs. Hobson had moved to Marquette to be near her son and brother, while renting out the house on Mackinac Island. She refused to live with Eric but instead found herself an apartment in the new Hutter Flats. Both the Lewis brothers had passed away, Charles following James by just a day. As for the Mitchells, each had aged, but their dispositions remained unchanged.

All summer, following their wedding, Tom and Mags seemed enormously happy. Then in the autumn, they decided they would start inviting friends over for dinner, and soon they were the most hospitable couple in Marquette, which surprised me since Mags could barely cook and was not at all domestic. Dad and I were invited over at least once a week, and if it weren't the two of us, it was Helen and I, or Mr. and Mrs. Lawson, or Mr. and Mrs. Hampton, or Eric and Mary. I soon realized the newlywed Hamptons never spent a single evening alone together. One night, apparently Eliza and Mrs. Graham canceled an invitation to dinner, so Tom asked Helen and I to come over; when I told him we already had plans to go to the opera house, he begged me, confessing he would be miserable if he spent all evening alone with his wife. When I asked why, he added, "We have nothing to talk about. We don't read. All we do is stare at each other." I laughed and told him winter was coming and then they could just have snowball fights, but he didn't find that amusing. Instead, he said he was worn out doing everything—that Mags would not do a lick of the cooking or cleaning. She had warned him before they married that she wouldn't cook, but he had not expected her to refuse housework. Every morning when he left for work, he suggested she sweep the floor or dust the living room, but she would reply that she felt sick and then go back to bed.

After he complained to me several days in a row, I finally told Grandma what was happening between them.

"Never mind, Robert," she said. "I'll take care of it." She went over to visit Mags that afternoon, although I would not know the result of the conversation for several more weeks.

I have neglected to mention Eliza yet in this update. Yes, she was a widow, but she did not seem to mind. Aunt Carolina's money had left her financially set for life. She had become involved in several women's organizations, focusing on fundraising for charities. But what made her equally happy was continuing Aunt Carolina's annual Christmas parties at the Ridge Street mansion. Those Christmas parties were some of the merriest I've ever known, far surpassing the ones Aunt Carolina had hosted. Instead of community leaders and snobs, Eliza invited friends, who actually used the time to enjoy themselves rather than to network for social advancement.

But during that year's Christmas party, Tom and Mags had their first major fight when he repeatedly asked her to dance with him and she refused.

"No!" she finally shouted so all the room heard her. "No, Tom!"

"Why not?" he asked. "I'm your husband."

"It—it won't be good for the baby."

And then she burst into tears, fully embarrassed, but everyone else broke into laughter, and Grandma winked at me; I then understood what had been said between her and Mags.

Mags continued to cry, even when her mother and Mrs. Hampton congratulated her and said how excited they would be to have their first grandchild.

"But I don't want babies!" said Mags. "Being married didn't seem so bad, but I'm not fit to be a mother. What girl wants a tomboy for a mother?"

Tom kissed her on the cheek and told her she would be the finest mother a girl ever had, and who was to say it would be a girl and not a boy, and what boy wouldn't love a mom like her? Later, he told me he had convinced Mags she would be a perfect mother since her own mother had taught her how not to raise a child.

Mary chose that same moment to announce that she and Eric were expecting, which caused Mrs. Lawson nearly to faint at the thought of two grandchildren, and Mrs. Hobson became so excited she trembled for the next hour.

"Mary's just as spiteful as ever, trying to steal my thunder," Mags whispered to Helen. "I'm going to be a wonderful mother now, if only to prove I can do better than her."

I should have been very pleased for all my friends, but I felt a little sad that they were all so happy while Helen and I were still waiting for our happiness. That night, when I drove Helen home, I suggested that maybe we shouldn't wait to marry, but she replied, "No, we agreed to wait until we both finished college and could support ourselves. We have the rest of our lives to spend together so there's no sense rushing, and I would wait all my life for you, Robert O'Neill."

Such loving comments were sometimes all that kept me going that winter. I had graduated, but I'd had no success in finding a teaching position. I barely even got to substitute teach more than a few times a month. I helped my father in the fall, but in winter, no carpentry work existed for us. Then I spent the days in my bedroom, writing, sending out my novels and short stories, and continually collecting rejection letters until I felt more and more useless. Yet Helen never once doubted I would succeed.

Then on Helen's twenty-second birthday, I came home from a day of substitute teaching, feeling more depressed than ever. I had been called to teach art classes that day; the kids had been unruly, and I felt my education a waste just so I could teach finger painting. I could not even raise my spirits by thinking about the birthday party that evening, and I was afraid my low spirits would ruin the party for Helen.

"Robert, there's a letter for you on the dining room table," Dad said when he heard me come in the front door.

"Thanks, I'll open it later. I have to go change my clothes," I shouted back, heading toward the stairs.

"I think you'll want to open it now," he replied.

Annoyed, I went into the dining room. I picked up the letter and instantly saw it was from a publishing company. Another rejection letter, I figured, but curiously, the envelope was small, not a large one containing my manuscript. Thinking a rejection letter was the last thing I needed today, I ripped open the envelope.

A full minute passed before I realized my father was behind me, reading over my shoulder. Then his hand squeezed my arm and he said, "Congratulations."

My book had been accepted! Enclosed was a check for a small advancement and a contract to sign. I was requested to contact the publisher upon receipt of the letter. But those were just minor details. What mattered was that I, Robert O'Neill, was going to be a published author! After beginning to fear I would die before I realized my dream, now it was manifesting before my eyes. I felt dazed, as if the entire world had changed. After years of writing and hard work, it suddenly had become easy; it seemed so impossible to believe my good luck.

"Congratulations," Dad repeated while I stared at the letter in awe.

"Thanks," I said.

"I knew it would happen for you. Soon you'll have written enough books to fill an entire shelf of the Peter White Library."

"Dad, this means—it means—Helen and I can get married now."

"I know," said Dad, and then he gave me a bear hug. "Why don't you tell her tonight? Surprise her."

"I will," I said.

"Hurry up now. We're supposed to be there by five o'clock."

I changed my clothes and was back downstairs in five minutes.

"Do you have the ring?" Dad asked.

"In my pocket," I smiled, patting the breast of my suit. I had bought the ring months before, without telling Helen, waiting for the appropriate moment to present it to her. I had longed to give it to her. I could not believe the moment had now finally come.

When we arrived, Helen was greeting her guests and feeling awkward as the center of attention. She would have preferred helping out in the kitchen to playing hostess.

"Robert, I'm so glad you're here," she whispered, rolling her eyes, "Aunt Elaine has fussed over me all day, but she won't dare to with you here to protect me. You and your father go sit on the sofa and save me a place between my two favorite gentlemen."

I was powerless to object; I was her prisoner of love that night. I quickly obeyed, then acted more jovial toward everyone than I had ever done before because I was under her spell. I did not know when the magical moment would come, but I was keeping my eyes open for it. When Eliza and her mother arrived, I remember thinking Eliza was still beautiful, perhaps having grown more so as the years passed, yet it was Helen only whom I now loved. I watched Helen warmly greet each guest, despite her discomfort; someday soon, she would make a splendid hostess in our own home.

When Helen came to sit beside me, I could barely restrain myself from grabbing her in my arms, but I let a peck on the cheek suffice before Grandpa Carter started quizzing her.

"So, Helen, how does it feel ta be twenty-two?" he asked.

"Not much different than twenty-one," she replied.

"But there is a difference," I said, taking her hand in mine. "Every year you become more lovely."

"Oh, Robert." She squeezed my hand. No longer was she that lonely, unloved, little girl, but a brave, proud woman, willing to wait forever for me, unaware the wait was now over.

I would have claimed her that moment, but Mrs. Lawson shouted, "You can all come and eat!"

Aunt Louisa May came into the parlor and shooed us all into the dining room. I ended up seated between Helen and Florence Mitchell. I was so elated I was nearly ready to tell Florence she looked lovely that night, even after she snapped at me for not paying attention when she tried to pass me the potatoes. I was paying attention—to Helen plopping potato salad on her plate in the most adorable way potato salad had ever been plopped. Everything tasted like ambrosia that night, and when I told Mrs. Lawson so, she blushed while Tom raised his eyebrows as if I were nuts and Dad beamed and winked.

"Elaine, let me help you clear the dishes," offered my aunt when supper was finished. "Then you can get the cake."

Mary and Florence Mitchell had a little tiff over trying to light all the birthday candles without burning their fingers—but after all, there were twenty-two candles. When Helen blew them all out in one great puff, Grandpa Carter said, "Ya sure ya wouldn't like bein' a hot air balloon instead of a teacher?" Helen was the only one to laugh at his sorry joke, but this kindness made me love her all the more. Then he asked what she had wished for, but she refused to tell from fear it wouldn't come true.

"Let me help with the dishes," Helen said when the cake was eaten.

"No," said Mollie. "We'll do the dishes later. You open your presents."

Mrs. Lawson carried the gifts to the table.

"I want to open yours last, Robert," Helen whispered, squeezing my hand under the table. "Yours are always the best."

Helen's Uncle John and Aunt Helen gave her green bedroom slippers. The Mitchells gave her salt and pepper shakers, "for when you and Robert set up housekeeping." Oh, little did they suspect how soon that would be! Helen's Aunt Elaine gave her a new dress. She got knitting needles from Aunt Louisa May, who was determined to teach her to make sweaters. Grandma and Grandpa Carter gave her books, and Mags and Tom gave her a necklace.

The last present was from me, and I felt how inadequate it was for the woman I loved, although I knew she would love it, if only because it came from me.

"You did a good job wrapping it this time," Helen said while struggling with the tape.

"What is it?" asked Grandpa Carter as she finally pulled off the paper.

"*The Man in the Brown Suit* by Agatha Christie," said Helen, holding it up for everyone to see.

"I never heard of her," said Mrs. Graham.

"You haven't?" said Helen. "Why Agatha Christie's the greatest murder mystery writer of all time."

"Murder mysteries!" gasped Florence Mitchell. "How can you read such dreadful books? You young people have no sense of morality these days."

"We have morals," I said, not wanting her snappish tongue to ruin Helen's birthday.

"How can you say that?" Florence continued. "Look at the young people these days! Girls wear skirts cut above their knees, just like dance hall hussies, and that new dance everyone is doing; why it's just disgusting."

"You mean the Charleston?" asked Mary Mitchell. "I think it looks like fun."

"Yes, the Charleston," said Florence. "They do it in those Chicago nightclubs, same places where the mafia commits all those murders just like in that book you got. It's just dreadful how society is falling apart ever since the war."

"Florence, have you actually read any of Agatha Christie's books?" Grandma asked.

"No, I wouldn't taint my brain with them," said Florence.

"If you haven't read them," said Grandma, "then how do you know whether they're horrid or not? If anything, they are moral because they explore why people commit crimes, and the criminals are always caught and punished."

"Robert also gave me a pair of earrings," said Helen, lifting them up to stem the argument.

"Those are just lovely, Helen," said Aunt Louisa May. "They'll go perfectly with your new dress."

"Now that the presents are open," said Mary Mitchell, "I'll help with the dishes."

"Wait a minute," I spoke up. "I have one more present for Helen."

"Oh, Robert," said Helen. "You shouldn't have. You know we're trying to save money, and we—"

But when I went down on one knee, her face froze and she could not speak.

I pulled the box from my pocket, opened it, took her precious white hand in my own, slid on the ring, then pressed her hand to my lips.

"Helen, I could never deserve a woman as wonderful as you, but if you'll have me, I'd be honored to call you my wife. Will you marry me?"

"Oh, Robert," she said, tears forming in her eyes, "but—but I thought that we—"

"We don't have to wait any longer," I said. "I just found out today that my novel has been accepted for publication."

Everyone let out a murmur of congratulations, but I paid attention only to Helen.

"Oh, Robert," Helen said, "that's wonderful. It's—"

"But are you going to say 'yes'?" I demanded. A man can only bear so much suspense.

"Yes, I'll marry you," she said.

Everyone cheered as I stood up. Then I whispered in her ear, "I love you," and kissed her lips, oblivious to the crowd of well-wishers.

"Well," said Florence Mitchell, although I think this time she was only half-serious, "such a scene in front of everyone. Wasn't I right? Young people don't know what's proper anymore."

"Maybe not!" Tom laughed, "but we sure know how ta kiss." And grabbing a very pregnant Mags, he pressed his lips to hers.

Chapter 23

A Wedding and a Honeymoon

"I'm so happy for both of you," said Mollie, on the front steps of St. John's, following the wedding.

"You make a beautiful couple," said Grandma.

"I hope you'll both be very happy," said Mary Mitchell.

Congratulations followed from strangers neither Helen or I knew, but whom her Aunt Elaine had invited so we would get more gifts. We had let Mrs. Lawson arrange the wedding since she had done so well arranging Mags and Mary's ceremonies, and Helen and I would not have cared if we were married in a stable and had no reception, so long as we were together.

"We'll meet you at the reception," said Dad, walking Aunt Louisa May to his car.

"Okay," I said.

Eliza told my wife, "You're so lucky, Helen. Robert is more handsome than even Mark was."

What a surprise after all these years that Eliza should think me attractive. But she'd had her chance. Now her charms were powerless over me.

"We better get going," I said to Helen. "I want to spend some time alone with you before the reception."

"Wait!" said Mags. "You can't leave until Helen throws the bouquet."

"Here goes!" cried Helen, once all the women had gathered at the foot of the church steps. She turned around and sent it flying over her shoulders.

"All right, Mrs. Hampton!" a boy hollered.

But when we all looked, it was not Tom's mother, nor Mags, but the other Mrs. Hampton, Eliza Hampton, who had caught the bouquet and stood, looking embarrassed.

"I didn't even try to catch it—I just—it nearly hit me in the eye so I had no choice," she laughed. "I was hoping Mollie would catch it."

"I don't want it," said Mollie. "I'm never getting married."

"Helen, it's a good thing you're going to be a teacher," said Grandpa Carter, "cause you'd sure make a lousy baseball pitcher."

"Come on, let's go," I said, aching to be alone in the car with my wife where I could kiss her to my heart's content.

We had hired a driver to take us around town and then out to Presque Isle where the wedding photos would be taken. The driver must have seen many weddings because he did not blink an eye as we drove away from the church, me kissing every inch of Helen until she pushed me away, laughing and scolding that I was mussing her dress.

"I'm sorry," I said, "but we've waited so long I'm just overcome knowing this day has now arrived. Are you happy?"

"I couldn't be happier," she said. "As a child I was always so depressed I never dreamt this much happiness was possible."

"I used to worry about you because of that," I said, "but now I'm happy making you happy. I feel like the happiest man in the world."

"I'll do my best to love you and be a good wife," she promised.

"I know," I replied. "I don't deserve someone as wonderful as you."

I will spare the reader the rest of the conversation since it is probably nauseating to anyone but me. Suffice to say, we were filled with joy, and on that drive, we planned for the future, where we would live, what would we do, how many children we would have, and what we would name them. Now when I look at the black and white photos we had taken that day at Presque Isle, they look so cold compared to the bliss I remember.

After the photographs were taken, we drove to the other end of Presque Isle where our reception was being held at the Pavilion.

"It's about time ya two got here," said Tom at the door. "I was beginnin' ta think ya might just go straight to the hotel, Helen, the way Robert was lookin' at ya durin' the ceremony."

My bride only laughed while I punched my best man in the arm.

"Helen, it's a beautiful wedding cake. Come see it," said Mags, ready to yank Helen away from me, but the cries of her baby boy pulled Mags away herself.

"He sure can scream for only two months," Tom beamed, "and he's so big I just know he's going to be a football player."

"I wish he was grown up already," said Mags, taking him from Mrs. Lawson's arms. "I'm so tired of changing diapers. Enjoy today, Helen, because here's what'll soon be in store for you."

"Not yet, I hope," I said, squeezing Helen's waist. "I want to keep her all to myself for a little while."

By now we had been spotted by a roomful of people. Soon all the guests began to mob us.

"There the two of you are," said Grandma. "I'm so happy for you both, and I'm just chomping at the bit to have great-grandchildren."

"It won't be too soon," I repeated.

"How're ya enjoyin' married life?" asked Grandpa Carter.

"It's wonderful," I said. "I doubt I'll ever be unhappy again."

"You will be," said Florence Mitchell, stepping up to us. "Life works that way."

Mary Mitchell said, "You'll be fine just so long as you help one another."

"Listen to Mary acting as if she knows anything about marriage," laughed her brother.

Once everyone had given us their congratulations, we sat down to dinner, complete with a three tiered wedding cake. At some point, we finally finished eating, and then began the dancing. I know I danced that night with Grandma, my aunt, Mrs. Lawson, and Mags, but all the while, if Helen were not in my arms, I had my eyes glued to her. I have never seen anyone so beautiful as my wife was that night. I wish I could have captured her forever like that. We were so drunk on love I felt as if I were in a fairy tale, with all my future days to be lived happily ever after.

Somehow Helen and I made it to the Clifton Hotel to spend our wedding night, and then in the morning, we got up early so Dad and my aunt could take us to the train station to leave on our honeymoon.

"Thank you for the honeymoon, Aunt Louisa May," said Helen, hugging her.

"Well, I doubt I'll ever have one of my own, so I wanted to spend the money on the two of you."

"No one could have a better aunt," I said, kissing her cheek.

"When you get back," said Dad. "We'll find you two a house."

"Thanks, Dad, but we can find one on our own," I replied.

"No, your aunt and I have been saving for years, and we're determined to help you out."

"Thanks, Dad," said Helen, kissing his cheek.

I was not going to argue further, although I wanted to be self-sufficient. We could think about it after the honeymoon.

The train ride was the longest I had been on since my first trip to Marquette from South Carolina with Aunt Louisa May. We were seeing the country, all the way to New York. Then we embarked on a ship to take us to our honeymoon destination of England.

"It'll be such a nice long voyage to London," said Helen, settling into our stateroom. "Think of all the books we can read."

"I hope we do more than just read," I said.

"You need to work on your next novel."

"Not on my honeymoon," I smiled.

"I feel almost guilty being away so long when Aunt Elaine depends on me, and she only has Mollie at home now."

"Too bad," I said. "She'll have to get used to you not being there because you have a terribly selfish husband who wants you with him all the time."

Every day of that journey was better than the next. I had known Helen for years, but only now, when I was living with her each moment, did I get to know all her endearing little ways. I loved to watch her sleep. I would purposely wake early so I could sit in the chair and watch her cheeks puff as she breathed, her chest rise and fall, her eyelids flutter as they stirred awake. And once she woke, I would crawl back into bed beside her. I loved how thoughtful she was, how she would iron my pajamas, how she would set out my toothbrush for me, how in the dining hall, she would always say I was the most handsome man in the room. I never once felt I deserved such happiness, such love from her, and the only sad thought I could have would be to lose her. I tried in every manner to please her. Sometimes in the evenings when we read, she would set down her book and write a little—poetry she told me, and finally, when I asked to read it, I found they were love poems about me. "No one will ever read them but you," she said, "because no one else would believe you're as wonderful as you really are."

And then we arrived in England—we had come to find the land of English literature, and we were not disappointed. After taking the train to London and checking into our hotel, we scarcely rested a minute. We walked through Westminster Abbey, and filled with goose bumps as we stood over Dickens's grave in Poet's Corner. We went to the British Museum to see the Elgin marbles Keats had written about, we toured the Tower of London, and we saw the changing of the guard. We walked through Kensington Gardens and stood outside J.M. Barrie's house for an hour, wondering whether we dared knock on his door, and then seeing a shadow in the window that we were convinced was him, we went back to the hotel, filled with glee. Finally, we went to Dickens's house, and when we saw his laundry room, we wished we could have done his laundry just for a second to be near the great man.

Then westward we went—goggling at Windsor Castle, visiting Winchester to tour the cathedral, to lay flowers on Jane Austen's grave. In Bath, we had high tea in the Pump Room, recalling our favorite scenes from *Northanger Abbey*, and laid more flowers on the grave of Fanny Burney. Then it was north, to Stratford-on-Avon, visiting the bard's birthplace and watching a play of *A Midsummer Night's Dream*, a play I nearly felt I was living because I was so intoxicated by Helen's presence. Then to the Lake District, to Grasmere, the home of Wordsworth, where we fully understood how the poet had felt as if he were one with Nature, for we felt the same when we walked beside Lake Windermere. Finally, we went to York, to visit the Bronte Parsonage, to stand on the moors by Penistone Crag and quote from *Wuthering Heights*, surrounded by heather, rain pouring down upon us, and laughing far more than Emily Bronte would have approved.

All too soon it was back to London and then on to home, reinvigorated with aspirations to write great books in our little attic rooms in Marquette. On the return voyage, it rained constantly, so we cuddled in bed, drinking Earl Grey tea, reading Trollope, dreaming of our future life together. The reader may find all this happiness tedious, but yet I wish it to every reader; those moments became for me more Wordsworthian "spots of time" to sustain me during difficulties to come.

On a cold, drizzling October day, we returned to Marquette, thinking the gray, dark looking town the most beautiful place we had ever seen and perfect for a married couple beginning their life together.

Dad met us at the train station and brought us directly to his house, where he informed us we were to unpack and make ourselves at home.

"I'm going to stay with your grandparents and aunt until you can get yourselves a place of your own," he said. "I've already moved what I need over there, so no arguing. You newlyweds don't need me in your way. Once spring comes, we'll see about building you a house of your own."

I was too tired from the journey to argue, and Helen accepted his offer before I could object.

Blessed. Happy. Lucky. Loved. We were all these. With such a family and Helen as my partner for life, I could not be otherwise. Life was everything I could ever want it to be.

Chapter 24

Marriage

Christmas 1927. Surrounded by family and friends, Helen and I enjoyed a magical holiday season in keeping with everything that was wonderful in our lives. Following Eliza's splendid Christmas Eve party, we spent the holiday itself at Grandma's house, with both our families. But the best moment of Christmas was when we returned home that evening, and I built a fire for us to sit in front of, wrapped in each others' arms, completely content together.

"Our families are so good to us, Robert," said Helen, her cheek against mine, "but even if we had nothing but one another, I think I would be eternally happy."

"Then you'll always be happy," I promised, "because I'll never leave you."

"Just think, Robert; by this time next year, I bet you'll be famous. I can't wait to find out how your book sold during the Christmas season. I bet you're a household name across the nation now."

"If I make enough money to put a down payment on a house, I'll be happy," I replied.

Rather than build a home, we decided to buy one. We had looked at several in the weeks leading up to Christmas, but only the day after did we find one little ramshackle house, only two upstairs bedrooms, a little kitchen and a living room. The house was the smallest we could imagine, definitely all we could afford, but perfect for just the two of us.

"It'll need a lot of work," said Aunt Louisa May.

"We'll have it fixed up in no time," Dad said.

Dad, Tom, and I devoted every minute of that week to making repairs. Helen insisted the spare bedroom be my study. I wanted her to take it, but she had been offered a teaching position when another teacher had left the school to have a baby, and the school system wanted to keep Helen on permanently. "I'll be the breadwinner until your royalties start to roll in," she said. I tried to keep my masculine ego in check, promising I would do my best to become a famous writer so she could quit teaching and write as well. Yet, for her to earn mere money was a cruel reason to keep me parted from my wife most of the day. Helen painted the study blue, and in return, I graciously consented to our bedroom being pink, although Grandma gave me a hard time over it— remembering how I had complained about my first bedroom in Marquette. After pausing to celebrate the New Year, we planned to move into our house on January 2nd.

Eliza had been particularly generous at entertaining that year and insisted on a New Year's Eve party as well as her Christmas Eve party. Helen and I were a bit envious that our new home wasn't like the giant playhouse of our childhood, yet we never could refuse an invitation to Aunt Carolina's old mansion.

At the party, as we were standing beside the staircase drinking eggnog, I said to Helen, "Quick, while no one's looking, let's slide down the banister."

"Oh no, Robert," Helen laughed. "I'm afraid it would break under my weight now."

"Why, you're as light as a feather," I said, and to prove it, I set down my drink and picked her up from behind so her cheek was level with my lips.

She giggled, but was embarrassed when Eliza, who had partly overheard us, came up to ask, "What are you going to break?"

Perhaps something was in the eggnog, although it was still prohibition time. I imagine I was just drunk on love again for I confessed, "We're afraid we'll break the banister if we slide down it. That summer you let me watch the house, Helen and I used to come over and slide down the banister all the time."

"Mark and I," Eliza smiled, "slid down it many times until his grandmother caught us. You can imagine the terror we felt then."

"Definitely," I said. "Aunt Carolina was always a bit frightening."

"Well, I'm glad you two enjoyed the house that summer."

"I don't think," said Helen, "that Robert and I would have gotten together if we hadn't spent that summer playing inside this house."

"It should have children playing in it," said Eliza. "I never will understand why fate chose to leave me a childless widow in this giant house."

"You're still young, Eliza," I said. "You'll find someone yet to love."

"No, I'm content now to make others happy by throwing parties and helping anyone I can."

"Hey, Eliza!" Tom shouted from the parlor. "When's the music gonna start? Mags and I wanna Charleston."

"I'll have to make sure Florence Mitchell is out of sight first," Eliza whispered to me before going to fulfill Tom's request.

We young people soon were dancing, and none of the older generation said a word about it—if they had, it would have only been from envy. Florence Mitchell watched without a word, but I did see her poke her sister in the ribs for tapping her feet to the music.

Then came my and Helen's first fight. We were moving furniture into the house. Outside was a blizzard, and having to wear coat and boots, and strain under the weight of the furniture, I was shivering and sweating at once, and consequently, a little cranky. When Dad and I placed the sofa in three different places, and Helen still could not decide where she wanted it, I'm afraid I lost my temper.

"Until you make up your mind for good, it's staying in the middle of the room!" I said.

Helen looked at me in dismay. Instantly I regretted my words.

"Helen, dear," said Aunt Louisa May, trying to make peace, "come help me unpack the dishes while we let the men take a break."

My wife and aunt went into the kitchen. I felt like a heel. Dad said nothing. I went outside in a fury, mad at myself for losing my temper; in my anger, I picked up a marble table, far too heavy for me to carry alone, lugged it inside, then straightened my back, feeling I had broken it, then went outside and held in my tears of self-loathing. When I went back inside, Dad was resting on the sofa. My aunt returned into the living room to say Helen was making supper, and the sofa was to go against the wall. Dad and I moved it there, where it seemed to leer accusingly at me. During supper, only a few awkward words were said. My aunt offered to help wash the dishes, but Helen insisted she could do them and that my dad and aunt should go home to rest. Sensing it best to leave Helen and me alone, they soon departed, abandoning the beauty to her beast.

"Helen, I'm sorry. I—"

But she ran upstairs and slammed the bedroom door before I could say another word.

I wished Dad had stayed. He would have known whether I should go after her or let her anger cool. Then I felt angry—how dare she run away from me like that? After all, she had been the thoughtless one not to consider how tired Dad and I were because she had been indecisive over the sofa.

I decided I would not go upstairs. I decided she was as much at fault as me. I sat down on the stupid sofa, in perfect view of the stairs. She would have to come down eventually, and I would be sitting there, waiting for an apology. That lasted a minute. Then I ran up the stairs, pounded madly at the door, threatened even to break it down if she would not open it. I shouted that I was the worst man in the world, and she a princess, and I hated myself, and she could come out and slap me and call me names, if only she would open the door. I vowed impossible promises to be the perfect husband from that day on.

And then I was smart enough to try the door and find it was not locked.

I went to the bed. She lay facedown in the pillow.

"Helen, please," I begged, preparing to lie down beside her.

"Go away, Robert," she said, turning over, swinging out her arm to wave me away, not realizing I was leaning over her.

SMACK! She struck me in the nose!

"Oh, Robert, I'm so sorry!" She looked horrified.

It hurt terribly, but my tears expressed relief that she was speaking to me.

"Helen, can you forgive me?"

"If you can forgive me for slapping you. I didn't mean to."

"I know," I said. "It's all my fault. I shouldn't have lost my temper."

"I should have been more considerate," she replied.

I don't know how in all the years we had gone together, we had never had such a terrible fight before—but I loved it for the joy of making up. It was a wonderfully new, excruciatingly exquisite feeling to go from the low of despair to the blissful warmth of her unconditional love—to know even if I were a bit of a beast, she would not leave me. Yet everyday after that, I kept that beast caged in.

We settled down now, happy as we formed a daily routine. Helen taught each day while I stayed home to write. I found writing so exhilarating when it went well, yet other days I felt exhausted, not from effort but from writer's block. I always felt energetic after five or six hours of pouring my soul onto paper. Then I would make supper while Helen came home and graded papers. After we ate, I did the dishes so she could plan her classes for the next day or spend a couple hours doing her own writing, although she usually reserved that for the weekends. We made a life this way, and a living.

My first book's sales were disappointing, but the publisher was willing to take a chance on a second book, so I worked furiously to finish it. We lived primarily on Helen's income while my meager royalties covered groceries. We had little money for extras, but we occasionally entertained our friends and felt grateful when we were their guests. My grandparents invited us over frequently, as did Helen's two aunts and my father; occasionally, Eliza would have a dinner party, inviting all the young couples. Once a week we were regularly invited to Tom and Mags's house, and we were constant guests at Eric and Mary's table; Eric and I enjoyed a strong friendship, while Helen tried not to let Mary's superiority complex annoy her. Only when Mary had a baby and would talk about nothing else did Helen find it difficult to be around her, for by then, we wanted a child of our own.

Many evenings, when the dishes were done, and Helen had no more papers to grade, we would just sit together, my head on her shoulder as we listened to records. Sometimes, I would read her a chapter or two of the novel I was working on while she lay with her head in my lap; I would stroke her hair with one hand while holding a page with the other.

These were peaceful, idyllic times for us until we seriously began to wonder when we would have a child. At Christmas 1928, Grandma remarked she wasn't getting any younger and hoped her great-grandchildren would be coming soon. The remark caused Helen to burst into tears. Grandma quickly apologized, although Helen told her it was not necessary. Peace was restored, but we were starting to fear we would never be parents. We were afraid even to discuss it with one another since we felt awful enough when other people mentioned it to us. Mags told us bluntly, "Count yourselves lucky. Not that I don't love my kids, but two of them, only a year apart, is too much, and I'm sick of cleaning diapers. I'm sure Tom will be a good father when the boys are old enough to run around, but he's not much help now." When Helen told her I would be a good father from the start, Mags said, "Humph, all men are alike when it comes to child-raising—they leave it to the women." Tom did admit to me he wished his children would quit startling him awake at night with their constant screams. Yet Helen and I would have paid to lose sleep at night. To us, a child would be the ultimate expression of our love.

The publication of my second novel in the spring of 1929 finally brought me some recognition in the book world. My novel was reviewed in newspapers across the nation, and the local *Mining Journal* ran a feature story on me. The only reason I had to be more proud was when Helen had a little book of poems accepted for publication the next year. Our emerging literary careers made us feel financially stable now, and once children were granted to us, we thought we would move into a bigger house. But that same spring, Helen began to complain she was tired. I feared she was overworking herself between writing and teaching, but she insisted she was just being lazy.

After a couple weeks, I found her seriously ill one morning and insisted she not go to school but let me take her to the doctor.

I waited patiently for over an hour in the doctor's waiting room. When she finally came out, she looked pale, and I grew frightened, but she refused to say anything until we were alone in the car.

"Tell me what's wrong?" I insisted.

"Robert, you're going to be a father," she said. I was dumbfounded, as if she had spoken a foreign language. And then her paleness, which must have come from being stunned that her dream was to become reality, was replaced by a smile.

"Robert, aren't you going to say anything?"

"I love you," I said. "When is it due?"

"Late October."

I was ecstatic. Rather than go home, we drove to my grandparents' house to tell them their great-grandchild was on its way. I had not thought I could be happier than I already was just being married to Helen, but now—I can't even now after so many years find words to describe my joy.

Chapter 25

Autumn

October 1929! A glorious month, destined to make Helen and I the proudest of all parents.

"I finished my novel this afternoon," said Helen one evening at supper.

"That's wonderful," I said. "Now you have to promise you'll rest until the baby comes."

"I can't just sit around the house, Robert. Who's going to do the housework?"

She was due in a couple weeks, and the doctor had ordered her to stay in bed and take it easy; she had quit teaching for the time being, and I absolutely refused to let her do any housework, but even if it meant lying on her back in bed, she was too obstinate to lay down her pen.

"I wish you would at least let me do the cooking," she said. "I know Aunt Louisa May means well, but I hate her always running over with dishes every night."

"It's either that or suffering through my cooking," I smiled. "Besides, that's what family is for; it makes my aunt happy to do it, and it gives us more time together."

"I'm not an invalid," she said. "You worry too much, Robert."

"Only because I love you."

We finished supper without any more fussing—she knew I would not give way. When she offered to wash the dishes, I only frowned until she said, "Fine," and went into the living room to put up her feet and read the newspaper.

When I joined her later, she showed me the day's headlines.

"Isn't it horrible?" she said. "Millions were lost on the stock market today. It's the biggest financial crash in history."

"It's too bad," I said. "I'm glad we didn't have millions to lose."

"Analysts are predicting this will send the nation into a depression."

"I don't think we have to worry," I replied. "All our money is safe in the bank, not in stocks. We have a pretty good income now and with my next book coming out and your poems being published in the spring, we should be comfortable. I'm sure the baby will have everything it needs."

"I don't know," said Helen. "If a depression comes, no one will have money to buy our books."

"Let's not worry about it until it happens. Let's go on with reading Dickens."

We started reading aloud from *Our Mutual Friend*, taking turns with the different characters' dialogues, still encouraging the dramatic side of our personalities. We were just finishing that unhappy scene where the Lammles, newlywed, each in the belief the other is rich, each secretly poor, undeceive one another. I thought how foolish the characters were to value money so much when loving one another would get them further. I vividly remember those final paragraphs, the sound of Helen's voice speaking the wife's lines, then my turning the page to go on to the next paragraph when the telephone rang.

Helen moved to answer it, but refusing to let her get up, I rushed to the phone.

"Robert?" said my aunt.

"Hi, Aunt Louisa May. How are you?"

"Listen, Robert, there's been some kind of tragedy. I don't know what it is, but your grandparents are very upset. I just called your father but he's not answering his phone. Can you come over right away? Maybe they'll tell you what's going on."

"All right," I said, her tone made me unwilling to waste time asking further questions.

"I'm going with you," said Helen when I explained the situation. "They're like grandparents to me as well, and if there's trouble, I want to know, not sit home in dread."

"Helen, if it's something truly bad, it might not be good for the baby if you—"

"Robert, will you quit fussing at me? It was endearing at first, but now it's becoming annoying."

I never heard Helen say harsher words to me, and if she had not been pregnant and worried about my grandparents, I doubt she would have even said those. Knowing she would win if we argued, I fetched her coat and put her shoes on her while she remained seated. Then I put on my own coat and shoes and walked her to the car.

On the way, I tried to imagine what could be wrong—did one of my grandparents have a serious health problem? They were in their mid-seventies now—I knew I could lose them at any time, although I tried not to think about that, but rather focused on the pleasure I would soon know of their seeing their newborn great-grandchild. I didn't dare speculate out loud what might be wrong with them from fear of upsetting Helen.

When we reached the house, I was relieved to see my dad coming up the sidewalk. My aunt must have gotten ahold of him after she called us.

"Do you have any idea what could be wrong?" I asked him after knocking on the door and waiting for my aunt to answer.

"No," he said. "I'm almost afraid to know."

My aunt let us in the door, shook her head to show she still knew nothing, then led us into the parlor where Grandma sat on the sofa, her arm wrapped around Grandpa Carter, seated beside her. He was slumped back on the sofa, wringing his hands. He raised his head when we entered, then lowered it again like a puppy that knows it has been naughty and awaits its punishment.

"Grandma, what's wrong?" I asked.

Helen sat down at my aunt's insistence while Dad and I stood to await dreadful news.

"Ruined," muttered Mr. Carter. "I've ruined us all."

"What has he done?" I asked Grandma.

"He lost some money in the stock market," she said. "It's nothing to be too concerned about."

"How much money?" asked Dad, while Aunt Louisa May covered her mouth. Her reaction recalled to my mind the newspaper headlines that day.

"It's not enough to worry over," said Grandma. "Please, just all of you go home."

But now that his secret was out, Grandpa Carter could not stand the guilt and told all.

"Every penny I had practically," said Mr. Carter. "I don't think any of ya know just how rich I really am—or was. I inherited thousands from my pa, and when I sold Marble Hill ta move up here, I invested every penny from that property, and it jus' kep' growin'. I know I never appeared ta have that much, but when a man don't have any family, he ain't got much need ta show off, so I jus' kep' savin' and hopin' someday I'd have someone ta care for. Then ya came along, Katy," he said, taking Grandma's hand, "and not havin' children of my own, I began ta think of y'all as family."

"We are your family," said Aunt Louisa May.

"So I wanted ta leave y'all comfortable when I'm gone, so I kep' investin' and tryin' ta make it grow, and added more ta it from my regular income and now—now it's all gone like that 'cause of a crash on Wall Street."

"It doesn't matter, Barney," said Grandma. "We've lived without it all these years. We can live on my income."

"But ya let me invest lots of that too," he said. "Ya trusted me with it, Katy."

"I still trust you, Barney. You didn't do it on purpose—it's not your fault if the financial world has come tumbling down. I know I gave you a lot of money to invest, but—"

"Mother, how much?" asked my father. "You were already on a fixed income before you married Mr. Carter. You can't expect to support the two of you and Louisa May on it, and if part of it is now gone—"

"Don't worry about me," said Aunt Louisa May. "I have my own fortune that Aunt Abigail left me—remember, Cynthia and I both inherited equal shares of her fortune. That money is very safe in government bonds and gold and other investments."

"Cynthia and I," said my dad, "used her inheritance from Aunt Abigail to buy our land and build a home. That house was sold to buy our house here, so I have nothing extra."

"I saved nearly every penny of mine," said my aunt. "It's far more than I'll need for the rest of my life."

"I'm not touchin' Weesa May's money," said Grandpa Carter. "We won't steal from our own young'uns."

I could not resist smiling—Aunt Louisa May was far from a young'un. To keep from laughing I said, "Helen and I can help too."

"Of course," said Helen, "we'll all pull together."

I was proud of Helen for saying so. We had a child coming, yet we were all family.

"Mr. Carter," said my dad, "did you invest in anything perfectly secure, or even hide some in a safe or sew some into a mattress. You know stocks and even banks aren't reliable always. You must remember the panics back in '73 and '93."

"I was goin' ta pull the money out when I thought we had enough," said Mr. Carter, "which I figured would be in a couple more years."

"John," Grandma said to my father, "forget the panics of '73 and '93; Barney and I saw far worse times than those when the Yankees wreaked havoc on the South, burning our homes and crops and leaving us to starve. That war taught me to be prepared."

I had never heard a pinch of a Southern accent in Grandma's voice, but now as she recalled the hard years of her youth, she sounded almost as if she had traveled back in time.

"I learned," she said, "that God helps those who help themselves. Plenty a night I thought I'd starve ta death, when if I hadn't hid food from the Yankees, we'd have had nothin', when if I hadn't hid the family silver in the well the slaves woulda run off with it, or the Yankees confiscated it, and when my mama was on her death bed and could do nothin'—and when if I hadn't had my head about me, I probably woulda dissolved inta grief over her sickness and not thought about the future—why if I hadn't had my head about me, I woulda starved right then and there, but I didn't 'cause I was clever, far more clever than those damn Yankee soldiers was. And after that, why I vowed I'd never find myself unprepared for anything. Tomorrow mornin', why we'll just go out in the backyard and do a little diggin'."

"What are you talking about, Mother?" asked Aunt Louisa May.

"I mean that ever since I married your father, Louisa May, I've saved nearly every penny I ever had, and I put them in old metal cans, and buried them around the yard. Why there's gotta be a thousand dollars in Indian head pennies alone beneath the maple tree. You didn't really think I liked gardenin' that much did ya. We'll have plenty, Barney. Maybe not be rich, or even comfortable like we was, but we'll be jes fine, ya jes wait an' see."

Mr. Carter looked amazed.

My father, shaking his head, said, "You are a wonder, Mother."

I had a new appreciation for my grandmother after that—she had never spoken to me of the war before, but I realized she had become the strong, determined, yet kind woman she was from living through that experience. Life would be very hard over the next several years, yet in moments of greatest need, Grandma's Indian head pennies never ran out, and a good number of silver dollars, liberty nickels, and even two-cent pieces were also dug up from the backyard and garden. Sometimes I wonder whether there might not still be a few jars of money buried around that house, now valuable rare coins doubtless. But rather than my bringing them to the attention of the house's current owners, they can remain there for some future generation to find.

"I never thought I'd be thankful to say my wife is smarter than me," said Grandpa Carter, "but it don't make up for the wrong I committed."

Grandpa Carter would feel guilty for a long time after that, but he gradually realized he was not as foolish as many others. In the following days, we heard many stories of former millionaires who committed suicide by jumping out of ten story windows. And what hit home hardest of all was to learn that the prominent local banker, Lysander Blackmore, shot himself through the skull, presumably because he had lost a fortune in the crash. My family had patronized his bank for many years, so we attended the funeral; I remember watching his wife, young son and daughter at the funeral; Mrs. Blackmore looked so miserable I imagine she would have thrown herself into her husband's grave if not for her children. I never did hear, however, that the widow or her children ever hurt for money. However much Mr. Blackmore lost in the stock market, it was not enough to commit suicide over. But money does strange things to people.

Life became frugal after the stock market crash. We pinched our pennies so hard we made Lincoln cry, yet we were all determined my grandparents would not be destitute in their old age, or that my and Helen's child should know severe poverty.

Helen worried a lot as we heard stories of people losing their jobs or their farms and having to move away to the big cities for work, only to find matters were worse there because at least around Marquette, many knew how to live off the land. Eliza spent a whole day crying when she had to let her two maids go, and I can only imagine the fear felt by the maids over their situations.

I worried most, however, that Helen was worrying and how that would affect the baby. When November came, the baby was a week overdue, and a few days after that, the doctor decided Helen would have to have a caesarean section.

I sat in the waiting room of St. Mary's Hospital for hours that day. Eventually, Grandma and Grandpa, Dad and Aunt Louisa May came to sit with me. The doctor came out to tell us when the operation would begin and promised to let us know how Helen was doing. But hours passed without word. We had chatted together with excitement at first, but as the day dragged on, we became exhausted, then worried, burying our faces in magazines we found we could not read, or wandering restlessly while drinking coffee we did not want.

"Mr. O'Neill?"

The doctor spoke. I quickly rose from my seat, tossing the magazine onto a table, anticipating the news that I would be a father.

"Mr. O'Neill, there have been some complications. I'm sorry to tell you this. It's always hard for me. I—I—"

I stared at him dumbly as he faltered for words. I understood before he said, "I'm afraid the baby has been lost."

But I was not prepared to hear, "And I'm afraid your wife is in very critical condition. We still have hope she'll pull through, but—"

"Can I see her?"

"She knew that childbirth could kill her. I told her that the first time she came to see me, but these last few weeks, we thought everything would be fine." He was talking, more trying to understand the situation himself than to explain it to me. Then he recollected himself and said, "I'll take you to her while there's still time."

My father stood up. His hand found my shoulder, but I ignored him and followed the doctor down the hall to where Helen rested in a private room.

"Helen, dear, how are you?" I asked, sitting down beside her, taking her hand in mine. She did not even open her eyes until I leaned over and brushed the hair from her forehead.

She gave a couple gasps. As I continued to speak her name, her eyes fluttered a little.

But then, as if her spirit had been released, I saw her body heave up, then fall so that she seemed to shrink. Without a parting goodbye, my beautiful wife had left me.

I was in too much shock to cry; I sat there, holding her hand, remembering all our happiness, then feeling suddenly overwhelmed with grief and despair, finding all those happy days were only a fleeting, half-remembered dream. The nurses and doctor left the room, left me alone, shutting the door behind them. I remembered my and Helen's childhood, years and years of friendship, then our courtship, our wedding and honeymoon, moving into our new house, our dreams of being writers and parents. And then the tears streamed down my face—couldn't the baby have survived at least so I would still have some part of her with me? After a little while, my father came into the room and drove me home. I walked about like a zombie as he helped me into bed, where I slept heavily.

When I woke in the morning, the room was filled with sunlight, and for a second I felt joyous, until I remembered. I could not believe it—I stumbled from my bed, realizing Helen was not beside me. I went downstairs, wandering listlessly, until I found my father in the kitchen. He told me to sit down and he fed me breakfast, as if I were a child all over again, just as he probably would have done had he been there when Mama died—I think to this day, the pain of my mother's loss only made Helen's death even worse for me. My father sat and listened to me and occasionally muttered a word or two of understanding. Grandma called and spoke to my father as I finished breakfast. She was bringing over food for all the visitors who would come, and Mrs. Lawson had said to give me her love and she would be over shortly too.

"Helen's aunt has probably told the whole town by now," said my father. "You better go get dressed."

I did not want to see anyone right then. I did not care whether I ever saw anyone again when the one I most wanted to see was gone. While dressing, I looked at my clock and realized already twelve hours had passed since Helen's death—how could the world have gone on for a full twelve hours already? How many, many more hours would it go on? I was only twenty-five. I might live fifty, even sixty more years, and how would I bear this grief for that long? I could not believe such heart-rending grief would ever pass.

I went downstairs as I heard my family starting to arrive. Everyone was trying to distract my thoughts from Helen by pouring me coffee, asking how it tasted, did I want cream or sugar, did I want to go to the funeral home to pick out the caskets—I would have to pick out one for the baby as well—how could I bear that? Yet I did—a tiny little casket for a child I had never seen, could not bear to see, a little girl we had planned to name Amelia. I hoped my little girl was with Helen now—that gave me some comfort, that Helen might get to be with our child—the only other comfort I could imagine was that I might purposely choose to join them.

I remember only fragments of that day—the visit to the funeral home, the visit from the priest, all the guests who flooded the house, my father speaking of how he had first learned of my mother's death and how hard it had been for him to endure, and that he doubted he would have survived if he had not had me to come home to—what comfort was such a statement to me when I had no child? Mrs. Lawson came and engulfed me in her arms, crying that she had loved Helen as much as her own daughters. Tom and Mags sat quietly with me, not knowing what to say—I found that a relief compared to all the chatter about me. Eliza came and told me, "Robert, you must go on. You're a writer, and that's a fabulous gift, and you can use this experience to help others get through this same pain; you can make it easier for them." I knew she was right, but I told her I did not care to help anyone anymore. "Remember who you are,

Robert," she replied. "Don't let the pain of this world change who you are." And then I thought how she must have suffered when Mark died, when she had been so much younger than me, so much more scared, and I felt a little comfort for the first time.

And then came moments when I almost forgot what had happened. Mr. Williams would be telling a story, and I would find myself smiling, and then turn to see whether Helen was equally amused, only to realize she was not in the room and never would be again. Mary Mitchell brought us potato salad, and knowing how Helen loved it, I started to say I would save some for her, only to remember she could not eat it now. I saw Dad clear the coffee table; he accidentally dropped *Our Mutual Friend* on the floor and its bookmarker fell out; I was about to warn him how upset Helen would be if he lost our place in the book until I remembered we would never read together again.

The morning after the funeral, I lay in bed late, weeping and alone in a lonely house. During his lunch break from school, Eric came by, knocked and received no answer, then opened the unlocked door and searched the house until he found me in bed, sobbing. He nearly dragged me downstairs and tried to make me a sandwich, but I refused it, so he made me tea that I only sipped once, then let grow cold.

"Robert, you have to go on with life. You are so loved by all of us, and you write such wonderful books—think of how many lives you touch with those books."

"There won't be any more books," I said. "I can't write without Helen. She was my inspiration. She's the one who first gave me the idea to be a writer."

"She would want you to carry on that dream."

"No," I said. "I'm not going to do anything now, except maybe kill myself."

Eric reached across the table and slapped me so hard I fell from my chair. In a second, he was sitting beside me on the floor, his arms wrapped tightly around me.

"Robert, I love you like a brother, but I'll hit you again if you even think about harming yourself."

And then I felt calm, and I knew I would go on.

The worst had passed. The pain would never completely leave, and it would be a long time before I felt alive again, yet I continued to live.

Chapter 26

Depression

Christmas came again. The happiest time of year, for people whose hearts are filled with love; my heart held only grief and despair. My first holiday without Helen only reminded me of the happy ones with her and the many empty ones to come before I joined her. At age twenty-five, I felt I had outlived my time on earth, yet I would not hurt those who loved me by departing before my natural time. At first, I wished I had been taken in Helen's place, but then I realized I would not want her to suffer the agony of losing me. I tried to persuade myself that God had a plan, that I had to trust Him, but most of the time, I felt I was only trying to trick myself with such thoughts.

"Robert," said my father a couple days after Christmas. "Helen's been gone nearly two months now. I know you have to work through your grief, but you can't just mope around the house. You haven't written a word since she died, yet you've always wanted to write—try it again—even if you only journal about your grief. You have to pull yourself out of this despair."

"I can't write," I moaned. "It's too introspective; I'm afraid if I go that deep into my soul, I won't be able to bear it."

"All right," said my dad, "but you need to do something. I'd put you to work with me, but with winter and this economic depression, there isn't much work."

"I think," I said, for I had been thinking of it for some time, and been waiting for the holidays to end before I decided, "I want to go away for a little while. Marquette has too many reminders of Helen for me right now. I feel trapped by my past here, and if I go away for a little while, maybe see some new scenes, then I'll be able to write again, to live normally again. I just need some time, away from everyone else, to work through my grief alone."

"I'll worry about you being away," said Dad, "but you're a grown man now. And only you truly know what's best for you. If you go, just drop us a line once in a while so we know you're okay."

"I don't know how long I'll be gone," I said. "It may be days; it may be months."

"Do you have enough money?"

"Yes, plenty. Helen and I saved for the baby; now I have all that extra, and I'll let you know where I am so if you or the family need money, I can wire it to you."

"We need you more than we'll ever need money," said my dad. "Just make sure you come back."

"I will," I promised.

I departed a few days into the new year of 1930. At first, I told myself I did not know where I would go. I just knew I wanted to get away from all the sympathetic words and expressions I received from everyone I met on the streets of Marquette. I knew I was not running away from my grief; I was just uncertain about where I was running. Part of me feared, despite my promise, that I wouldn't come back, but I knew I loved my family too well to stay away for long.

I went first to Chicago, feeling it my responsibility to talk with my and Helen's publisher, for when the staff there had originally heard my wife also wrote books, they had agreed to look at her work, then decided to publish her poems. But when I got to Chicago, I found myself unable to talk about business; for a few days, I just wandered about the city, then returned to my hotel, to eat alone, to cry myself to sleep. Finally I went down to the publishing house, unannounced, afraid if I set an appointment, I would not keep it.

"Hey, I'm sorry to hear about your wife," said Dave, my publishing representative. "Maybe you'll feel better when you see her book of poems published. We've got the book cover done. Here, I'll show it to you."

The cover was beautiful; Helen would have been pleased.

"Do you want to see the proofs? We can send them to you wherever you are."

"No," I said. "I'm sure they'll be fine. I can't read those poems now."

"Oh," he said, "that's right—some of them are about you—she sure did think the world of you."

"More than she should have," I muttered.

He looked uncomfortable, not knowing what more to say. He was a man obsessed with his work, but not good at personal relations. I left soon after to make it easier for him; I did not enjoy the discomfort my grief brought everyone.

"Your sales are going well. Between the last two books, I'm guessing you'll have sold a quarter million copies by the end of this year. Did you see the review in *The New Yorker*? No? It said you had more dazzle than Fitzgerald and more strength beneath the dazzle, and the *Cleveland Plain Dealer* said your stories were as endearing as those of Edna Ferber."

"That's good," I said, and I felt pleased for a moment before the agony settled back in.

"You'll write again. You can't let all those readers down," Dave said as I departed. "Take it easy a couple more months and I'll bet you any money you'll come back with material that's stronger than ever. We may even see your next book out by Christmas if you can write one by spring."

"I can't promise I'll ever write another book," I replied.

"You will," he said.

I actually had a complete rough draft of my fourth book, but I had not touched it since Helen died. It seemed trite and pointless now beside my grief. Of course, my readers know I have written many more books, but that novel, a love story, written during the happiest period of my life, became far too personal for me ever to finish, and I will probably destroy it before I die.

I did not know what to do after that. Chicago's noisy, busy, buzzing liveliness grated on my nerves. I longed for solitude, and for warmth and sunlight, for summer along Lake Superior, but it was the dead of winter.

And then that night, I dreamt of home, not Marquette, but my childhood home in South Carolina, of swinging in the backyard, of humid summer nights, and of magnolia trees. I woke to realize what I had somehow deep down always known—that the day would come when I would need to return to the South, to understand that Southern part of myself I had left behind years before, yet would always be with me. I felt flooded by memories of the South, not by specific events, but the feel of it, the scent of its rain showers on the rich red soil, the Spanish moss trees, the constant buzz of insects on sultry humid evenings, the overcast skies and long suffocating heat spells. The South called me, and I went, not sure what to expect, but seeking a part of me I had nearly forgotten.

I enjoyed driving to South Carolina, the freedom of it, the ability to stop wherever I liked for as long as I wished, unlike when I rode the train as a child. I was stunned by how beautiful Kentucky was in early March, how impressive the Smoky Mountains were, how green the Upstate of South Carolina. But once I reached the Upstate, I did not know what to do.

I found a hotel room in Anderson, and then I drove out toward my parents' old house. I doubted anyone in the neighborhood would remember the little O'Neill boy who had once lived there, and I did not know that I would tell anyone about my connections here. I stopped at a gas station and saw a young man who looked somewhat familiar; looking at the nametag sewn onto his overalls, I knew him to be one of my old classmates, but I did not reveal my identity to him.

I found my parents' house, my childhood home. The roads had not been altered, but I nearly missed the house for it had changed. No one appeared to be home, so I pulled into the yard and sat in my car looking at it, not feeling right wandering about the property when my family no longer owned it. The house had been white, but was repainted green; a new roof had been put on it, the old porch expanded, although the swing taken down. The magnolia trees I had dreamt about were gone, as was my swing in the backyard, which I could just see from looking around the side of the house. No sign existed that children lived there now. The name on the mailbox was unfamiliar to me. This place was not my home any longer.

I then drove to Marble Hill, although I feared I would feel the same disappointment. Once the finest plantation in the county, Mr. Carter had long ago sold the land and a developer had since come in. In my childhood, forty vacant acres had surrounded Marble Hill, but now neighbors' houses clustered within a hundred feet of it. The main house looked an eyesore amid the little houses built in the last decade. No one had bothered to paint it since Mr. Carter had sold it, and considering its ostentatious size compared to its neighbors, I just knew it would be demolished before many more years passed. I would never mention this visit to Grandpa Carter.

Trying not to cry, I drove away, wondering why I had come to the South at all. I felt alone now, more than just missing Helen, missing everything, crying for the past, for my mother—I thought of going to the cemetery where she was buried, where she would lie alone for all time, for I would rest in

Marquette beside Helen and I imagined my father would be buried in Marquette as well.

But then I thought of Nellie, and leaving thoughts of the melancholy cemetery behind, I sought my old friend. Did she still live in the house she and Martin had bought when they were married? I soon found their house. I parked in their yard and went up their steps to knock on their door. I saw a curtain part and Martin's scowling face stare out at me; then the door opened. Nellie was older, her hair starting to turn gray, although she could not be much more than forty. A little girl hid behind Nellie's skirt.

"Yes?" she said.

"Nellie," I smiled.

"Yes," she said. "What is it?"

"It's Robert," I said.

She looked blank.

"Robert O'Neill, John and Cynthia's son. You worked for my family."

"Oh." She cleared her throat. "Cindy, go back inside." She pushed the little girl back into the house, then stepped onto the porch and shut the door behind her.

"Hello, Robert. How are you?" she asked, wiping her hands on her apron.

"Fine," I said, wanting to hug her, but I sensed she felt awkward seeing me. Instead, I extended my hand to shake hers. She was just surprised, I thought. In a minute, she would be her cheerful old self. "It's good to see you."

She just stared at me. She looked tired, as if she had been up since early that morning.

"You have a little girl?" I said. "Do you have any other children?"

"No, just Cindy," she smiled. "She's four. I named her after your mother, although Martin didn't like it."

Then she clamped together her lips, realizing she had said something she shouldn't.

"How are you?" I asked.

"Fine." She kept staring at me. I did not know what more to say.

"Where's your wife?" she asked. "Your father wrote to me when you got married."

"Oh," I said. I had forgotten that. How could I explain except to say, "She died this fall."

"I'm sorry to hear it," she said, but she said it like a stranger, to be polite.

"She died in childbirth," I added, although she had not asked how. "I just had to get away from Marquette, from everything that reminded me of her, so I thought I would come and see my old haunts. Things sure have changed here since I was a boy. I barely recognize this area anymore."

The door opened and Martin stuck out his head.

"What is it?" he asked.

"It's Robert, John and Cynthia's son."

"What does he want?"

"I just stopped by to say 'hello'," I said. Martin glared at me, as if I had stepped out of line by addressing him.

"I have my meeting tonight," he told Nellie. "You better get supper on the table."

"I'll be there in a minute," she said.

As he shut the door, I said, "I'm sorry. I didn't realize it was that close to suppertime."

"It's all right," she said. "It was nice to see you."

Was our reunion over this quickly? The old Nellie would have invited me to stay for dinner.

"You too," I said, politely, and turned to go down the steps.

"Things have changed since you were a boy, Robert."

"I see that," I said, but I felt she was speaking of herself.

"Here," I said, turning back and reaching for my wallet. "Let me give you a silver dollar for Cindy. You can save it for when she goes to college."

"Robert," she shook her head. "Things have changed. I can't take your money. Martin wouldn't like it."

"I've published a couple novels," I tried to explain. "I know things are getting hard with this depression settling on the country. I just want to take care of my friends."

"Your heart is in the right place. You were always a generous boy. But times have changed. Maybe up north, you don't understand that—you haven't been here to see it, or maybe it's just that I've changed. But—anyway, I thank you, but I can't take your money. I hope you have a safe trip back home. Give my best to your father."

"I'll do that," I said. For a second, I wanted to protest, to ask what was wrong, to ask what she meant by "things have changed"—what had changed? Was it Martin who made her so aloof? Or was it just the passing of time that made us strangers—was I just a Yankee to them now? "Have a good evening," I said.

"Goodbye," she said. She tried to say it kindly, but I heard relief in her voice that our meeting was over.

I did not know what I wanted now except to get away from the Upstate. I drove to Charleston the next day, seeing the sites, half remembered from my childhood when twice as a little boy I had gone with Grandma to visit her Aunt Abigail, a woman I only remembered as shriveled and mean. I could not even have found Aunt Abigail's house had I wanted to. I walked the streets of Charleston all that next day, past high steepled churches, beneath arching Spanish moss trees in a park, and along the harbor. I thought about how Charleston had once been a major slave-trading port—Nellie and Martin's ancestors had probably arrived here in chains. I was a free man; my people had always been free. In Marquette, I could almost forget Negroes existed at all; I certainly had no reason to think about slavery, save for when I thought of Aunt Carolina, and occasionally of Jenny and Jones, whom she had treated like slaves. Slavery—is that what had changed—is that what Nellie had meant by things had changed? But she had never been our slave—fifty years had passed at that time since the war, sixty-five years now. Scarcely anyone was still alive who had been born into slavery or fought in that terrible war. Yet Charleston was full of the past. When I went into a restaurant and ordered, the waitress asked me, "Are you from the North?" How could I explain where I was from? I was from Marquette. I never identified myself as being "from the North" as these people identified themselves first and foremost as being "from the South," before they would say South Carolina or Alabama, New Orleans or Richmond. I felt as if they thought that war had still not ended.

I went on to Atlanta the next day, hearing it was a modern, bustling city. I wanted to see the South of the present and the future, not the past. I drove North from Charleston, halfway back toward the Upstate, then turned westward toward Georgia. I passed through a little town whose name I recognized because my aunt had told me it was close to where my great-grandparents, Edmund and Dolly O'Neill had lived, not terribly far from where I had grown up, but far enough away that I had never visited it. Then I remembered the picture of the farmhouse I had seen in Great-Aunt Carolina's bedroom. I doubted that house could still be standing, but curious, I drove into town to ask about it. At a little country store, I inquired whether anyone knew where the O'Neill farm had been.

"Never heard of it," grunted the storekeeper, and I knew from his tone that my "Yankee" accent offended him, although I have often been asked about my Southern accent in the North.

"My family is originally from around here," I tried to explain. "That would have been my great-grandparents' house. I just wondered whether it was still standing."

"Can't help ya," said the storekeeper. "Will that be all, ma'am?"

He turned to his next customer. I started to leave, but as I passed out the door, I heard someone say, "Sir."

I turned around and saw an elderly Negro walking toward me. He motioned that we could talk outside.

"I heard ya askin' 'bout the ole O'Neill farm."

"Yes," I said. "I wondered whether someone knew how to get there. I'm just curious to see the place. My great-grandparents owned it."

"Yo name O'Neill?" he asked.

"Yes," I said. "Robert O'Neill."

He reached out to shake my hand.

"I'm mighty proud to meet you, sir," he said. "My name's O'Neill too. I was born on that farm ta slaves. Yo people, dey owned my people."

I was taken aback by this sentence. I had never thought about my family in connection to slavery, other than that my great-grandfather had thought it wrong, which is why he had set his slaves free and moved North. But for how many years had my family owned slaves, closing their eyes to its evils until my great-grandfather could not close his eyes to it any longer? The thought of it disturbed me deeply.

"I'll show ya where the house is if you'll drive me out there," said this Negro Mr. O'Neill, looking me in the eye. "It's 'bout a five mile drive."

I was nearly frightened to take him up on his request, for he looked feeble, at least eighty years old, somewhat hunched over, stumbling about with an old wooden cane. But I did want to see the house.

"Thank you," I said. "I would greatly appreciate it." I walked him to the car and opened the door for him. He looked surprised by my courtesy, yet climbed in.

"Lor', we ridin' in high style now!" he said after I got in on my side and pulled away from the store. Once he told me which direction to go, I asked him whether he remembered anything about my family.

"Not a lot," he said, "but I was born at dat farm. My parents, and me too I guess, though I was too young to know it, we was set free by Mastuh O'Neill. My folks, dey was born in Georgia, and Mastuh O'Neill bought dem dere while on a trip. Dey only worked at da farm a few years 'fore dey set free. Dey always say yo granddaddy da bes' white man dey ever known."

"He was my great-grandfather," I corrected, "but do you remember him?"

"No, not really," he said. "I was jus' liddle den, but I remember young Mastuh Robert and Miss Carolinee."

"Robert was my grandfather," I said. "I was named for him, but he died before I was born."

"Oh, he was a good one too," he told me. "He and I used ta play all duh time when we was liddle. Some of duh older boys dat was slaves, dey tole me he wouldn't be no friend a mine when he was older, but I dunt know 'bout dat. He moved away when we was still liddle, so I dunt know."

"I think he would have still been your friend," I said, "at least, from what I heard about him. I do remember my Great-Aunt Carolina. What was she like when she was a girl?"

"Lor' she was a whiny chile. I never seen no one who could set off a cryin' over da liddles' thing. She was a pretty thing, but always pouty. My mama said she wished she could spank Miss Carolinee, but she never dared."

I couldn't help but laugh and say, "Yes, she was ornery when she was older too, though she's dead now as well."

"Sorry ta hear it," he said.

We were silent then as we drove. I thought again of that picture in my great-aunt's bedroom, painted by my great-grandmother, but treasured by Aunt Carolina. She must have had fond memories of her childhood here, although I wonder whether she had only romanticized the past when she was older—I began to wonder whether I had romanticized my own Southern childhood, or simply not been aware of the tensions that must have existed. How could Nellie have been so cold to me? Her husband must have changed her, or had she never been my great friend as I had thought, but just simply been doing her job as a servant in caring for me? Yet she had named her daughter after my mother, so she must have felt affection for my family. Her emotions must be far more complicated than I could analyze. I realized Mr. O'Neill, beside me, was also complex. The South had done that to us all, made our lives, our understandings complex, raveled our lives together, intertwining friendship with slavery, making a mess of it all. I grew angry at history. I felt sorry for us all, Nellie, Aunt Carolina, my grandmother who had married a Yankee, Aunt Abigail, who had hosted Yankee soldiers in her home, probably more out of fear than friendship, only to be ostracized by Charleston society, and for Mr. O'Neill beside me, who apparently had found it hard to be born into a world of slavery, only to be forced to fend for himself as a free man.

"Dere it is," said Mr. O'Neill, as a farmhouse came into view. I pulled up to it, but parked on the road. It had a large porch with little pillars on the front, pretending to be grander than it really was. To Aunt Carolina as a very little girl, it must have seemed prominent, and she had remembered it through a four year old's eyes, not the eyes of an adult—had she seen it as an adult, she would have scorned it for being smaller, less ornate than her Ridge Street mansion.

"It sho good ta see it 'gain," Mr. O'Neill said. "I don't get ta dis area much anymore. Brings back good mem'ries, it does."

"I don't think anyone's home," I said. "I'm going to get out and look around."

"I think I'll jus' sit here and res' a spell then," said Mr. O'Neill.

I had come to see the house, but I also needed a moment away from Mr. O'Neill. I was touched that he thought my family had been good, but they had been slave owners nonetheless. I had never thought about what that truly meant until today, when I met a former slave, not only born on my family's land, but owned by my family, even bearing my family name. I walked up to the house and stood on the porch, looking at the timbers that had seemed like great columns to a little white girl named Carolina. I saw the magnolia trees blossoming on the edge of the yard. I saw how green was the grass, how magnificent the giant oaks, and in the distance, I could see fields, and I tried to imagine a handful of slave cabins in a clearing before the fields. It was a beautiful place—I would have found it hard to leave had I been my great-grandfather, Edmund O'Neill. But I still did not know why I had come here.

I went back to the car.

"Ya know," said Mr. O'Neill, "dere's a liddle somethin' 'bout ya dat remind me a Mastuh O'Neill. So many year since I seen 'im, it prob'ly my 'magination, but I think I can tell ya 'is fam'ly."

"I wish I had known them," I said, turning the car around to head back to the store.

"Ya should be proud a 'em," said Mr. O'Neill. "Dey was fine people. Only ones in dese parts dat set der slaves free. I 'member once we free we had ta leave these parts, but we sho didn't mind none jus' ta be free, and den aftuh da war, we come back here. I 'member duh udder slaves was 'fraid dat when Mastuh go up Nort', he was gonna sell us all, but he done freed us."

"I'm glad," I said.

"My ma said da udder white folks round dese parts was mighty upset 'bout it, but yo family done it anyhow. Dat's bravery, dat's what dat is. I'd be mighty proud if I was ya."

"Thank you," I said. "That means a lot to me."

"Lots dem white folks so uppity. Dat dere man in the store for zample. He ain't from nothin' but white trash, dat what he is, not good white folk like yo' fam'ly. Yet he think he good as ole Gen'l Lee. I woulden say dis ta no one else, but ya's a Yankee, so I can tell ya. I'd spit in mos' da white folks faces 'roun' dese parts, but yo people was fine, dey was. Dis a proud day for me, ta meet ya."

We had returned to the store now. I got out of the car and opened the door for him and helped him get on his feet.

"I sho proud ta shake yo han', sir," he said once he was standing up, "and ta say thank ya for yo folks freein' me and mine." I felt equally honored to shake his hand and told him so, for I could not imagine the adversity this man had undergone in his long life, and if he would like to spit on most white people, well, I could not hold that against him.

"Thank you for showing me the place," I said. "Let me give you something for your trouble."

I reached into my wallet and began to extract a ten-dollar bill.

"No, suh, ya put dat 'way. Dese is tough times in dis countree. White man see me wid dat much money I likely ta be lynched. No thankee, but I do 'preciate it, suh. Yo have a good day, suh."

He hobbled back to the store. I watched him for a minute, then got in my car and continued on my way.

I drove to Atlanta, that great, growing city. I have often wondered whether perhaps I passed Margaret Mitchell on its streets, the young woman who at the time was writing *Gone With the Wind*. Many times I have attempted writing about the South, but each time I feel I've failed. My life has been a strange mixture between my roots in the South and in the North, an inability to decide to which land I truly belong. Margaret Mitchell captured the South far better than I could, which is why I have taken a passage from her monumental work as the title and epigraph for my own book, for land has mattered to me deeply, the land of Marquette just as much as the South mattered to her, and had we ever met, I think we would have understood one another. Although Gerald O'Hara states that land is the only thing that lasts, I think he meant more specifically, it was the sense of belonging to a place, as Scarlett belonged to her Tara, so I belonged to Marquette and to its people, and even long after the City of Marquette and all who have ever lived there are equally gone with the wind, the love I knew there will continue to expand and touch the lives of millions who come after me, as each generation bequeaths to the next a little bit of what its lives have been. So also the South will always be part of me, as will my mother, and my Helen, their influence immeasurable—and equally, the influence of myself and my books upon others.

With this realization, my grief began to dissipate.

I only stayed in Atlanta a few days. Then one bright spring morning, I got back into my car and drove home to Marquette.

I was welcomed by the family, and grateful to be with them, grateful for the time remaining to spend with each of them before they would also leave me; yet I knew with each loss that I would be wiser and stronger, until I could join them in the next life.

By the end of that summer, I began to write again, this time to write a great family saga, to write about the South I remembered from my childhood, showing how innocent children can be happy there, until they become aware of the underlying secrets, the prejudice, the discrimination, the pains of the past that lay beneath, forgotten by the younger generation. I have never written to disparage the South, although my critics have accused me of it, but rather, I wanted to explore the complexities of its culture, how it remains haunted by its past, and why that is so. That novel became the most popular and controversial book I had written so far, and William Faulkner, himself, said he admired it. I was less interested in praise, however, than the relief of knowing I could write again.

That summer, I also rented out my house, less to escape memories of Helen than to provide additional income for the family. I moved in with my father, who had always been rather lonely since I had married; he was glad for the company. Whenever I had writer's block, or temporary bouts of grief that made me unable to write, I would go on carpentry jobs with him and Tom, although the Great Depression made such jobs rare now; pounding nails did as much to relieve my grief and anger as anything. My evenings I often spent with Grandma and Grandpa Carter, aware I needed to treasure every moment of these last years with them. I did not look for happiness or success, or dream of the future during this time; I simply tried to live one day at a time, and at night, I recounted the good events of the day, finding they always outweighed the bad. And so four years passed away.

Chapter 27

The Reader and I Part

The telephone rang one snowy December afternoon in 1933, just as I was going out the door. It always will ring at the most inopportune times. I had tons of Christmas shopping to do, and I wanted to finish it before I went over to Mags and Tom's house for supper that night.

"Hello," I said, picking up the receiver.

"Hello. Is this Robert?" asked a female voice I recognized as Eliza's.

"Yes. Hello, Eliza," I replied.

"Your dad fixed the banister on my staircase yesterday, but he left one of his hammers here. Do you want to pick it up for him?" she asked.

I agreed to stop by on my way downtown, although I felt irritated to make an extra trip when I had so much to do. I hated Christmas shopping. It would be my fifth Christmas without Helen, and having lost her just before the holidays made them still difficult for me. I felt frustrated and sad as I drove to Eliza's house.

Eliza greeted me at the front door. Until the Depression, a servant had always answered the bell, but now Eliza only had a lady who came to clean for her once a week. "Thanks for coming by. Do you want to come in for a minute and have a cup of coffee? I was just wrapping up some trays of cookies. I can have yours ready in a minute if you can wait."

Politely, I agreed to stay a few minutes.

I sat down at the table in the kitchen, which she had stacked with both material and baking supplies. She cleared a space for me, pushing away Christmas stockings she said she was making for the children at the Holy Family

Orphanage. Then she handed me a cup of coffee and gave me a plate full of frosted cookies shaped like Santa's face. "I'm baking twelve trays of cookies to bring over to the orphanage with the stockings," she said, "and more for a party for my and your aunt's women's group. Then I need to save some for my Christmas Eve party, besides the ones for all my neighbors and family and friends."

"That's amazing," I said, sipping my coffee and watching her wrap up the plates. "It's as if you're a one woman assembly line."

"Well, it keeps me busy," she said. "I haven't even started to wrap the packages for my nephews and nieces." Eliza had no nephews and nieces of her own, but since she had been married to Tom's brother, she counted Mags and Tom's many children as such, and she often babysat for them.

"You have an awful lot of energy," I said, "especially considering you lost your mother last month."

"Yes, well, that's why I keep busy," she said. "I learned when Mark died that it's pointless to mope about. It won't help those orphans any, and rather than feel sorry for myself, I can do things for others."

I thought how I had moped so much when Helen died. I had not actively served the community like Eliza, but I hoped my books in some way helped others.

"We'll miss your mother," I said. "I can still remember my first full day in Marquette was on Thanksgiving. You came over to my Grandma's house to say your mother couldn't come to dinner because she was sick, so Grandma sent you home with two plates of food."

"Funny, I don't remember that at all," said Eliza. "When was that?"

"The first year I was here, during the war, before you were married to Mark—1917."

"That seems so long ago," said Eliza, done with wrapping up plates and sitting down across from me with her own cup of coffee. "It's almost impossible to think both my mother and Mark were alive then. Life seemed a lot easier in those days."

"It's good that you keep busy," I said, staring into my coffee cup.

"I try," she said, "although I sometimes wish I had my own family to look after. Now that my mother is dead, the only real family I have is her brother, and he doesn't live around here, so it is a little lonely."

"Do you think you'll ever marry again?" I asked, only because it was the obvious question. I understood what she meant by being lonely, even with all my family around me.

She laughed. "I'm an old widow now. Who would want to marry me?"

"You're not old," I said, "just a few years older than me; I'll only be thirty next spring."

"I'll be thirty-three," she said. "That seems old to me. And besides, all the men my age are married."

"I bet there are some eligible bachelors out there if you looked for them. I don't think Mark would want you to be lonely."

"Do you want more coffee?" she asked.

"No, thank you."

She got up to refill her own cup, then started covering more cookie trays.

"You can't preach to me, Robert," she said, "the U.S. economy has not been as depressed as you've been since Helen died. Why don't you remarry?"

I didn't know what to say. Of course, the thought had crossed my mind that I might remarry, but I felt I would be unfaithful to Helen to do so. Yet somehow I found myself now saying, "Perhaps someday I will if any woman ever wants to take me on."

"I don't need a husband," she said, sitting back down. "What I need is advice on how to sell this house."

"Sell your house? Why?" I asked. I was astonished.

"I thought I could go live in my mother's house. This house never should have been mine to begin with. I wanted Tom and Mags to take it, but they said they couldn't afford the taxes in this part of town."

I was sure Eliza had plenty of money, despite the Depression. How could she part with such a house? I looked out the kitchen doorway into the beautiful dining room, and beyond that I knew was the splendid library.

"I wish I could afford to buy it from you," I said.

"You?" said Eliza. "You're only one person as well. It's too big for one person, even for two really, but I daresay with all the money you make from writing your books, you can afford it."

"I'm not hurting for money," I admitted, "but book sales have declined a lot in the last few years."

"I would think the Depression would make people buy more books, only for momentary relief from their own lives, and your last book must have given so much hope to people."

"Thank you," I said, munching on a cookie with embarrassment. I was used to being praised in the papers by critics, but I still did not know how to take a compliment from someone I knew. "Well, I better get going. I have a lot of Christmas shopping to do." Then, looking into the dining room, I added,

"You know, I would hate to have anyone else live here. It sounds silly, but this house reminds me so much of Helen."

Eliza laughed. "Yes, I remember you telling me how the two of you played here that summer I was away. Maybe I should tell your father to send you the bill for repairing my banister."

"Maybe," I laughed.

"Well, Mark and I slid down it too, and we were older, so our weight probably weakened it more."

The mention of Mark's name made me recall the old enmity I held for him, and that Eliza had been the cause of it. I had thought her a goddess then, and looking at her now, I realized she was still remarkably beautiful.

"Thank you for the cookies," I said, after putting on my coat and taking the tray she handed me. "I guess I'll see you at your Christmas Eve party."

"Yes," she said. She smiled, but it seemed forced. She was going to leave in a minute to bring the cookies to the orphanage, to bring those children Christmas cheer, but she did not look cheerful herself. I imagined she was lonely when she did not have company. I quickly went down the front steps and to my car. I felt cowardly, as if I were fleeing from the gloom of that large house and its lonely occupant.

I arranged the cookies on the car's back seat, hoping I had put them where they wouldn't slide off. Then I got in and started up the car, only to remember I had forgotten to get my dad's hammer from Eliza.

I left the car running and went back up the porch steps. I was just about to knock on the door when I heard a loud thump followed by the sound of glass crashing. I flung open the door and rushed into the front hall. Eliza was sitting on the floor in the middle of the room, laughing hysterically.

"Eliza, what happened?" I asked.

She gave me her hand, and I helped her to her feet.

"What happened?" I repeated.

"I'm sorry," she said. "You'll think it's silly, but I couldn't resist. I slid down the banister. I just didn't think I'd fly so far that I'd crash into that ugly old vase."

"It was an ugly old vase," I said, joining in her laughter.

"It didn't hurt at all, even though I am an old widow now," she said, standing up and smoothing out her skirt.

"I wonder whether it would hurt an old widower?" I asked.

"Only way to find out is to give it a try," she said, her eyes twinkling.

And so I did, and I think I enjoyed sliding down that banister more than when I was a boy. Then Eliza had another run, but near the bottom, she nearly fell sideways. My reflexes made me grab her before she tumbled over.

We both laughed until it hurt.

"I better go," I said. "Don't try it again without someone to catch you."

"I won't," she promised.

After that, I found myself looking forward to Eliza's Christmas Eve party. I almost wished I were the only guest so the two of us could slide down the banister again.

What I did not expect at the party was for her to ask me whether she could have the first dance.

Politely, I said, "Yes." I had not danced since Helen died. I had not held a woman in my arms since then. Eliza was more beautiful that night than I had ever seen her, and when the dance ended, she held onto my hand and led me to a corner and chatted with me, neglecting all her other guests. I found myself telling her all about Helen, and she told me about Mark, and then I admitted to her how jealous I had been of Mark all those years before.

"Now your rival is out of the way," Eliza said, "and so is mine."

"What do you mean?" I asked.

"You were just a boy when I first met you, but you grew into such a fine man. I was always jealous of Helen getting to be with you. Not that I ever wished her ill, just wished I could find someone like you. Maybe it's just because you're Mark's second cousin and look a little bit like him, but God forgive me, I think you're more handsome."

She took my hand in hers, and then I said, "Eliza, I don't think you should sell this house. I think there's a good chance there will be children to fill it some day soon."

She smiled. We were sitting behind the Christmas tree where no one could see us, and we took advantage of the privacy, although no mistletoe was nearby.

That happy moment was nearly sixty years ago. I never imagined then all the happiness to come as a result of that kiss. Eliza and I married the following spring, and even in the most difficult times after that, our love has carried us through. Helen will always be dear to me as my first true love, but Eliza has been my wife for over fifty years, the mother of my children.

I am too old to write more of my life—if I do not stop now, I will never complete this book. I do not wish to discuss all the novels I wrote, the ideas behind them and how they came to be. And I do not know how I could perfectly describe a life with such a wonderful woman as Eliza, a woman constantly occupied with making school lunches, patching our children's bleeding knees, organizing birthday parties and charity functions; I certainly cannot adequately describe those quiet moments when we sit together in the library on a Sunday morning, drinking coffee, not a word spoken between us but completely understanding one another.

I began this book to tell the story of my life, but now I leave it rather incomplete. What I believe I have accomplished is to capture that point in time, of Marquette during the First World War, of the people I knew, of a world that has passed away, perhaps changed for the better in many instances, yet passed away, as I shall soon do myself. I have tried to capture that world in all my books, but I think I succeeded best here by describing the simplicity of my childhood. As I wrote, I heard all those friends' voices; I was amazed to find I could so clearly recall their conversations, their smiling faces, each one so vivid. Not one of them is with me now save Eliza, but I leave this as a memorial of appreciation for them all. I leave it as a gift to my son, Bernard, to my daughter, Helen, and to my grandchildren, so they may know their family's past.

And I leave it as a parting gift to my millions of loyal readers. I trust I have captured some warmth and courage in these pages, and even if my books are forgotten, I trust my readers gained some joy and knowledge from them, which they will pass on to others, so that when Robert O'Neill's name is lost to history, what little good I have done will live on as a murmur beneath the surface of many future lives. That murmur is my gift to future generations; it is small return for the happiness I found when I was first welcomed to Marquette by strangers who became my family.

BE SURE TO READ ALL OF TYLER R. TICHELAAR'S NOVELS:

IRON PIONEERS:
The Marquette Trilogy: Book One

When iron ore is discovered in Michigan's Upper Peninsula in the 1840s, newlyweds Gerald Henning and his beautiful socialite wife Clara travel from Boston to the little village of Marquette on the shores of Lake Superior. They and their companions, Irish and German immigrants, French Canadians, and fellow New Englanders face blizzards and near starvation, devastating fires and financial hardships. Yet these iron pioneers persevere until their wilderness village becomes integral to the Union cause in the Civil War and then a prosperous modern city. Meticulously researched, warmly written, and spanning half a century, *Iron Pioneers* is a testament to the spirit that forged America.

THE QUEEN CITY
The Marquette Trilogy: Book Two

During the first half of the twentieth century, Marquette grows into the Queen City of the North. Here is the tale of a small town undergoing change as its horses are replaced by streetcars and automobiles, and its pioneers are replaced by new generations who prosper despite two World Wars and the Great Depression. Margaret Dalrymple finds her Scottish prince, though he is neither Scottish nor a prince. Molly Bergmann becomes an inspiration to her grandchildren. Jacob Whitman's children engage in a family feud. The Queen City's residents marry, divorce, have children, die, break their hearts, go to war, gossip, blackmail, raise families, move away, and then return to Marquette. And always, always they are in love with the haunting land that is their home.

SUPERIOR HERITAGE
The Marquette Trilogy: Book Three

The Marquette Trilogy comes to a satisfying conclusion as it brings together characters and plots from the earlier novels and culminates with Marquette's sesquicentennial celebrations in 1999. What happened to Madeleine Henning is finally revealed as secrets from the past shed light upon the present. Marquette's residents struggle with a difficult local economy, yet remain optimistic for the future. The novel's main character, John Vandelaare, is descended from all the early Marquette families in *Iron Pioneers* and *The Queen City*. While he cherishes his family's past, he questions whether he should remain in his hometown. Then an event happens that will change his life forever.

*

NARROW LIVES
A Novel

Narrow Lives is the story of those whose lives were affected by Lysander Blackmore, the sinister banker first introduced to readers in *The Queen City*. It is a novel that stands alone, yet readers of *The Marquette Trilogy* will be reacquainted with some familiar characters. Written as a collection of connected short stories, each told in first person by a different character, *Narrow Lives* depicts the influence one person has, even in death, upon others, and it explores the prisons of grief, loneliness, and fear self-created when people doubt their own worthiness.

*

To order autographed copies and to view Marquette Fiction's complete book catalog, visit:

www.MarquetteFiction.com

www.ingramcontent.com/pod-product-compliance
Lightning Source LLC
Chambersburg PA
CBHW030356020726
47493CB00003B/847